A MILLION DECEMBERS

L. B. JOYCE

A Million Decembers ~ 2nd edition
ISBN 978-0-9600311-4-6

ALSO BY L. B. JOYCE

This book is the first book in the series,

Twelve Months, Twelve Love Stories.

A Million Decembers

For the Love of July

February's Angel

Promise Me November

An Unexpected June

A January to Remember

September's Moonlight Serenade

Goodbye Heartbreak, Hello May

Holidays in White Oaks Valley

A Grand Slam Kind of Christmas

I never thought I would write a book. And I never thought I would write what I did. But evidently it was a story that wanted to be told, because once I started writing, I couldn't stop. So, to all of you out there who've been telling me I should write a book – and you know who you are – here it is.
I hope you like it.

A MILLION DECEMBERS ~ BOOK 1

Once in a while,
right in the middle of an ordinary life,
Love gives us a Fairy Tale.

~ Unknown

CHAPTER 1

$\mathcal{N}$icholas—formally known as Nicholas William Edward Hanover III, a fact he shared only when absolutely necessary—wasn't in the best of moods.

Because, come on… this was by far the worst overseas flight he'd ever experienced.

And he had been on quite a few.

He glanced down at the woman who was mostly responsible for this. A vice-like grip on his arm and her face pressed into his shoulder, she occupied the seat next to his. She'd been like this since the weather took a turn for the worse halfway through their flight.

He sighed, giving her hand a reassuring pat when yet another jagged streak of lightning illuminated the sky, sending the interior lights of the plane flickering. He wasn't too happy with this turn of events, either. But he'd been on enough flights to know they weren't in danger. The pilot had everything under control.

Hadn't he made this perfectly clear in his announcement of only a few minutes ago?

He knew he should also be more understanding. Many people had a fear of flying. But this woman had been a thorn in his side from the moment she'd first claimed the seat next to him.

What is it with so many American women? Why are they so forward? And why were you so unlucky to be seated next to one on this flight?

She just wouldn't stop talking. For some reason, even though they were complete strangers, she'd felt the need to fill him in on everything about her life in general. Starting with the rude behavior of the taxi driver who brought her to the airport.

Not to be mean, but he didn't care.

After an uneventful take off from Heathrow and they were in the air, he'd pulled out his laptop. Making a big production out of signing in, he kept his eyes glued to the screen, hitting the keys as though he was in the middle of closing a huge business deal.

When, in fact, he was catching up on his personal emails.

He'd foolishly thought this would send the hint he had no time for any of her social chit-chat. And she would leave him alone. Read the celebrity magazine he could see sticking out of her bag. Watch a movie. Or even catch up on her sleep. He would've been happy with any of these.

But yeah, you guessed it… he'd thought wrong.

There hadn't been even the slightest dent in her constant chatter. Or in her annoying inability to remain in her own seat, instead leaning over the arm-rest into his. And he'd swear her voice had become louder, her laugh even more shrill.

This meant he hadn't been able to accomplish a damn thing.

So, he gave up.

Shoving his laptop back into his briefcase, again making a big deal out of this, he leaned back in his seat and closed his eyes.

She finally seemed to get the hint. And there was silence… a sweet, blessed silence.

But almost as if to mock him, the turbulence started up. And it hit with a vengeance, every jolt and bounce of the plane bringing on another of this woman's hellish screams. This, along with her nails digging into his arm, was how he spent the rest of the flight.

He must have dozed off, waking as the flight attendant began her announcement for landing. He shot a glance over at his seatmate. Her head thrown back against the seat, and her mouth wide open, she was dead to the world. But even in her sleep, she hadn't let go of his arm. After he untangled himself from her grip and fastened his seatbelt, he raised the shade to look out the window of his first-class seat.

The reflection of his scowling face said it all.

Not a pretty sight, by all means.

His view blurred by the driving rain, he watched as they began the descent for landing at the Chicago O'Hare airport. The heavy rain, along with the angry grey waves of Lake Michigan, didn't offer a very promising outlook as far as the weather was concerned. But since it was now early December, this was to be expected.

He hoped this wasn't an omen of what was to come.

Leaning his head back against the seat, he closed his eyes. He was ready for this part of his journey to be over.

Good Lord, you are so ready.

Hopefully, Chicago was ready for him.

The plane on solid ground, Nicholas extended his arms and legs in a long stretch, quite a feat for his well-toned and six-foot frame in the limited space. As he massaged the muscles in the back of his neck, he could feel some of the tension leave his body.

Unfortunately, going by the heated gaze of his American seatmate, these moves had been a bad choice, triggering her immediate reaction. A reaction he wanted no part of.

What the hell? She looks like she's going to throw herself right at you. You need to get out of here... fast.

He groaned, and dragging his hand through his hair, he gathered up his belongings. His plan was to make a quick exit. But, as had been the case until now, luck wasn't on his side. She latched on to his arm, and leaning against him, she issued a gushing offer to buy him a drink. This would be for his "strong manly presence" during what had been such a "terrifying and life challenging experience" on their flight.

She gazed up at him and, running her tongue slowly over her lips, waited for his answer.

Good Lord... really?

He refused. Firmly, he did this.

He turned to leave, but insisting he wait, she began searching through her humongous purse. After she pulled out a pen and what looked like a crumpled up napkin from a fast-food restaurant, she proceeded to ever so slowly, write out her name and number. This, she informed him, was in case he later decided to take her up on her offer.

With her watching his every move, he stuffed the napkin in the pocket of his overcoat. Then, after sending her a brief smile, he left. Just barely avoiding her attempt at a more amorous farewell.

Moving at a brisk pace, Nicholas tried to ignore the twinge of guilt brought on because of the way he'd behaved. But in his defense, this woman had tried his patience, her abrasive personality sending out all kinds of red flags.

Claire would shake her head at this. As his younger sister, already married with twin daughters, she worried about his single state. His expectations were too high, she'd told him. This was because he was afraid to commit.

Yes, she would agree it was great he was so successful at what he did. But when he came home after a long day at work, he couldn't cuddle up with contracts and year end profit reports, could he?

And as much as she hated to remind him, he wasn't getting any younger.

Hmm... You wonder what she would have to say if she knew what you had in the works now...

But enough of that. Right now, he was a man on a mission, focused on three things. One, head over to the baggage area to claim his luggage. Two, hail a taxi. And three, check into his hotel. Only then would he be able to get back into somewhat of his normal routine.

Was this too much to ask?

He didn't think so.

But first, there was something he needed to do. He stopped at the first trash container he saw. He took the napkin the woman had given him out of his pocket and, without a second glance, tossed it into the container.

He felt better already.

From only a few feet away, she watched him throw the napkin into the trash, wondering if she should be insulted, or just plain out angry.

After deciding she was a little of both, she tossed her head, a look of determination on her face.

Okay, so maybe this was a bit of a setback as far as her plans went. But she wasn't worried. At least not yet, she wasn't...

He obviously didn't have a clue with whom he was dealing with.

If he had, he would know she always got what she wanted.

And this would be him.

Settled within the quiet confines of the taxi and en route to his hotel, Nicholas finally relaxed. He was back in control, a feeling he was the most comfortable with in his hectic life.

Pulling out his phone, he began scrolling through his itinerary for the week ahead. He'd scheduled only one meeting for today, his plan to use the remaining time to catch up on any calls and emails. Then, after a well-deserved drink and dinner in the privacy of his room, he would follow with an early night.

As he double checked the details of his meeting, this is when he realized the time difference here in the states had completely slipped his mind. This meant his day was just beginning.

He dragged his hand through his hair, staring down at his phone.

How the hell did you forget something as important as this? It's not like you've never traveled to the states before.

He sighed, massaging his forehead with his fingers. Why was he surprised? As of late, his mind hadn't been functioning as it should. But he wasn't going to start thinking about this. Not now.

He put his phone back in his pocket and, resting his head against the back of the seat, he stared out the window.

In his preoccupied state, he didn't even notice it was still raining.

Maybe harder than it had been before.

After Nicholas checked into his room and had made a few calls, he wandered over to the window, taking in the hustle and bustle that was Michigan Avenue.

He turned, gazing around at the room.

He felt trapped. What he needed was some fresh air, inclement weather, and all. The rain might even wash away some of the restlessness that hadn't left him since this trip began.

It sure as hell couldn't hurt.

A glance at his watch showed he had a little over an hour before his meeting. If he left now, he would have plenty of time to get in a decent walk.

He needed to clear his mind, stop thinking about the real reason he was here. Or what he now thought of as a possibility that could change his life.

He scratched his head, a wry smile on his face.

You've got to stop reading so much into this. You know damn well this a one in a million shot.

He exchanged his sweater for a shirt and tie suitable for a business meeting and pulled on his coat. After he slipped his room key in his pocket, he was out the door.

Yes, a walk and fresh air should do the trick.

Not even half a block from Nicholas's hotel, Anna Jameson pushed open the door of the fashionable boutique.

A powerful gust of wind came whipping around the corner of the building. The rain of earlier had now turned to sleet. Ducking her head against the icy pellets stinging her face, she jammed her hat even farther down on her head.

But she was smiling. Not even the wild and unpredictable Chicago weather could dampen her mood.

Nope, not today. Not with a check tucked deep inside the bag she was carrying. A check written out to her as a generous down payment for one dozen of her original designed and hand painted ornaments.

She peeked into the bag to make sure the check was still there.

Yep. There it was.

She looked up at the sky, a shiver racing through her. There was no getting around it, she was going to get soaked. She pulled up her collar and was just about to make her move when another blast of wind slammed into her, reaching out to snatch the bag out of her hand.

Before she even realized what happened, the bag took off, sailing up into the air like a runaway kite. Leaving her staring open-mouthed at her now empty hand. Another gust of wind, this one even stronger, was enough to shock her back to life.

"Oh no, no, no… my bag. If you see it, please grab it."

Yes, she knew she was screaming like a lunatic. But she didn't care. She needed that bag. A sample ornament and her designs were inside, along with the check.

Oh my God… the check!

Carried by the wind, the wildly dancing bag had now made a sharp turn, heading in the direction of the late afternoon traffic, now bumper to bumper down Michigan Avenue.

She had no choice but to take off after it, zig-zagging her way through the crowded sidewalk. She was only inches away from grabbing it out of the air when, as unbelievable as this sounds, she collided with an enormous wall of greenery coming from out of nowhere.

Ommmmmph.

"What the…?"

The force of the impact was enough to send her flying backwards onto the sidewalk. Her hat sailing into the air, her head hit the pavement, the loud cracking sound giving her every reason to be concerned.

As if this wasn't enough, as though it was falling from the sky, the enormous mass of evergreen came crashing down to land right on top of her.

Then… nothing.

CHAPTER 2

"**I** say, are you all right? Please… open your eyes."

If only to please the voice calling out to her, Anna struggled to pull herself out of this half-conscious state she was floating in. But this was slow going.

It was a man's voice, a deep and soothing voice. And even in her confused state, she noted it had a distinct, yet very charming, British accent.

Have you died and gone to heaven? Is this God speaking? He's British?

Barely opening her eyes, she searched in the direction his voice had come from. Overwhelmed by the sea of faces peering down at her, she grew dizzy, her lashes fluttering shut.

You don't even know what you're looking for. And for all you know, he could have left already.

But miracle-of-miracles, his voice came at her again. "Thank God it looks like you're coming around. If I give you a boost, can you stand? We need to get you off this wet pavement."

Before she could even respond, she was lifted to her feet, held steady in his firm grasp. And though his hold was gentle, she could feel the powerful strength hidden under the heavy fabric of his overcoat, his muscles flexing under her hands.

8

She leaned against him, seeking the warmth he provided against the wintry weather. The comforting scent of just ironed cotton, along with the spicy citrus fragrance of his cologne, had her pressing her face against his shoulder, breathing it all in.

She wanted to melt right into him.

Overcome by a sudden need to see his face, she tilted her head to fall right into the most amazing blue eyes she'd ever seen. A mesmerizing shade of blue, they reached deep, sending a riot of emotions sweeping through her. She couldn't look away for the life of her.

A few seconds passed. Or maybe it was more like minutes they remained locked in each other's eyes. They were completely oblivious to the wind and rain… or the comments of the few disgruntled pedestrians as they skirted around them. It was when a strong gust of wind almost pushed her even further into his arms, Anna's brain finally kicked in, her gaze going on to roam over the rest of his face.

Good grief, was anyone actually this handsome?

Not handsome in a fake-made-up-movie-star-handsome kind of way. No, this man was beyond that, every feature of his face perfectly aligned. His entire presence radiating confidence and strength, he gave the impression he was a person you would always want on your side.

Raindrops sparkled like diamonds in his dark auburn hair. This, along with the slightly windblown, yet extremely sexy look he had going on, had her gripping his arms even tighter to keep from running her fingers through the tousled waves.

In order to ignore this tempting thought, she lifted her chin, only to find his mouth was a mere whisper away. This sent her right into imagining how it would feel like to be kissed by such sensuous lips.

There was no doubt in her mind it would be an unforgettable experience.

Addicting even…

Run your fingers through his hair? Kiss his sensuous lips? What in the world is wrong with you? You don't even know this man! Exactly just how hard did you hit your head?

But it now appeared this eye-searching thing they had going on between them was over. His expression had changed. If she had to guess, she would say he was alarmed. Maybe even in shock. Either way, it certainly didn't bode well for her.

She tightened her hold on his arm. "Oh, no… what's wrong?"

He seemed to hesitate. Then he cleared his throat. "I, uh… I'm sorry. Nothing is wrong. You look fine. Smashing in fact, when you consider your impact with the pavement. I guess for a minute, well… I thought you were going to go out on me again."

Slowly shaking his head, he brushed his finger over her cheek. "I can't believe you don't have any scratches with that enormous pile of greenery landing on you. But I'm more worried about you hitting your head. Are you sure you're feeling all right?"

Her breath had caught in her throat, a warm tingle racing through her at his touch. To the point, she couldn't think. Wrapping her arms around herself, she took a deep breath. "Yes… No… I mean, I don't know. I'm a little shaky. I think I might only need a minute or two."

This is so far from the truth. You are not all right, not by a long shot.

So, she tried again. "I'm sorry… I guess what I'm trying to say is I'm not really sure?"

She knew this probably wasn't the answer he was hoping for, wishing he was anywhere else, but it would have to do. At least while he was standing so close, those blue eyes so intently watching her.

After another searching look, he took her by the arm. "We need to get you somewhere where you can sit down."

Giving her no chance to resist, he guided her through the crowded sidewalk and into a little coffee shop. He found a vacant table, pulled out a chair, and gestured for her to sit.

After sinking into the chair, she sent him a cautious smile. He tilted his head. "Coffee? Tea?"

On the verge of shaking her head, she saw what appeared to be a hint of a challenge in his eyes. She glanced away, confused.

My goodness, can he read your mind? No, of course not. You're imagining this.

She gave him a bigger smile. "Tea would be lovely. Thank you."

He studied her for what felt like several seconds. Then he slowly smiled back at her.

Oh my...

Her world tilted, throwing her off balance and right into a spin, making her feel almost giddy. Gripping the edge of the table, she almost couldn't breathe, while her heart soared right into high gear.

She bowed her head, closing her eyes. Only when she sensed he was gone, she glanced over to see he was placing his order at the counter.

Thank goodness...

She leaned back in the chair and, after taking a deep breath, she decided this was her opportunity to check him out even further. Because it was obvious, by her strange behavior, he'd made quite an impression on her.

And now she wanted to know more.

Let's be honest... after that smile he just gave you? You want to know everything about him.

Chin in hand, she studied him. From what she could see of his outward appearance, he was a person of importance. She was going to go out on a limb and say very important, almost in a lordly kind of way. My goodness, if he had ties to royalty, Prince William would tumble far down on the scale compared to the regal handsomeness this man possessed.

His shoes appeared to be handcrafted and of the softest Italian leather. She couldn't see much of his suit, but judging by the perfect cut and luxurious fabric of his overcoat, undoubtedly the finest cashmere available, both articles of clothing screamed hand tailoring and the best money could buy.

But his tie... only able to catch a glimpse, she was puzzled by his choice.

Definitely silk. No surprise there.

It was the pattern on the tie that caught her attention. Various sized paintbrushes, spattered with different colors of paint, were scattered across the dark blue background. Definitely not a style she expected after her assessment of the rest of his attire.

Was he also an artist?

Ha... of course not. Nope, you can't picture this.

Unless he was an artist who dabbled in art for the fun of it? When he wasn't caught up in the many engagements required because of his social standing. Or running his multi-million-maybe-even-billion-dollar company, making more money than he could ever need.

She shook her head.

You can't see this happening, at least not the dabbling. This would be too frivolous of a hobby for him.

Maybe he was a patron of the arts? This seemed like more of a possibility. But certainly not one who traveled in the same art circles as she did.

He was definitely out of her league.

Becoming annoyed, and not knowing why, she glanced over to where he was chatting with the blushing clerk behind the counter. She watched as he laughed at something she said, bringing her to turn an even brighter shade of red.

Now she was even more irritated. Not only was he out of her league, but it appeared he was also a man who wouldn't hesitate to use his good looks and charming ways to get what he wanted. And she, of all people, knew men like this were not to be trusted and better off left alone.

But wait a minute... why are you so angry with him? He's done nothing to deserve this.

Yes, this was true. He had been nothing but nice. In fact, he was almost too flawless to be real.

And this was the problem.

Exactly.

She needed to cut this meeting short.

Anna watched as, a cup in each hand, he made his way back to the table.

This had her sitting up straighter in her chair, combing her fingers through her tangled hair. She decided to go for a sophisticated look, placing her hands in her lap, a reserved smile on her face. As if having a man pick her up off the sidewalk was not a big deal.

No, she was cool with it.

Men came to her rescue all the time.

After he set the cups on the table and sat down beside her, he searched her face. Very seriously, he did this.

Nervously wrapping her hands around the cup, she responded by sending him a timid smile. "Thank you for the tea. You're very kind."

Yes, this was very basic. Maybe even a little vague. But at least it was polite.

He simply nodded, the corner of his mouth turning up in a slight smile.

She waited.

He remained silent.

Good grief, is he going to help you out at all?

She found this puzzling. He didn't come across as a man who would be tongue-tied around women.

Because, seriously? Look at him. No doubt women flocked around him wherever he went, hanging on to his every word.

If he ever came out with any, that is.

Hmm… maybe this explained why he was still single? If he was, in fact, still single. A quick glance at his left hand confirmed there was no ring. A fact that, for some odd reason, had her feeling very relieved.

Hoping he hadn't noticed this, she sent him a quick glance. Settled comfortably in his chair, as if he had no intentions of going anywhere, he nodded. So, now she was flustered, searching for something to say… something safe.

Her gaze came to rest on his tie. Perfect. This would give her the opportunity to find out the reason for his choice.

She gave him another timid smile. "*Umm...* I like your tie. It's very whimsical. And colorful." Again, there was no reason for him to find fault with a comment like this, was there? What man didn't like a compliment?

He glanced down at the tie, almost as if he'd forgotten he was even wearing one. Then he looked up at her, and this time, he gave her an actual smile.

"Thank you. It was a gift from two special ladies in my life."

What?

Her smile immediately disappeared. What did he mean? Was he trying to impress her? Letting her know he had no trouble attracting women? Or was this his way of informing her he wasn't available?

And she was irritated all over again, a curt response flying out of her mouth. "Ha, I bet it was."

As soon as she saw the puzzled look on his face, she realized how sarcastic she sounded. And now she was beyond flustered. Rather than meeting his gaze, she grabbed her cup and took a big gulp of tea.

It was hot... almost boiling hot. Snatching the napkin from the table and holding it up to her mouth, she closed her eyes.

Another impressive moment, but at least you didn't spit the tea across the table. Think of it as a blessing in disguise, putting a stop to any more of your stupid comments.

When she finally opened her eyes, he was still watching her, that concerned expression back on his face.

He leaned forward in his chair, tilting his head towards her. This had her leaning closer to him in return, her lips parted.

His voice was hesitant, almost as if he was afraid to ask. "Are you okay?"

She blinked, her mouth snapping shut.

Was she okay?

She closed her eyes. No, of course she wasn't okay. In fact, she hadn't been okay since she first heard his voice. But she certainly wasn't going to tell him this. There was no reason to inflate his ego any more than it already was.

She sighed, suddenly feeling very weary. To think this was all happening because she hadn't been able to hang on to her bag.

Her head jerked up, her eyes going wide.

Her bag.

Oh no, no...

Why was she sitting here drinking tea, with a man who happened to be British and one she knew nothing about, when her bag could be just about anywhere? This was certainly not the time for an afternoon tea party.

She came up out of her chair, bumping against the table and sending her cup teetering. A startled look on his face, he also stood. After he reached over to right the cup, he grabbed hold of her arm.

"Whoa… What are you doing?"

"My bag. The one I was trying to catch. I have to find it. My samples are in that bag." She groaned, her look frantic. "And the check… I can't lose that."

She tried to free her arm from his hold. But he held on tight, and reaching under the table, he held up a bag for her inspection. He raised an eyebrow. "I assume this is what you're looking for? Someone handed it to me while you were still out."

He set the bag on the table in front of her. "You'll find your hat is also in the bag."

Yep, it was definitely her bag. The same bag that was beginning to make her think she'd fallen into some kind of crazy dream.

She nodded, slowly sinking back into her chair. The color draining from her face, a sudden wave of dizziness washed over her. In a desperate attempt to fight it off, she dropped her head down on her arms and closed her eyes.

Oh please, no... you can't pass out on him again. Once was way more than enough.

For a long moment, there was only silence.

Had he left?

With the way things were going, she wouldn't blame him if he had. Then she felt the brush of his fingers to her hand, sending another one of those warm tingles racing through her.

His sharp intake of breath had her almost raising her head.

Did this mean he felt it, too?

She didn't move. Nor did she trust herself to speak. Instead, she held her breath, waiting to see what he would do.

This was if he even planned on doing something. Because other than keeping those amazing eyes of his focused on her every move, the rest of his behavior until now certainly hadn't been very responsive.

He finally released a long, drawn out breath. "I'm worried about you. I think we should get you to a doctor. You may be more injured than you think."

Just as she allowed herself to sink into the comfort of his words, he continued, the tone of his voice becoming more exasperated with each word. "Just what the hell were you doing, charging through the crowded sidewalk like that? Were you even paying attention to where you were going? And what is in that damn bag of yours that would warrant the risk of not only injuring yourself, but someone else?"

This was followed by a brief pause before his voice rose in disbelief. "Do you always act so crazy?"

Anna couldn't have been more surprised than if he'd thrown a huge bucket of ice water over her.

She was also very confused. What brought this on?

Why is he so angry at you?

Did he somehow feel responsible for her?

If so, she needed to let him know this wasn't necessary.

She did not need his help.

Very slowly, she lifted her head from her hands to tell him this. Only to become caught right up in his eyes.

Oh, dear God... you need to get away from this man, the sooner, the better. You don't need another angry man in your life. No matter how beautiful his eyes are. Or how incredibly handsome he is.

She shook her head.

This wasn't fair.

Not fair at all.

He was still watching her, but now his look was troubled. No doubt he was worried about what she might do next, having already determined she was crazy.

So she needed to prove him wrong. And she was going to do this by making a dignified exit before he had the chance to say another word.

Or, heaven forbid, give her another lecture.

Her hands shaking, she reached into her coat pocket for her wallet. Taking out a five-dollar bill, she pushed it across the table in front of him.

This brought on another puzzled look from him.

Unsteadily coming to her feet, the room feeling like it was swaying right along with her, she picked up her bag. She turned to see he'd also come to his feet.

She almost groaned out loud. Not only was the guy irresistibly attractive, had a smile that could melt butter, and was no doubt made of money, it appeared he was also one of the few men left on this planet with manners.

And how had she responded to all of this in the short time they were together? She'd managed to convince him she was totally insane.

Good job... you really know how to impress a guy, don't you?

Now beyond frustrated, she pulled her hat out of the bag. After she jammed it on her head and picked up the bag, she sent him a bright smile. "I'll be fine. And I don't need to see a doctor."

With a regal lift of her chin, she sent a nod towards the five-dollar bill. "This should more than cover the cost of the tea. Consider the change as a tip for your help."

The brief thought flitted through her mind, this comment may have been just a wee bit too much, when she saw what suspiciously looked like a smile tweak the corner of his mouth.

Great, just great. Oh, well, at least you got a smile out of him. Finish up with what you want to say so you can leave and forget any of this ever happened.

She sent him another smile as she began backing away from the table. "Now I really need to go. I have a lot of things to do. Maybe not as pressing as what you have planned, but very important to me. So, thank you and enjoy your day."

With this being said, she turned around and ran right into the table behind her.

Oh, no... don't look back. Just keep walking. You'll never see him again, so it doesn't matter if your exit isn't perfect.

"Anna?"

She froze. Did he just call out to her? But how was this possible? There was no way he could know her name.

And this time, she did groan aloud. It was obvious this whole experience was messing with her mind, letting her imagination take over. Resisting the urge to turn around, she pushed her way through the maze of tables, almost breaking into a run to get out of the little shop.

Once the coffee shop was a safe distance behind her, Anna slowed her pace.

Her mind was in an uproar. The more she thought about what happened, the worse she felt about how she'd behaved.

He had gone out of his way to help her. He'd been more than nice. And how had she responded? By throwing it all right back in his face. Most notably, the bit with the five-dollar bill.

Could she have even been more insulting?

But come on, if someone hints they're pretty sure you're crazy, you might as well live up to their expectations, right?

She shivered, huddling deeper in her coat. The rain had now turned into a mixture of snow and sleet, the wind whipping it up in a frenzy. As she stopped to pull up her hood and put on her gloves, she was relieved to see she was almost home. Besides suddenly feeling very weary, she'd also developed a pounding headache.

Maybe he was right, she should see a doctor. Not that she would admit this to him if given the chance. But it really didn't matter, did it? Because she would never see him again.

Briefly closing her eyes, she was overcome with such a strong feeling of regret. And sadness.

As if by leaving, she had walked away from something very special.

Possibly still waiting back in that coffee shop…

CHAPTER 3

A photo can be a reminder of the past.
Or, if you choose,
It can give you a glimpse of the future.
~ Unknown

*N*icholas watched Anna walk away.

No, he'd have to say it was more of a stagger than a walk. Which gave him every reason to be concerned.

He should go after her, hail a taxi, and get her to a doctor. This is what a normal and sensible person would do.

But she hadn't turned around when he called out her name. Instead, she began walking even faster, almost running in her haste to get away from him.

There was also the fact he wasn't feeling like the normal and sensible person he usually was.

No, he'd have to say he was almost in a state of shock.

Seriously? What the hell just happened?

As he began his walk back to the hotel, there was only one thing he was sure of... he'd totally screwed things up.

Badly.

19

He should have stayed in his hotel room. Because his decision to go out for some fresh air had only resulted in a catastrophe of sorts. But come on, what was the probability he would pick up, off the sidewalk of all places, the woman who was part of the reason for his trip to the States in the first place?

Admit it... this woman is the main reason you made this trip.

He ran his hand through his hair, a frustrated sigh escaping him. He needed to go over again what happened.

When he'd first noticed a woman running at full speed through the crowded sidewalk, he didn't know what to think. But as she drew closer, and he heard her screams, he became concerned.

Was she running from someone? Chasing someone?

He watched as, her face raised to the sky, she began coming right at him. Giving him no choice but to either step aside or try to catch her.

But, this decision was made for him when she abruptly changed course and went flying right past him.

And... BAM!

She sailed right into a cart piled high with Christmas garland.

His sight hindered by the heavy load, the man who was pushing the cart didn't even see her coming. She crashed into the cart with such force, she was sent flying backwards, her head hitting the pavement... hard.

This was right before the entire pile of garland came tumbling down on top of her.

Along with the help of the now almost hysterical man who had been pushing the cart, Nicholas began pulling away the garland. When they finally uncovered her, it was to find she was out cold.

It wasn't until she gained consciousness and he'd helped her up off the sidewalk, she turned to gaze right into his eyes. And this was when he received the shock of his life.

Anna...

The woman he was holding in his arms was none other than Anna.

A woman who, until a few months ago?

He hadn't even known she existed.

. . .

But first, let's backtrack a little here...

Anna is a friend of Katy's. The same Katy who is also the fiancée of Stephen Burns. And it turns out Stephen is an American business associate and also one of Nicholas's closest friends.

It had been late September when Katy and Stephen came to London for a brief holiday. And it was during this visit Nicholas met Anna.

But they hadn't met in person.

No, of course not. Things couldn't be that simple, could they?

Oddly enough, the connection was made through a photograph.

The memory of that night would be forever ingrained in his mind. While sitting out on the patio of a local wine bar and enjoying the unusually warm autumn weather, he and Stephen had reminisced about how their friendship had come about.

This prompted Katy to talk about her best friend, Anna. She brought out a photo, taken last New Year's Eve, showing the two of them smiling into the camera.

Instantly, Nicholas had been hit with a strong and binding connection to this Anna. As though she was the missing piece of his life he'd been waiting for. That he hadn't even known he was waiting for someone made this sudden awareness even more mind-boggling.

It was then he knew he had to meet her. When he told Katy this, he knew she was amused, but he didn't care. At his insistence, it was decided when he made his next trip to the states, Katy and Stephen would have a cocktail party so he and Anna could meet. Anna didn't believe in blind dates, Katy told him, so a party it would have to be.

She also made it clear this would be the extent of her involvement.

What happened after that would be all up to him.

Now let's swing right back to the present...

Over the past two months, Nicholas hadn't been able to get the image of Anna out of his head. And even though he knew he was reading too much into the situation, his mind refused to let it go.

Good Lord, who looks at a photo of someone they've never met and reacts like this?

Someone who has taken complete leave of his senses, that's who!

But now, instead of meeting tomorrow night at Stephen and Katy's party as planned, this mind-boggling encounter happened. He then had to go and cap it off by insinuating she was crazy.

He had to smile at this.

It appears you and this Anna may actually be suited for each other? She seems a little crazy and you are a tad out of your mind. A perfect match, wouldn't you say?

And the lecture he gave her?

He decided this had been brought on by the shock of finding out she was the Anna of the photograph. It had also scared the hell out of him when she hit her head so hard on the pavement.

He groaned. It's no wonder she stormed off the way she had. But this was only after she left him a generous tip.

Another smile quirked his lips at the memory of the righteous expression on her face when she did this. Trying to remember the last time anyone had tipped him, and in such dramatic fashion, he came up empty.

He made a mental note to let her know she would never need to tip him in the future. This was if she even agreed to talk to him tomorrow night...

He groaned.

My God, what in the world had come over him?

Oh, come on... you know what it is.

He came to a complete standstill, right in the middle of the crowded sidewalk. With everything he didn't know if he yet understood, coming at him all at once.

He'd been lost from the very first moment he had gazed into Anna's eyes. If he'd thought seeing her in a photograph rocked his world, meeting her in person had sent him flying over the top.

The connection was still there. But this time, it hit deeper. As though a shot of adrenaline had heightened his senses, everything coming at him in a more clear and brighter light. Everything having to do with Anna, that is.

Because she was all he could see.

His mind had emptied, any attempt at conversation eluding him. He had wanted to stay right there in that coffee shop and study her forever.

And this is what he should have done. Instead, he went and opened his big mouth.

Yes. He'd bungled this one. Big time.

Damn.

Well, there wasn't anything he could do about it now, was there? It was over and done with. He would have to hope, when he and Anna met up again tomorrow night, he would have the chance to make things right.

Yeah, like this is going to be easy…

Someone was trying to get his attention. Completely caught up in his thoughts, he'd miraculously made his way to the gourmet wine and cheese shop in his hotel. And now, much to the amusement of the sales assistant, he was standing in the middle of the aisle, staring blindly at the wine selection. Embarrassed, he enlisted her help in putting together a basket of wine and cheese to send to Katy and Stephen for the party.

The details of the gift basket worked out, he began making his way over to the elevators.

He groaned, coming to an abrupt stop. He smacked his hand to his forehead.

Your meeting… Good Lord, what about your meeting?

A quick glance at his watch showed if he hurried, he could still make the meeting, arriving only a few minutes late.

He took off in a run.

He needed to get his priorities in line. And his first order of business would be to put this situation with Anna on hold until tomorrow night. Even though he couldn't ignore how she'd now settled deeper in his mind than before.

But he was okay with this. Yes, he was actually looking forward to what was going to happen next.

He had a good feeling about this.

A really good feeling.

Anna climbed the three flights of stairs leading to her third-floor loft apartment, the pounding in her head intensifying with each step. Arriving at her door, she rested her forehead against it in relief.

Once she was inside, a bundle of tan and white fur came charging across the room and began circling her in excitement. Dropping to her knees and closing her eyes, Anna braced herself for the sloppy puppy kisses eagerly planted across her face.

She hugged the ecstatic little dog. "Oh, Mia. You don't know how lucky you are! You would never get messed up in a crazy situation like I did this afternoon."

After a few minutes spent running her fingers through the little dog's silky fur, she placed her bag on her worktable and removed her coat. She sank into the cushions of the sofa with Mia snuggled close beside her and closed her eyes.

Within minutes, she was asleep.

Her cell phone was ringing.

The sound jerked her awake, wincing at the shooting pain in her head at the move. Groggily stumbling over to her coat, she pulled her phone out of the pocket just as it stopped ringing.

The call was from Katy.

Oh no, you can't talk to her now. Not when you feel like this.

She sent her a text.

If she didn't, it would be like Katy to come rushing over to check on her.

Can't talk right now... call u tomorrow.

Katy replied almost at once.

Ok?

Relieved, Anna set the phone on the nightstand as a reminder she needed to call her in the morning. Then she crawled into bed, and pulling the quilt over her, she closed her eyes.

She needed to get some sleep.

Maybe then her headache would go away.

Along with the unshakable memory of a certain someone's beautiful blue eyes.

CHAPTER 4

It had been a very productive morning. And now Nicholas was looking forward to meeting Stephen for lunch.

He stepped outside to find the sun was shining. The sky a brilliant blue, there wasn't a cloud in sight. After taking in a deep breath of the invigorating breeze coming in from the lake, he set off for the restaurant, a smile on his face.

This is more like it! Let this beautiful day be an omen of good things to come.

Walking at a brisk pace, he vowed no matter what the outcome, he was going to embrace the rest of his stay with all the enthusiasm he could muster. If Anna took one look at him tonight and turned her back on him, so be it. It wasn't meant to be.

But this wouldn't happen, would it?

Nah, things will work out.

And let's just say they didn't?

Hello? Where's that enthusiasm you were just throwing around a moment ago?

"Hey, Nicholas…"

He looked over to see Stephan was standing in front of the restaurant, trying to catch his attention.

After an enthusiastic greeting, they entered the restaurant.

They'd been seated and, without looking up from the menu he was studying, Stephen was the first to speak. "Did you get any work done this morning? Or are you still re-living what happened yesterday?"

What?

His head jerking up, Nicholas groaned.

How the hell does Stephen know about your run in with Anna?

His reaction was enough for Stephen to glance over at him, an inquiring expression on his face.

Nicholas gave him a nonchalant glance. "And this would be because of?"

His selection made, Stephen snapped his menu shut and put it aside. He slowly shook his head. "Katy told me about your flight. Travel is becoming such a hassle, isn't it? Bad weather... crazy passengers... cancellations and so on. I feel your pain, buddy. Believe me, I've experienced it all."

Leaning back in his chair, he massaged his chin. "But now, because of you, my good man, Katy says she's done with flying. I almost had her sold on it, too. This puts a damper on future holidays abroad since boating across the pond, as you Brits refer to it, is not really an alternative. At least not for me."

Nicholas was relieved. *Very relieved.* The flight. Stephen was talking about the flight, not Anna. Thank God he hadn't gone and blurted out something stupid.

But he also felt guilty. Thinking back on his call to Katy, confirming he would be there for the cocktail party, he recalled doing more than his share of complaining about his flight. He should have remembered her fear of flying.

And here we have it... another incident to add to his long and recent list of blunders. All because of a silly whim.

Good Lord, what's next?

He ran his hand through his hair. "Hell, I'm sorry. When we talked, I was still wound up. Since I know how you want to do more traveling together, I'll do whatever it takes to get Katy back on a flight to London again."

The server interrupted to deliver their drinks and take their lunch order before Stephen could respond. "Hey, anything you do will be appreciated. Because as it stands now, nothing short of a miracle will get her back on a plane. Especially going overseas." He held up his drink in a toast. "But enough of that. Here's to a great week ahead."

Nicholas had just taken a swallow of his drink when Stephen went on to add. "Speaking of Katy, are you still up to meeting Anna tonight?"

Nicholas nearly choked on his drink.

In fact, he did choke.

Which turned out to be an extremely embarrassing situation, with Stephen leaping out of his chair to pound him on the back. Finally able to laugh at himself, Nicholas waved him back to his seat.

Slowly sinking back in his chair, Stephen regarded him with concern. "What the hell is going on with you? Almost everything I've said has you reacting in the most unusual way. I'm beginning to wonder what's going to set you off next."

Nicholas's smile was distracted. "Sorry, I guess I've got a lot going on in my mind right now."

Good Lord, steer the conversation away from Anna. Because now, even the mention of her name is wreaking havoc with your behavior.

After taking a fortifying, but more cautious swallow of his drink, he set his glass on the table. "And yes, I'm still looking forward to meeting Anna. It will also be nice to reconnect with people I haven't seen in a while. Fill me in… is there anyone or anything I need to know about?"

Stephen leaned back in his chair to think about this for a few moments. He frowned. "We have a new Chicago rep, Megan King. From what I've seen so far, she excels at only two things. She can be so loud and annoying. I'll be interested to see what you think when you meet her."

He shook his head. "Whoever hired her must have seen something the rest of us can't. And now I heard she's back in town, so she'll probably show up at this party. Invited or not."

He grimaced. "I guess I should also add aggressive to her list of traits. You'll know who she is as soon as she walks into the room. Her loud, grating voice makes everyone scatter in order to avoid her. Even Katy. This should tell you something, since she likes everyone."

Nicholas grimaced. "She sounds like the woman I had next to me on my flight."

A look of horror came over Stephen's face. "God, I hope not! Wouldn't that be your luck?" Then he suddenly grinned. "I've also heard she's on the hunt for a husband, so you'll be fair game."

Taking another swallow of his drink, Nicholas shook his head. "Since the odds of us being on the same flight are pretty low, I'm not worried. And from what you've told me, it sounds like she really isn't my type."

Stephen chuckled. "I don't know about that. It seems even with your pompous British upbringing, every woman on this earth thinks you're the one and only man for her, practically swooning at your feet. Why, I don't know. It can't all be because of the accent."

As the server set their entree in front of them, Nicholas wondered what Stephen would have to say if he knew about his encounter with Anna.

Yeah, your pompous British upbringing definitely made an appearance. A bloody, unfavorable one. And swooning at your feet? I guess you could call it that.

He grinned, giving a dismissive wave. "You'll never figure it out. But I'd be glad to give you a few pointers if you like. It wouldn't hurt to learn a thing or two about charming the fairer sex."

Hmm... sort of how you turned on the charm with Anna?

Stephen shook his head. "I'll pass. Katy is the only woman I need to charm, and believe it or not, she likes me just the way I am."

He looked at Nicholas, his smile slightly puzzled. "Go figure."

After he and Stephen parted and with his next appointment not until late afternoon, Nicholas began a leisurely stroll back to his hotel. And yes, he was sure about the time of this next meeting, having checked this out more times than he wanted to admit.

His thoughts drifted to Stephen and Katy and how they seemed to be so well matched, their personalities bringing out the best in each other. This led him to mull over this whole concept of falling in love.

How was it two people were able to find each other and know it was true love? Did this happen by chance? Was there really such a thing as a chemical attraction between two people? Or was it merely being in the right place at the right time?

He had no idea. Absolutely no idea at all.

Considering, over the past ten years of his life, he'd devoted his life to growing his business, pursuing the 'perfect relationship' hadn't even been an option. Good Lord, any free time he did have, he'd rather chill out alone and in the privacy of his own home. And he, along with everyone else, appeared to be fine with this.

Until lately, that is.

The subtle, and sometimes not so subtle, hints by his family it was time for him to think more seriously about settling down, hadn't escaped him. This, along with the mention of grandchildren, seemed to be their favorite topic of conversation. The responsibility of producing the next generation of Hanovers was something not to be taken lightly. At least not according to his parents.

Hmm… maybe someday he would be ready for children, but not yet. His life now was predictable, everything running smoothly and in the correct order. So, the last thing he wanted was to complicate things.

Though he'd be the first to admit he enjoyed spending time with his sister Claire's six-year-old twins, Clementine and Emily. If anyone could make his day brighter or bring him to laugh, it would be those two.

So, why do these thoughts keep taking over your mind? And why did you schedule this trip around this party tonight?

Reluctant to admit this and only to himself, mind you, over the past few months, he'd been hounded by a sense of urgency. Time was flying by all too fast, his business dominating his life.

And this was making him wonder if he was missing out on what was really important.

After all, what's so great about building up a business, one surpassing even your highest expectations, if you have no one by your side to share in your success?

He frowned.

Since when did the fact he was alone start to feel so wrong?

And, more importantly, why couldn't he stop thinking about Anna?

CHAPTER 5

*A*nna's cell phone was ringing.

Slowly opening her eyes, she was surprised to see the sun shining down through the loft high windows. This meant she'd slept straight through the night.

She made a grab for the phone. Instead she hit it with her hand, sending it flying off the nightstand. She watched as it hit the floor and went skidding under her bed.

Where it continued to ring.

Mia, who was sprawled out on the bed beside her, let out a loud yelp and went diving off the bed, barking up a storm.

"Mia… it's okay, it's just the phone."

When the barking continued, she sat on the edge of the bed. This sent the room spinning around like she was on one of those whirly-twirly kind of rides at an amusement park. She lowered her head to her knees and began taking in deep, gulping breaths.

Finally, with the help of Mia, who had burrowed her way into her lap to shower her face with encouraging puppy kisses, the dizziness began to subside.

She retrieved the now silent phone. Just as she thought, the call was from Katy.

But first things first. What she needed was a hot shower. And coffee. Yes, definitely lots of coffee.

Only then would she call Katy.

Seated at her kitchen counter with a cup of coffee cradled in her hands, Anna realized this was the first time in the past twenty-four hours she'd felt normal.

Well, almost normal.

Unfortunately, her headache was slowly making a comeback. But she was counting on the coffee to take care of that. She only needed to give it time.

Her gaze traveling around the room, bathed in the light of the early morning sun, her thoughts drifted to her grandmother. She'd passed away unexpectedly only a few months ago and Anna missed her so much. She had been her only family and her biggest fan. Even now her love and support lived on. The bequest of this apartment and the promise of financial security for years to come now made it possible for Anna to pursue her dream of starting her own business.

After approaching several local boutiques and shops throughout the city about stocking her original hand painted glass ornaments, she was finally beginning to see results. Yesterday's order was not her largest, but coming from a well-established and popular boutique, it was sure to open more doors in the future.

She hoped this meant her life was finally headed in the right direction.

Is it? Then why do you feel so empty? And why can't you stop thinking about the stranger who came to your rescue yesterday? Remember his blue eyes? And his smile?

There was less than a million in one chance she would ever see him again, so why even go there?

Chin in hand, and staring into space, she sighed. She just couldn't shake the memory of the intensity of his gaze, his eyes holding hers. As though he knew what she was thinking. Or could sense her every need.

It was almost as if they were connected in some way.

Even now, with no clue of his whereabouts, this feeling was still so strong inside of her.

You must be losing your mind...

This actually made her laugh out loud. Maybe he was right. Maybe she really was crazy.

A rapid knocking at her door sent Mia off the couch and in a scramble across the room. Following the excited dog, she opened the door to find it was Katy.

Her expression was one of relief, bordering on anger, she crossed her arms over her chest. "I have been calling you all morning. I thought something horrible happened. Especially after the text you sent last night. It wasn't like you at all."

Anna gave her a hug. "Oh Katy, I'm so sorry, *really* sorry. I was out in that awful weather and when I got home, I had such a headache. I only wanted to crawl in bed, pull the covers over my head and go to sleep."

Katy frowned. "You do remember you promised to be at this cocktail party tonight. You know I need your support. So many of Stephen's business associates will be there and I need to make a good impression. If only for Stephen's sake."

Anna laughed. "You will be just fine And I'll try my best to be there."

Katy shook her head. "Try? That's not even an option. In fact, just to reassure me, tell me what you're planning to wear."

Anna looked at her with surprise. "Why should what I wear matter?" Then she sighed. "Oh Katy, you're not trying to fix me up with someone, are you? Please tell me you're not. You know how I feel about this."

Katy was immediately flustered, avoiding her gaze. "Ah... no, no. There will probably be some interesting types that show up, but I had to invite everyone. I couldn't take the chance of offending someone by not inviting them. You can't fault me for that, right?"

Anna gave an exasperated sigh. "I know my life may seem boring to you, but I'm happy. I don't want to be fixed up, not even with one of Stephen's friends. This would only complicate things. We both know Marc would go crazy if I started dating someone."

She shuddered. "I don't even want to think about what could happen."

Already searching through Anna's closet, Kay turned to make a face at her. "Anna, every man out there is not like Marc. For heaven's sake, you need to be thankful it's over and move on."

Anna stared at her, eyebrows raised. "Move on? Katy, if he left me alone, I would. But again, I'm not the least bit interested in staring up a new relationship."

Unless this would be with your handsome blue-eyed stranger. A man who made you feel like you've never felt before.

Anna closed her eyes, shaking her head. Where had that come from?

He wasn't hers. Nor did she want him to be.

Right?

She could hear Katy talking to herself. Then her voice grew louder. "Anna? Did you hear me? I asked if you want to wear this red dress? The tags are still on it. If not, I'll just keep on searching to see what else I can find."

Anna sighed, and massaging the back of her head, she went to see what dress she was talking about.

Once Katy was on a roll, there was no stopping her.

With a long sigh of relief, Anna leaned back against the door she'd just closed behind Katy.

She loved Katy dearly, she really did, but her high energy level was hard to take sometimes.

Like today, with this headache that was refusing to go away.

Katy had gone through her closet like a small hurricane. Even though Anna was relieved with how quickly she decided on a dress, along with the perfect accessories to match, she was worried. The serious way she went about this could only mean she was up to something.

She scooped up Mia in her arms, and once she was settled with her on the sofa, she closed her eyes. Her headache wasn't going away. If anything, it seemed to be getting progressively worse. How could she go to Katy and Stephen's cocktail party tonight when she felt like this?

She sighed. She would be there. Wearing the dress Katy had chosen. Because, honestly? She would do anything for Katy.

When Anna was only eight years old, her whole world had been turned upside down with the sudden death of her parents. She'd moved in with her grandmother, but had been so lost, something Katy quickly picked up on. They became inseparable, even going as far to make a pact they would be friends for life. And to this day, they were still the best of friends.

When she broke off her engagement with Marc, Katy had helped her through the whole horrible ordeal. And when her grandmother died only a few months later, once again it was Katy who was there for her, even though she'd just become engaged to Stephen.

While watching Katy go through her closet, she'd tried to ignore the garment bag still hanging there, holding her wedding dress. She could still remember how she, Katy and her grandmother had so much fun choosing what she thought would be the perfect dress for one of the most important days in her life.

But the dress had never been worn. The tags still attached, it had been packed away in the bag it came in,

After she gave Marc back his ring, she hadn't intended to keep the dress. But caught up in a struggle to put the shattered pieces of her life back together after her grandmother's death, she'd shoved it even further back in her closet.

Out of sight, out of mind, right?

And this is where the dress had remained. A sad reminder of how something so wonderful could change so quickly, her dreams destroyed in an instant.

No, getting married isn't for you. Not for a long time. Let Katy be the one to do that.

But right now she had work to do. Pushing herself off the sofa, leaving Mia to burrow even deeper in the cushions without even opening her eyes, she turned on her favorite Christmas playlist and got to work on her new orders.

But first she was going to check out the dress Katy had chosen.

She hoped it didn't need to be ironed.

Nicholas was ready.

More than ready.

In fact, he was starting to obsess about things he shouldn't be obsessing about. Like a few minutes earlier, when he began to question if his choice of tie was appropriate to wear to a cocktail party.

This moment of indecision was not like him. Especially since the tie in question, a whimsical design of snowflakes on a deep blue background, was his favorite to wear during the holidays.

Thank goodness, he'd talked himself out of making such a ridiculous move. And since when did he even give a hoot about what anyone else thought about his choice of attire?

Oh, come on, admit it. There's definitely someone you want to win over tonight. If only to remedy the shoddy impression you gave earlier.

He sighed. He clearly had his work cut out for him.

When he realized he was pacing back and forth, he sank down in the chair by the window where he could keep an eye out for his taxi. In a further attempt to keep his mind off what he shouldn't be thinking about, he pulled out his phone to check his messages.

Claire had sent him a photo of Clementine and Emily holding up a handmade sign, the message—Don't forget, Uncle Nicky!—decorated enthusiastically in crayon.

He laughed, thinking how they must have pestered Claire to send this.

How could he forget the deal he made with them? Shaking his head, he made a note to call them in the morning. With the time difference, they would now be in bed and sound asleep.

Checking his watch, he saw he still had a good twenty minutes before his taxi's arrived. A perfect excuse for a short nap. He rested his head against the back of the chair and closed his eyes.

And as had been happening more times than he'd like to admit, a vision of Anna settled again in his mind.

He dozed off… his dreams bringing a smile on his face.

Anna gave one final check in the mirror.

The hazel hue of her eyes picked up the blue of her dress and her cheeks were still flushed from the hot bubble bath she'd indulged in for way too long. But it had felt so good, allowing her to forget her headache for at least a little while.

After she slipped into her heels, she settled on the sofa to wait for her taxi. Smoothing her hands over the silky fabric of her dress, the shade of blue brought to mind someone's eyes.

Stop it! You need to think of something else. Anything!

Gazing around the room, she saw the ornaments she'd worked on for the boutique setting on her worktable, ready to be finished.

And what a surprise… they were all done in a certain shade of blue.

Oh dear… you're pathetic.

Her cell phone rang.

Her taxi was here. Now she wouldn't have time to think. Or get lost again in the memory of a certain smile.

A smile that seemed to reach out to touch every inch of her.

Twenty minutes later, Anna walked into Katy and Stephen's condo. The busy hum of conversation putting her in a festive mood, her headache was momentarily forgotten.

The beautifully decorated great room, with its high ceilings and wall of windows that showcased a magnificent view of the city, glowed in the candlelight.

As she slowly made her way through the crowded room, searching for Katy, she wondered how Stephen could possibly know so many people.

Eventually making her way into the kitchen, she found Katy, a tray of appetizers in her hands as she tried to maneuver her way around the crowd gathered there.

"Katy!" She almost had to yell to get her attention.

Katy turned, a relieved look coming over her face before she set the tray on the island. "Oh Anna, I'm so glad you're here." After she wrapped Anna in a big hug, she stepped back to look at her. "You look stunning. I knew this was the right choice."

She waved her hand around at the crowded kitchen. "Why is everyone in the kitchen? There is far more space in the great room and it's also quieter. Here you can't even hear yourself think."

Anna smiled, gazing around the room. "People always seem to gather in the kitchen. After all, it's where the food is. Like this amazing display of appetizers here on the island. Please don't tell me you did all of this yourself."

Katy winked at her, a mischievous grin lighting up her face. "Not all by myself, of course. I had a little help from Martha."

They dissolved into laughter, both remembering the time after college when they shared an apartment. During this time, obsessed with Martha Stewart, Katy began making her own soaps, mixes, and throwing theme parties. To this day, they still joked about how intense she was.

"Well, I guess it paid off." Anna gestured to both the island and Katy. "Look at all of this and look at you! Why, you're actually glowing. Being engaged certainly suits you."

Katy gave her a startled look before she sent her a smile. "Oh Anna, now I know why I wanted you here. You always make me feel so much better about myself."

She nodded towards the island. "Now, what can I get you? Would you like something to eat? Or a glass of wine"

Anna nodded towards the tray of appetizers Katy had set on the island. "I want something to do. Let me pass around these appetizers. Since I really don't know anyone here, this will keep me busy and I'll meet people at the same time."

Katy frowned, crossing her arms. "I didn't ask you to be here tonight to work! I want you to have fun!"

Anna shook her head as she picked up the tray. "No, trust me, I want to help. I can have fun and hand out appetizers at the same time."

As she started towards the great room, she smiled back at Katy. "I'll be back when these are gone!"

Nicholas had arrived at Katy and Stephen's about forty-five minutes ago and he already felt like he needed a break.

Badly.

His head was starting to ache from all of the introductions and social banter this type of event involved. Since he arrived, it had been non-stop and he was beginning to wonder what had possessed him to encourage Katy and Stephen to throw this event on his account.

To make things worse, Anna hadn't even made an appearance yet. While he was already exhausted and ready to return to the peace and quiet of his hotel room.

What he needed was a drink. And something to eat was sounding like a good idea, too. This way, when Anna arrived he would be in a better frame of mind. This was imperative if there was any chance of making things right between them.

Of course, this all depended on if she even agreed to talk to him. Knowing this was probably a long shot, he rubbed the back of his neck in frustration.

How did everything get so damn crazy?

Yep, he definitely needed that drink.

He began to make his way towards the bar just as a shrill laugh came from across the room. The familiarity of this immediately set off a warning bell in his mind.

No... it couldn't be.

He turned around to see the laugh was coming from the person he thought it was... the annoying woman from his flight. This meant she was indeed, the Megan Stephen had warned him about. Her gaze darting about as if she was searching for someone, he watched as she began making her way across the room.

She couldn't possibly be looking for him, could she?

Nah, come on. Get over yourself.

But deciding he wasn't going to chance it, he quickly ducked behind a large group of people engaged in a heated conversation about politics. His hope was, in her attempt to avoid them, Megan would pass right by and not even notice him.

He checked out his surroundings. He was by a wall of windows overlooking the city. He gazed longingly at the chair next to him, the plush cushions an invitation to relax and enjoy the view.

It was too tempting to pass up. Only a few minutes, he promised himself. Then he would fall back on his original plan of getting a drink and something to eat.

But a loud and husky voice coming from behind him put a halt to his plan. Her voice, falling right below his ear, was a loud and irritating purr. "Darling! I've found you! I was so hoping that I would run into you again!" He briefly closed his eyes.

Damn... this woman is going to be the death of you.

Pasting a smile on his face and bracing for what he knew would be an aggressive greeting, he turned to her. Sure enough, she came right at him, her fingers reaching up to run through his hair. It was when she attempted to plant a kiss to his cheek, he swiftly turned his head.

And this is when he saw her.

Anna.

As Anna wandered among the guests with her tray of appetizers, she was beginning to regret her offer to help. Her headache had returned with a vengeance, leaving her feeling even a bit lightheaded. The air in the room felt heavy, the combined scent of the different perfumes, food and alcohol making her feel nauseated.

She glanced longingly over at the front door. If only she could slip outside to breathe in some fresh air. She would only need a few minutes. Maybe then she would feel better.

You only have one shrimp puff left on the tray. As soon as it's gone, you can make your escape. So, hang in there.

She took a deep breath, and gazing around the room, her attention was captured by a voluptuous and heavily made-up woman, the form fitting black knit dress she was wearing straining at the seams.

Only a few feet away, she was draped up against a tall, dark haired man, her hand clutching his arm. She appeared to be whispering something in his ear.

Anna was overcome by a sudden anger. Why she found this so upsetting, she had no idea. For heaven's sake, she didn't even know these people.

But seriously? Why was it some men were only happy when they had a woman fawning over their every move?

Against her better judgment, she began moving closer, if only to get a better look at this man who would encourage such behavior.

In a crowded room, no less.

Her breath catching in her throat, she came to an abrupt stop, almost sending the shrimp puff sliding off the tray. There was something about this man that was so familiar. As she tried to search her memory as to why, he looked over and right at her.

In less time than it would take to blink, she became lost in his eyes.

It was him...

The man with the beautiful blue eyes.

The same stranger that had her ready to walk right into his arms when he aimed that slow smile of his at her.

Uh, hello... the same stranger who also thinks you're crazy. Let's not forget this one important fact.

CHAPTER 6

For Nicholas, everything had come to a grinding halt. Frozen in space, his eyes locked with Anna's.

Whirling around to see why Nicholas's attention was no longer on her, Megan spotted Anna holding the tray. Snatching up the shrimp puff and turning back to him, her shrill voice instantly shattered the connection between him and Anna.

"Look! There's only one appetizer left, so it must be meant just for you! Let me feed it to you, darling!"

As she began waving the shrimp puff in front of his face, he tried to push her hand away in order to focus his attention more closely on Anna.

Because, from what he could see, it appeared something was terribly awry.

Anna gazed down at the tray she was holding.

Then she glanced up to fall right back into those blue eyes. As she tried to form the words to let him know something was wrong, the floor shifted beneath her feet. At the same time, the lighting in the room dimmed. Her fingers losing their grip on the tray, she sank into the darkness coming up to meet her, only one thought playing over and over in her head.

Oh no, oh no, oh no... not again.

Having watched all of this happen, Nicholas launched into action, shoving Megan aside in his haste to get past her. Judging by her shrill scream, a sound he'd hoped to never again hear in his lifetime, his push was far from gentle. But this was the least of his worries. After watching Anna crumple to the floor, his only objective to get to her as quickly as possible.

He gathered her up in his arms, pushing his way through the crowded room. In a quest to find a more secluded area, he came to Katy's and Stephen's bedroom. He laid Anna on the bed only seconds before the concerned voice of Katy came from behind him.

"Nicholas! What happened? Oh my, do you think it's serious? Should we call an ambulance?"

He turned to her, his voice deep with concern. "I don't know. One minute she was standing there, the next she hit the floor. I told her she needed to see a doctor. Do you know if she did?"

Sitting down on the bed, Katy's expression was puzzled as she reached over to hold Anna's hand.

"A doctor? Nicholas, whatever are you talking about? What do you know about all of this? What happened?"

They were joined by Stephen, who came running into the room, a worried look on his face. "My God, Katy! What's going on? Someone just told me a woman fainted, and I thought it might be you. But it's Anna? What happened?"

His eyes never leaving Anna's face, Nicholas filled them in on his encounter with Anna the previous afternoon.

"I know I should've said something about this before, but it was all so unreal." He shrugged, a pained expression on his face. "And I didn't help matters by giving her a lecture. But I could only think of how much worse it could have been. Good Lord, she wasn't even looking where she was going. She could have run right out into traffic."

He groaned, dragging his hand down over his chin. "I should have insisted she go to the hospital. Even if I had to take her myself. How could I have been so stupid?"

Katy and Stephen glanced at each other, surprised at his distraught state. Katy reached over to squeeze Nicholas's hand. "Don't worry, it will be okay. Knowing Anna, she wouldn't have gone along with that, anyway."

But Nicholas wasn't listening.

His attention was focused on Anna, who was beginning to stir.

Anna wasn't quite sure where she was or what happened. She tried to think back on what landed her in this state, but everything in her mind seemed to be in a total state of confusion.

What she did know, she didn't want to open her eyes. At least not until everything stopped this ridiculous spinning around her. Nor did she want to move, the painful throbbing in her head becoming almost unbearable when she did.

Someone took hold of her hand. "Anna?"

She felt a tremor go through her at the touch. And this voice? Why did it sound so familiar? Struggling to remember, she had a sudden flashback of being in the crowded room and holding the tray. She could see the annoying woman taking the appetizer. And then …

Oh my God… it was him… it was really him.

Her eyes flew open and there they were. Those blue eyes. The same blue eyes she hadn't been able to get out of her mind since the first time she became lost in them.

How was it even possible they had come back into her life?

Was this really be happening? Maybe she was dreaming?

She struggled into a sitting position, shaking her head in disbelief. This immediately bringing on another wave of dizziness, it was a few moments before she could focus on his face.

"You again… who are you?" This was barely a whisper.

Nicholas glanced over at Katy, getting a cautious smile in return. His gaze shifting back to Anna, he opened his mouth as if he planned to say something. Instead, after a frustrated sigh, he turned and walked out of the room.

Once he was in the hallway, he glanced in her direction before taking out his phone.

A bewildered expression on her face, Anna watched this before she turned to Katy. "Katy, who is he? And why is he here?"

Katy squeezed her hand. "Oh Anna, first things firsts. Why didn't you tell me what happened?" She eyed her closely. "You really should go see a doctor and get this checked out. I'm so worried about you."

When Anna only continued to stare at her, the confused expression still on her face, Katy sighed. She gestured over at Nicholas, who was now talking on his phone. "And who's that?" She smiled. "That's Nicholas. He's the Nicholas we spent so much time with when Stephen and I went to London in September. Didn't I tell you about him? He and Stephen are good friends."

She glanced over at Stephen, receiving his affirmative nod.

"Nicholas lives in London but travels here often." She smiled. "I'm sure you've noticed his charming British accent? And now he has told us what happened yesterday. What a coincidence the two of you met in such an unusual way."

Anna was having a hard time concentrating on what Katy was chattering about. There were only three things registering in her mind right now.

This man from yesterday was not a stranger. At least not to Katy and Stephen.

His name was Nicholas.

And he was the same Nicholas who had come to her rescue yesterday, picking her up off the ground… or off the floor, or wherever. Did it really matter? Because either way, it wasn't good.

But it now seemed this Nicholas had more important things to do. What could possibly be so urgent that he needed to be on his phone? While she was practically at death's door?

Okay, maybe this was a bit of an exaggeration. But seriously? Could he show a little more concern? After all, wasn't he partly responsible for this state she was in?

Come on, give the guy a break. He can't be all that bad. And as far as what happened? It certainly wasn't his fault.

His final words to her in the coffee shop popped into her mind. She hoped there wasn't going to be a repeat performance of this now. She certainly didn't need another lecture. This would send her head spinning even more than it already was.

There was only one thing she needed right now, and this was to go home.

She turned to Katy to tell her this, but darn if this slight movement didn't set off another round of dizziness. She put her head down and weakly waved her hand in Katy's direction. "Katy, you should go back to your guests. And I need to go home. Don't worry about me. I will be fine."

But evidently this wasn't going to happen. At least not as far as this Nicholas was concerned. Slipping his phone back in his pocket and confidently sauntering back into the room, his eyes zeroed right in on her. The serious tone of his voice indicated he meant business.

"I will be taking you to the hospital."

She opened her mouth to protest, but he swiftly held up his hand to stop her. Her mouth snapping shut, she glared at him.

Unfazed by this, he stared right back at her.

After a short silence, he continued, his voice becoming softer. "I called for a taxi and the driver said he would come as quickly as possible. I don't know what I was thinking yesterday when I let you leave. I should've insisted you did this then."

Anna closed her eyes, her hands clenching in her lap.

Insisted? He should have insisted? Just who does he think he is?

How was it he thought he could tell her what to do? If she wasn't feeling so absolutely wretched, she would have plenty to say in response to this.

And none of it would be good.

When Katy saw the furious expression on Anna's face, she grabbed her hand. "Anna, he's right. And I'll go with you."

But Stephen wasn't at all in favor of this. He put his hand on Katy's shoulder, shaking his head. "Katy, Anna will be fine with Nicholas and with a houseful of guests, you need to stay here. But for now, stay with Anna until the taxi arrives. I'll take care of everything else until then."

He planted a quick kiss to her cheek before he turned to smile at Anna. "Don't worry, Anna. You're in good hands with Nicholas."

After he left the room, there was only silence. Katy glanced over at Anna, to see her stubborn expression was almost a carbon copy of the look on Nicholas's face. Hoping to lighten the mood, she searched her mind for something to say. But a loud voice beat her to this, shattering the silence in a very unpleasant way.

"Darling! Here you are!"

Startled, Anna glanced over to see this was coming from Nicholas's let-me-whisper-sweet-nothings-into-your-ear girlfriend, who was now hanging on to his arm.

She was confused. This was the kind of woman he was attracted to? Really? It just didn't seem possible. But then again, why was she even surprised? With his good looks and suave demeanor... and don't forget that accent of his... he probably had many girlfriends. All styles, shapes and sizes of them.

Nicholas smothered a groan. Good Lord, this whole incident was turning into a three-ring circus! Unable to pry Megan's grip from his arm and not wanting to make a scene, he slowly turned to her, his greeting strained. "Megan, you should go join the others. There's no need for you to be here."

Megan ignored this, leaning even more provocatively against him. She was practically purring as she gazed up at him.

"*Oh puh-leeese...* I've spent entirely too much time looking for you to leave, darling." Her voice turned into an annoying whine. "After telling everyone about our horrible flight and the way you took such good care of me, I realized you'd disappeared. I was so worried you might have left without me."

She followed this with an exaggerated pout before she shot a quick glance around the room, almost as though she was seeking approval for her performance. When her gaze fell on Anna, she gave a dramatic gasp, tightening her grip on Nicholas's arm

"Oh my, is our little server ok?" She gave a dramatic frown. "I'm so thankful you had an empty tray. Otherwise you might have spilled something on me or one of the guests. I consider myself very fortunate this wonderful man kept you from toppling over onto me."

This earned Nicholas another loving look, her fingertips dancing up the lapel of his jacket. She glanced over at Katy and shook her head, a look of pity on her face. "It's sort of scary, not knowing how experienced the catering help will be, isn't it?"

Katy's laugh was strained. "Megan, Anna is my dearest and best friend. And she's been kind enough to offer her help. Nicholas, with this being said, why don't you escort Megan back to join the other guests? Anna and I will stay here and wait for you to let us know when the taxi arrives."

Anna hid her smile at the expression on Nicholas's face. He certainly didn't look very happy about being dismissed so firmly by Katy. But he merely nodded before he took Megan's arm to briskly escort her out of the room.

Katy was surprised to see what looked like a smile on Anna's face. But when their eyes met, Anna quickly ducked her head and closed her eyes.

They sat in silence, Katy absentmindedly patting Anna's hand. She couldn't wait to see what was going to happen next.

CHAPTER 7

$\mathcal{A}$nna was exhausted. Her eyes closed, she was huddled in the corner of the backseat of the taxi.

She felt like they had spent hours in the hospital, traveling from one room to the next, for one test after another. The doctor who had finally examined her had been no help at all.

Her headache was worse than before, and any move she made still made her dizzy.

The medication they gave you certainly isin't doing any good, is it?

She was almost too worn out to be mad about anything. But she was still trying to hang on to some of her anger. She couldn't risk the chance all the emotions swirling inside of her would take over, terri-fied what might happen if they did.

And this was all because of this beautiful blue-eyed man who she now knew as Nicholas. The same Nicholas who was still with her and only inches away in the close confines of this taxi. So close, she could reach over and touch him if she wanted to.

And for some crazy and unknown reason she found herself so desperately wanting to do exactly that.

What can you possibly be thinking? Remember? You don't like him. And it certainly wasn't your choice to have him here.

She had been so relieved when she finally talked the doctor out of an overnight stay at the hospital. But why had she thought this would work in her favor? Because she then had to turn around and promise she wouldn't be alone. Someone would stay with her.

At the look of determination in Nicholas's eyes when he told the doctor he would be that someone, she'd seriously wanted to scream. And she probably would have if she hadn't been so completely drained from trying to convince him and everyone else she only wanted to go home.

So, she could crawl into her bed and go to sleep.

Alone.

But of course, this didn't happen. And now here they were, in route to her apartment.

Could things get any worse?

She cautiously turned her head to look in his direction, her breath instantly catching in her throat. With his head resting against the back of the seat and his eyes closed, he looked totally done in. And this, she realized with a small twinge of guilt, was all because of her.

As she continued to study him, her anger slowly began to fade.

Even with exhaustion etched on his face he was still so unbelievably handsome. She was hit with the sudden urge to reach over and brush her fingertips down his cheek, if only to smooth away some of the worry she could see there. When this craving grew even stronger, she quickly turned to stare out of the window, her hands twisting together in her lap.

Within seconds her gaze was drawn back to him, this time moving down to where his hand was resting on the seat between them. Impulsively, she reached over to lightly brush her fingertips over his wrist.

Instantly, he turned to her and his eyes, his beautiful eyes, opened to look right at her. And as with every time she'd found caught up in his gaze, she was unable to look away.

Say something... something nice for a change. Give the guy a break.

"Thank you." This came out in a husky whisper.

The corners of his mouth slowly turning up into a smile, he cleared his throat.

His response was also a whisper. "You're welcome, my love."

Linking his fingers with hers and bringing her hand to his mouth, he brushed his lips over her knuckles in a soft kiss before he rested their hands back together on the seat. She watched as he settled his head back against the seat and closed his eyes, the smile still on his face.

In a daze, she stared down at their hands, hers still tingling from the touch of his lips. She was afraid to move, fearful she'd wake up to find this was all a dream.

My love? He didn't actually say that, did he? Oh my God, this bump to your head is making you imagine way too many things.

Suddenly more tired than she could ever remember being in her life, it became a battle to stay awake. She finally gave in and closing her eyes, she nodded off.

Her hand still tucked in his.

Nicholas was dead tired.

He felt like he'd been up for twenty-four hours straight.

Which, if he stopped to think about this, he probably had.

It hadn't been until after all the tests they gave Anna at the hospital confirmed she only had a slight concussion, he'd finally been able to relax.

And now in the hushed darkness of the taxi, fatigue hung over him like a heavy cloud.

A small smile on his face, he thought back to the smug look on Anna's face when she convinced the doctors she didn't need to stay in the hospital overnight. But how she quickly became so frustrated when she then had to promise someone would stay the night with her. When he stepped in to say he'd be the one to take on this role, the look she gave him made it quite clear spending more time with him was the absolute last thing she wanted to do.

For some reason and he wasn't quite sure why, she seemed to blame him for everything that happened. As if he'd planned it all. As if any sane person would set up this progression of events! But if he stopped to think about it, had anything been at all normal since they met?

No, undeniably it had not. And the way things were going, it didn't look like anything was about to change.

No sooner had they settled in the taxi, she informed him she was fine and there was no need for him to stay with her.

He shook his head, no.

When she brought this up again a few minutes later, he stopped her in mid-sentence, informing her would be staying with her whether she wanted him to or not. It was settled and there was nothing more to discuss.

Period.

This had brought on her enraged look, along with a very loud and dramatic sigh. She then turned her back on him to settle into the far corner of the seat. Where she stayed, Where she remained, completely silent.completely silent.

He rested his head against the back of the seat and closed his eyes.

He smiled.

He couldn't help but wonder what was going to happen next. Because with the way things were going, it appeared he was in for one hell of a wild ride with this woman. And surprisingly, he was actually looking forward to the journey, whatever the outcome.

But let's be honest here. This isn't completely true. About the outcome, that is.

Yes, somewhere in the back of his mind, he already had an inkling of what he wanted. Something was happening here. Something he knew he wouldn't be able to explain even if he tried. And believe it or not, he was okay with this.

So, it's pretty much official. You are completely out of his mind.

Why else would he be so drawn to a woman who seemed to dislike him so much? Good Lord, she didn't even know enough about him to feel the way she so obviously did! And the way things were going he was beginning to wonder if this opinion of hers was ever going to change.

But like the soft flutter of a butterfly's wings, she trailed her fingers across his. At first, he thought it was his imagination, her touch was so light. But he turned to find she was staring at him, her eyes wide and her expression one of total exhaustion.

His first impulse had been to pull her into his arms, if only to hold her close and reassure her everything was going to be fine. Instead he held his breath, waiting to see what she was going to do.

In a whisper, so soft he almost missed it, she thanked him.

After he finally managed to respond, he linked his fingers with hers. And the simple sweep of his lips over her hand? Honestly, that came out of nowhere, surprising even him.

When she fell asleep, her hand was still in his.

And now here he was, suddenly wide awake and wondering why such a small thing felt so right.

CHAPTER 8

Anna opened her eyes to the bright sunshine filling the room. At first it felt like any other morning, but when she raised her arms to stretch, the ties on her sleeves, sweeping across her face, told her otherwise.

Uh oh... what's this? What are you wearing? And why?

Now she was wide-awake.

She shot up into a sitting position on the bed to find she was looking directly at a disheveled, but wide-awake Nicholas. She closed her eyes, thinking she had to be dreaming. But when she opened them again, he was still there.

And he was very, *very* real.

Casually leaning against the kitchen counter, he was holding a coffee cup in one hand. His face showed traces of dark stubble covering his cheeks and chin and his hair was slightly mussed. Minus his suit jacket and his tie, his sleeves were rolled up and the top two buttons of his shirt were unbuttoned.

There was one thing that remained consistent. This was those beautiful blue of his eyes.

And they were aimed right at her.

He looked completely at ease, as though it was a common occurrence for him to hang around all night, waiting for a woman to wake up to his irresistible good looks. And yes, even though she didn't want to admit she was even thinking this, he was still so unbelievably handsome, even in his slightly disheveled state

He held his coffee cup up in a salute before flashing one of those slow smiles she was now beginning to know so well. "Well, well, well… good morning, Sleeping Beauty. I was just wondering what step I should take next if you didn't wake up soon."

His head tilted, a smile still lingering on his lips, he proceeded to study her.

This made her nervous. Tossing the quilt aside and scrambling out of the bed, she dragged her hands through her hair.

Not good… there was certainly no princess look going on there.

After an attempt to tame the tangled mess with her fingers, she aimed for a casual shrug. As though waking up to an extremely handsome man in her apartment wasn't really all that big of a deal.

She had this.

Which unfortunately was a big fat lie?

Because come on… with those eyes and that smile coming right at her? It was taking every ounce of control she possessed to keep from diving right into his arms.

Fortunately, the excited bundle of fur that came leaping up against her legs put an immediate stop to the possibility of this happening

"Mia!" She laughed, scooping up the wriggling dog. As Mia rained kisses all over her face, she glanced over at Nicholas.

He was watching her, a smile still on his face.

She smiled back at him. "Did Marie just bring her back?"

He cleared his throat, a somewhat distracted look on his face. "She showed up with Mia about an hour ago. She seems like a very nice lady. We got along quite famously."

He gestured to the cup he was holding. "In fact, you can thank her for making this coffee. She also mentioned something about whipping up a coffee cake to bring over later."

A faint frown flitted across his face. "But you should also know she was very upset you didn't tell her what happened yesterday. I hope you don't mind that I had to fill her in. If only to explain why I was the one to open your door when she stopped by earlier."

He reached over to put his coffee cup on the counter. Casually crossing his arms, his gaze slowly swept over her before coming to rest on her face. And after clearing his throat, darn if he didn't go and give her another one of those smiles.

But at the same time, he threw this bit of information at her. "It's only fair I should let you know the sunlight is making your gown quite transparent."

Anna wanted to run right out of the room. Instead, after throwing Mia on the bed, where she landed with a yelp, she almost yanked the quilt out from under her. The little dog immediately dove off the bed and went scrambling across the room to leap right into Nicholas's arms, burrowing her head into his chest.

Avoiding Nicholas's gaze, Anna wrapped the quilt tightly around her. This morning certainly wasn't starting out in her favor. How was it everything, as she knew it, was now beginning to spiral completely out of her control?

What happened to normal? Remember? You want normal.

She cautiously glanced over at Nicholas. His eyes were on her, his smile still there. He was also still holding Mia, who had now settled comfortably in his arms, the look she was sending Anna, wide and accusing.

Anna groaned.

Great. Even Mia has been caught up in his spell.

As Nicholas slowly ran his hands through Mia's fur, his expression grew serious. "It's such a relief to see color in your face, Anna. I must say you had me quite worried last night."

This was a reminder she needed to find out why she was wearing the nightgown her grandmother had made for her. Intended for her trousseau, it now hung in her closet. Right next to her wedding dress.

Well, at least until now it had.

Her eyes closed, her next words came out sounding quite desperate. "Please tell me that I was the one who put this gown on last night."

That slow smile came over his face again. "Why, yes. Yes, you did."

She gave a sigh of relief. But when she saw the smile was still lingering on his face, she knew this probably meant he had something else to tell her. Something she really didn't want to know.

She waited.

He smiled. "Eventually you did."

Her hand slowly went to her throat. *Eventually?* Ah yes... this was exactly what she so not wanted to hear.

She eyed him nervously as he began making his way across the room, only stopping to put Mia on the bed before he slowly strolled over to stand next to her. A faint smile on his face, he reached for the ties at the neckline of her gown and working very slowly and carefully, he tied them into a bow.

He took a few moments to admire his handiwork. Then his eyes smiling into hers, his voice was so soft, "There, now you look like a princess in a fairy tale. The perfect Sleeping Beauty."

A princess? Sleeping Beauty? Oh my...

She had no words. Absolutely none.

But the eventually comment he made wasn't going to let her enjoy this moment. It was bouncing around in her head, seeking an explanation.

Slowly backing away from him, her words came out in a breathless mess. "About what you said... before this." She indicated the bow he'd just tied. "You said eventually. What did you mean by this?"

After studying her for a moment, he smiled. "*Ah Anna...* let's just say there was quite a bit of persuading on my part to get you to change into what you're now wearing, rather than what you so adamantly insisted you wanted to wear. This being the very elaborate wedding dress hanging in your closet. Correct me if I'm wrong, but I'm pretty sure this wouldn't have been a good choice, at least not for sleeping. Wouldn't you agree?"

Sinking down on the bed, she dropped her face into her hands.

Oh no, no, no.

Her mind went right into overdrive, her imagination taking over. A vision of her parading around the room, wearing the dress and singing 'Here Comes the Bride' immediately began to play in her head.

Then an even worse scenario came to mind. What if she'd tried to convince him to marry her?

Oh my God... what have you done?

When he sat down next to her she didn't move, a tiny part of her hoping if she ignored him, he would leave. But after a long silence, finally broken by his long sigh, the bigger part of her couldn't believe how relieved she was he hadn't.

"Anna, I believe the medication they gave you was too strong for you. It played tricks on your mind before it finally put you into a deep and healing sleep that lasted through the night. And from what I've seen so far this morning, you appear to be much better. Which was exactly what we had set out to accomplish?"

She knew his eyes were on her, waiting for her to react in some way. But she wasn't sure this was a good idea. It seemed a bit too risky.

He sighed again. "I promise it wasn't a night of scandal, despite what you might be thinking." He smiled. "If anything, it was an experience I will always remember."

Not sure how to answer this, she stayed silent. Then she felt his fingertips graze her arm. "Anna, love..."

Her head came shooting right up out of her hands, bringing her right where she shouldn't be, her face mere inches from his. And as if an invisible thread was pulling her, she felt herself leaning in even closer, thinking how nice it would be if he kissed her.

Evidently, he was thinking along the same lines. He reached over to stroke the hair back from her face before he placed a soft kiss to her forehead. His lips were so soft, the warmth of his breath brushing against her skin like a caress. Moving her hands up to his shoulders, she wanted more, her mouth tentatively searching for his.

But as luck would have it, a cell phone started to ring close by. Right between them, in fact. Almost in a daze and her hands dropping into her lap, she watched him take his phone out of his pocket to check the number. He smiled. First at the phone, then over at her.

"I need to take this. But before I do..." He took her hand and pressed a deep kiss into her palm, sending a tremor zinging all the way from the top of her head down to her toes. After he pressed her fingers over the kiss as if she was holding it in her palm, he cupped her chin in his hand.

His eyes scanned her face. "Hold on to that until I get back, love."

With that, he was gone... across the room and speaking into his phone.

She didn't move, her fingers clenched in her palm and holding on to his kiss like this was the most important thing she'd ever been asked to do in her entire life.

She blinked.

This is crazy. What are you doing? It's an imaginary kiss, for heaven's sake!

She slowly, but only slightly, relaxed her fingers before she sent a cautious glance over at Nicholas. She was curious. What was so important about this phone call? Maybe this was something she needed to find out?

She scooted across the bed to get closer, shamelessly listening to his side of the conversation. By the warm tone of his voice, it was obvious she was talking to someone who was very special to him.

A girlfriend?

For a moment, she let this possibility sink in. Then she quickly pushed it right back out. She wasn't sure if she wanted to know what she was up against.

Whoa... hold on a minute.

This was not a competition. *Oh no, no, no.* Definitely not. She had no interest in him along those lines. Of course, she didn't.

But it certainly couldn't hurt to listen to what he had to say, could it?

She leaned in closer.

He chuckled. "Yes, lovey... I haven't forgotten."

Lovey? Ah... so, it is a girlfriend.

"I promised I would. Have you ever known me to break a promise?"

She frowned.

No doubt he makes oodles of promises. And if he breaks one? He just throws out that killer smile of his and he's forgiven. Poof! Just like that!

"Be patient. Not much longer and your dreams will come true."

Seriously? He thinks he's what women dream of?

"Ok, Princess. You too. But for now, blow me a kiss for me to hold on to until I get home. And tell Clemi I missed talking to her. Bye sweetheart."

Ah... kisses seem to be flying everywhere! And who is Clemi? Another girlfriend? Good grief, just how many does he have?

And now Anna was beginning to get angry.

Nicholas had just slipped his phone back in his pocket when there was a knock on Anna's door.

After he watched Mia dive off the bed to go charging over to the door, he glanced over at Anna. Her back was turned to him, as if she was trying to ignore him.

Wondering what brought this on, he followed Mia over to the door.

Marie was the first to come marching in, a big smile on her face. Carrying a cake that sent the tantalizing scent of cinnamon throughout the room, she flashed a big smile at Nicholas before she set the cake on the counter. She then began pulling plates and silverware out of the drawers and cupboards.

Katy came next. After she gave Nicholas a kiss to his cheek, she made her way over to Anna.

Nicholas turned to smile at Anna, only to find she was glaring at him. His hand going to the back of his neck, he shook his head.

Ah... and here you were foolishly thinking everything was going so well. What the hell could have happened in the past few minutes to bring on her sudden change of mood? Evidently the spell has been broken?

He watched as Katy plopped down on the bed next to Anna before she turned to give him a big smile. Which made him feel a little better. At least someone appreciated him.

Her comment was even more of a balm to his bruised ego. "Oh Nicholas, Anna looks so much better. I was so worried, but Stephen wouldn't let me call you. I should've known you would take good care of her."

He gave a brief laugh before he walked over to the where his suit jacket and coat were draped over the chair by Anna's worktable. As he rolled down the sleeves of his shirt and slipped into the jacket, he nodded in Katy's direction.

"Thank you, Katy. It's nice to see someone has faith in my abilities, as it has now come to my attention Anna may think differently."

He suddenly grinned, shooting a quick glance over at Anna. After reaching into his pocket for his wallet, he pulled out a five-dollar bill and set it on the table.

His words were directed right at her. "Which reminds me, a tip wasn't necessary, sweetheart. In fact, I'll never expect you to tip me for my services."

With a wink, he turned back to Katy. "As you just noted, Katy, she does have more color in her face, which is a very good sign. But since my work here is now done, I need to leave. Unfortunately, I have a lot going on today."

He pulled on his coat, hesitating a moment before he walked over to cup Anna's chin in his hand. His kiss was soft, his lips lingering over hers as he spoke. "I will call you, my Sleeping Beauty."

And with what looked like a very pleased expression on his face, he gave a quick wave before he closed the door behind him

A silence had fallen over the room.

Katy put her hands to her cheeks. "Anna! My goodness! What was that? Sweetheart? Sleeping Beauty? How romantic! If he'd kissed me goodbye like that, I would've followed him right out the door!"

She grinned. "Of course, this would only happen if I didn't already have Stephen."

Anna gave her a blank look. She wasn't talking.

No, she was too busy trying to figure out what just happened.

Sleeping Beauty? The kiss? Yes, what did it all mean?

Katy leaned in to peer into her face. "What exactly went on last night? And what's with this beautiful gown you're wearing? You look like a princess out of a fairy tale."

Her eyes opened wide. "Oh my gosh! Is this why he called you Sleeping Beauty? Does he think he's your prince charming?"

Anna had absolutely no idea of how to answer this. Thank goodness Marie caused a distraction when she set a tray with cups of steaming hot coffee and fragrant slices of coffee cake, on the table. After pulling a chair next the bed, she reached over to put her hand on Anna's arm. "Anna, I remember this gown so well. Your grandmother showed it to me right after she finished it. She was so proud of how it turned out."

Anna shot her a grateful smile, extremely relieved the conversation had taken a different turn, no longer about Nicholas. "I know. It is beautiful, isn't it? It was meant for my trousseau."

As she absently fingered the ribbons at her neck, the memory of Nicholas tying them into a bow only a short time ago sent a tremor running through her. With both Katy and Marie watching her so closely, she looked down, hoping to hide the heat she could feel flooding her cheeks.

Katy, under the impression Anna was caught up in memories of her grandmother, quickly reached over to hug her. "Oh Anna, I'm sorry. I know how much you miss her. And it is such a beautiful gown. Is this why you decided to wear it last night?"

Anna slowly ran her hands over the fine fabric of the gown before she looked up at them. "I can't believe I'm going to share this with you, but I had no idea I was wearing it until I woke up this morning. According to Nicholas, I wanted to wear my wedding dress to bed, but he persuaded me to wear this instead."

She grew flustered. "I don't know all of the details, because to tell you the truth, I was afraid to ask. But I got the definite impression I gave him a hard time."

She shook her head. "I'm so embarrassed. I guess the pain pills they gave me at the hospital made me a little crazy before I finally passed out on him. I don't even want to think about what else I might have done. Or what I said."

With Katy and Marie both staring at her, their mouths hanging open, Anna knew she only had to wait. And sure enough, after one look at each other, they burst out laughing.

Katy's words were barely discernible. "Oh no, no! Poor Nicholas!" Falling back on the bed, she laughed even harder. Finally, she wiped the tears from her eyes and reached over to give Anna a hug.

"Oh Anna, I'm sorry I'm laughing, but I can just picture it. Nicholas, the proper English gentleman, suddenly finds he's wrestling with a woman who is drugged and wants to wear a wedding dress to bed. This had to be so out of his comfort zone. He probably didn't have a clue of how to handle the situation."

She grinned. "Well, he asked for it."

Anna shot her a quick glance. "What do you mean, he asked for it?"

Suddenly intent on brushing something off her sweater, Katy avoided her gaze. "Oh, you know. Taking you to the hospital and all. But I want to hear more of what happened last night. Did he tell you any more about what happened? And what's this about a tip? You tipped him? For what?"

Anna slowly shook her head. "If there was anything else, he didn't share it with me. The one thing he did say, was nothing scandalous happened. He had me so flustered I didn't even ask what he meant by that. And the tip comment?" She gave a dismissive wave of her hand. "This was just a little joke of his, I think."

There was absolutely no reason to let them know how that all came about. She didn't even want to think about how badly she acted towards Nicholas in when they were in the coffee shop. In fact, even the thought of how she'd behaved since he showed up in her life, she groaned.

"Oh God, I bet he's having a good laugh right now, thinking about what a great story this will be to share with his friends when he returns home. His encounter with a crazy American woman."

Katy frowned. "I haven't known Nicholas for all that long, but from what I do know, I don't think this is his style. If anything, the kiss he gave you and the Sleeping Beauty remark leads me to believe he's very interested in you."

Marie nodded, obviously in complete agreement with Katy. "I think Katy's right, Anna. He such a polite young man. And oh, so handsome. Those gorgeous blue eyes… *hmm.*" She winked. "Ah, to be younger. Just let go and enjoy, Anna."

Anna shook her head quite vigorously. "Oh Marie, I don't think so. I bet he puts on this charming act of his all the time. I'm just someone new. Someone to add to his harem or whatever he has going on. A collection, I assure you, I have no desire to join."

Katy smiled, wondering if she should tell Anna about the photo. Then she shook her head. No, not yet. Because something was happening here. And she certainly wasn't one to mess with fate.

And, from what she could see, although this modern-day Sleeping Beauty hadn't caught on quite yet, she may had found her prince.

The moment Nicholas closed the door behind him, he was hit with an overwhelming weariness. He massaged the back of his neck, wondering how the hell he was going to get through everything he'd planned for the rest of the day.

He ran down the steps and pushed open the door to the outside. The light snow coming at his face like a soothing mist, he began walking towards the nearest L-Station. Maybe instead of taking a taxi, the combination of cold air and exercise would wake him up.

And even more importantly, clear his head.

He started to laugh. Seriously? How many more miles did he need to rack up to get a handle on this restlessness that had a hold on him? Because so far, nothing seemed to be working. If anything, he was now more unsettled and confused than before.

Never before had a woman touched his heart, awakening a passion inside of him evidently just waiting to surface. Then along comes Anna. And now, after this night they spent together, as crazy as it was, he'd fallen even deeper under her spell.

After they had left the hospital and arrived at her apartment, where he had to carry her up the last flight of stairs, he'd suggested she change out of her dress so she could get some sleep. She disappeared into her closet, to come back out carrying a wedding dress. Throwing herself on the bed, still holding the dress, she burst into tears.

From that point on, she never stopped crying.

From what little he could understand of the gibberish of words coming out between her sobs, she had been engaged, but her fiancée cheated on her. Then things had gone even more downhill when he started drinking. He also took it quite badly when she ended the engagement.

He realized the only way to get her to stop crying would be to get the dress away from her. So, he checked out her closet to find what he was pretty sure was a nightgown.

Unfortunately, this had only resulted in more drama.

How could he have known this had been a gift from her grandmother shortly before she passed away? Bringing on yet another onslaught of tears?

Fortunately, it had also turned out to be a distraction, enabling him to get the wedding dress back into the closet where it belonged.

After he'd finally persuaded her to change into the gown, she curled up on the bed. This was followed by a few more muffled sobs before she became silent.

The medication had finally kicked in. And once again he was in possession of an unconscious Anna.

But this time, he more than welcomed her silence.

Shaking his head, a smile tugged at the corner of his mouth

Yes, this was definitely a night you'll never forget.

His thoughts jumped to this ex-fiancée of hers.

What the hell had he been thinking?

Obviously, someone needed to set him straight.

In fact, the prospect of searching for the cad and knocking him senseless was suddenly sounding very appealing to him. That this was coming from him was absolutely absurd. Solving problems with physical violence wasn't his style.

It would have to be an extremely serious situation to get him riled up enough to resort to that kind of behavior.

Good Lord, now you're starting to imagine you're some kind of damn hero in the making? Charging in to rescue your woman from any evil coming her way?

Again, this wasn't his thing. And as much as it pained him to admit this, she also wasn't his woman. A fact she made quite clear with the look she gave him when he left this morning.

He sighed.

Nope, it appeared her opinion of him was no longer favorable. Why? He had absolutely no idea. Unless it was because he'd taken the call from Clementine and Emily. But why would this upset her?

He shook his head. It looked like he was right back to square one.

He grinned. If there was a bright side to all of this, it would have to be his exit. Both the kiss and Sleeping Beauty comment were a brilliant touch. His favorite, of course, being the kiss.

Emily and Clementine would be so proud of him. They were both firm believers that every man, prince or not, should have a princess of his own to share a kiss with.

He found he couldn't agree more.

CHAPTER 9

You have no idea how hard it is
to force myself to stop thinking about you.
~ Anonymous

$\mathcal{A}$nna was sitting at her worktable, chin in hand.

Her mind was stuck on one thing.

And this was it had been almost two days since Nicholas had walked out of her apartment.

And also, it appeared, out of her life.

She'd tried to be very nonchalant when she asked about him in her phone call to Katy this morning. She made sure to let Katy know her inquiry was merely because of her concern Nicholas had left his tie behind. Nothing more. After all, he could be wondering where it was.

Almost like she was wondering the same about him.

Seriously, what happened to him?

Had he already returned to London? Or was his schedule so busy he had no time for calls?

Oh, come on... how long could one call take? Maybe five minutes

Katy seemed clueless. In fact, she seemed preoccupied, as if she wasn't even listening to what Anna had to say.

She'd been absolutely no help at all.

Anna groaned. How could one person shake up her life like this? And why was she letting him get away with this?

She glanced over at the tie in question, draped over the back of the chair. The unwanted thought popped in her head it was possible a woman gave him this tie. A woman he'd known forever and was now waiting patiently for him to finally propose.

This made her feel extremely irritated and very depressed, all at once.

She picked up the tie. She knew this was silly, but she loved the design. An iridescent, deep blue silk, it had a simple design of snowflakes randomly drifting down to land in a pile at the bottom of the tie. When she turned it over, she found his name, Nicholas William Edward Hanover III, embroidered down one side. She traced his name with her finger, wondering if he even remembered he'd left it behind.

Or worse yet, if he even cared.

She stared down at the tie in her hands. For all she knew, he left ties all over the place. With scores of unsuspecting women moping around and wondering if they'd ever see him again.

And look at you... you've become one of them.

She groaned.

Stop it! You need to stop thinking about him. Move on.

She clasped her hands above her head in a long stretch and glanced over at the ornaments lined up on her worktable. Once she added the bows, they would be ready to be tagged, boxed and delivered to the boutique even earlier than she'd promised.

The designs had flowed from her paintbrush like magic, each one better than the last. And though she was finding it hard to believe she accomplished all of this in two days, she knew this only happened because she'd worked almost non-stop during that time.

Would this have anything to do with all of this nervous energy you have? So much that you can't sleep?

For when she finally crawled into bed, totally exhausted and Mia stretched out next to her, the instant her head hit the pillow she became wide awake. Too many thoughts began running through her mind, most of these she had no reason to be thinking about.

Yes, your mind has become fixated on Nicholas. He's managed to get under your skin and you have no idea how to deal with it.

After tossing and turning, becoming even more frustrated by the minute, she'd dragged herself back out of bed to go right back to work.

And now she was beyond exhausted.

She leaned back in her chair and looked out the window to see it had started to snow. Big, fluffy snowflakes already beginning to accumulate on the rooftops and tree branches.

She sighed… just like Nicholas's tie.

And with this simple thought, a new design began to take shape in her head. She reached for her brush and began to paint, singing along with the Christmas music she'd turned on earlier.

Abruptly, she sat back, holding the paint brush in midair.

She smiled. What if she were with him all of the time?

Oh my, oh my, oh my… just imagine. The possibilities were endless!

And once again, she was off and dreaming.

Over the past two days, Nicholas had tried like the dickens to immerse himself in his work.

Well, this had been his initial plan, but his mind was refusing to go along with this. Instead it seemed to be functioning at a snail's pace.

This was frustrating him to no end.

He found himself in a constant state of confusion. He didn't even want to think about the number of times he'd drifted off while in a meeting with a client, his mind at a complete loss of the business at hand.

And this was all happening because of a woman?

Yes… yes, it was. And you can't deny this even if you try.

Before Anna, his life had run like clockwork, predictable, always in an orderly manner and with no surprises. But somehow, she'd managed to throw him completely off balance.

During the day, thoughts of her constantly invaded his mind. At night, she slipped into his dreams. Some of these dreams so real, when he woke to find she wasn't beside him, he felt empty and so completely alone.

He wanted to hold her in his arms. He wanted to be able to kiss her. And make love to her. Mad, passionate love.

But what it all came down to, he wanted to be with her. And this would be all of the time.

As it stood now, it had been almost fifty-two hours since he'd walked out of Anna's condo. And yes, he'd actually been counting the hours since he last saw her.

Dear God, was this pathetic, or what? This infatuation you have with Anna is taking over every aspect of your life.

He shook his head.

So, why aren't you able to make this happen?

These thoughts were occupying his mind as he sat in his client's office, watching him read over a contract. Unable to sit still, he ran his hand through his hair before he glanced again at his watch. It was when he began drumming his fingers on the arm of the chair, annoying even himself with the sound, he finally cracked.

He closed his eyes, his fingers stilling. He couldn't do this anymore. He didn't give a damn about the project. In fact, right now, he couldn't even remember what it was all about. The only thing he did know was every minute he was sitting in this office was a waste of his time.

Time he should instead be spending with Anna.

Mumbling some lame excuse about a forgotten engagement, with the promise of a follow-up call the next day, he walked out of the office, leaving the poor man in a state of shock and staring after him.

The next thing he knew, he was standing outside Anna's building, instructing the taxi driver to wait. By the time he arrived at her door, he'd convinced himself he had every right to be there. After all, he was just a friend checking on another friend.

Right?
Because they were essentially friends, weren't they?
Maybe?
He ran his hands through his hair, straightened his tie and took a deep breath. He had this. But as he raised his hand, ready to knock the door flew open. And he found himself face to face with a very surprised Anna.

Ah... you should've known something like this was bound to happen.

Anna had been working all morning on her orders. And now, all of the ornaments were packed into her two carryall bags, ready to be delivered to the boutique. Except for one ornament which was not quite finished.

She glanced over at the snowflake designed ornament, inspired by Nicholas's tie, where it was in a box and on her table. She still couldn't understand why she hadn't been able to finish it. Her other designs had come to her so easily.

She'd stayed at her worktable for the longest time, gazing down at the blank space waiting for her design. But nothing had come to her. And she'd tried, she really had.

She tucked the tie in the box with the ornament and shoved the box as far back on the shelf as she could before she eyed the clutter of ribbons, containers of glitter and bottles of paint strewn all over the table and even on the floor.

That would have to wait. She needed to get out of her apartment. Maybe the fresh air would help bring on a night of desperately needed sleep, a night without dreams of you-know-who. Dreams so real, upon awakening, she felt like she hadn't slept at all.

She slipped into her coat, picked up the bags and opened the door.

And who was standing right in front of her, his hand raised and about to knock?

Nicholas...

CHAPTER 10

A riot of feelings swept through Anna.

She was surprised, if only because he'd just been in her thoughts. But this was very concerning, suggesting they were connected in some way. And she wasn't too sure how she felt about this.

She was relieved to know he hadn't left Chicago. Though of course she wasn't going to tell him this. That would make it look like she cared. Which she did… but only a little.

Now she would also be able to give him back his tie. Something she definitely planned to do. Maybe not right this minute, but soon.

But most of all, she was furious, the one emotion that always seemed to surface when she was with him. In fact, she was so angry, she almost shouted out the words. "What are you doing here? And how did you get past the doorman?"

Nicholas took a quick step back.

Hmm… she doesn't seem all that thrilled to see you.

No, she certainly did not.

But he should have expected this. After all, this was Anna he was dealing with. And opening the door to find him standing right in front of her must have been quite a shock.

It had certainly been a surprise to him.

It looks like you need to proceed very carefully here.

He tilted his head to study her more closely. Should he just lean in and give her a kiss? Would this help? Because this was what he'd really like to do.

Hmm... maybe not. A more casual approach might be better.

He smiled. "Well, hello. In answer to your question, I guess I'd have to say I'm here to make sure you've recovered from the other day."

Leaning against the doorframe, arms crossed, he let his gaze travel slowly over her before coming back to rest on her face. There he could see, even though her expression hadn't changed, color had begun to flood her cheeks at his inspection.

Hmm... maybe she's more affected by your presence than she's letting on? This blush she has going on, along with the fact she hasn't yet slammed the door in your face, is definitely encouraging.

He raised his eyebrows, his gaze still on her face. "And how did I get up here? Well, it seems I now have a new friend in your concierge, Louis. I believe he sees me almost as a hero type of guy. Or your knight in shining armor, one who was gallant enough to bring you home safely the other night."

His grin was smug. "So, today he was more than welcoming."

Anna could only stare at him in disbelief.

How was it everyone was so completely won over by this man? First Marie and now Louis. And forget Katy. As far as she's concerned, he could walk on water if he so desired.

With her heart now pounding almost out of control, she tried to avoid his gaze by staring intently over his shoulder.

Undaunted by this, he reached over to run his fingertips lightly down the side of her face, a trace of wistfulness in his voice. "Seriously Anna, I only wanted to make sure you're okay. After all, you did have a concussion."

He shrugged, a slight smile coming to his face. "And I guess I was hoping maybe, just maybe, you might be a bit happy to see me. Even though for some reason, I get the distinct impression you blame me for everything that happened."

And then if he didn't top this off with a very mournful sigh.

She gripped the handles of her bags even tighter, fighting the urge to just drop them. If only so she could take his hand and bring it up to her face again.

Oh my God, what are you thinking?

Now even more flustered, she took a step back, throwing a string of words right at him. "There was absolutely no need for you to come here. Because I'm fine. Just fine. And I want you to know I do appreciate all you've done for me. For coming to my rescue, like the knight in shining armor you and everyone believes you are."

She paused to catch her breath. "And to put your mind at ease, I don't blame you for what happened. So now, if you will let me get by."

Her only goal to get away, she tried to squeeze around him. Granted, this wasn't making much sense, but she had to do something.

Because for her, it was all so clear.

He was dangerous, way too charming for his own good, and definitely too much for her to handle. And this was scaring her to death.

Nicholas took a step closer, his hand going to the doorframe to block any chance of escape. His sigh was weary. "What's really going on here, Anna? What are you so afraid of? Is it me?"

In the silence that followed, she tried to convince herself this was only a coincidence he'd just voiced her thoughts.

Then, as nonchalantly as she could, she began sliding down against the doorframe, her plan to eventually duck under his arm and run. But he countered by moving his hand down further to keep this from happening. Unable to keep her balance and hindered by the bags she still held in her hands, she slid down to her knees on the floor.

Totally mortified, she closed her eyes.

Oh no, no... now what do you do?

Nicholas squatted down beside her, taking the bags and setting them aside. Holding her hands, he waited for her to open her eyes.

Anna couldn't even imagine what he was thinking about this latest predicament she literally just 'fell' into. She slowly opened her eyes to see he was studying her, that concerned expression on his face again.

A look she was beginning to see entirely too much from him.

She shook her head, her voice barely a whisper. "I don't know, I honestly don't know." And much to her horror, she felt a tear begin to slide down her cheek.

He let out another big sigh. "Ah, sweetheart, what am I going to do with you?"

It was when he went to swipe away the tear with his thumb, Anna's anger returned with a vengeance, any additional tears halted in their tracks.

Sweetheart?

He had to be kidding, right?

It was clear he needed to know she wasn't going to become yet another "sweetheart" to add to his collection. No matter what he thought.

She yanked her hands from his. "I'm not your sweetheart. And please don't waste your concern on me. In fact, it would be best if…"

And this was as far as she got before his mouth came down on hers with a kiss that sent the rest of what she'd been planning to say flying right out of her head.

When he lifted his head, she gave this soft little sigh, and gripping his arms, she pulled him closer. A smile touching his lips, he captured her mouth in another kiss.

And this was all happening, on the floor and in the middle of the hallway. Where at any moment, someone could come up the stairs.

This was a bad move… a really bad move.

Yes, Anna realized this was a huge mistake. But she didn't care. Not while his lips continued to work their magic.

She was lost.

A faint cough came from behind them.

Anna's lashes flew open. Marie was standing a few feet away, a surprised look on her face.

Her gaze sweeping over Anna and Nicholas, she nervously cleared her throat. "Well, hi there. I don't mean to interrupt, but since it's such a nice day, I thought I would take Mia for a walk. But it can wait. I'll come back later."

"No… it's okay." After batting away Nicholas's attempt to help, Anna scrambled up off the floor. "And this isn't a bad time. I'm sure Mia would love to go for a walk. So, I'll go get her."

Slipping into her condo, Anna snatched up a dozing Mia. After she put on her leash, and with the little dog leaping in ecstatic circles around her feet, she casually sauntered back into the hallway and handed Marie the leash.

She sneaked a quick glance over at Nicholas.

Did he look like, only a few minutes ago, he'd been in the midst of a passionate kiss?

No, he certainly did not.

He looked as though this was just another ordinary incident that could happen at any time and on any day in his perfectly charmed and organized life. In fact, standing there, his arms crossed and a smile on his face, he appeared completely at ease and extremely pleased with life in general.

He turned to her, a teasing glint in his eyes. "I'd have to agree with Marie. It's a beautiful day. The kind of day to take chances… embrace life while you can."

A huge grin appeared on his face. "Wouldn't you agree, Anna"

After Anna sent a curt nod and smile in his direction, Marie, who had been watching them with a great deal of interest, turned to smile at her. "Anna, you can stop by whenever you want to pick up Mia. I have no plans for the rest of day, so there's no rush."

She scooped Mia up in her arms and headed for the stairs, her voice floating back to them. "I'll be going now, so carry on with what you were doing."

When she realized what she'd implied, she made a hasty retreat down the stairs.

The silence in the hallway was overwhelming. Sneaking another glance over at Nicholas, Anna saw he hadn't moved, his arms still crossed. But now the look on his face was guarded. No doubt he was expecting another outburst from her now they were alone.

Well, she certainly wasn't going to give him the satisfaction of knowing he just might be right. She'd show him she could be just as cool and collected as he was.

Like you were in the coffee shop? Or in your condo the other morning? Or even a few minutes ago? Yeah, those all went over well, didn't they? So, let's see how you calm and collected you can be this time.

She was beginning to think it would be for the best if they parted for good. This would be her only chance of hanging on to what little sanity she had left. Out of sight, out of mind? Isn't this what they said?

Yes, this is exactly what she was going to do.

She gave him her brightest smile. "Again, I'd like to thank you for stopping by, but I'm afraid I really must be going." She nodded towards her bags. "I want to deliver these to the boutique before it closes. I originally told them Monday, but since they're finished, I decided to deliver them now. With only a few weeks until Christmas, I ..."

Her words trailed off. She was babbling again. And by the bemused expression on his face, he wasn't going to be much help.

Good grief, it's the coffee shop all over again.

She held out her hand, in what she felt was not only a very casual gesture, but also a peace offering of sorts. "I'm sure you have lots of places to go, people to see. You know, like the saying goes"

Stop! *What's wrong with you? If he needs any more proof that you're crazy, this should just about do it.*

There was still no move from Nicholas. Instead he was studying her very seriously, almost as though he was trying to read her mind.

Which meant he should know she was wondering if he was ever going to reach out and take her hand. And if he didn't do this soon? Then he should also know she was going to turn around, walk into her condo and shut the door.

And even though she knew this was exactly what she should do, she couldn't seem to make a move in that direction.

Instead, she looked directly into his eyes and shrugging her shoulders, she gave him a tentative smile.

He blinked, and slowly uncrossing his arms, he reached for her hand. He turned it over to study her palm, a puzzled expression coming over his face.

"What happened? Did you lose it?"

She looked at her hand. Then she looked at him.

Lose what? When? And where?

One eyebrow raised, his gaze stayed on her face. "I distinctly remember giving you a kiss to hold here in the palm of your hand. Now, I don't give these out lightly, you know."

Anna started to smile.

But then she frowned. "Really? I'm afraid I find this very hard to believe."

"Well, believe it, love." His mouth turned up in a slight smile. "Now I'm afraid you'll have to try even harder to earn the next one."

With this being said, he winked at her.

Then, still holding her hand, he glanced down at the bags by her feet. "I see you have plans to venture out. And with two bags this time, it appears."

He slowly shook his head. "*Ah*, Anna... this isn't a good idea, is it? If one bag caused as much trouble as it did, I shudder to even think what could happen with two."

He studied her for a few moments before he shook his head again. "Nope, this won't do. I'll escort you to this boutique, if only to make sure history doesn't repeat itself. Otherwise I would never forgive myself if, God forbid, something happened."

Then he gave her what could only be taken as a very mischievous grin. "Because as it now stands, you've already passed out on me more times than I want to think about."

Anna was still trying to wrap her mind around his comments about the kiss to her palm. Bewildered, she glanced down at the bags before she looked back at him.

She had to earn it? What did he mean? And how was she ever going to be able to think straight if he kept coming up with comments like this?

Her hand still in his, he reached over to close the door to her apartment. He handed her a bag, and taking the other one, he began pulling her with him towards the stairs.

It was obvious she didn't have a choice as to whether or not she was going with him.

But for some odd reason, she found she was all right with this.

Well... at least for now, she was.

CHAPTER 11

$\mathcal{N}$icholas wandered aimlessly around the little boutique.

The prospect of shopping had always been overwhelming to him. But it was even more so in a store like this. From what he could see, there appeared to be no more than a collection of a lot of fluff and sparkle.

Definitely not his thing.

But knowing Anna was only a few feet away, meeting with the owner in her office, this experience was more than bearable.

Since they'd arrived, the boutique's only sales assistant had been sending him furtive glances. When he finally caught her eye and gave her a smile, she turned a bright shade of red and went darting behind the counter where she began re-arranging one of the display cases. Since then, she'd ignored him completely.

It seems you have an unusual effect on women. Maybe you should concentrate on business instead. How you even managed to wind up here with Anna is a miracle in itself.

When he'd offered Anna his company, he thought for sure she'd refuse. When this didn't happen, he'd quickly rushed her down the stairs and into the waiting taxi before she even had a chance to think about it.

From that point on, her only words had been directed to the taxi driver and this was to give him the address of the boutique. After that, she appeared to have nothing to say, her gaze fixed out the window. But, he was okay with this. Because even though she was ignoring him, he realized there was no other place he'd rather be. A silent Anna was better than no Anna at all.

If anything, he'd have to say he almost welcomed the silence. It seemed when either of them did venture to open their mouths, this was when the trouble started. He said something to bring out a deluge of angry words from her because she didn't believe him. Or she voiced an opinion of him, usually not at all favorable, which he in turn had to prove wrong. But somehow, they always managed to settle their differences with an unspoken truce.

Like they had now.

At least, you're pretty sure this is what happened. Only time will tell.

So, now here in the boutique, after having checked his phone for any important emails or messages, he had plenty of time to mull things over.

And what was he thinking about? This would be what it was going to take to convince Anna he was a pretty nice guy and definitely not the cad she seemed to think he was.

Good Lord, this was so far from the truth it was laughable.

First of all, his total commitment to his business absolutely forbade such behavior. Secondly, his personal life could only be described as uneventful. Ask any of his family. Or friends. They would attest to this in a second. Let's face it, if anything, he was downright boring.

He laughed aloud at this, drawing a concerned look from the sales assistant. Merely giving her a big smile in return, he checked his watch again. It was beginning to feel like Anna had been gone for a ridiculously long time.

He glanced down at the items arranged on the top shelf of the display case he was leaning against. A pair of delicate sterling silver angel pins immediately caught his eye. Almost identical in design, their whimsical design reminded him of Emily and Clementine.

Displayed right next to these two pins was yet another angel pin. Larger in size, this angel had her hands clasped to her heart and an expression of joy on her face. Perfect for his sister, Claire.

He cleared his throat to get the attention of the sales assistant. Once he indicated he wanted to make a purchase, he finally received a genuine smile from her, before she began chattering non-stop about what a great choice he made. After she removed the pins from the display case, she hurried off with his credit card to write up the sale.

A sharp laugh came from behind him.

Anna?

He turned to see that, yes, it was indeed Anna. But the look on her face was far from happy. Instead she looked extremely annoyed. And he had a hunch whatever brought this on, it had something to do with him.

Again...

Good Lord, now what?

Crossing her arms, she gave a curt nod towards the display case. "I see you haven't wasted any time in finding a few trinkets for the many women waiting at home for you." She tossed her head, giving him an exaggerated smile. "How excited they will be!"

His eyes narrowed, his smile disappeared. *What the hell?* Many women? Him? He looked at her more closely, thinking she must be joking. But no, she wasn't. Not by a long shot. She looked dead serious.

He gave her a long look as he tried to figure out how to answer this. "Me? Many women? You actually think this?" Then he shook his head. "Believe me when I say you couldn't be more wrong."

He ran his hand through his hair, giving a frustrated sigh. "Anna, I'm not a man who would give out affection that easily and certainly not to these many women you're implying I might be hoarding away somewhere. I find it puzzling as to why you'd even think this."

Recalling his phone conversation in her condo, she was powerless to stop the next words from tumbling out.

"Well, I wonder what 'Princess' and 'Lovey' or the many others you've graced with such cutesy little nicknames, would have to say about this? But then they're probably willing to settle for whatever they can get, even if it's only a phone call. After all, the competition must be pretty stiff."

Nicholas slowly leaned back against the counter.

My God, so it was the phone conversation you had with your niece that made Anna so angry that morning?

She was jealous of his six-year old nieces? They were the competition?

Ah... it suddenly all clicked in his mind. His arms crossed and his eyes holding hers, the slightest suggestion of a smile played at the corners of his mouth.

"Let me see if I've got this right. You believe I've got what could possibly be a harem of adoring woman at home. And by merely showering them with a few gifts every so often, I'm able to keep all of them happy and satisfied."

He nodded. "*Hmm...* how very interesting."

Anna was starting to feel a little nervous. This didn't look like it was going to end well, at least not for her.

He was shaking his head. "Well, I don't know what to say except I find this to be absolutely ridiculous. In fact, I'm wondering if the real issue is you might be jealous of these many women? Which, again I assure you, aren't even a remote possibility. Seriously, Anna, take a moment to think about this."

Anna didn't need to think about anything. He was right on both counts. She was being ridiculous. And even more horrifying? She was definitely acting like she was jealous.

And again, you've given him even more of a reason to think you're crazy. You've got to stop talking.

His gaze was so intense, she couldn't even think. Shifting her gaze to the counter, she nervously fingered the pile of scarves on display.

Somehow, she had to fix this. She needed to say something. "Ok, so maybe there aren't a lot of women. But I find it hard to believe there isn't at least one or two." She rolled her eyes, giving an irritated sigh. "Oh, come on. I bet there's maybe even more. Good grief, just look at you. You're, well... you're..."

Her words were spilling out so fast, she was actually starting to stutter. But did this stop her? Of course not. Even with the warning flashing wildly in her head, she was probably going to say something incredibly stupid, she just couldn't give it up.

"You're just… well, you're just too perfect."

And yes, those words actually came flying out of her mouth.

When the corners of his mouth turned up slightly at this, she laughed nervously. "Don't get me wrong. I'm not the one who thinks this. I don't think you're perfect. Of course, I don't. In fact, I'm sure you have many faults."

She nodded vigorously, if only to convince herself this is what she really believed. "And you're insinuating I might be jealous? Well, don't flatter yourself thinking this. Because why would I be? I have no claim on you, nor do I ever want to."

Her mouth snapping shut, she was done.

At least for now, you are.

He was silent, his gaze still on her face.

The salesperson had brought Nicholas his purchases and was waiting for him to sign the receipt. When he turned to her, Anna took this as her chance to slip away.

She made her way to the entrance of the boutique. She couldn't believe what a mess she was. Her heart was pounding in her chest and glancing down at her hands, she saw they were shaking.

Never had she felt so out of control, her emotions so fragile. And she didn't like this feeling like this. She wanted it to go away.

But there was only one problem.

She had absolutely no idea how to make this happen.

Nicholas came to stand next to her, cupping her cheek in his hand. His eyes searching hers, he slowly shook his head. "Hey, are you okay?" At her faint nod, he took her arm to lead her out of the boutique.

She finally found her voice. "Nicholas, I…"

He put a finger to her lips. "*Shush…* no talking, okay? I think it's

about time I show you I'm not the bad boy you seem to think I am."
He grinned. "Come, we can easily walk to where we're going. Your
ornaments have been safely delivered and as Marie noted earlier, it's a
beautiful day. So, let's enjoy it."

"But I…" She had to say something, even if it was only just a simple
sorry.

He abruptly leaned in to press a soft kiss to her lips, his mouth
lingering over hers as he spoke. "Ah… look what you've made me go
and do again. I'm beginning to think this could become quite a habit
with us, no?"

He aimed another one of his smiles at her and tucking her hand
under his arm, he started off at a brisk pace.

Anna was completely silent.

Not because she was afraid if she wasn't, Nicholas would kiss her
again.

No, this wasn't the reason at all. As a matter of fact…

Oh no, you don't. You can't even start thinking along these lines.

And this, she realized, was the problem. She was doing entirely too
much thinking.

And it was always about him.

But she honestly didn't understand. Why did he keep coming back
into her life?

She certainly hadn't given him any reason to seek out her
company. She didn't fawn over him, or hang on to his every word. She
didn't flirt with him. And she disagreed with just about every single
word that came out of his mouth.

Hadn't he been the one to point out she was crazy? Something
she'd given him every reason to believe with the way she'd behaved up
until now.

You'd think all of this would have sent him off and running.

So why do you think he's still here?

She had no idea. She really didn't.

Maybe he considered her a challenge? If so, he was in for a big surprise. After Marc, she was no longer the trusting and naive girl she used to be. She could take on any man, Nicholas included.

Hmm... Not so sure about this. You haven't done a very good job so far, have you?

She sighed.

It was obvious she didn't know what she was doing.

And she was definitely in way over her head.

Totally caught up in her thoughts, Anna was totally unprepared when Nicholas came to a stop, and opening a door, ushered her into what could only be described as a madhouse of activity.

Giggles and excited shrieks coming from little girls of all ages, it was like a huge pajama party, minus the pajamas. Instead, most of the girls had on their best outfits, and the dolls they carried were dressed to match.

They were in The American Girl Store?

Anna gazed up at Nicholas, her lips parted in surprise.

She didn't understand... why had he brought her here?

He grinned, and leaning in close, he put his mouth to her ear. Even so, she almost couldn't hear him. "Now do you see why I brought you here? I'm way out of my element, Anna. And definitely in need of a your help. Do you think you can help me pick out two dolls, along with whatever you think two six-year old girls would need for these dolls? I promised my nieces, Clementine and Emily, I would get each of them one of these dolls for Christmas. They would never forgive me if I didn't follow through on this."

He took her hand and began pulling her further into the store. After a few steps, he turned to put his mouth to her ear again. "For the record, these are the nieces I refer to as 'Lovey' and 'Princess' most of the time. Along with any other 'cutesy little nicknames' I might come up with."

His grin widened. "And I'm pretty sure they're very happy and satisfied with these nicknames. Along with any trinkets I might toss their way."

Anna was smiling. She didn't care if he was teasing her. Instead, she had the urge to throw her arms around him.

His nieces?

The American Girl Store?

Really?

Hmm… maybe he wasn't quite as bad as she thought.

CHAPTER 12

When Anna and Nicholas finally emerged from the chaotic store, they were greeted by the early evening sky and softly falling snow.

Not wanting to lose Anna in the evening crowds rapidly taking over the sidewalks, Nicholas reached for her hand, tucking it securely under his arm.

He glanced down at her, hit with the urge to stop right where they were, right in the middle of the sidewalk.

Then, in full view of everyone, he would pull her into his arms and kiss her.

Thoroughly.

He wondered … what would she do?

Umm... maybe not a good idea. Things are going pretty good right now. Why screw it up.

He sighed, tightening his hold on her. He was beginning to wonder why he was doing so much thinking while he was with her. Good Lord, if he went about making decisions in the same way when it came to his business, it would have tanked a long time ago.

So, what the hell is your problem?

Glancing down at Anna, he had his answer.

He didn't want to goof this up. It had become very clear he was holding on to something far too precious to be rushed. So, for now, kissing her would have to wait. When the moment was right, he would know.

He smiled, thinking about the time they spent together in the American Girl Store. Emily and Clementine were going to be ecstatic when they saw what Anna had chosen for them. And he was thrilled, maybe even more relieved, to know his promise to the girls was now taken care of.

Though honestly? He really had no recollection of what he purchased. Trailing after Anna in the store, he had been so captivated by her every move, he'd nodded his approval to everything she showed him. No matter what it was or what the cost. Yep, he would have followed her around the store forever if it had come to that.

Whoa ... imagine that. Since you're not the shopping kind of guy.

But now he needed to come up with a plan. They couldn't keep walking forever, as appealing as this sounded.

He didn't want this time with Anna to end. Not when they appeared to have come to an understanding, fragile though it was, and comfortable in each other's company.

Gazing around at the Christmas decorations on display everywhere around them, just like that, he had his answer.

He knew the perfect place.

Lovey and Princes, otherwise known as Emily and Clementine, were Nicholas's nieces.

Anna couldn't stop smiling as this information danced in her head. According to Nicholas, they were six-years old and identical twins.

She knew they were going to like what she picked out for them in the American Girl Store. What little girl wouldn't? Nicholas had certainly turned out to be an easy person to shop with, agreeing to almost everything she showed him.

It had been fun. But now what.

She glanced down at her hand tucked securely under his arm, then up at him. Their eyes met. A message of such tenderness in his, she had to look away.

No one had ever looked at her like this. Maybe Marc had at one time. But this was when they first started dating and fell in love. At least she thought they were in love at the time. But he'd changed, turning into a man she no longer knew.

She frowned, a sliver of uncertainty working its way into her mind,

"Anna?"

Concerned when he saw the anxiety clouding her eyes, Nicholas pulled her closer, giving her another smile.

The smile worked its magic, sending her doubts scattering.

You could almost say she was bewitched.

Nicholas brought them around a corner, a quaint wooden sign announcing they were in front of the Old City Tavern. Almost hidden between two sleek and modern high-rise office buildings, this storybook styled establishment had miraculously escaped the ongoing attempts at modernizing the city over the years.

The stone front, the weathered wood front door and brown shingled roof gave the impression it was straight out of an English countryside.

Candles beckoned from the windows, pine boughs and holly over flowed the window boxes. The ornate rod iron fence surrounding the property was draped with an evergreen garland and twinkling fairy lights.

The whole effect was magical, reminiscent of an earlier time.

Anna fell in love, enchanted by everything about it.

Pleased with her reaction, Nicholas smiled. "I take it you've never been here before? This is your city, Anna. How can it be I know about this and you don't?"

She smiled, her eyes sparkling. "I don't know. But it's so charming. Not at all what you'd expect to find in the middle of the city! I love it!"

"Ah, Anna ..." The sudden longing to always be the one to make her

this happy, he pulled her against him. Surely this had to be a moment that called for a kiss?

Hmm...

She tilted her head, gazing up at him. She wanted him to kiss her. Or she would kiss him. It didn't matter, just as long as they kissed. But his expression was hesitant, the look in his eyes so uncertain, she held back.

Then he slowly leaned in to brush his lips over her cheek. She closed her eyes, the warmth of his breath mingling with the icy sting of the falling snow sending a shiver through her. Giving a soft sigh, she tilted her head, bringing her face even closer.

Another couple, also on their way to the restaurant, bumped into her as they passed. Her eyes going wide, she pulled away.

He groaned.

Another missed opportunity. Again because of too much thinking.

When she leaned her head against his shoulder, he pressed a soft kiss in her hair.

He reached for her hand. "Evidently this wasn't meant to be." He smiled. "But I believe it's a great beginning. Come on, let's go inside where it's warm."

They entered the restaurant, greeted by the warmth of the fire burning in the huge stone fireplace taking up one wall. A Christmas tree, all decorated with ornaments and lights, was set up in the corner. The rest of the room was divided into groupings of tables and chairs, each set into their own private little nook. The soft glow of candle light filled the room, while music played softly in the background.

A man came to greet them, his face lighting up in recognition. "Nicholas! You've come back! How good to see you again! And who is this you've brought with you tonight?"

"Andy, it's good to see you, too." After he shook his hand, Nicholas smiled down at Anna as he put his arm around her. "This is Anna. And even though she lives here in the city, she had no idea you were here."

Andy laughed as he reached out to shake Anna's hand. "It's so nice to meet you, Anna. And don't let this guy make you feel guilty. He's only been here once. If I remember correctly, it was with his sister."

After escorting them to one of the few vacant tables, he waited until they were seated before he handed them each a menu. "Take some time to get comfortable before you check out the menu. In the meantime, I'll get one of our servers to bring you a complimentary glass of our special mulled wine to sample. It's perfect for this snowy night."

Once he left, Nicholas smiled over at Anna. He was pretty sure he knew where her thoughts had taken her. Reaching across the table, he took her hands in his.

"The answer is yes to what you're thinking. It really was my sister who was here with me last time. Her name is Claire. Emily and Clementine belong to her."

Anna could feel her cheeks burning. She just couldn't win with this man. He didn't miss a thing. But she suddenly found she didn't care about winning. Or losing. Or even if he was teasing her. She only wanted to get lost in the intoxicating feeling of being with him.

She looked up at him and smiled. "I believe you."

He let go of her hands before he leaned back in his chair. "You do?" The expression on his face was one of complete astonishment.

Still smiling, she nodded.

He studied her for a few seconds before he spoke. "Well, I believe we're making progress here. Which means we definitely have a reason to celebrate."

The urge to touch her becoming stronger with each passing second, he took her hands in his. As he caressed her fingers with his, he hesitated, the expression on his face now serious. "May I ask why this sudden change of heart?"

She looked down at their hands. If he kept doing what he was doing, she certainly wasn't going to be able to give him a sensible answer. Gently untangling her hands from his, she clasped them together on the table. Only then did she look over at him. He was studying her so intently, she almost forgot what she wanted to say.

Oh boy... you need to just dive in.

She swallowed nervously. "Oh Nicholas, I realize I've been so wrong about you. All this time you've been so nice, while I've been so horrible in return. And I'm so sorry for that. I guess this is because, lately, I've been having such a hard time trusting anyone. It's gotten so I don't even trust myself anymore."

He remained silent, his eyes fixed on her face

Her smile was wistful. "I wish I could be like you! You know what you want and you're not afraid to go after it. I can't even imagine being able to do that."

She shrugged her shoulders. "But then I don't even know what I want any more. I thought I had the best of everything when I was engaged. Instead, everything turned out so terribly, horribly wrong. So, I've sort of put up this imaginary wall, if only a way to keep me safe. I know this may seem extreme, but I don't want to get hurt again. I couldn't handle this."

She swallowed. "I can't promise you anything. I'm sorry, I really am. Because even though sometimes it might not seem like it, I really like being with you."

She unclasped her hands and slid them across the table closer to him. As if she was reaching out to him, trying so hard to let him know how much she wanted this with him.

Which, she realized, was exactly what she was doing.

She gazed down at her hands. Talk about feeling vulnerable. My God, she'd just poured out her most private thoughts and fears to him. What made her tell him all of this? What if he thought she was being overly dramatic? Or he'd been right all along, she really was crazy?

Or, the unthinkable, what if he decided to get up and leave.

The silence was almost unbearable. When he finally reached across the table to take her hands, she wanted to drop her head down on their joined hands in relief. She closed her eyes, letting out the long breath she hadn't realized she was holding.

Nicholas could feel her hands trembling. His voice rough, he tightened his grip. "Anna, look at me, love."

She gazed up at him, all the fear and anxiety she was so desperately holding inside, slowly starting to fade at the look of tenderness in his eyes. When he leaned closer, she leaned in to meet him, her lips parting in anticipation.

His words came in a whisper against her cheek. "Anna, I will never hurt you. I promise you this. You only need to trust me, sweetheart."

His kiss was gentle, searching… his mouth lingering over hers as if he didn't want it to end. No matter how simple of a kiss it was.

To Anna, if felt like a promise.

For Nicholas, it was.

Abruptly leaning back in his chair, Nicholas cleared his throat. "Hey, love…"

Her lashes fluttering open, Anna saw the server was standing by their table. An indulgent expression on his face, he was holding two glasses of wine.

Flustered, she glanced over at Nicholas.

He winked at her.

She tried to hide her smile, but failed.

And Nicholas?

He was still holding her hands.

It seemed the more he held them, the harder it was to let go.

CHAPTER 13

$\mathcal{A}$nna was having a really hard time trying to stay awake.

Seriously, she could barely keep her eyes open. She was going to blame this on that last glass of wine she now realized she should've refused.

The wine also had to be the reason for her present failure to stay in an upright position. Why else would she be curled up next to Nicholas in the taxi, her head on his shoulder and with his arm around her, holding her close?

She sighed.

She couldn't think of anywhere else she would rather be right now. If only she wasn't so, so tired. Was it really only this afternoon she'd found him standing outside her door?

She gave in and closed her eyes.

Nicholas decided it was official. Anna was a perfect fit in his arms. And, what was happening between them was real. *Very real.* And even though this meant his life had now begun to spiral completely out of his control, a feeling he certainly wasn't accustomed to, he was more than eager for what was to come next.

Yes, he was more than ready to take on the next step in this relationship with Anna.

But her passionate confession at the restaurant was a sign he needed to slow down, step back and let her start making some of the moves.

How the hell are you going to do this?

With everything else in his life, this wasn't his style. If he wanted something, well, he went out and got it. Letting others take the lead wasn't the way he was used to getting things done.

But this was different.

He groaned in frustration. He knew things were moving all too fast, but he was pretty sure he could handle this.

And Anna?

He shook his head. She definitely needed more time, maybe more than they had. But he wasn't going to start thinking about this. Not when he had her here and in his arms.

She stirred against him. Smiling, he placed a kiss to the top of her head, breathing in the intoxicating floral scent of her hair. When she sighed and snuggled even closer, all kinds of thoughts began whirling around in his head, most having to do with kisses and where these kisses could lead them.

Damn. This is certainly more than you bargained for. And definitely more than you're prepared for. But then again, is anyone ever ready for something like this?

He smiled, shaking his head.

Determined to enjoy the rest of the ride, he rested his cheek in her hair and closed his eyes.

When they pulled up in front of Anna's building, Nicholas helped Anna out of the taxi, all the while ignoring her protests.

She didn't need his help. He could just go on to his hotel. He didn't have to walk her upstairs. It was late. She was fine. Really. A little tired, that's all.

Nicholas glanced over at the taxi driver who was watching this with amusement. After he signaled to him he should wait, he put his hand to the small of Anna's back and proceeded to guide her, still protesting, into the building.

When they reached the stairs, he put his finger to her lips. "Anna, stop. Not seeing you safely inside would go against everything I was taught. Which means I'm going to escort you all the way to your door whether you want me to or not. So, come on, let's get going."

Navigating the steps required Anna's complete attention, so she was silent right up until they came to the landing of the second floor. It was there, for her, the next step suddenly appeared to take on one of mountainous proportions.

"Oh my…"

She came to an abrupt halt and sinking down onto the bottom step, she put her head down in her knees. As Nicholas settled next to her, his smile carried over into the teasing tone of his voice.

"Anna? Will I need to carry you up the last flight of stairs? I've done it before, if you remember." His smile grew. "Oh, that's right. You don't remember, do you? A pity, it was quite an experience."

Anna lifted her head from her hands to stare at him before she blurted out exactly what she really had no business asking.

"I don't understand. Why aren't you already married?"

Wait, did you really just ask him that? Seriously?

Again, this had to be because of the wine. In fact, she was going to blame everything on the wine. Heaven knows she needed some kind of excuse for all of these crazy thoughts whirling around in her head right now.

For example, throwing her arms around him and asking him to kiss her was sounding quite appealing to her right now. As she took the time to imagine the outcome of this, she stared at him, a wistful smile on her face.

But then here was a frightening thought … what if he really was able to read her mind? Instantly becoming flustered, she blurted out the rest of what she'd wanted to say. "Because look who you're stuck with." Eyes wide, she placed her hands to her cheeks, her voice turning into an exaggerated whisper. "Crazy, crazy me."

When he smiled, she gave him a brilliant smile in return. Then her expression turned serious and reaching out to run her fingertip lightly down his cheek, her words came out in a whisper

"I don't get it. Do you?"

Nicholas didn't answer. Not because he didn't want to. Oh no, this wasn't the reason. He just couldn't. The most he could do was stare at her.

How was it that he, of all people, had now been rendered completely speechless?

It had to be because they were alone in the hushed stillness of the empty stairway. Where every move, every touch and every single word seemed so significant, their sudden awareness of each other so transparent.

Yes, he'd admit she was a little bit drunk. And him? Not that much. Well, maybe he was, but not from the wine. No, he was high on her. Her eyes, her lips, the sound of her voice and the intoxicating scent of her perfume. They were all drawing him in, making him oblivious to everything else. He was almost hesitant to touch her, lest he lose any control he had.

In the past few hours they'd spent together, something had shifted between them, especially with her. He could only hope her earnest outpouring of feelings meant she was beginning to trust him, something he wanted so badly. This would be the start in pushing down the wall she claimed to have built up around her. God knows any barriers he had in place had come crashing down the very first moment he'd looked into her eyes.

But now what?

He decided this was one of those times he needed to step back and let her carry them through.

Mesmerized by the look in Nicholas's eyes, his beautiful blue eyes, Anna decided it was important she let him know this. A dreamy expression on her face, she tilted her head towards him. "You have the most beautiful blue eyes I've ever seen. When I look into them, I become lost. I just want to…" She quickly put her hand to her mouth. "Oh no, no, I can't even …"

Her eyes quickly traveling over the rest of his face, they finally came to settle on his mouth.

How you love his mouth, something you should also probably share with him. Heck, why not? You're on a roll here.

Her smile was big. "And when you smile at me?" She stopped to shake her head. "I feel like I'm going to melt. Right at your feet."

She leaned over to look down at his feet. When she slowly started to topple over, he pulled her back until she was leaning against him. She gazed up at him, a dreamy smile on her face.

Nicholas was beginning to have a really hard time with all of this. It was almost too much, this bemused expression on her face, now topped off with holding her in his arms.

God, he just wanted to kiss her. One mind blowing kiss, this is all he wanted. Was this really all too much to ask?

Umm, yeah … like you'd be able to stop at that. Come on, this isn't the time. Or the right place. You're in a deserted stairwell, for God's sake.

He tightened his hold on her. "Ah, love… thank you. I must say it's been very flattering to hear all these compliments coming from you. With all of them coming in one evening, it has been somewhat over-whelming, to say the least."

He traced her lips with his finger. "And just so you know, a compliment coming from these lips will always mean far more to me than any others combined. In fact, they're the only ones that matter."

Anna's smile grew bigger.

Wow, you really like the sound of that.

In fact, she was beginning to like everything he said. It must be the deep velvety tone of his voice. Then if you add in his accent? Together they made everything sound, well, almost enchanting.

He reached over to tuck her hair behind her ear. "And you're wondering about my marital status?" He smiled. "I guess I've never found that 'special someone' yet." He studied her more closely, a thoughtful expression coming over his face. "Though as of late, there seems to be a glimmer of hope in that direction."

Anna's eyes widened. Really?

Really?

She closed her eyes. *Please...* she just wanted him to kiss her.

Really kiss her.

Pulled in by her thoughts, his hand went to cup her cheek, bringing her face to his. A whisper apart, the delicate scent of wine mingled with each breath they took.

He traced her jaw with his thumb, his voice low and so soft. "Sweetheart, I'm not sure what's happening here, either. But I do know I want to be with you. It just feels right."

His lips met hers with the gentlest of touch. Not at all what you'd consider overly passionate. Or a kiss you'd expect to find described in great detail in a romance novel. No bells ringing out, no voices singing in harmony or lights flashing brilliantly across the sky. No, there was none of this.

But it was a good kiss. A kiss filled with the promise of so much more to come.

A kiss settling deep within her soul.

After drifting apart, Anna and Nicholas gazed at each other in silence before she reached over to trace his lips with her fingers.

Then she just couldn't help it ... she yawned. And it was a huge yawn. A genuine wide-open-mouthed yawn she knew she didn't have a chance of holding back.

Nicholas burst out laughing. "Ah, I don't know if I should be insulted or what. I can only hope this yawn was brought on by the wine, or because you're simply very tired. Because it's certainly not the reaction a man wants to get when he gives a kiss to a beautiful woman. At least not this man."

He stood, pulling her up with him. "Come on. We need to get you up this last flight of stairs so you can go to bed."

Anna was almost too muddled to even think about feeling embarrassed. Well, almost, but not quite. And now there was something even more for her to think about.

Beautiful? Did you hear this right? He thinks you're beautiful?

Well, she certainly managed to ruin that moment, didn't she?

Again, she was going to blame it on the wine.

They climbed the remaining steps in silence. After she fumbled with her keys in an attempt to find the right one, Nicholas finally took them from her and unlocked her door. He turned to find her eyes were on him, a dreamy expression on her face.

He smiled. "Anna?"

Startled, she gave him a guilty smile. "Sorry, I'm so sorry. Obviously, I'm just really tired. And, it seems, a little bit drunk on too much wine. But you needn't worry. I'll be fine."

This was so, so far from the truth. She wasn't fine. Her head was spinning and it was taking everything she had to remain standing. And as much as she tried to convince herself otherwise, she knew this wasn't all because of the wine.

Which turned out to be a very sobering thought. And a sign she needed to say goodnight. Before she did something really stupid, such as throwing herself right at him.

She pressed a quick kiss to his cheek and started to back into her condo. "Thank you for a wonderful day, Nicholas."

He reached out to take her hand. "Anna, what are your plans for this weekend?"

She stared down at their hands, desperately trying to think. This weekend? In her present state, it was a struggle to even remember what day it was. Thursday? Yes, she was pretty sure it was Thursday. Or wait … was it now Friday? It very well could be.

She shook her head, her expression questioning, her eyes wide.

Unable to resist, he brushed his fingers down the side of her face. She swayed towards him, her eyes drifting shut.

He blinked.

Hurry up and say what you want to say. Then you need to get the hell out of here before things get out of control. Remember? With her, you need to take this slow.

He took her arm, prompting her to open her eyes. "There's an annual social event this Saturday night, hosted by long-time friends of my family. It's held at an estate outside of the city, one of the several they've renovated into luxury resorts. Since it always takes place during this time of year, everything is done in a very festive Christmas holiday theme. I know you'd love it and I'd be honored if you would agree to be my date. Stephen and Katy are also planning on going, so it should be a fun evening."

Anna could only stare at him.

This brought a tentative smile from him. "I know this is short notice, but it would really mean a lot to me if you said yes."

She continued to study him. Was it her imagination, or did he actually look nervous as he waited for her answer? Because this wasn't at all an expression she'd expect to see from him.

Because, come on ... how could any woman in her right mind think of turning down an invitation from him? No matter what it involved.

She hesitated. Even though his invitation was tempting, at the same time it was a bit daunting. An annual social event? She always found these to be such pretentious and stressful affairs.

But evidently it really didn't matter what she thought because it appeared she'd already started nodding, her voice coming out right out behind. "I would love to go with you, Nicholas."

And darn if he didn't throw that smile of his right at her, giving her no chance to even think about what she just did.

He reached out to give her a quick hug. "Thank you, Anna. You can talk to Katy. She'll be able to give you all of the details. And now, I really should go. Until Saturday night, then?"

She nodded, watching as he began to walk away.

He abruptly turned back to her. "*Ah...* I almost forgot. I do believe I owe you something." He took her hand to press a leisurely kiss to her palm before he folded her fingers over the kiss. As he had done that morning in her apartment.

"This time, try to remember to hold on to it, love." He followed this with a wink.

He headed for the stairs. And once again, he turned to her. "One last thing. You'll need to pack an overnight bag. Since it will be such a late night, we'll return on Sunday."

And with this simple, yet eye-opening announcement, he went running down the stairs. Leaving her standing by her door, frozen in in place.

"Nicholas, wait…"

It didn't really matter this came out in only a whisper.

Because he was already gone.

She closed the door and leaned back against it, her eyes closed.

You can't go to this party.

You can't spend a weekend with him.

It's out of the question. Absolutely.

Whatever possessed you to say yes?

Flashbacks of the events she'd been forced to attend with Marc came flying at her. How he lectured her repeatedly on what to say and how to act until she hadn't been able to function at all. This had always been followed by his anger. His sarcastic criticism bringing her to tears, the evening would invariably end in disaster.

This even more of a reason she shouldn't have accepted Nicholas's invitation, she decided she would go visit Katy tomorrow to let her know she wouldn't be going. She'd changed her mind.

But Katy isn't going to go along with this. If anything, she'll be beside herself with excitement.

Between the wine and her lack of sleep over the past few days, she didn't have the energy to it was time to call it quits. She changed into her pajamas and crawled into bed.

The palm of her hand still tingling with the memory of his kiss, she pressed it to her lips.

A smile on her face, she closed her eyes.

And this is how she fell asleep.

As the taxi made its way to his hotel, Nicholas couldn't stop thinking about how much more enjoyable it had been when Anna shared this same space with him only a short time ago.

He smiled, thinking back to their conversation in the stairway.

There was no doubt she was a little drunk. Yes, maybe even more than a little. But even so, from what she said, he was pretty confident they were heading in the right direction. And even though he wasn't all that good at reading women, especially when the woman in question was Anna, it was more than obvious she'd wanted him to kiss her.

Ah, the kiss ...

He wondered what would have happened if he'd gone with his gut feeling and kissed her like he'd wanted to? He shook his head. If he had, he wouldn't be here in this taxi. No, he would still be there with her.

Good Lord, you need to put this completely out of your mind. Otherwise you'll have a long and sleepless night ahead.

He was feeling a bit guilty about how he'd sprinted down the stairs, leaving her still standing by her door. But he hadn't wanted to give her the opportunity to tell him she'd changed her mind. When he'd given her the information they wouldn't be returning until Sunday, the expression on her face was a definite warning this might be a possibility.

So, he bolted.

He needed to put some kind of plan in place so he could be with her again. He ran his hand through his hair, worry beginning to creep into his mind.

You're running out of time...

He was set to fly back to London Monday night. As it was, the time he blocked out for this trip had already stretched out longer than he'd planned. Thinking about the work no doubt piling up on his desk and waiting for his attention, he leaned his head back against the seat.

He exhaled a long sigh. Well, so be it. Whatever... whenever. Eventually, it would all get done.

And... *BAM!*

For the first time, in he didn't know how long, work was no longer his number one priority?

It appeared Anna had now moved into that top spot. And miracle of miracles, she was going to be with him this weekend.

He leaned his head back against the seat again and closed his eyes. But this time he had a smile on his face.

Life *really* was good.

Even though it was quite late when he arrived at his hotel, he was too wired to sleep. Deciding this would be the perfect opportunity to finish some of the work he'd neglected, he removed his tie, rolled up his sleeves and brought out his laptop. Flexing his fingers, he signed in.

And nothing.

He stared at the screen, his mind completely blank. You'd think he never used a computer before.

Instead his thoughts drifted to Anna. How right it had felt to have her curled up next to him in the taxi. Or how soft her lips had been against his when they'd kissed. And even now in his hotel room, he could still catch the lingering scent of her perfume.

He glanced over at the time displayed on his computer screen. They'd been apart for less than an hour. And already, how much he missed her.

How was this possible?

He groaned.

Looks like you're in trouble.

Snapping the top down on his computer, he pushed it away. He leaned back in his chair and closed his eyes.

Big trouble.

CHAPTER 14

*A*nna took Mia with her when she went to see Katy.

The crisp December air, along with the added bonus of the bright sunshine filled morning would do them both good.

Again, she hadn't slept well. Every time she fell into, what turned out to be a restless sleep, she went right into another dream. And of course, Nicholas managed to pop up as the main character in every single one of them. It was almost as if he hadn't left her last night.

Good grief, how could one person shake up your life like this?

As she trailed behind Mia, her thoughts drifted to what it might be like to actually spend the night with him.

She came to an abrupt stop, bringing a yelp from Mia, who nearly somersaulted backwards through the air.

What was she thinking?

Oh no, no, no … this is not what she wanted.

Was it?

She decided to run the rest of the way to Katy's.

Katy opened her door to find Anna and Mia standing there, both panting and out of breath from their short run. She reached out to give Anna a big hug. "Anna! I've missed you! Come in. I hear we have a lot to talk about."

They both watched as Mia trotted over and curled up in front of the fireplace. Once they were settled on the sofa. Anna glanced over at Katy, who was watching her, an expectant expression on her face.

Uncomfortable with this close scrutiny, she glanced over at the Christmas tree in the corner of the room. She recognized quite a few of her ornaments hanging from the branches.

She gave Katy a big smile. "With all the people that were here for your party and everything else that went on that night, I didn't even get a chance to appreciate all of the decorating you've done." She waved her hand towards the tree. "Everything is beautiful."

Katy nodded. "Yes, yes… very festive. But I'd rather talk about you. What's new with you?"

At the teasing tone in Katy's voice, Anna began fluffing up one of the decorative pillows on the sofa, her answer coming out entirely too loud and cheerful.

"Well, I finished up the order I got from the new boutique I told you about and the owner is now planning to order more for her other stores. It probably won't be a big order since it's already December, but she did mention they would probably do well on their web site. So, it looks very promising for next year."

She then started arranging all of the pillows on the sofa as if it was very important they were in a certain order.

Katy studied her for a few seconds, her smile growing. "That's nice. But what else, Anna? Anything new?" She put her finger to her mouth as if in deep thought. "*Hmm…* let me see. Anything to do with a certain gorgeous and sexy man we both know? And don't try to deny he's all of these things, Anna. Because you and I both know he is."

She was grinning from ear-to-ear, excitement dancing all over her face. "And now I've heard you're going to be his date for tomorrow night! I'm really beginning to think he's falling in love with you!"

Anna could feel her cheeks growing hot. She tried to avoid the expectant look on Katy's face, horrified when she felt her bottom lip start to quiver. Foolishly, she attempted to mask this with a smile.

Instead she burst into tears.

What's this? Do you even know why you're crying? What happened to that casual approach you were going for.

Katy's expression quickly turned to one of concern. She left the room, to come back with a box of tissues she placed on the sofa next to Anna.

Her dramatic display of tears having dwindled down to a few sniffles, Anna leaned her head against the back of the sofa and closed her eyes. She pulled out one and then another tissue from the box, absentmindedly wadding them up and throwing them on a pile beside her.

"I'm sorry." She smiled weakly at Katy." I don't know what brought this on."

This was followed by a huge sigh as she pulled out yet another tissue, only to throw it on the pile.

"Oh God... yes, I do. Everything happening between the two of us is scaring me to death. It seems too good to be true. He seems too good to be true. Which means it can only end badly. Like it did with Marc."

Katy shook her head. "Anna, listen to me. Nicholas is absolutely nothing like Marc. In fact, put that thought completely out of your mind. Nicholas is such a gentleman and most women would kill to be with him. In fact, it really is a mystery some woman hasn't already snatched him up by now."

She grinned at the alarmed expression now on Anna's face a this even being a possibility.

"Come on, admit it. He's so handsome. And so darn sexy." She gave a dramatic sigh, fanning her face with her hand. "If you stop to think about it, he's the perfect man."

When she saw Anna start to smile at this, she nodded. "Out of all of Stephen's friends, he's my favorite. And I am not just saying this. He's so genuine. And smart. Honestly, I could go on and on. For starters, he is very successful and I also believe, quite wealthy. I wouldn't be surprised if his family descended from royalty or something."

Her eyes going wide, she clasped her hands together. "Maybe he's a prince! Or a lord of some kind! If you married him, you could be a

Princess! Or a Lady! I'd have to curtsey when you walked into the room."

She jumped up off the couch and with a very solemn expression on her face, curtsied in front of Anna. "So happy to make your acquaintance, Lady Anna." Her hands going to her cheeks, she gasped. "Oh my! Listen to that. Lady Anna! It even sounds right!"

They both dissolved into laughter.

After Katy settled back on the sofa, Anna grinned at her. As usual, Katy had found a way to make her feel better.

She sighed, pulling yet another tissue out of the box to ball it up in her hands. "Nicholas lives in another country, for goodness sakes! How can I possibly handle a long-distance relationship? Look at the mess I made out of the one I had here."

As she began shredding the tissue to pieces, Katy reached over to take it out of her hands.

Anna merely shrugged her shoulders. "And Katy, I'm sure his family has a girl already picked out for him, one from a suitable family and just waiting for him to propose. Can you even imagine what would happen if he arrived home with me thrown over his shoulder, so ordinary and boring? I'm sure this wouldn't go over very well at all."

Katy was beginning to wonder if this might be the time to tell Anna about the photo. After all, they never kept secrets from each other. She sighed. At least not until lately, they hadn't. But something was telling her she should wait. So, this is what she was going to do.

She gave an exasperated sigh. "First of all, you're not ordinary. And you're not boring. Nor would he throw you over his shoulder. I really don't think this is his style." Eyebrows raised, she gave Anna a long look. "And come on, aren't you overreacting just a bit? Just because you'll be going to this party with him, doesn't mean you're obligated to marry him. At least I don't think so."

Anna reached for yet another tissue, only to draw her hand back with a guilty smile. "I know. I guess, well, I wish I wasn't starting to like him so much."

Then, in an attempt to come across as merely curious, even though she knew she probably wasn't fooling Katy one bit, she asked her about what she was most worried about. "And I'm sure he'll be leaving soon, right?"

Katy sent her a quick glance. "I'm pretty sure he's flying home Monday night."

A sick feeling settling in her stomach, Anna closed her eyes. Monday night? But it was already Friday.

What had she done?

Katy jumped up from the sofa and reached for Anna's hand. "We'll worry about that when the time comes. Right now, we need to find you the perfect dress. Since we wear about the same size, I'm sure we can find something for you in my closet. This is when I appreciate all these business events Stephen drags me to, because I've acquired just about every kind of dress you can imagine."

She grinned. "Come on, we'll pick out something that will knock Nicholas right off his feet. He'll be so stunned by your beauty, he'll forget about every other woman in his life. Every Elizabeth, Isabella and Margaret. Whatever their names are, they'll be history."

When Anna hesitated, Katy grabbed her hand. "Oh, come on, Anna! We're going to have so much fun!"

Anna had no choice but to trail after Katy, who was now almost prancing down the hall with excitement.

Nicholas was leaving on Monday. This was only three days from now.

Then what?

CHAPTER 15

nna was a mess.

She couldn't seem to hold on to things, for heaven's sake.

Like now. She dropped one of her earrings, well, one of Katy's earrings, only able to watch as it skittered across the floor and disappeared under the bed. Carefully getting down on the floor, not an easy maneuver while wearing a long evening gown, mind you, she patted the floor with her hand until she found it. With hands she realized had now started to shake, she finally managed to get the earrings on.

She slipped on a pair of wispy high-heeled silver sandals, also compliments of Katy. She was pretty sure this was a huge mistake on her part. She was definitely flirting with danger with these shoes, no matter how stunning they were. If she had to make any fast moves while wearing them, the outcome wouldn't be good. And the last thing she wanted was Nicholas coming to her rescue.

Again.

But for now, she was ready.

She checked out her reflection into the full-length mirror. As she ran her hands lightly over the floating layers of shimmering silver chiffon, she could only think how thankful she was for such a generous friend as Katy.

Because the dress was absolutely gorgeous. Any woman lucky enough to wear it couldn't help but feel beautiful.

She watched the tiny crystals and rhinestones, scattered over the fabric, sparkle in the light as she did a slow spin in front of the mirror. The delicate diamond necklace, bracelet and matching earrings she wore completed the look to perfection.

Her hands going up to the sweetheart neckline, she wondered… maybe it was too low? She shrugged. Even if it was, there wasn't much she could do about it now, was there?

There was also the fact she now had something even more important to worry about. This would be the phone call she received only minutes ago from Stephen to let her know he and Katy would have to cancel because Katy wasn't feeling well. After he assured her Katy would be fine and she wasn't to worry, he ended the call by telling her to go with Nicholas as planned. And have a great time.

Go with Nicholas as planned? And have a great time?

Really?

He made it sound so simple, didn't he? How she wished she could be just as nonchalant about this sudden change of plans. But going by the nervous flutter having now settled permanently in her stomach, it was obvious she wasn't.

She removed a vintage white fox stole from her closet, worn by her grandmother so long ago on her wedding day. Once she draped it over the chair, the only thing left to do was wait for Nicholas. She glanced over at the clock.

She closed her eyes. In fifteen minutes, he would be here.

Lord knows she wasn't one to pray, but maybe now might be a good time to start.

Nicholas was irritated.

If anything, he was beyond irritated. And yes, he knew he was overacting, but come on. For just once, why couldn't things go as planned? Was this really too much to ask?

He ran his hand through his hair and gave a quick tug to his collar.

Obviously, this latest setback was going to test his patience to the max.

Why the hell aren't the cars in front of you moving?

Usually cars were racing down this highway, zipping in and out of the lanes as if they were all in a rush to the finish line. Nothing at all resembling this complete standstill he was now caught up in.

He gave a frustrated sigh. Why was it when you had to be somewhere by a specific time, you promptly found yourself caught up in a traffic jam.

Damn. Damn. Damn...

He began drumming his fingers on the steering wheel of the Lexus he'd rented for this weekend. If the traffic in front of him didn't start moving, he was going to be late. He was trying not to look at the clock on the dashboard. The thought of Anna sitting, waiting and maybe even starting to wonder if he was even going to show up made his stomach churn. A bad start to the evening like this would certainly not be in his favor.

He shook his head.

No. Tonight, everything needed to be perfect.

Normally these events meant nothing to him. Good Lord, he'd attended what was probably dozens of these affairs. All with the same people, same conversations and the same promises of future deals and possible meetings

But this particular event was a pleasant change from all of this. A very extravagant and festive affair, it was always held in December and had become an annual affair not to be missed.

And this year he would be sharing this experience with Anna, a beautiful and very intriguing Anna. And don't forget sexy. She definitely had him there.

Or, Lord help you, if she gives one of her soft little sighs, making you lose your mind. Every single time.

A smile slowly settled on his face, just thinking about this. There was no doubt in his mind she'd somehow managed to cast a spell over him, something he doubted she even knew she'd done.

He was still finding it hard to believe she'd agreed to be his date for the evening. And now that Stephen and Katy wouldn't be joining them, his feelings were mixed. There was no doubt the four of them would've had a great time, but the thought of being with Anna alone, now spoke of so many possibilities.

But don't forget... with Anna, expect the unexpected. Meaning, you need to be ready for anything.

Yeah, yeah, yeah… he was well aware of this.

A horn sounded behind him, jerking him back to reality. He glanced ahead to see the cars were still at a standstill. His frustration mounting, he ran his hand through his hair again. He turned the radio on. He turned it off.

Finally, the cars in front of him began to move.

In what seemed like only minutes, he'd pulled up in front of Anna's building. After a quick greeting to Louis, he went sprinting up the three flights of stairs. Before he raised his hand to knock on Anna's door, he pulled back the cuff of his shirt to look at his watch.

He grinned.

Imagine that… he was right on time.

Every horn, every car going by and about every single noise in general made Anna jump. She was trying not to look at the clock because if Nicholas was late, she didn't want to know. This would only add fuel to the feverish state she'd worked herself into.

Perched on the edge of the sofa and her eyes closed, she was trying to talk herself into a more relaxed frame of mind. But this wasn't happening. Instead, thoughts of the weekend ahead kept swirling around in her head, making her almost dizzy.

Startled by the knock on her door, she practically dove off the sofa. As she walked over to the door, she took a deep, calming breath and once again, tried to tell herself there was no reason to panic. As if attired in an evening gown and diamonds, with her date for the evening an extremely handsome and charming man … well, this really wasn't all that big of a deal.

If this were true, you wouldn't be such a wreck right now, would you?

After nervously smoothing down the layers of her dress with her hands, she opened the door.

A beautiful vision of silver and sparkling diamonds greeted Nicholas when the door opened. He swallowed.

"Whoa…"

Dear Lord, what kind of greeting is that? Is it the best you could come up with?

Evidently, it was. Because in the silence that followed, he could only gaze at her, unable to utter another word.

A warm glow settling over Anna at his reaction, she smiled. Her soft response was almost a question. "Nicholas?"

Coming to life and his eyes never leaving her face, he moved until there were only inches between them. When he brought her hands to his lips for a kiss, he could feel they were trembling.

He cleared his throat. "Anna… you look absolutely beautiful. As you can see, you've rendered me almost speechless, love."

Anna wanted to say something clever but having him so close and looking so amazingly handsome in a tuxedo, well… she considered it a miracle she was even still standing.

When she realized she was actually starting to sway towards him, she stepped back, pulling her hands from his. Quickly hiding them in the fabric layers of her dress, she hoped he hadn't noticed they were shaking,

Nicholas took a step to erase the space between them. "So, what do you think, love?" His eyes held hers, his voice husky. "Do I also pass your inspection?"

She wanted to tell him he'd passed her inspection the very first time she looked into his eyes. Instead, she reached up to adjust his tie. It didn't need to be straightened, something she was pretty sure they both knew, but it was a way for her to get close to him.

Something she so desperately wanted.

She smiled into his eyes. "There. Now you're perfect."

As she went to back away, he was unable to resist pulling her into his arms. With a soft sigh, she leaned into him, her hands drifting up the sleeves of his tuxedo.

His lips pressed in her hair, he gave a deep sigh. He closed his eyes, wanting nothing more than to close the door, pick her up and carry her over to the bed.

The hell with the party...

The hell with everything...

He blinked.

My God, you've more control than this. At least you've always had in the past.

Fortunately, this was when his common sense kicked in. Exhaling a deep, ragged breath, he brushed his lips over hers before he pulled away. "Ah, Anna, we have to leave. Now. We have an obligation to attend this party." His smile was wistful. "You have me thinking things I shouldn't be thinking right now, all of which involve you. But we really do need to get on the road."

Completely bewildered by this sudden change in him, at first Anna didn't move. Then she slowly stepped back from him and turned to almost run over to get her stole.

As if an invisible thread was pulling him, he swiftly moved to her side to drape the stole over her shoulders. When he brushed his lips over the back of her neck, the shiver he felt course through her made him close his eyes. Touching her... and kissing her was suddenly all he could think about. But pressing one final kiss in her hair, he reluctantly stepped away.

Now, as you can imagine, this had Anna even more confused. And again, no surprise here, a little bit angry.

Exactly what was going on here?

She didn't understand. One minute he was pushing her away, the next he was pulling her back.

She wrapped the stole more tightly around her, her anger building. It looked like she needed to make it very clear to him she wasn't the least bit affected by this behavior of his. Which was pretty laughable since everything in her was telling her to grab hold of the lapels of his tuxedo and pull him close. Then she would kiss him. Or he could kiss her. Once again it didn't matter who initiated the kiss.

Did she dare?

No, obviously this wasn't an option. After all, hadn't he made it perfectly clear they had no time for something like this?

She pasted an expression of indifference on her face and turned to him. "Yes. You're probably right. We probably should get going."

Uh oh...

Nicholas interpreted both the expression on her face and the tone of her voice as a sign she wasn't happy. He swiftly moved to take her hand. "Anna, I want this to be a wonderful evening for both of us. So, please, can't you try to relax?"

At first, she could only stare at him.

Relax?

He had to be kidding.

Seriously? Maybe she needed to come right out and inform him the only way she might be able to 'relax' would be if he walked right out the door and never came back?

Never mind the fact she knew he could be right. Okay, she'd come right out and admit that yes, he was right. But he certainly wasn't helping matters, was he? Not when he kept doing everything he did. Or saying all the things he said. Or, for God's sake, kept on being, well … just him.

That familiar rush of anger now coming at her full force resulted in her exasperated sigh. "You know, you're absolutely right. We have a long evening ahead of us, don't we? So, let's get on with it." She followed this with an angry toss of her head.

His hand going to the back of his neck, Nicholas watched as she went marching over to the door.

Well, there you have it. The evening has barely just begun and already you've managed to somehow upset her.

As he'd feared, everything was off to a rocky start.

He picked up her overnight bag, and shaking his head, he followed her out the door.

It was then he realized he was smiling.

Why was he even surprised?

After all, this was Anna he was dealing with.

CHAPTER 16

$\mathcal{A}$nna had been staring out the passenger window for the past twenty minutes. One would think this was because there was something interesting to see. But once they left the city behind, other than a few random snowflakes coming at the car's headlights, or an occasional light in the distance, it was as though the car had been swallowed up into the night, heading into the middle of nowhere.

She closed her eyes.

She hoped he knew where he was going.

Nicholas didn't remember the drive being this long when he attended this same event last year. But then again, he'd made that trip alone. He wasn't with what now was a very irate and silent Anna. An Anna who made it quite clear she was in no mood to talk to him. Or, for that matter, even look at him. His few attempts to start a conversation had been met with only a nod or a one-word answer, her attention riveted out the window.

It's quite obvious your company is not a top priority on her list right now.

He sighed.

The complete silence coming from her side of the car, along with the anger and frustration vibrating in the air between them, wasn't the emotional response he'd been hoping for this evening.

No, not at all.

He began drumming his fingers on the steering wheel.

Ah… what to do, what to do.

Anna was still fuming over Nicholas's suggestion she should try to relax. She was also beginning to feel a bit worried. The way things were going, it didn't look good. Not only for this evening, but also the rest of the night and tomorrow?

Oh Lord, what is wrong with you? What were you thinking?

How had she ever thought accepting his invitation was a good idea? Apparently, she made the worst possible decision this time.

Her gaze still fixed out the window, she gave a rather loud and dramatic sigh.

Nicholas glanced over at Anna, a smile tweaking the corner of his mouth. He was curious what could be going on in her beautiful, yet extremely fired up mind, to bring on such a tragic sigh.

He hoped she wasn't regretting her decision to be with him tonight. This had him wondering why he hadn't kissed her like he wanted to before they left. Because, even though he had patted himself on the back for being the perfect gentleman, things weren't looking all that great right now, were they?

Oh, what the hell.

He was overthinking things again. It was time for him to dive right in and go with his gut feeling.

He reached over to take her hand.

And he waited…

Well, so far, so good. She hadn't pulled away.

At least not yet, she hadn't.

He decided to wait a little longer.

Finally, he sensed she'd turned to look in his direction.

Hmm... she was becoming a little curious, was she?

He caressed her fingers with his. "So, Anna, tell me... have you been able to find out if any of your ornaments have been sold?"

The question was so unexpected Anna could only stare at him for a few moments before she could respond.

"I... I don't know. Why?"

Encouraged she'd responded with more than a simple yes or no answer, he smiled. "I'm only curious, since I know you're so passionate about what you do. You are very talented, love. You put so much work into your designs and it shows."

She continued to stare at him, wondering where he was going with this. If he was really interested.

And if so, why?

Stop it. You're doing it again, assuming the worst. And you know where this can lead. So be nice.

For once and for all, she needed to let go of this anger she was holding inside. It was taking too much out of her. And it was so unfair to him.

Her mouth curving into a smile, the tone of her voice was almost teasing. "May I ask how you know all of this?"

He sent her a smile. "If you recall, I spent the entire night in your condo and since I was awake almost the entire time, I checked out the work you left on your worktable. I hope it's all right I did this?"

Anna continued to study at him.

Was it all right? She supposed it was.

Wait a minute. Of course it is. It's more than all right.

Marc considered her work as a hobby. A way to pass the time when she wasn't with him. He'd also bluntly informed her it would never become a successful business. Or be profitable. When Anna told him this wasn't her primary goal, he had become angry. So, you can understand why this genuine interest from Nicholas was almost too hard to believe.

A surge of happiness filled her, bringing on another smile. "Why yes, of course it's okay. I guess I'm surprised you're even interested."

Now having braked for a red light, he gazed over at her, those blue eyes of his pulling her right in.

"Ah, Anna, everything about you is interesting to me. How could it not be?" His eyes locked with hers, he brought her hand up to his lips for kiss.

A feeling swept through her. One she couldn't quite identify, leaving her with a deep longing to go right into his arms.

Her words caught in her throat. "Nicholas, I'm sorry. I don't know what's wrong with me. Or why I act like this, I just... I can't seem to stop..."

Untangling his hand from hers, he reached over to cradle the side of her face in his palm. "It's okay, love. It can be overwhelming. Trust me, I know."

His attempt at a kiss was interrupted by a horn sounding behind them. The light had turned green. But this didn't stop him from reaching over to reclaim her hand as they resumed their drive.

He smiled over at her. "So, tell me more. I imagine the Christmas holidays must be very special to you. Do you do a lot of decorating? Do you put up a tree with all of your own ornaments?"

Her head resting back against the seat, and her mind still whirling from the conversation they shared, she almost missed what he said. So, the smile she sent him was a little preoccupied. "No, I haven't. Not yet. I'll do it soon, though. Maybe Monday?"

Monday...

The word settled like a dark cloud between them.

Nicholas drove down a long driveway, illuminated by what had to be thousands of lights twinkling in the pine trees lining each side. This brilliant display continued to the covered entrance of a regal and massive red brick estate.

All decorated for the season, it was an incredible sight.

Candles were glowing in each of the many windows, each anchored with an evergreen swag and a red bow. A magnificent two story arched window showcased a towering Christmas tree sparkling with ornaments and lights. More lights adorned the two large pine wreaths hanging on the massive double front doors, each sporting a huge red bow.

The entire setting, made even more perfect by the snowflakes drifting down from the sky, could be an opening scene for a holiday movie.

They pulled up behind a horse-drawn sleigh to watch as a party of guests began to board. Once everyone was settled, the driver began guiding the sleigh down the driveway for a trip around the estate. The jingling bells, and clip-clop of the horse's hooves against the brick pavement echoed in the crisp winter air.

After Nicholas pulled the car up to the entrance, he turned to Anna. He was almost holding his breath as he waited for her reaction.

She gave him a radiant smile. "Oh Nicholas, everything is so beautiful! I feel like we've driven right into a painting on a Christmas card."

He leaned over to kiss her cheek. The thought flitted through his mind, kissing her had now become quite a habit with him. He didn't know how this happened, he only knew he liked it.

He smiled. "I knew this would make you smile. And it's even more impressive inside."

He winked at her. "You'll have a wonderful time, even with me."

He came around to open her door. Again taken with her beauty, he took her hand. When what he really wanted, was take her into his arms.

This is when it occurred to him. For the next few hours, he would have to share her with everyone else. With no chance for them to be alone.

He almost groaned aloud. This was going to make for a very long evening.

But until then, he was going to treasure every single second.

Starting right now…

CHAPTER 17

*A*nna was feeling a bit overwhelmed.

From the moment they arrived, almost everyone they came in contact with, seemed to know Nicholas. Never leaving her side, his arm lightly encircling her waist or his hand holding hers, he made it a point to include her in every conversation.

He made her feel, well… beautiful. And even though he didn't say this aloud, he made it known to both her and to everyone else, she was the only woman he wanted to be with.

She sighed. How easy it would be to get used to this kind of attention.

When he tightened his hold on her waist, she glanced up at him. A bemused expression on his face, his hand drifted across her shoulders in a gentle caress before he leaned in to whisper in her ear.

"Have I told you how absolutely gorgeous you are? And that I'm so glad you're with me tonight?" This, along with the brush of his lips against her skin, sent shivers down her spine.

Her mouth fell open in shock. How did he do this? How did he always know what she was thinking? My God, he had her in a constant state of anticipation, becoming so flustered she couldn't even think straight.

By her reaction, one would think she was falling in love with him.

No. No. No. This is crazy. You can't let this happen. A million times, no.

In a panic, she turned away, feigning interest in the conversation going on next to them.

Nicholas smiled at Anna's initial reaction. But when she abruptly turned away, a thoughtful look came over his face.

He wondered… what the hell went on with this ex-fiancé of hers? Evidently, he'd managed to beat down her confidence on every level. Because it was obvious, with how rattled she became, she wasn't used to compliments of any kind.

He decided this was going to change. From this moment on and with every chance he got, he was going to let her know just how beautiful and desirable she was.

He watched as she chatted with a colleague of his, her eyes sparkling as she laughed at his comment. Which made him wonder if maybe now might be a good time to start? After all, there were plenty of other women this man could be talking to right now. He had to know Anna was already taken.

Hmm…

Moving closer, he wrapped his arm around her waist and pressed a kiss right below her ear.

Anna drew in a sharp breath after another shiver zipped through her. And this time, she didn't pull away. Instead, she leaned back into the shelter of his arms, the warmth of his body surrounding her.

She sighed, her lashes drifting shut.

Then, with a jerk, she pulled away, her eyes going wide.

What are you doing? More importantly, what was he doing?

She didn't understand. Up until now he had been the perfect gentleman. But first, the compliments.

And now this?

Something was going on, this she knew for sure.

Was it because she was talking to another man? But she quickly put this out of her mind. She didn't even want to think about how Marc had always been so quick to accuse her of flirting, this sending him into a rage.

She closed her eyes, taking a deep breath. She was with Nicholas, not Marc. She was safe with Nicholas, the promise he'd made to her in the restaurant safely tucked in the back of her mind. A promise she knew he'd never break.

But if he wasn't jealous, what could it be? Maybe, just maybe, he was also caught up by this overwhelming force working so hard to pull them together? The same pull she was trying so hard to resist?

She needed to find out. She wasn't quite sure how, but she had to do something.

Are you sure? What if you don't like the results of this little test of yours? Then what?

She wasn't going to think that far ahead. She only knew if she did nothing, she would surely lose her mind.

At that moment the orchestra began to play their first song of the evening. As she watched the couples fill the dance floor, she wondered if this could be the opportunity she was looking for.

She took a deep breath.

She leaned into Nicholas, giving him a seductive smile. At least she hoped it was seductive. Because contrary to what Marc had believed, flirting had never been one of her best attributes.

Lightly dancing her fingertips across his shirtfront and under his jacket, she kept her voice a breathy whisper. "Nicholas? Remember? You promised me a dance when the orchestra began to play."

And just to make things interesting, she formed her lips into a dramatic pout. After all, if that Megan could do this, she should certainly be able to pull it off, shouldn't she?

If Nicholas's reaction was any indication, it looked like she'd nailed this little experiment of hers.

Big time.

For Nicholas, to say this move of hers was unexpected would be the understatement of the year.

Dear God, what brought this on?

He closed his eyes, searching his memory. Had he promised her a dance? If he had, he certainly couldn't remember doing so. But now, with the state he was in, he very well might have and simply couldn't remember.

He didn't understand. Did she really want to dance? Or was there something else going on?

He gazed down at her to see she was watching him very closely. Too closely. Almost in a challenging kind of way. His brain kicking into gear, he .

Hmm... obviously this is some kind of test? Well, she's going to find out very quickly she's messing with the wrong man.

He slowly removed her hand from under his jacket. After he linked her fingers with his, he leaned in to murmur softly in her ear. "You're playing with fire, sweetheart. When you come at me like you just did, you'd better be prepared for the consequences."

Anna's eyes grew wide.

Uh oh... maybe this wasn't such a good idea after all.

Before she even knew what was happening, Nicholas had made their excuses to the others around them and was leading her across the room and out into the hallway. He was moving so quickly she almost had to run to keep up. This definitely made her regret her decision to wear these ridiculously high heeled sandals of Katy's.

Again, what were you thinking? It seems you've made a lot of bad moves so far this evening, haven't you?

If he didn't slow down, she was going to wind up on the floor. And by his current behavior, she had a feeling if this did happen, he might just leave her there. In fact, he seemed so determined to get to wherever he was going, he probably wouldn't even notice if he had left her behind.

She tried to pull her hand from his. "Nicholas, please. You need to slow down. I can't keep up with these heels I'm wearing."

He slowed his pace, an amused expression on his face.

Was she stalling? Rethinking her actions?

He decided to tease her a bit. "Ah… this certainly isn't good, is it? Would you like me to carry you? Because I can, you know. Very easily."

She gasped. He wouldn't dare. Or would he? Imagining the reaction from the other guests if he did this, she quickly shook her head.

As usual, things aren't going that well, are they?

She searched for another excuse. "Nicholas, this is silly. Shouldn't we go back? I'm sure everyone is wondering where we are."

He kept on walking.

Giving a frustrated sigh, she pulled at his hand, much harder this time. He glanced over at her, one eyebrow raised.

Her smile was desperate. "Is this all because you don't want to dance with me? If so, just tell me. Because we don't have to dance. Really, we don't. It was only a suggestion. I just thought …"

If he didn't go and aim one of those slow smiles right at her, bringing her to trip over her own feet and fall right into him. She couldn't even blame this one on the shoes. Her cheeks growing hot, she refused to meet his eyes as he steadied her, holding her tightly against him.

His laugh was a soft brush of breath against her cheek. "*Ah... Anna.* It was a wonderful suggestion. Of course, I want to dance with you. Anything that involves holding you in my arms sounds like heaven to me. But I believe we need to talk first, love. Something's going on and I want to know what it is."

Then he was pulling her into a small sitting room. She glanced around to see, unfortunately for her, it was empty of guests.

She gave a frustrated sigh.

Honestly, where is everyone when you need them?

She was beginning to think everything about this evening was going to turn into one mishap after another. Maybe she should suggest they call it a night and leave? If nothing else, this would keep her from making any more stupid moves.

Before she had a chance to act on this, Nicholas had shut the door and had her backed up against it with only inches between them. His hands sliding up her arms, he pressed them down to her sides and against the door, holding her captive. Though his hold was gentle, she could feel the control he was trying so hard to maintain.

For a few seconds, the only sounds in the room were the crackling of the fire in the fireplace, the ticking of the grandfather clock and Anna was quite certain, her own wildly beating heart.

Completely unnerved, she closed her eyes. If there was ever a time she needed to remain calm, this was it. After all, she was the one who brought this on, so she had to at least pretend she knew what she was doing.

If only she could get her mind to step it up and help her out Instead, it appeared to have shut down completely.

Nicholas almost smiled, watching the expressions flit across her face. God, he just wanted to kiss her. But first he needed to find out what she was up to.

"Anna, open your eyes. I want to be able to look in your eyes, love."

She did this to find he was gazing down at her, the burning intensity in his eyes almost stealing her breath away.

Yep, she was definitely way in over her head right now.

Way, way in over your head...

She swallowed.

He leaned in closer, their lips almost touching. Feeling as if her heart was in her throat, again she swallowed. "Nicholas, please, I..."

He stopped her in mid-sentence. "Anna, have you any idea what you're doing to me?"

"This..." He slowly brushed his lips lightly across hers.

"And this..." He teased her lips with his tongue.

His mouth hovering over hers, his voice was deep and so, so seductive. She couldn't believe how sexy it sounded.

"This is almost all I'm able to think about when you are with me. In fact, even when we're apart, these thoughts fill my mind. Then you go and tempt me like you did back there in the ballroom and my God, it's almost too much to take. You are dealing with a very desperate man, love. Do you even have any idea of how much I want you?"

The best she could manage was a weak shake of her head as his lips had now begun pressing slow, hot kisses down her neck and along the neckline of her dress. She gave a soft moan, and resting her head back against the door, she closed her eyes.

"Do you want me to go on, Anna?" His voice seemed to be coming from far away.

Did she? She wasn't quite sure. What did pop in her mind was she'd been right in thinking the neckline of her dress was too low, his lips finding way too much of her bare skin to work their magic. She should have done something about this when she had the chance.

If only she could push him away, just enough to catch her breath. Then she might be able to give him an answer. Slowly opening her eyes, she swallowed again. Even then, she was barely able to get the words out. "I… I…"

His lips came back to brush against her mouth in a husky whisper. "What? Tell me Anna. What is it you want?"

Oh my, exactly what did she want? Because, honestly? With her mind now in such disarray, she wasn't even sure what her name was, let alone what she wanted.

And how was he dealing with all of this? From what she could see, he was as cool and in control as ever. Which meant he knew exactly what he was doing. And she was willing to bet he also knew the effect he was having on her.

Let this be a lesson for you. Don't think of going up against him again. You'll never win. Never, ever...

She just blurted something out.

"I don't want you to feel the need to flatter me with empty compliments. Like you do with all the other women in your life."

But wait… this wasn't what she'd intended to say. Granted, it would be nice if this were to happen, but there was something she wanted even more. It was the one thing she hadn't been able to stop thinking about since the first time she'd looked into his eyes.

She searched his face, her words finally coming out in a whisper. "When you kiss me… I mean, if you… what I want… is for you to kiss me like you really mean it."

His expression became puzzled.

Eyes locked, they both remained completely still, the silence in the room surrounding them. It was a log falling into the fire with a loud hiss that finally broke the spell.

Nicholas let out a long, ragged breath as he brought their hands up between them, his gaze never leaving her face. "Anna, we're never going to get anywhere if you don't let go and start to trust me."

His smile was wistful. "Believe me when I say I want the same from you, love. I want your kisses filled with passion and given from your heart. I want them to be meant for only me. So much more than you can even possibly imagine."

He slowly shook his head. "This shouldn't be so hard, sweetheart."

The tenderness in his voice was almost her undoing. She glanced away, blinking to stop the tears.

And, of course, he noticed this. Bringing her hands to his mouth, he placed a soft kiss in each palm. *"Ah…* don't be upset. Together we'll work this out. But not now, and certainly not here."

Suddenly, he grinned. A very wicked grin, she would have to say. "Also, if I recall, this all came about because of your claim I made a promise to you. So, how about it… would you like to share a dance with me?"

She gave him a tremulous smile, impulsively brushing her lips lightly over his. "I would love to dance with you, Nicholas."

She felt him go still against her before he exhaled a long sigh. "Ah, Anna… someday we'll look back on this and smile. Trust me with everything. Just trust me."

He was about to open the door when he turned, his expression serious. "And when I give you a compliment? Believe me when I say, the words that come out of my mouth are exactly what I'm feeling in my heart. Every single word, every single time."

His eyes still fixed on her face, it appeared he had something else to say. "And for the last and final time, there are no other women. Okay?"

When she nodded, that wicked grin of his made a comeback. "Good. Because honestly? With you alone, I've got all I can possibly handle." He slowly shook his head. "I've never met a woman who makes me feel as crazy as you do."

Her eyes going wide, she started to laugh. "Crazy? *Hmm…* where have I heard that before? But it's nice to know I'm not the only one who's falling…"

Her mouth snapped shut. Horrified at what she almost blurted out, she closed her eyes, afraid of what she'd see in his.

Honestly, with your mouth so out of control, you need a censor button of some kind.

When she finally, and slowly, opened her eyes, it was to find he was studying her, a thoughtful look on his face. He cleared his throat. "*Hmmm… falling.* I don't think I could have said it any better myself. And do you know what? I'm damn sure it's a good thing."

Without another word, he took her hand and they headed for the ballroom.

Anna wasn't quite sure what happened, but it appeared Nicholas had done it again. He'd turned the situation into something entirely different from what she'd planned. Leaving her dazed and aching for more.

And now they were going to dance. After all, this is what she'd asked of him.

So, she should be happy, right?

But she wasn't. Not now. Not after what just happened. Instead, she was wondering why she hadn't been brave enough to tell him to stop talking and kiss her.

She had a feeling if he had, his kiss would have been everything she imagined it would be.

It would be amazing.

And Nicholas… what was going on in his mind right now?

He was confused.

Unfortunately, this was an emotion he was becoming entirely too familiar with.

What had Anna told him she wanted? For him to really mean it when he kissed her?

Good Lord, where was this coming from?

He thought they had worked this all out. Did this mean she still wasn't convinced his feelings for her were real?

It certainly didn't look like it, did it?

And how did they get back to the topic of all these women supposedly coming and going in his life? There were no other women in his life. None. Nada. Not a single one.

Hell, he didn't want any more women in his life. Which was a good thing, since going by what just happened, he wasn't doing a very good job at handling the one he had. This is if he even had her, something now looking very doubtful.

He was frustrated. And tired of playing games. He wanted everything between them to be real. And to have this happen, he needed to gain Anna's trust.

Completely.

Then everything would fall into place.

He was trying his best to be patient. But this latest confrontation made him want her even more. My God, it had taken everything he had not to take her right there in the sitting room. But he'd held back, knowing even though he was ready, he wasn't sure if she was quite there yet.

Even though she'd completely floored him with her 'falling' comment.

He smiled. Yeah, they were definitely falling. With him at a much faster rate than her. Which meant it was up to him to make sure she held on tight. Because he had the feeling this could be the most exhilarating ride of their life.

But now? She wanted to dance.

He smiled. He could do this.

He only had to find a way to keep the music playing.

A mega-watt smile pasted on her face, Megan King sashayed out of the powder room.

She came to an abrupt stop when she saw Nicholas.

Well, what do you know. Maybe you got lucky after all. Just as you'd hoped, Nicholas was also here.

Her smile quickly disappeared. It appeared he wasn't alone.

No, he was with the woman who fainted at the cocktail party the other night. Katy's friend.

She watched as he and the woman, whom she liked to think of as her competition, made their way to the ballroom. For a brief moment, she considered catching up to them, if only just to shake things up a little.

Boy, wouldn't he be surprised?

She didn't understand.

What did he see in her? She certainly wasn't what you'd call the sophisticated type.

This was the kind of woman he should be with. An ambitious woman like herself. A woman who would work right by his side, helping him grow his business into the multi-million-dollar empire she knew he was capable of running.

A man who would certainly be more successful than her date for this evening would ever be.

This immediately brought up an unwanted thought. Exactly where was her date right now? He'd headed straight for the bar when they arrived and she hadn't seen him since.

She frowned. She should probably make the effort to find him, if only to make sure he wasn't drinking too much. Just because they were staying for the night wasn't an excuse for him to do this.

But now, after seeing these two holding hands, and all googly-eyed over each other, it was obvious she needed to up her plan of attack. She certainly wasn't ready to throw in the towel yet.

She looked around for the nearest exit. She needed a cigarette to calm her nerves.

Only then would she go find her date

When Nicholas and Anna entered the ballroom, the band was about to start a new song.

As he guided her on to the dance floor, Nicholas was smiling. The lyrics couldn't be more fitting.

At last ...
My love has come along.

He took Anna into his arms. When he felt her relax against him with a soft sigh, he pulled her even closer. They began to dance, his cheek resting in her hair as he softly sang along with the words to the song.

My lonely days are over,
And life is like a song.

Anna leaned back in his arms, her lips parted in a smile. After pressing the softest of kisses to her mouth, he continued to sing, his lips caressing her cheek with each word.

I found a dream that I could speak to,
A dream that I can call my own.

She closed her eyes. She wanted nothing more than to stay right where she was and forever in his arms.

I found a thrill to rest my cheek to,
A thrill that I have never known.

As they continued to move to the music, Nicholas tightened his hold on her, his only thought he never wanted to let her go.

And here we are in heaven,
For you are mine, at last...

CHAPTER 18

The orchestra finished their last song of the evening, the notes fading into the ripple of applause from the guests as they slowly drifted off the dance floor.

As they made their way around the small groups gathered in the room and in the hallway, Nicholas and Anna bid their goodnights. Her hand in his, they walked down what seemed to be one hallway after another before Nicholas finally found the room he was searching for. He inserted the old-fashioned brass key into the lock and swung open the door with a flourish.

With a slight bow, he waved his hand for Anna to enter. "After you, my love."

The room was beautiful. Like the rest of the house, it reflected the decor of the early twentieth century when the home had originally been built. It was welcoming and regal at the same time, offering all the comforts of home, but on a much grander scale.

From the high ceiling bordered by an intricately carved molding and centered with an elaborate crystal chandelier, to the luxurious fabrics and rich mahogany furniture, the effect was one of both luxury and nostalgia.

A fire burning in the gas fireplace, along with a small bedside lamp, cast a warm glow over the room, giving the large space an intimate feeling.

As she glanced around the room, Anna quickly averted her gaze from the beautiful, as well as what appeared to be the largest, king-sized fourposter bed she'd ever seen. It was the focal point of the room. You couldn't miss it.

At least she couldn't.

Then there were their overnight bags, sitting side by side on the luggage rack. Which got her to thinking. Maybe she shoul have told Nicholas she preferred her own room.

Oh, come on... really? It's a little too late for this, no?

She crossed the room to a small sitting area. She leaned against the arm of the sofa, and kicked off her shoes, giving a sigh of relief. Only then did she finally glance over at Nicholas.

He'd already removed his jacket. She watched as he undid his tie, pulling it off before he unbuttoned the top two buttons of his shirt. After he unfastened his cufflinks, he began rolling up his sleeves. He was humming one of the songs the orchestra had played.

Only then did he turn to Anna, his humming quickly replaced with a smile when he saw she was watching him. He also noticed how she was perched precariously on the arm of the sofa. As if she was ready for a quick getaway. Possibly without shoes, if need be.

He smiled.

Well, this is something that isn't going to happen. Not if you have any say in the matter.

He glanced over at the wet bar to see there was a bottle of champagne chilling over ice. He briskly rubbed his hands together. "So, what do you think? Should we cap off a wonderful evening with some champagne?"

Embarrassed to have been caught staring at him, she smiled, giving him a nod.

Not the least bit uncomfortable with her silence, he went to work uncorking the bottle. At the same time, he began to talk casually about some of the people they'd met and how he knew them.

She tried to follow along, but wasn't able to concentrate,

completely caught up in what he was doing. As if the whole process of opening a bottle of champagne and pouring it into two glasses was the most interesting thing she'd ever witnessed in her life.

She sighed.

In a way, it was. And this was only because he was the one who was doing the opening and pouring.

The more time they spent together, the more she was drawn to into him, captivated by everything about him. He was just so smooth, his body language radiating such confidence and authority. Yet at the same time there was a gentleness and sincerity about him that made her feel all was well when she was with him. And even though he was so easily able to keep her off balance, he always managed to remain steady and in control for both of them.

Ah... but maybe not?

What about earlier this evening? When she surprised him with her request for a dance? Granted this had been a very short-lived victory on her part. But she was going to hold on to this little bit of power for as long as she could. Good grief, she needed to have some leverage when it came to dealing with him, didn't she?

Nicholas cleared his throat. Anna glanced up to see he was standing in front of her, a champagne glass in each hand.

She gave him a brilliant smile

Taken aback, he stared at her, a completely bewildered look on his face. Then, after a slight shake of his head, he handed her one of the glasses.

He smiled as he tipped his glass against hers. "To us, love."

Anna was careful to take only a small sip of the champagne. She certainly didn't need a reminder the combination of alcohol and Nicholas was a risky combination. That she'd agreed to be his date for the evening was confirmation of this.

She smiled up at him. "Champagne is so wickedly tempting, isn't it? But indeed, such a welcome refreshment."

Oh my God... you sound like you've just stepped out of a Victorian romance novel. Wickedly tempting? Indeed, such a welcome refreshment? Where did this come from?

She took a gulp of champagne, followed by another. When she saw Nicholas trying to hide his smile as he watched this, she dropped her gaze to her glass, appalled to see it was now half empty. Or half full. Or whatever, it really didn't matter. What mattered was she needed to slow down.

You'll be running over to drink it right out of the bottle next! Remember, you have a whole night to spend with this man!

She gripped the glass tightly in her hands, nervously licking her lips. She needed to start talking. About anything she could think of. And she needed to do this fast.

She smiled. "It was such a beautiful evening, Nicholas. I had a wonderful time and everyone was so nice. Thank you for asking me to come with you."

He was twirling the stem of his glass between his fingers, his gaze now having settled on her mouth. Suddenly the only thing he could think about was how badly he wanted to take her in his arms and capture her mouth in a kiss. Again, he would do this. And again. And yes, even again.

He cleared his throat, giving a slight bow in her direction. "Ah, but the pleasure was all mine, Anna. With you by my side, I'm sure I was the envy of every man here tonight."

He moved closer, his knuckles gently tracing the line of her jaw before brushing over her cheek. The tone of his voice dipped to a husky drawl. "And look. Here you are, still with me. So, it is I who should be thanking you."

His gaze holding hers over the rim of the glass, he took a drink of his champagne. He topped this off by throwing out another one of his smiles, right at her.

She was speechless. Yes, believe it or not, she was unable to utter a single word, not even a thank you. She could only stare back at him before she gazed down at the glass in her hand.

Dear God... will you ever become immune to his smiles? Or the compliments that come flowing so smoothly out of his mouth?

She wanted to toss her glass over her shoulder, walk right into his arms and tell him to do with her what he wanted. She was all his.

Immediately becoming flustered at the possibility of this actually happening, she lifted her glass to her lips and drank the remaining champagne in her glass.

Well, so much for keeping your cool. But let's be honest here, this is what he does to you.

Every...

Single...

Time...

Without a word, Nicholas took her empty glass and placed it on the table next to his. He reached for her hands and pulling her up from the sofa, he brought them over to the chair by the fireplace. He sank down into the chair and pulling her with him, she fell into his lap.

"Nicholas!" This, for some reason, came out in a hiccup-like-giggle.

He gave a soft chuckle, putting his finger to her lips. "*Ah...* hush, love. This feels so comfortable, no? It feels like heaven to me. Only the two of us, finally free of those people we spent so much time with this evening."

He pressed a kiss to the top of her head and inhaling the familiar floral scent he now associated only with her, a feeling of utter contentment flowed through him. It felt like heaven holding her in his arms He closed his eyes, his imagination keeping them like this forever, their hearts beating almost as one.

Well, maybe... because that bed does look pretty inviting.

In an attempt to clear his mind of this, at least for now, he smiled at her. "I don't want champagne to blur your opinion of me, not tonight. I want you to see the real me. Which, I assure you, is not the man you still seem to think I am."

Anna nodded against him. She was trying to figure out how it was even remotely possible she felt so lightheaded from only one small glass of champagne.

And so quickly, too.

But maybe the champagne wasn't the problem?

She only knew she was having a hard time trying to deal with the sensation of being so completely surrounded by him. Between the heat radiating from him, and his arms holding her close, she felt like she she was melting right into him, becoming a part of him.

It was all too much. Resting her head on his shoulder, she closed her eyes.

And this is how they stayed, not speaking, not moving.

For Nicholas this was because, believe it or not, once again he was unsure of his next move.

While Anna was waiting and wondering what he was thinking. This a reminder there was something she needed to tell him.

She stirred, giving a small sigh. "He was here tonight."

What? Who was here? Nicholas was confused, while at the same time, his whole body shifted into an alert mode. When he saw her fingers nervously twisting the fabric of her dress, he linked her fingers with his, keeping his voice even. "Tell me more, love."

He waited, her words finally coming at him so softly, he had to lean in closer to hear them. "He was with the woman who was at Katy and Stephen's cocktail party. I think her name was Megan? I saw them leave the ballroom while we were dancing."

She didn't tell him Marc and Megan had been in a heated argument at the time.. Even now, remembering the anger on Marc's face, she felt herself slipping back to a time she didn't want to remember. She tightened her grip on his fingers.

Nicholas tried to quell his feeling of unease. He'd caught a glimpse of Megan once during the evening, but hadn't given her another thought. In fact, he'd gone out of his way to stay as far away from her as possible.

But this news she was with Anna's ex-fiancée had him regretting his actions. Together, the two of them could only mean trouble.

Why the hell hadn't he paid more attention to what was going on around them tonight?

Because you really didn't care about Megan or anyone else, did you? Your eyes were only for Anna.

He kept his voice calm, sensing her uneasiness. "When you say he, I assume you're referring to your ex-fiancée?"

She gave a slight nod against his chest. He brought her hand to his mouth, brushing his lips over her fingers. "Sweetheart, why didn't you let me know?"

She curled up closer to him, almost as if she was trying to hide deeper in his arms. Gripping his hand tightly, she spoke in a soft, shaky voice.

"Oh Nicholas, I was afraid of what he'd do. Especially if he saw I was with you. He has such a terrible temper, always fighting with someone. He wasn't always like this, not in the beginning. But then he changed, becoming so angry and moody all of the time. No matter what I said or did, it was never enough. And now, the thought of coming face to face with him makes me feel physically ill."

For a few seconds she was silent, before her next words came out in a whisper. "He frightens me. I don't think he'll ever leave me alone."

His uneasiness had now turned to rage. It was an anger so intense, his throat tightened up. He honestly felt like he was choking. Lightly running his fingers through her hair, he tried to calm down.

You need time.

Yes, he needed time to think of the right thing to say to her without sounding like a crazed maniac. Because from what she told him, this was exactly the kind of behavior she'd experienced with this Marc.

If he'd come face to face with him tonight, he wouldn't have hesitated to warn him Anna was off limits. And if his advice had gone unheeded? Well, he would have dealt with him personally, right then and there. He didn't care about his temper, nor was he afraid of him.

He would do whatever was needed to keep Anna safe and sheltered within his love.

His love?

This hit him like a lightning bolt coming from out of the blue.

It happened... he'd fallen completely and madly in love with Anna. Somehow his heart had taken the leap without his knowledge and now there was no turning back.

The photo had sent him on the right course, and now she was here, what they had was real.

She was real.

And his plan was to never let her go.

He wanted it all, to have, to hold, to love and to honor. He wanted to share a lifetime with her. He would be her prince and her knight in shining armor, all rolled into one.

God willing, he'd do anything for her.

Anything.

Anna felt a flicker of uncertainty. Why wasn't Nicholas saying anything? Deciding maybe it was better she didn't know the reason for his silence, she closed her eyes.

Lulled by the warmth of his embrace, the steady beat of his heart and the light touch of his fingers in her hair, she drifted off.

When Nicholas realized she'd fallen asleep, he pressed a kiss in her hair.

His head resting against the back of the chair, his mind was racing as he stared into the flames flickering in the fireplace.

So, this was love. This wonderful everything-was-right-with-the-world feeling now inside of him.

He knew he was grinning, but he couldn't seem to stop. Good Lord, this was all so new to him. He had no idea a person could feel this way. Why, right now he felt like he could take on the world.

What he'd once thought of as a one in a million chance at love, had now become the real thing.

He, Nicholas William Edward Hanover III, had fallen in love.

CHAPTER 19

A shrill beeping sound pierced the silence. Instantly coming awake, Anna's eyes went wide with shock.

At the same time, startled by the dreadful noise, Nicholas jumped up out of the chair, nearly spilling her onto the floor. He glanced wildly around the room, to finally sprint over to turn off the alarm clock on the bedside table, unplugging it for good measure.

Rattled, he massaged the back of his neck. "What a God-awful noise. Why the hell would anyone choose to wake up to that?"

Then he remembered Anna.

He turned to see she was wide-eyed and starting to giggle as she slowly sank back down into the chair. Swiftly crossing the room, he pulled her up out of the chair and into his arms.

"I'm so sorry, love. This certainly wasn't the best way to wake up, was it? But I'm quite confident I've put that nasty old alarm clock out of commission and we won't have to worry about it going off again."

She pressed a quick kiss to his cheek. Her smile was teasing. "*Ah, my hero. Or maybe you'd rather I refer to you as my knight in shining armor?*"

His laugh was soft, his gaze tender. "*Ah… Anna, for you, I hope to always be both.*"

A look of unmistakable longing on his face, he trailed his fingertips across her cheek and along her jaw. When he felt her shiver at his touch, he slowly released his hold on her and stepped back. His eyes searching her face, his expression was uncertain.

"It's late. I guess we should think about going to bed."

Anna glanced over at the bed, then looked back at him, color rising in her cheeks.

He quickly reached out to smooth her hair back from her face. "It's okay, love. I can easily sleep on the sofa." He gave it a quick glance, running his hand through his hair. "It looks pretty comfortable as far as sofas go."

But this was certainly not what he was thinking.

Good Lord, how was it even remotely possible you could wind up sleeping on the sofa with Anna so close by in this big bed? A bed meant for two people, not one.

A bed meant for them.

If you do have to spend the night on the sofa, it's a safe bet you won't be getting any sleep while you're there.

Yes, in the series of events since they met, this could be the final test that might finally put him over the edge. But he had to give her the option of deciding what would happen next. No matter how much he wanted her.

He uttered a short laugh. It would probably kill him, but this was the chance he had to take.

At the resigned expression on Nicholas's face, Anna was hit with a rush of panic.

This was not what she wanted. She wanted to be with him and in his arms. So he could ease this hunger inside of her.

She looked over at him to see he hadn't moved, waiting patiently to see what she would do. But this was so out of her comfort zone, she wasn't even sure how, or where to begin.

She took a deep breath. He wouldn't let her do this alone. This she knew for sure.

She removed her earrings. After she placed them on the dresser next to his tie and cufflinks, she attempted to take off her necklace.

But her hands had begun to shake and she couldn't undo the clasp. Frustrated, she closed her eyes.

Breathe. Just breathe. You can do this. This is Nicholas you're with. A man you can trust. How many times has he already told you this?

He was suddenly behind her, gently moving her hands aside so he could unfasten the necklace. His lips went on to leave a trail of soft kisses up her neck before they ended with a soft whisper in her ear. "Anna … everything about you is so desirable. You must know this, don't you?"

A shudder running through her at his words, she leaned back against him, her heart beating so out of control, she was afraid it was going to leap right out of her chest.

When his hands slid down to her waist to pull her even closer, in an almost desperate move, she turned to face him. She made sure she kept her eyes on the buttons going down the front of his shirt. If she got caught up in his eyes, she knew she'd be lost.

She began to slowly undo the buttons, her voice barely audible. "It doesn't seem right you should have to sleep on the sofa when the bed is more than big enough for both of us …" Her voice trailed off in a faint whisper.

He gathered her hands in his. "Anna …"

She swiftly untangled her hands from his and put her fingers against his mouth. "Nicholas, no. Let me do this. Please."

He nodded and after dropping a soft kiss to her forehead, he watched her hands move slowly down the front of his shirt, stopping to undo each button.

She glanced up at him. Emboldened by the desire in his eyes, she pulled his shirt free from the waistband of his trousers. Her hands slipping under his shirt, she pushed it down his arms to fall to the floor.

Her fingertips drifted over his bare skin and up over his shoulders She wanted to explore very muscle, each contour, anywhere she could reach. Breathing in the intoxicating scent that was him, she pressed a soft kiss to the pulse beating at the base of his neck before she leaned against him with a sigh.

He pulled her even closer. And suddenly, for Anna, it was all too much, uncertainty taking over her desire.

She didn't think she could do this.

No, she couldn't.

With a shaky sigh, she dropped her hands to his waist. "Nicholas, I'm trying, but I don't think I can do this. I'm not good at it."

Bewildered, he pulled away to search her face.

Not good at this? How could she even think this?

He framed her face in his hands, his eyes searching hers. "Ah, Anna. No, no, no … tell me, why would you even say this?"

She had to close her eyes before she could give him her answer. "Marc … he said I …"

Damn...

He swiftly covered her mouth with his in a kiss. He didn't want her to feel the need to repeat the words Marc had used in one of what was probably his many attempts to humiliate her. Again, fury began to build inside of him at what this man had done to her. It was only when she began to tremble against him he put his anger aside.

Her face still cradled in his hands, his eyes held hers. His voice, so deep and soothing, flowed like a river to settle inside of her.

"I'm not Marc. I'll never be like him, think like him or act like him. And I will never, ever be disappointed in you. Never. My God, love, how could I be? Just look at me... being with you has my head spinning and my heart racing almost out of control. You are all I can think about, all that I want. So, trust me when I tell you you're doing everything right. Everything."

For a few moments, they regarded each other in silence before she let out a long, shaky breath. The fear and anxiety clouding her eyes began to fade, leaving her gazing up at him in whole different way.

Her hands moved up to grip his shoulders.

"Oh, Nicholas, kiss me." Their lips almost touching, her plea was a desperate whisper. "Please, please, I just want you to kiss me."

His mouth turning up in a small smile, he pulled her against him. *"Hmm...* I'm going to kiss you like, what was it you requested earlier? *Ah, yes...* I remember. You wanted me to kiss you like I really mean it."

Before she could respond, his mouth came down on hers in a bruising, deep kiss that took her breath away. It was a kiss so demanding, she had to tighten her hold on him to keep from sinking to the floor. She leaned into him, molding her body to his as the kiss deepened, fearful she would spin away into nothing if she lost his touch.

Finally…

She had no idea a kiss could make her feel this way. Yes, she'd been kissed before, but never, ever, ever like this. Not with such passion, such fire. In her struggle to keep up, her only thought was if he were to stop, she might possibly die.

For Nicholas, the constraint he'd battled over the past week completely shattered the second his mouth came down on hers.

Yes, finally…

He wanted to hold her like this forever.

He wanted a million nights just like this.

For she was everything he'd imagined.

And all he would ever want.

Anna wanted more.

She wanted to touch him everywhere.

She trailed her fingers slowly across his chest and down over his stomach until she came to the waistband of his trousers. After she managed to unbutton them and undo the zipper, she ran her hands down over his bare skin, pushing at his clothing until it all fell to the floor. He quickly kicked the garments aside.

He took her back into his arms. He pressed a trail of kisses down her throat, brushing across her collarbone and above the neckline of her dress. When she pressed even closer, a soft moan rising from low in her throat, he captured her mouth in a deep kiss.

And now, he was the one who wanted more. He ran his hands over the silky layers of her dress, watching as they floated back in place. Gazing down at her, his voice was rough. "Anna, you're driving me mad. Look at us. How is this fair? With all of these layers, I'm at a disadvantage here."

She reached up to caress his cheek. "Then I guess it's up to you remedy this…'"

Needing no further invitation, he pulled down the zipper. This sent the dress drifting down over her shoulders before it fell into a soft whisper of chiffon at her feet. After his fingers made quick work of removing the rest of her clothing, his mouth searching for hers, the kiss he gave her was even more demanding, more passionate.

He'd foolishly thought he would be able to remain in complete control when he was with her. But never could he have known what it would feel like to finally have her in his arms like this. Her soft curves, fitting so perfectly against him, evoked a feeling like nothing he'd ever experienced. A moment so sacred, it was almost as if they had already become one.

Almost in a prayer, he whispered her name.

"My God… Anna…"

He was lost…

Nicholas gazed around the room. The bed… this was where they needed to be. He gathered her up into his arms, her sigh disappearing into the kiss he gave her.

Gently setting her down on the bed, he moved over her, resting his hands on either side of her head. His eyes, dark with passion, glittered into hers.

He was so close, yet not close enough to ease the deep ache inside of her, this desperate hunger for him. She whispered his name, and tangling her fingers in his hair, she pulled him down against her.

Lifting his head, he smoothed the hair from her face, his voice like velvet. "Tell me, love… tell me what you want."

Her lips sweeping over his mouth, she struggled to get out her answer. "Kiss me again."

He gazed long and thoughtfully at her before he finally responded, his answer coming in a whisper instead of a kiss. "Anna, are you sure? Because once I do, I won't be able to stop with just a kiss. I need to know you want all of this as much as I do, love."

She could see the desire in his eyes. And a tenderness so real she knew this was where she was meant to be. She pulled him closer, planting soft kisses across his face between her words. "I want you... I want all of you... So please, please... just kiss me."

Together, they became lost in the fierce tide of hunger that consumed them. With each whisper, every touch and each kiss that followed, they reached a level of passion they never could have imagined.

It was the sweetest of surrenders.

With the promise of a new beginning.

Nicholas knew from this moment on, he would always belong to her. The emotional response she brought from him was one he didn't know he was even capable of giving, taking him beyond anything he'd ever experienced.

She would forever be a part of him.

And Anna?

Adrift in the feel of him, she was floating in a world she never knew existed. She had no idea it could be like this. And now, nothing would ever be the same.

How could it be?

Because this was what she should have been waiting for all along.

Nicholas's hand drifted lazily over Anna's shoulder before traveling down her arm to pull her closer. Feeling a shiver run through her at his touch, he pressed a kiss in her hair.

She caught his hand in hers, her eyes searching his face. For a few moments, they remained wrapped up in each other's gaze.

Then, she brought his hand to her lips. "Nicholas... I..." She slowly shook her head.

"I know, love. My God, how I know." Burying his face in the curve of her neck, he followed this with a kiss.

She settled closer to him, her gaze traveling around the room. She wanted to remember everything about this night... *everything.* The soft glow of the fire in the fireplace. The feeling of being in the shelter of Nicholas's arms. And the sound of his heart beating so close to hers, almost echoing in the stillness of the night.

She wanted to gather up the memory of every kiss, every caress, and each of his whispers, all meant for her alone. So she could hold on to them forever, tucked safely away in her mind and in her heart.

She gave a long, contented sigh.

He smiled, and bringing her hand to his mouth, he brushed a kiss over each finger before he pressed a deep, smoldering kiss in her palm.

After he folded her fingers over the kiss, a smile tweaked the corner of his mouth. "Seriously, love? This is the third time I've given you one of these kisses. And you've yet to hold on to even one of them. Will I have to have to keep reminding you about this for the rest of our life?"

She searched his face.

The rest of your life? Together? You and Nicholas? This is only wishful thinking, right?

The thought of this even being a possibility was overwhelming to Anna. Her heart beginning to beat in a frenzy, she closed her eyes as she tried to fight off the panic building inside of her.

What had she been thinking?

How had she let herself get so carried away?

More importantly, what was going to happen now?

Nicholas watched the different expressions flash across Anna's face. This, along with the sudden frenzied beat of her heart, pounding against him, was confusing to him.

He pressed a soft kiss in her hair. "Anna, all of these expressions on your face, love. I don't know what to make of them. And your heart… it feels like it's about to leap right out of your chest. Tell me… what's going on."

When Anna saw the worried expression on his face, she pushed her fears into the furthest corner of her mind. She wasn't going to drag him down with her uncertainty. No… now, more than anything, she wanted to sink into the strength and comfort of him. Where she finally felt safe.

Her hands framing his face, she gave him a lingering kiss. "Oh Nicholas, it's okay. I'm fine. Really, I am."

She studied him. It wasn't fair, no matter how disheveled he'd become, he was still so handsome. With his face showing a five o'clock shadow, and his hair all mussed, he seemed more relaxed and not so perfect.

She snuggled back against him. "You know… I think I almost like you better this way. Scruffy. Mussed up. But oh, still so very, very sexy."

He chuckled. "Sexy, huh? *Hmm…* it's settled then. If this is what it takes to keep you with me, I'll never shave again. Or comb my hair."

"Hmm… I don't know if that's wise. I remember when Marc… " A look of panic on her face, her voice dropped to a whisper. "I'm sorry, I didn't mean…" She shook her head again.

For a long moment, Nicholas was silent, his eyes searching hers. Then, gently brushing her hair back from her forehead, he sighed. "Anna, I know it must be hard for you to talk about him. And I also want to apologize for my silence when you brought him up earlier. But I needed to get my feelings under control. The last thing I want, is to bring more anger into your life."

She turned her face into his shoulder, her reply muffled. "Oh, Nicholas. It's okay."

"Oh, Anna… no. No, it's not. Whatever hell he put you through is not okay." He cupped her chin in his hand, gently forcing her to look at him. "I don't want you to think this. Because there is absolutely no excuse for his behavior."

His kiss was gentle. "You'll always be safe with me. Nothing you do will make me angry with you. Nor will I ever hurt you."

She reached up to stroke his cheek "Oh Nicholas, I know you won't." She leaned back, her eyes searching his face. She opened her mouth to speak. Then closed it again.

His eyes never leaving hers, he waited.

Her words were soft. "What's going to happen next? With us?

You're going to be leaving and I don't know what you're planning. Or if we…"

Her words trailing off, she closed her eyes. But not before he saw the worry pooling there. Burying his face in her hair, he tightened his hold on her. He was suddenly unsure of what to say, his fear he might overwhelm or even possibly scare her.

He knew what he wanted. And this would be a lifetime with her. For all their days and the nights that followed. So, he could love her, take care of her, and keep her safe. But he didn't know if she was ready to hear this so soon. She'd been given promises before, only to have everything come crashing down in the worst possible way, leaving her with an overwhelming loss of trust.

He framed the side of her face in his hand, his gaze holding hers. "I don't know for sure what's coming next. But I do know no matter what happens, we'll find a way to be in this together. I can't imagine it being any other way. Again, with us, everything feels right. *So* right."

He could see the struggle in her eyes as she tried so hard to believe him.

She finally reached up to clasp her hands behind his neck. Her eyes bright, her request was barely audible.

"Promise?"

He leaned his forehead against hers, overcome with emotion and almost unable to speak. "Oh, love… yes, I promise you this."

His name coming from her in a sigh, she lifted her mouth to his. He pulled her close, taking over the kiss with a passion he knew she would expect.

And once again, she surrendered to all he gave.

Her heart beating so sure and steady with the promises he made.

CHAPTER 20

The kiss was soft, but insistent.

"Hey… Sleeping Beauty. Come on. It's time to wake up."

Anna's eyes flew open. Nicholas was sitting next to her on the bed, his hair still damp from the shower.

His smile was so genuine, an unexpected feeling of pure happiness spread through her. She now understood what people meant when they said they were on cloud nine.

Because this is where she was, in a place overflowing with everything good.

And this was all because of Nicholas.

She gave a slow, lazy stretch, a drowsy sigh escaping her. When Nicholas reached over to brush the hair back from her face, she put her arms around his neck to pull him down next to her.

"*Umm… good morning.*"

He settled beside her. "Good morning, love. I've been wanting to kiss you awake like this ever since I stayed that night in your condo." He shook his head. "God, what a night that was. I was so worried about you."

His gaze was searching. "But you didn't seem to be very fond of me. So, who knows what you might have done?" He tilted his head, a grin spreading across his face. "I think you may have returned my kiss, even though now you would probably try to deny this. *Hmm... maybe like this?*"

He was kissing her again. A slow, sweet kiss. And like every other time he kissed her, she fell right into it. Sliding her fingers through his hair to keep him close, she didn't want it to end.

She opened her eyes to his smile.

He rested his forehead against hers. "How amazing it was to wake up this morning with you beside me, all cuddled up in the blankets and sleeping so peacefully. I didn't want to wake you. And since there is no need for us to hurry..."

His voice trailed off into a deep intake of breath. This was because Anna's hands had slipped beneath his robe, her fingertips skimming over his bare skin.

He closed his eyes.

Anna wouldn't be able to tell you where this out-of-character behavior of hers was coming from. In fact, she had no clue how she even knew how to do what she was doing. It was as if this overwhelming need for him had taken over her senses, making her blind to everything except for how much she wanted him. And she couldn't rein it in for the life of her.

Nor did she want to...

It wasn't helping that he looked so incredibly handsome this morning. And if you stopped to think about it, he was the one to start it all off with the kiss he just gave her. Sleeping Beauty should be so lucky to be awoken by a kiss from him.

Nicholas groaned as she pressed a trail of feathery kisses across his face, his body reacting to her touch with a hunger he was almost powerless to control. How was it she could make him become so helpless? Wasn't he supposed to be the one to initiate the moves? The one in charge?

Well, if so, you certainly aren't doing your job.

As much as he wanted everything she was promising with her touch, there was something he needed to do. Gently pushing her back into the soft bedding, he gathered her hands in his.

"Anna…"

Her eyes closed, a long purring sigh was her response. Untangling her hands from his, she reached up to run her fingers through his hair.

He tried again, this time cupping her chin in his hand. "Anna, love… listen to me for a minute. Then I'll be more than happy to go along with whatever you seem to have in mind."

This got her attention. Her lashes flying open, color flooded her cheeks.

He was smiling as he planted a quick kiss to her mouth. Then his expression turned serious, his words hesitant. "I don't want to leave you, love. I want you to come with me."

She blinked, her hands slowly falling to his shoulders.

Come with him? Right now? Where?

She didn't want to go anywhere. She wanted to stay right here. In this bed and in his arms for as long as she could. Didn't he just say they had as much time as they wanted?

Yes… yes, he did.

Her eyes searched his. "Where?"

Edging a strand of hair from her face, a faint smile played about his lips. "I want you to fly home with me. So you can meet my family and see where I live. I'll take you to all of my favorite places, give you a tour of the city. You'll love it during the holidays. But most of all, I just want you with me."

He watched the confusion clouding her eyes. When this turned to panic, he wondered if he'd made a mistake in bringing this up. Because this wasn't the reaction he'd been hoping for.

Dear God, are you ever going to know what you're doing with this rela-tionship thing?

He was beginning to think not.

Long after she fell to sleep, he'd stayed awake mulling over her question about what was next in their relationship. It was then he decided he would ask her to make the trip home with him. This would be the best way to keep the promise he gave her. But now he wondered if he jumped the gun.

Or maybe it was bad timing?

Anna was struggling. She'd been expecting a kiss. Yes, this would have been very nice. Never had she expected this.

"London? Fly?" Yes, knew she was repeating everything. But she wanted to be sure she heard him right.

His next words confirmed she had.

"Yes, London. And yes, fly. It's being done quite often these days, you know."

Not wanting to sing his own praises, but he was feeling quite pleased. His idea was brilliant. Surely, once she thought it over, she would have to agree.

Maybe you need to give her a little more time to think about it?

The possibility of this actually happening had slowly begun to register in Anna's mind. How easy it would be to toss everything aside and say yes. But let's be serious… she couldn't jump on a plane and go jetting across the ocean with a man she'd met only a little over a week ago.

If she stopped to think about it, she didn't even know all that much about him. Definitely not enough to just take off on a whim.

You just spent the night with him. And you did ask him what was next. It looks like he gave you an answer.

But what about her life here? Her work… her condo… Mia… What about these?

Her silence had Nicholas dropping a soft kiss to her mouth before he gave a long sigh. "Anna, If I could, I'd stay here with you. In a heartbeat, I would do this. Leaving you is something I don't even want to think about. And you have to agree what we have together is amazing."

He gave her a sweet, lingering kiss. "It's magic, love. Like a spell that shouldn't be broken. So, say yes… you'll come with me."

Anna closed her eyes.

This wasn't fair.

How was she supposed to make a logical decision with his words going straight to her heart, settling there like this was where they belonged?

And his kiss?

It was already obvious what his kisses did to her.

Yes, what they had was incredible.

But was it real?

Was it love?

Did he feel the same?

Did he love her?

Wait a minute... now you're thinking you might be in love with him?

Confusion clouded her mind. And suddenly, this was too much to deal with. She didn't want to think, and she didn't want to talk. She only wanted to get lost in the feel of him and in this time they had together. Maybe later she could decide, but not now.

She pulled his head down, seeking his mouth in a kiss. It could be taken as a hint at what her answer might have been had she spoken aloud.

This sudden move of hers sent Nicholas's thoughts scattering, his request forgotten. He was helpless, nothing making sense except getting lost in this moment with her.

Once again they became caught up in their hunger for each other, his hopeful plea and her unspoken response swallowed up in a kiss.

Ah... but it was a kiss of magical proportions.

Anna studied her reflection in the bathroom mirror.

Her thoughts drifting back to the night she and Nicholas spent together, she was overcome by a desperate longing to be back in his arms. Gripping the edge of the sink, she closed her eyes as she tried to catch her breath.

Yes, this is what he did to her.

You've become bewitched by this man. How can this be real?

So, maybe it wasn't real. But whatever happened next, she never wanted to lose this magical, dreams-really-come-true, feeling.

No, she was going to hang on to this for as long as she could.

But now she had an important decision to make.

Should she be on that plane with him tomorrow?

Her mind was in denial, all the reasons she shouldn't go with him tripping over each other to be heard.

While her heart was telling her to go for it, beating with a passion almost impossible to ignore.

And, as it had been ever since this whole crazy whirlwind with Nicholas began?

Her heart was still leading the way.

Nicholas stood by the window gazing out at, well… nothing.

If anyone were to ask him, he wouldn't be able to say what the hell was out there. No, his thoughts were all wrapped up with Anna.

He glanced over at the closed bathroom door. Even though it seemed she was taking forever to get ready, when he checked his watch, he saw it had been a very short time.

This was a sure sign he might be in trouble. If this is how he felt now, what frame of mind would he be in tomorrow if he had to return home without her?

Something that now looked like it could very well happen.

His forehead creased with worry, he ran his hand through his hair. How was he to convince her she was meant to be with him on a plane bound for London tomorrow?

If only she'd given him some kind of answer. Unless she had meant for it to be in the kiss she gave him.

If so, he'd take it. Because, dear God, what a kiss it had turned out to be. Shaking his head in amazement at this incredible Godsend that was Anna, his Anna, he again glanced at his watch.

Where was she?

Ah, finally...

Her blue sweater making her eyes shimmer like the ocean on a clear day, and a shy smile on her face, Anna walked right into his arms. Where she leaned against him with a long, contented sigh.

This was when he realized it didn't matter what her answer was. He would accept whatever decision she made. Even if this meant he would have to make the trip, as often as he could, to see her.

The bottom line... you want to be with her, no matter when, no matter where, and no matter how it came about.

It was this simple.

He pressed a kiss in her hair. "It was worth the wait. You look beautiful." Pulling slightly away, his eyes smiled into hers. "I don't know about you, but I'm starving. I also want to introduce you to Charlie and Susan, the hosts of this event. They are very special to me. I'm hope we'll be able to meet up with them at the brunch. Does this sound good?"

Anna reached up to clasp her hands behind his neck. "Sounds perfect."

She glanced around the room before she turned to him. "I wish we didn't have to leave. It was wonderful, being here with you. The party, last night, everything."

He was silent, a hint of uncertainty in his eyes.

This was a reminder she needed to give him the answer she knew he was patiently waiting for. Her hands sliding down to rest against his chest, she smiled up at him.

"Nicholas, will I be able to meet Emily and Clementine? I know how special they are to you."

The apprehension filling him only minutes ago?

Poof... it disappeared. Just like that.

He rested his forehead against hers. "*Ah, love…* this is wonderful. I believe you've given me an early Christmas gift. And the perfect gift, at that."

He leaned back to look into her eyes. "The girls are going to love you. They're very much into princesses and fairy tales. So, when I tell them you're my princess, they will idolize the ground you walk on. In fact, everyone will love you. How could they not?"

Framing his face with her hands, she kissed him soundly before she smiled back at him. "Oh Nicholas, I hope so."

He nodded. "I know so. You have nothing to worry about. And now, with all my fears at rest, I'm more than ready for brunch."

She nodded, once more glancing around the room. He smiled at her wistful expression. "And if you don't think it's too presumptuous of me, I'll see if I can put in a request for this same room for next year's party,"

Her smile was radiant. "Oh Nicholas, that would be wonderful. I would love that."

Deciding this called for another kiss, he pulled her back into his arms.

There was no doubt about it...

He was completely and totally head-over-heels-and-crazy-in-love.

CHAPTER 21

Nicholas was flying high, everything right in his world.

As he walked to brunch with Anna beside him and their fingers linked together, he greeted everyone they passed with a big smile.

When they reached the dining room, he came to an abrupt halt and pulled her into his arms. Much to her surprise and to the amusement of the guests around them, he proceeded to give her a thorough kiss.

But he didn't care what anyone thought. This was because Anna had given him the answer he'd been hoping for.

When you board the plane home tomorrow, she will be with you.

He chuckled.

His family was going to be in a state of shock when he came home with Anna. *Hmm...* maybe he should throw her over his shoulder and march in, making a grand entrance. As if she was the treasure he had set out on a quest across the ocean to find.

And by God … had won, fair and square.

He had to chuckle at the ridiculousness of this. Even though it was tempting, it certainly wasn't something he could ever imagine doing.

There was also Emily and Clementine. They were sure to love

Anna. After all, hadn't they both been after him for quite a while to find his princess?

Well, he'd accomplished exactly that.

Charlie and Susan Holmes were stationed by the main entrance of the dining room, greeting everyone as they arrived for brunch.

A friend of Nicholas's father since they had been children, Charlie had moved to the states about twenty years ago. A well-respected real estate investor, he'd started out by buying up large and abandoned estates around the country. Always careful to maintain the original style and design of the time period they were built, he then converted them into luxury resorts.

His wife Susan, an award-winning interior designer, came in to add the finishing touches.

This resort was their baby, their first renovation together, and now a huge success. Hosting the annual Christmas party had become their way of thanking all of the friends and clients who had supported them through the years.

Nicholas's relationship with Charlie was like that of a nephew to a favorite uncle, and vice versa. When Nicholas decided to expand his business into the states, Charlie was right there to pave the way with valuable advice and dozens of possible contacts.

Susan was born and raised in New Hampshire. She had met Charlie through a mutual friend and after a whirlwind courtship, they were married. Since they had no children, Nicholas's family had become their surrogate family.

When Charlie saw Nicholas and Anna, his face lit up with his huge smile. "Nicholas! We've been wondering when we would finally catch up with you!"

He gave him a big hug before he turned to Anna, his smile growing even broader. "And who do we have here?"

Nicholas smiled down at Anna as he drew her closer. "Charlie and Susan, this is Anna Jameson. I'm one lucky man to have her as my date for this weekend."

Without even thinking, he dropped a kiss to the top of her head before he turned to Susan. "Susan, I believe you two will have a lot in common. Anna is an artist and she designs beautiful Christmas ornaments. Her designs are almost, but not quite as beautiful as she is."

Charlie and Susan shared an amused glance, bringing a blush to Anna's cheeks as she reached out to shake their hands. "It's so nice to meet both of you. This has been such a beautiful weekend. Last night was absolutely magical."

Charlie winked at her. "*Ah,* so the two of you had an enjoyable time together last night? Your room was to your liking?"

This, of course, had Anna's blushing even more.

"Charlie! Behave!" Susan lightly swatted his arm before she turned to Anna. "Anna, ignore him. He can be such a tease sometimes. We're so glad you're here and I would love to see your work. I'm always on the lookout for something new."

She turned back to Nicholas, a mischievous sparkle in her eyes. "And, Nicholas… so you've decided to date an American woman? It looks like you Brits have finally accepted we're the best there is."

Charlie laughed, his arm wrapping around his wife in a hug before he turned to Anna. "I don't think Nicholas or I should let the two of you compare notes. Though I am sure it would all be favorable." He sent his wife a teasing glance. "Right, Susie?"

They all laughed when she merely shrugged, an impish smile on her face. Then she turned at Anna. "Oh Anna, I do hope we'll be seeing a lot more of you in the future."

Charlie chimed in. "Yes, but until then, you make sure Nicholas takes very good care of you, my dear. If he doesn't, let me know and I'll set him straight."

He patted Nicholas on the shoulder. "Hopefully we will see you again before you leave. Now go and enjoy the brunch."

Her hands wrapped around her coffee cup, Anna watched the snowflakes drifting past the window next to the table she and Nicholas shared.

She glanced over at Nicholas who was sprawled out in his chair, his legs stretched out. A look of complete contentment on his face, he was staring into the flames dancing in the huge stone fireplace.

He sensed her gaze, turning in her direction. Their eyes meeting, he gave her one of his slow smiles. And her heart melted even more.

He moved closer to reach for her hands. After he brought them to his mouth for a kiss, he linked their fingers together. "I'm sorry. I guess I was daydreaming. I seem to be doing a lot of that lately and always about you."

His eyes searched hers, his voice rough with emotion. "Still here with me?"

She removed her hand from his to brush her fingertips gently down the side of his face. "Yes, always."

She smiled, tucking her hand back in his.

He swallowed. "Happy?"

She leaned in to place a soft kiss to his mouth, her eyes shining into his. "With you, always."

Nicholas found he had no words. He wanted to tell her he was completely and madly in love with her. She'd become such a big part of him, he couldn't imagine now being without her.

But this didn't seem to be the right place. Nor did it seem like the right time. So, he had plans to do this when they were alone, in each other's arms. Again, he had the feeling he would know when the time was right.

Anna looked down at their joined hands. To be here with him should be more than enough right now. But she couldn't shake the feeling what they had together could so easily fall apart. No matter how many promises he made.

She didn't want to acknowledge this fear rooted so deeply inside of her. But it continued to haunt her, refusing to let go.

She was afraid.

So afraid...

The fire danced and crackled in the fireplace.

While snowflakes continued to drift past the window.

Anna's hand still tucked in Nicholas's, they sat in silence, filled with dreams of the incredible possibility of being together.

Not only now on this snowy December day...

But for a million Decembers...

CHAPTER 22

$\mathcal{W}$here was Nicholas?

He'd gone to put in a request for their car and Anna was beginning to wonder why it was taking him so long.

She couldn't believe how alone she was feeling. And even with the fire blazing in the fireplace, it felt as if all the warmth had gone out of the room.

She glanced around the room at the guests who still lingered at their tables. Enjoying both the brunch and the relaxing ambiance, it was obvious no one was in a hurry to return to their busy and hectic lives.

Again, she looked over to see if Nicholas had possibly come into the room.

She froze with fear, her heart beginning to pound frantically in her chest.

Oh God... no.

Marc was leaning casually against the door, his eyes slowly scanning each table.

Quickly bowing her head, she went completely still. As she stared down at her shaking hands, she frantically began praying he hadn't seen her.

But, in what seemed like only seconds, he was standing next to her. Her fear escalating, she kept her head down, her eyes closed.

He laughed, a sarcastic laugh. It was a laugh she could remember so well as a warning of bad things to come.

"Well, well, well… if it isn't my lovely ex-fiancé, hiding here in the corner. Anna, I had no idea you were here, but my date selfishly made it a point to let me know. Let's just say she's pretty upset with you, babe. She claims you stole her man."

As he moved closer, she could feel the anger radiating from him, the tone of his voice becoming even more sarcastic. "So, I guess this is a good indication you've already moved on, huh? But then why would I even be surprised at this?"

To Anna, it sounded like he was shouting, his words bouncing off the walls for everyone to hear. Desperately trying to keep her face turned away from him, again she glanced towards the entrance to the room.

Where is Nicholas?

Finally, she had no choice but to look up at Marc. Her heart sank when she saw he was hung over, a look she remembered all too well. His eyes were bloodshot and he was unshaven. He was also still in his tuxedo. All wrinkled, no doubt he'd slept in it.

Knowing how volatile he could be when he was in this state, she took a deep breath and tried to keep her voice calm.

"Marc… how are you?"

He responded by leaning in even closer, the smell of alcohol on his breath so overpowering she was hit with a wave of nausea. When she tried to turn her head, he grasped her chin and turned her face to his, leaving only inches between them.

She closed her eyes, giving a soft moan.

Oh please, please… where is Nicholas?

Marc's words were blunt. "How am I? What can I say except you pretty much ruined my life when you left me, Anna, I don't get it. We were so damn good together until you just up and decided you didn't want me anymore." He shrugged. "So maybe I slipped up a little. But, hell, things happen."

His face loomed in even closer.

"I say you let this new guy go back to Megan. Then everyone will be happy." He glanced around the room before he zeroed back in on her, his eyes mocking. "By the way, where is he? Left you already? If so, let's go find a room in this monstrosity where I can prove how much you need me. Come on, babe, it'll be like old times."

When his mouth came down on hers, everything in her recoiled. She gave a horrified cry and jerking her chin from his hand, she rose from her chair, pushing him away. This sent him stumbling sideways into the table, the sound of the impact echoing loudly throughout the room.

Marc, who somehow managed to stay on his feet, began coming at her, a murderous expression on his face. His words were a snarl.

"Damn it, Anna. What the hell do you think you're doing?"

As she began backing away from him, she gave another swift glance around the room. Everyone had now turned in their direction, their conversations coming to a halt. A few of the men had come out of their chairs, concerned looks on their faces.

Oh God, please... where is Nicholas

Finally, her prayers were answered.

Ringing out with authority, Nicholas's voice echoed throughout the now silent room. "What is going on here? You... I'm speaking to you. Do you know Anna?"

Marc spun around. They both eyed each other. Nicholas, his arms crossed and his eyes blazing with anger, Marc, barely able to stand, his body shaking with fury.

"Nicholas..." This anguished whisper came from Anna. She grabbed hold of the chair next to her and sagging against it, she closed her eyes in relief. She wanted to run to him, to sink into the safety of his arms, but she was paralyzed with fear.

Nicholas glanced over at her. He wanted so badly to go to her. But first he needed to deal with this hung over, pathetic excuse of a man.

He sent her what he hoped was a reassuring smile. "Anna, it will be okay. Just stay right where you are, sweetheart."

Turning his attention back to Marc, it was to see he was now, thank God, staggering in his direction and away from Anna. When he came within a few feet, he stopped to regard Nicholas with contempt. His words were slurred. "Who the hell are you?"

His eyes narrowed, Nicholas remained completely still for a few moments. When he finally spoke, his deep voice cut through, what was now, an almost eerie silence in the room.

"I'm with Anna. And this is all you need to know." He paused before he slowly delivered his next words. "It's very obvious Anna doesn't want your company. So, I suggest you leave. Now… before we get someone to escort you out of here instead."

Marc gave a nasty laugh. "Anna is mine. She needs someone like me to keep her in check. And let's face it lover boy, women like her never change. If she left me, she sure as hell isn't going to think twice about leaving you next. So, you might be getting what you want from her right now, but it will turn out to be a waste of time in the end."

He gave a curt nod over at Anna. "In fact, she was about to take off with me for a quick tryst before you came waltzing in here like some kind of damn hero. So why don't you go back to Megan and leave Anna to me."

Completely spent after this tirade, he stumbled, reaching out to grasp the back of a chair to keep from falling over.

He never made it.

Nicholas forgot all of the rules he'd set for himself, notably the one never to resort to physical violence in order to resolve a conflict. Everything Marc said made him see red, sending any intentions of remaining civil flying right out of his mind.

His fist shot out, coming in contact with Marc's face, before he even thought about the consequence of his action. The cracking sound of bone against bone was magnified tenfold in the dead silence of the room.

Arms flailing, Marc slammed back into the table, this time with such force it collapsed. The sound of breaking glass echoed loudly throughout the room as dishes, glasses and silverware hit the hardwood floor to shatter and fly in every direction.

Nicholas massaged his throbbing hand before he shot a quick glance over at Anna. She was motionless, her eyes closed and her arms pressed to her sides. As if she wanted to become invisible.

Dear God, you've got to get her out of here.

His gaze swiveled back to Marc, who was now trying to get his bearings. As he moved to stand over him, he clenched his fists to his sides in an attempt to keep his anger in check.

His powerful voice once again resonated in the silence. "Don't ever come anywhere near Anna again. If you do, you won't be as lucky as you are right now. I will personally see to this." He glared at him. "Do. You. Understand?"

Marc swiped his sleeve across his face in an attempt to stop the blood now streaming from his nose. Violently shaking his head, he glared up at Nicholas, almost spitting out his words. "No, Anna belongs to me. The sooner you realize this, the better. And if you try to keep her from me? I'll do whatever I can to ruin you."

He grimaced as he wiped his face with his sleeve again, his voice becoming louder and his words even more threatening. "I've done this to others and by God, I'll do the same to you. No one treats me this way and gets away with it." He jerked his head up, looking over at Anna. "Ask her, she knows."

Nicholas only glared at him, deciding he wasn't going to respond. He wasn't worth it. His only concern was for Anna, the desperate plea she was sending with her eyes making his heart ache.

In mere seconds, he was at her side to find she was shaking uncontrollably. Gripping her hands tightly in his and looking directly into her eyes, he spoke as calmly and softly as he could.

"Anna, listen to me. We don't want him to see how scared you are. So, we're going to walk out of this room like he isn't here. As if none of this ever happened. As long as you are with me, you'll be fine."

She nodded. Her gaze never leaving his face and her hand tightly gripping his arm, they left the room.

Leaving Marc behind, still mumbling angry threats.

Anna felt Nicholas stiffen beside her before he tightened his hold.

She glanced up to see Megan was standing in front of them. Her hands clutched dramatically to her mouth, she was shaking her head.

She held out her arms to make a move towards Nicholas. But, confronted with the furious expression on his face, she came to an abrupt stop, dropping her hands to her sides.

When she opened her mouth to speak, he cut her off, the icy tone of his voice revealing his anger.

"I don't want to hear it, Megan. In fact, nothing you have to say is of interest to either me or to Anna." He jerked his head towards the ballroom. "I suggest you go see to your date. No doubt he could use your help."

He placed his arm around Anna, and they turned and walked away.

A look of defeat finally on Megan's face, she watched them leave.

Anna and Nicholas arrived at the main entrance, where he was relieved to find the parking attendant was waiting with the car.

When he realized Anna was still shaking, he grabbed her stole from the back seat. After he wrapped it around her, he rocked her against him, murmuring soothing words of comfort between the kisses he pressed in her hair.

Someone called out his name. He turned to see Charlie hurrying towards them, Susan by his side. The concerned looks on their faces let him know someone had already filled them in on what happened.

He sent them a warning glance, shaking his head.

Charlie cleared his throat and fixed a huge smile on his face. "Anna and Nicholas, you're leaving so soon. We're so sorry we weren't able to spend more time together, but we're still so glad you came."

He took Anna's hand in his firm grip. "Our home will always be open to you, Anna. Never forget this."

Susan followed this by wrapping her in a big hug. "Yes, you're welcome anytime." She reached out to gently stroke Anna's cheek, a wistful smile touching her lips. "Since I can see Nicholas cares for you very much, you must come back for a longer visit so we can get to know you better."

The kindness from both of them was too much for Anna, her tears spilling over. She could only shake her head, the horror of what happened, crashing down on her.

It was everything she'd feared. And now she knew it would only get worse.

So much worse.

Nicholas took his hand from the steering wheel to flex it again.

The soreness was almost easier to bear when he brought up the vision, still so fresh in his mind, of Marc sprawled out on the floor. He was still furious about what happened but was now trying to push it all to the back of his mind.

His only concern was for Anna.

Since she'd started to cry, she hadn't stopped. Her head resting against the seat and her eyes closed, the tears continued to slip steadily down her face.

Earlier, when he'd reached for her hand and brought it up to his lips for a kiss, her only response had been a slight negative shake of her head. But he'd rested their hands on the console between them, unwilling to let go.

His only hope he was giving her some comfort.

He'd thought the drive yesterday was stressful, but this was much worse. Almost to the point he was beginning to feel scared.

It was as if the Anna he'd held in his arms only a few hours ago had ceased to exist, leaving him with only a shell of the Anna he'd known.

He glanced over at her, his sigh troubled.

Darkness was just starting to blanket the city when Nicholas pulled the car up to the entrance of Anna's building. After shutting off the ignition, he looked over at her.

"Anna?"

She turned to him, her eyes luminous in the darkness. He was relieved to see her tears appeared to have stopped.

Hopefully this was a good sign, right?

He reached over to gently frame the side of her face in his hand, his mouth curving into a smile when she rested her cheek against his palm and closed her eyes.

He pressed a kiss to her forehead, his words soft and reassuring. "Anna, I'm pretty sure Marc was still drunk from the night before, this being the reason for his wild threats. But it's certainly not an excuse for the way he acted. Or for that matter, for the way I responded. I never should've lost my temper and hit him like I did."

His thumb lightly caressed her jaw. "Good lord, I'm surprised I didn't go all out and challenge him to a duel at sunrise. It's a good thing handling a gun has never been something I've excelled at, or I might have stupidly done just that. I guess I felt the need to be your knight in shining armor again."

He saw this brought a glimmer of a smile.

Good.

His expression turned serious. "About Megan…"

Anna reached for his hand, holding it to her lips. She shook her head. "Oh, no, no, Nicholas… I know that wasn't true."

His smile was relieved. "Good. Because you have to know you're the only one I want to be with, love."

He reached over to tuck her hair behind her ear. "I never should have left you alone. I don't know what I was thinking. But I give you my solemn promise nothing like this will ever happen again. I was completely serious when I told Marc he'd have to answer to me if he ever came near you again."

He watched as her eyes began to fill again, a single tear slipping down her cheek. A faint smile on his face, he brushed it away with his thumb. "I'm surprised there are any tears left to fall."

She let out a long, quavering sigh. "I know… oh Nicholas, I'm so sorry. I've ruined the whole weekend for you, the whole incredible time we had together. I'm really sorry. So sorry about everything."

A wistful expression on her face, her eyes searched his face. "It was wonderful, wasn't it?"

At first, Nicholas could only gaze into her eyes as he tried to rein in his emotional response to her question.

Then he swallowed, his voice unsteady. "Oh, Anna, it was all that and more. It was magic."

He brought her hand to his lips to place a kiss in her palm. "Every moment we shared this weekend has been like a gift. An incredible gift I will treasure forever."

Holding her hand over his heart, his eyes caressed hers. "You are in my heart, Anna. And this is where you will always be."

She moved closer. Their hands pressed between them and over their hearts, her voice was barely a whisper. "As you are in my heart, Nicholas. And will always be."

She gave him a kiss before she rested her head on his shoulder. Her sigh was heartbreaking.

He held her, the same prayer repeating over and over in his head like a chant.

That this vow they made to each other would last a lifetime.

Hand in hand, they walked up the stairs to her condo.

As Nicholas watched Anna unlock the door, he was filled with this urge to take the key from her. Maybe even fling it as far down the hallway as he could to where it would be impossible to find. Then he would whisk her right back down the stairs and into the car, giving her no other option but to go back to his hotel with him.

He would wrap his arms around her and love her with everything he had. If only to prove she would always be safe with him.

This is what he wanted to do.

What he should do.

But what he didn't do.

He had an important business meeting in just a few hours. Involving a multi-million-dollar contract, the outcome was not only crucial to his company, but to so many others as well.

But right now?

Truthfully?

He found it hard to even give a damn.

Before the whole fiasco with Marc, he'd planned to ask Anna to go with him to the dinner planned after the meeting. Then he would convince her to stay with him at his hotel. Or he would come back to her condo to stay with her. He honestly didn't care where they wound up, as long as she was with him.

But now he was unsure of what to do. He knew attending the dinner would be the last thing she'd want to do after what happened with Marc.

So, he was worried. Very worried.

He didn't want to leave her. He couldn't shake the nagging fear in the back of his mind, once he did, nothing would ever again be the same.

Once they were in her condo, he took her into his arms. Holding her close, he tried to come up with the right words to convince her they should be together. "Anna, I don't want to leave you. Not now. Not after what happened. Let me stay here with you. I don't give a damn about my meeting. I know Stephen can easily handle it without my help. Just say the word."

When she shook her head, he didn't even hesitate. "Then come back to the hotel with me. You can stay in my room while I'm in the meeting, or I can stay with you. You can stay the night and we'll be together."

He leaned back to look into her eyes. "I'm so worried about you, love."

Pressing her fingers to his lips, Anna shook her head. "Nicholas, it's okay. Really. I will be fine." Briefly closing her eyes, she let out a shaky breath. "I want you to go. I really think I need some time alone. I also need to finish up a few last-minute details if I'm to go with you tomorrow."

She searched his face, her look suddenly desperate. "Everything will look better tomorrow, right?"

He studied her. Besides the fear coming through in her voice, there was something else that he couldn't quite figure out. It had to do with her eyes. There was something missing, almost as though the connection they shared had shattered into a million pieces, at least on her end. Leaving him scrambling at his end, grasping at whatever he could to keep them together.

Dear God, hopefully you're only imagining this.

He brushed her hair back from her face before he pressed a soft kiss to her forehead. "Everything will be fine, love. Just like I told you last night, we're in this together. But tonight, while we're apart, I want you to keep me in your dreams. And if you need me for anything, even if only to talk, call me. No matter the hour. Promise me this."

Resting her head on his shoulder, she nodded. She wanted to stay in his arms, but she knew she needed to let him go.

Somehow, she needed to find a way to make sense of everything. Her mind was in a haze, filled with thoughts of him, all they shared and of course, the one thing she wanted to forget, Marc. Her gaze roaming over his face, as if she was trying to memorize every detail, her plea was a whisper. "Kiss me just one more time."

As he kissed her, she tried to hold on to the kiss for as long as she could, hoping to draw from his strength.

After he gave her one long searching look, he made his way over to the steps. There he turned to find she was watching him. She held up her hand, her palm facing him.

In an instant, he was back at her side to press a soft kiss to her palm before he gently covered it with her fingers.

Again, he paused at the stairs to see she hadn't moved, her hand placed over her heart and still holding on to his kiss.

He smiled at her, the slow smile she loved so much.

Then he turned and was gone.

This was only because he didn't want her to see the look of despair he knew was on his face.

Lost in his thoughts, the sound of someone clearing their throat was what finally registered in Nicholas's mind.

Slowly focusing on his surroundings, he saw he was once again the center of attention.

For what was it? The third time since this meeting began?

The room was totally silent. As he looked around the conference table he saw all eyes were on him, a few amused, but most with concern.

Catching his eye, Stephen gave him a hesitant grin, one eyebrow raised. Running his hand through his hair, Nicholas shook his head at him.

This was insane.

No matter how hard he tried, he couldn't stop going over, and then over again, the events of earlier in the day. Wondering if there was something he could've done to prevent what happened.

No matter how hard he tried, he wasn't able to concentrate on anything but this. The image imprinted in his mind of Anna's terrified face wouldn't let him.

But this wasn't the time for this.

He needed to get his mind back on track and where it should be. And this would be on this meeting. If he didn't, there was a good chance he could completely make a mess of everything he and his team had worked on for so long.

But is this really all that important? What about Anna?

He groaned, his hand going through his hair again.

This is ridiculous. You need to get your act together.

He leaned back in his chair and cleared his throat. A sheepish grin on his face, he glanced around the table. "God, I'm sorry. Let's just say it's been one hell of a day."

"Must be something to do with a woman." This came from one of the men seated at the table, drawing a laugh from the group, Nicholas included.

But his laugh was forced.

Yes, as a matter of fact, it was about a woman.

But not just any woman... a woman you should be with right now. Instead of in this damn meeting.

Frustrated, his laughter came to a sharp halt. When he glanced over to see Stephen was now eyeing him, worry furrowing his brow, he bowed his head to study the papers spread out in front of him.

Hell, they might as well be in another language with as much sense they made to him right now. But determined to get the meeting back on track, he sent a glance around the table and clearing his throat, he dove in with all the confidence and authority he could muster.

Thank God, everyone followed his lead.

He gave everything he had, which turned out to be enough to seal the deal. With everyone satisfied with the outcome and handshakes all around, the meeting finally came to an end.

As soon as Nicholas was able to pull Stephen aside, he informed him he was leaving, giving no explanation. He gathered up his belongings and with Stephen's puzzled look following him, he left the room, secure in the knowledge the rest of the evening would go as planned.

God knows, he was in no mood for socializing. Or, an even worse possibility, dealing with questions from Stephen about the weekend.

The one thing he wanted to do more than anything was go to Anna. But she'd made it quite clear she wanted to be alone. So, even though this was the hardest thing he ever had to do, he was going to honor her wishes.

When Nicholas walked out of the building, the snow and brisk wind came at him, clearing away some of the fog he felt like he was floating in. He pulled up his collar and slipped on his gloves before he broke into a brisk walk, skirting around the holiday crowds caught up in the excitement only a city could bring during this time of year.

He groaned.

He was frustrated.

And he was angry.

He and Anna should be together right now, as part of this festive scene. But it had come to this, both of them so close, yet both so alone.

It didn't make a damn bit of sense.

As he passed by a brightly illuminated jewelry store, the window display caught his attention. Spread out on a blanket of blue satin, a display of snowflake themed jewelry sparkled in the light. There was every kind of pin, necklace, bracelet and ring you'd imagine. Gold or silver, big or little, simple or elaborate, jeweled or plain, there was something for everyone.

With the snow and wind swirling around him, he stared blindly at the display. A vision of Anna flashed through his mind, both her eyes and the dress she wore last night sparkling with such incredible light and beauty.

The image was so vivid he could almost feel the softness of her against him when he'd held her in his arms on the dance floor.

Within minutes, he was in the store deciding on a sterling silver necklace with a delicate diamond studded snowflake pendant. He would give this to her as a remembrance of the incredible time they shared.

Maybe it will help erase the memory of the horrible way the weekend had ended? You can only hope...

By the time he arrived at his hotel, he was completely done in. After he made new flight reservations to include Anna and set his phone alarm for his morning meeting, he practically fell into bed.

But sleep eluded him. His mind was filled with everything Anna.

My God... how is it that you already miss her so much?

Clasping his hands behind his head, he stared into the darkness. It was almost too much to take in, the weekend and all they'd shared. Then there was the most amazing thing of all, this being she felt the same, showing this with a passion that was beyond anything he could've ever imagined.

There was no doubt about it, she'd changed his life in a way he never would've dreamed possible.

But something wasn't right.

He couldn't shake the feeling she was somehow going to slip away from him. And no matter how hard he tried to block this out of his mind, he couldn't forget the last thing she said to him before he left her.

The words wouldn't stop echoing in his mind, fueling his fear.

Kiss me just one more time...

Wrapped in her favorite quilt, with Mia sound asleep on the sofa beside her, Anna stared into space. The Christmas music she'd turned on barely even registered in her mind.

She was still feeling a little guilty how she'd all but pushed Marie out the door when she brought Mia back a short time ago. But it was obvious Marie was hoping for details of the weekend and with her emotions so raw right now, Anna didn't want to talk to anyone. She also knew how upset Marie would become if she found out about the confrontation with Marc.

Everything in her was completely numb except for her racing mind. It was there, what happened with Marc kept playing over and over, his latest threats pushing her even deeper into a dark place she couldn't seem to escape.

During the time they were engaged, she'd witnessed first-hand how he would stop at nothing to get back at someone who crossed him or made him look foolish. And these were the very two things Nicholas managed to do the first time they came in contact with each other.

Which meant revenge would now be Marc's next move. He would set out to destroy Nicholas and everything he stood for.

And this would be all because of her.

You can't let this happen... you just can't.

She suddenly felt very cold. As she wrapped the quilt more tightly around her, how she longed for the warmth of Nicholas's embrace. Why had she told him he to leave? She needed him now more than ever.

A deep feeling of such hopelessness settling inside of her, she closed her eyes. There was a reason Nicholas couldn't be here with her. She had a decision to make, one that had to be hers alone.

And it had to be the right decision, as it could be the most important one she would ever make.

But right now, there was something she had to do. She took a box down from the shelf above her worktable. It held the ornament she'd been unable to finish, along with Nicholas's tie. Leaving the tie in the box, she sat at the table, the ornament in her hands. For the longest time, she stared at the blank space still waiting for her design.

She finally set the ornament back on the table. After she lined up everything she would need in front of her, she dipped her brush in the paint and began to outline her design. Her vision suddenly blurring, she slowly placed the ornament and her paintbrush back on the table.

Bowing her head, she let the tears fall.

CHAPTER 23

*N*icholas was at a loss.

He ran his hand through his hair, staring at the note the assistant had discretely handed him during his meeting. It was from Anna.

According to what he just read, she was asking him to meet her in the hotel restaurant at noon. He looked at his watch to see this was only forty minutes from now.

He read it again. And he still didn't understand.

Why does she want to see you now?

He closed his eyes. A fear settling in his stomach, his muscles clenched in response.

Kiss me just one more time...

He'd called Anna earlier this morning during a break in his meeting. Switched over to her voice mail, he left the message he would pick her up at six o'clock this evening. This would give them enough time to have dinner before checking in for their ten o'clock flight. He also told her how she could reach him if she needed to talk to him.

Now he was questioning the wisdom of giving her this last bit of information. Either she hadn't received his message or something was wrong.

And something told him it was the latter.
Something was very wrong.

Anna followed the hostess over to a table featuring a panoramic view of what was now a wildly churning Lake Michigan and a sky heavy with storm clouds. From what all of the local weather stations were predicting, a winter storm was now swiftly advancing on the city.

She placed a white gift box, tied with a glittered silver bow, at her feet. It held the ornament she'd worked on until the early morning hours, the design finally coming to her as she poured her feelings into each brush stroke and every detail she added. When it was finally finished, it was everything she wanted it to be. But now gazing down at the box, she was filled with only a deep sadness.

As she waited for Nicholas, she gazed around the room. At the next table, two women were laughing over gifts they were opening. On the other side was a mother, father and their two little girls who were just leaving. As they started walking away, the father swung the youngest girl up in the air, her excited laughter ringing out through the room

Anna gazed wistfully at them. Nicholas would be like this man. He would be such a wonderful father.

She shook her head.

Stop it! Don't let your thoughts go there.

She glanced over at the entrance of the restaurant to see Nicholas was making his way to their table. Even from across the room, the sight of him caused her heart to begin thundering with anticipation. As always, he looked so incredibly handsome, everything about him absolutely flawless.

As Katy had declared, he truly was the perfect man.

She watched all of the women who were in turn watching him. She found it amazing he had no clue of how attractive he was. But then again, maybe this was part of his charm.

Almost to her table, his eyes locked with hers, the look in his sending a wave of desire sweeping through every inch of her entire being, her breath catching in her throat. When he leaned over to give her a lingering kiss, she had to grip her hands tightly together in her lap so she wouldn't throw her arms around him. She closed her eyes, breathing in the intoxicating combination of scents that were him. Even here in the restaurant, they made her senses reel.

He sat next to her and taking her hand, he brought it to his mouth. After he placed a kiss in her palm, he gave her a long, searching look. "Anna, you look beautiful. As you always do."

He hesitated, his eyes searching hers. "I hope you've missed me as much as I've missed you."

Oh please, no, no, no...

This was not the kind of greeting she wanted to hear. Not now. Already she could feel tears beginning to gather in the back of her eyes.

Seriously? How could you have any tears left after all the crying you did yesterday and last night?

Blinking rapidly, she quickly glanced away, her gaze falling on the two women seated next to them. Their gift exchange over, they were now curiously watching her and Nicholas. Giving them a weak smile, she turned back to Nicholas.

"Nicholas." She stopped, suddenly unsure of how to continue.

After a short silence, he tilted his head, his eyes searching her face. "Tell me, Anna. Why did you want to meet here? And why now? You did get my message about the flight, didn't you?"

She couldn't seem to get her voice to work, finally managing a whisper. "Yes, yes, I did."

They sat in silence until he cleared his throat. "Then tell me what's going on, love." He swallowed. "Because you're beginning to worry me." This was a major understatement. If anything, she was scaring the hell out of him.

And now, her hands shaking in his and her bottom lip starting to quiver, he knew he had every reason to be worried. From his past experience with women of all ages, he knew neither of these things were a good sign of what was to come.

As if on cue, a tear began to roll down her cheek. She swiftly brushed it away before he did it for her. If he touched her now, she knew she would break down completely.

She looked down at her hands, her voice choked with emotion. "I won't be going with you tonight, Nicholas. I'm sorry, but I can't."

He became completely still, his eyes intent on her face. She could see the muscle twitch in his jaw, which was now tightly clenched.

The silence again stretched out uncomfortably between them. Still unable to meet his eyes, she spoke. "Nicholas, I like you a lot, but…"

His hand went to his head, his laugh coming out sharply. *"You like me a lot? What is that supposed to mean? My God, Anna, I thought we'd gone past the liking stage. I certainly wouldn't call what we've shared something that happens between two people who like each other… a lot."*

An expression of pain flashed across her face. "We have. I'm sorry, you're right. I should have said that differently. I … it's just so hard for me to say. I need you to understand."

She waved her hand between them. "We're not going to be able to make this work. Us… the two of us, together."

Abruptly letting go her hand, he closed his eyes.

Dear God, what was happening here?

On the verge of losing it, his fear had him wanting to lash out, if only to gain control of the situation. But he couldn't even think straight… the-clear-headed-I-can-solve-this-kind-of-guy that he usually was, eluding him. And he didn't like this… not one damn bit.

The only thing that registered was her use of the word 'work'. He didn't understand, she thought what they had together required work? How? Nothing had ever come easier to him than this love he had for her. Was he being unreasonable to expect her to feel the same?

Frustrated, he ran his hand through his hair. "I guess I wasn't aware what we did was work. I don't understand how you can even use that word in describing what we have together. Why, I…"

His words came to a halt. He needed to put a stop to this flicker of anger threatening to ignite inside of him. My God, the last thing he wanted to do was scare her, something he'd promised he would never do.

He took a long, deep breath. "I'm sorry if I sound angry. It's only that I'm having a hell of a time trying to make sense of what's going on here."

Taking both of her hands in his, his gaze was intense. "Sweetheart, what's happened to you between yesterday and now? I feel like you're not the same Anna I was with only hours ago."

He waited for her to say something, anything. Only because he so desperately wanted to understand. Then he could fix everything and they would be back to the way they were before.

But she only shook her head.

He tightened the grip on her hands. "This is all because of Marc, isn't it? I promised you I would make sure he never bothered you again, love. And I will never go back on that promise."

Clearly agitated, she pulled her hands from his to grip the edge of the table. "Nicholas, you don't know him. You've never seen how he can be. I have. I know how his anger can get the best of him."

Another tear started to slip down her face. "If he finds out we're still together, he will do everything he can to make our lives a living hell. I've seen him do this so many times. And to so many people."

She kept shaking her head, her next words barely audible. "He'll come after us. He'll come after you. *Oh God*, Nicholas ... especially you. He'll stop at nothing to get back at you."

She opened her eyes, more tears falling. "You have to understand. I'm so scared of what he might do. I don't want to get you involved in this mess with him. I can't do this to you. I just can't."

He reached over to gently brush the hair back from her face as he tried to fight the familiar surge of anger Marc brought out in him. Because this was not the time. He needed to remain calm and focused.

"Sweetheart, I can handle him for both of us. And I'm already involved in "this mess" as you call it. Whether you want this or not. After what happened yesterday I would never again let you face him without me by your side."

He reached into his pocket and pulled out a handkerchief. He wiped the tears from her face, before tucking it in her hand. "People like him never win in the end, Anna."

She began twisting the handkerchief in her hand, her eyes frantically pleading with him to understand. "Oh Nicholas, he always wins. Everything is a game to him. A game he has to win, no matter whom he hurts along the way. Can't you see this? What if he plans to do something really bad this time? Because he will, I know he will."

Even though she heard the hysteria rising in her voice, she was powerless to stop it. What happened yesterday had sent her spiraling back into a place of such overwhelming fear she was unable to think of anything except how she needed to keep Nicholas away from Marc.

Nicholas wanted to pull her into his arms. Maybe if he held her close, he could make her terrified expression go away. But with the agitated state she was in, he feared if he made the move to do this, she might react by pushing him away.

God, no... you couldn't handle that. Not now.

When he saw her hands were still shaking, he reached over to firmly grasp them in his as he desperately tried to come up with the right words. "Then you need to get on the plane with me tonight like we planned. You'll be thousands of miles and an ocean away from him. You'll be safe. I will make sure of this".

Anna shook her head. "No, he has too many business contacts in London. And if he found out I was there with you, it would only make things worse. So much worse."

She looked up at him, panic building in her eyes. "And your family, Nicholas. He wouldn't think twice about going after any of them. I would never be able to live with myself if this happened."

Nicholas cleared his throat. Everything was now so clear to him. He knew what he needed to do. "We'll have to make it so there are no other options open to him as far as you're concerned. We need to make it permanent, love."

With this being said, he slipped out of his chair to go down on one knee.

Anna mouth dropped open. What was he doing? Evidently, the women at the nearby table were just as surprised, a loud gasp coming from both of them.

The expression on Nicholas's face was serious, yet so tender as he took her hand.

"Anna, will you do me the honor of becoming my wife, to have and to hold? To love and to cherish?" He paused before he continued in almost a whisper. "To be mine, as I would be yours? For always?"

Anna was so tempted. How wonderful it would be to say yes. To go into the safety of his arms and let him carry her off to wherever he decided to take her. It would be like a modern-day fairy tale, with this ending being the happiest of all possible endings.

But it could also turn into a completely different version of a fairy tale. One with a tragic ending. With Nicholas the one to lose the most. And this was a risk she couldn't take.

She wouldn't let her heart be so selfish to overrule what was the right thing to do.

So… she looked into the blue eyes she loved and slowly shook her head. "No."

Nicholas abruptly leaned back, almost as though he'd been pushed. The expression on his face was a combination of pain and disbelief.

"No?"

This certainly wasn't what he'd envisioned would happen when he finally took the big step of proposing marriage to the woman he loved.

Where were the happy tears? The hugs and kisses?

And the joy… where the hell was the joy?

He didn't understand. Why wasn't this working out like it was supposed to… like in the fairy tales he read to Emily and Clementine? Or in the movies? There it all seemed so simple. Boy meets girl, they fall in love, get married and live happily ever after. The end.

Was it him?

Was he the problem?

It must be him. He evidently didn't know what the hell he was doing. But he had no idea of what more he could do. He didn't have a manuscript to fall back on. Or someone to direct him on how to act. He only had this deep love he wanted to share. Which unfortunately didn't seem to be enough.

Anna's voice came at him through a haze. "It won't work, Nicholas."

He exhaled a long drawn out breath as he ran his hand through his hair again. So, maybe it wasn't him. Because here she was again. Using that damn word... *work.*

But too weary to even comment on this, he got up off his knee and sank back into the chair. He picked up a spoon from the table and began tapping it against the surface. Then he threw it back down on the table

His voice was resigned. "Well, I really don't know what else to say other than I must be the fool here."

She wanted to reach over smooth away the sadness she saw on his face, but keeping her hands clasped tightly together in her lap, she shook her head. "Oh Nicholas, no. You're not a fool. Please never, ever think this."

His laugh was harsh. "I thought we had something special between us. Something most people could only dream of having in their lifetime."

After a few moments of silence, his eyes met hers, an expression of complete bewilderment on his face. "I actually thought we had fallen in love with each other. At least I know I've fallen in love with you. And I'm pretty sure I've felt this way ever since the very moment I first saw you. But it looks like this no longer matters."

He shook his head again. "So yes, Anna. I'm definitely the fool, thinking you had come to feel the same way about me."

Anna opened her mouth. Then she closed it, bowing her head. Everything she wanted to say, she couldn't.

Oh Nicholas, I do love you. But you deserve so much better than me.

The conversation she had with Katy about all of the women waiting for him back in London flashed through her mind. Surely one of those women would be able to make him happy?

This the only thing keeping her from completely falling apart, she managed to smile at him through her tears. "Nicholas, you'll be fine."

He looked at her in disbelief.

He was at a loss for words.

He would be fine?

How could this even be remotely possible?

And how could she even think this?

For him, this is when it slowly started to sink in. She wasn't going to change her mind. Which meant if he wanted to maintain any sense of dignity, he needed to gain some level of emotional control. After all, this is what he was known for, wasn't it? His ability to stay cool under pressure. No matter what the challenge, or how big the deal.

Are you crazy? Haven't you learned anything? This isn't a damn business deal. Your whole life is on the line here. Do something.

But he was at a loss. There wasn't anything else to say, was there? My God, he told her he would keep her safe. He told her he loved her. And he asked her to marry him. So, what more could he possibly do?

Obviously, nothing, as Anna was now standing in front of him, struggling to get into her coat.

He could only watch as, tears still streaming down her face, she reached for the box she'd put under the table and set it in front of him. But when she looked over at him, he refused to meet her eyes.

Her words were barely audible through her tears. "Nicholas, I made this for you. I hope you like it." After an agonizingly long pause, her final two words came out in a whisper.

"Merry Christmas."

Then she was gone.

Nicholas was in a state of shock.

My God... it actually happened

She'd turned her back on him and walked away. Out of the restaurant. And possibly out of his life.

He couldn't move. This paralyzing pain was like nothing he'd ever experienced before in his life, almost as though his heart had been ripped out of his chest. Closing his eyes, he tried to stop the overwhelming panic filling him.

And fear... a deep and numbing fear.

Kiss me just one more time...

He shouldn't have left her last night. Those words should have been a warning to him. Then maybe things would be different now.

What the hell were you thinking?

"Sir, is there anything I can get for you?"

Nicholas looked up to find a server standing next to him, a worried look on his face. Enough to invade the stupor he was, he shook his head, his gaze falling on the gift box in front of him.

He suddenly had the crazy desire to laugh.

Did she really think giving him a gift was going to make everything right?

Then, to add insult to injury, try to soften the blow by wishing him a Merry Christmas?

My God, this was certainly out of the question, wasn't it? A merry anything wasn't going to be happening anytime in his future. Certainly not without her.

How the hell was he going to return home now? As it was, he didn't think he even had enough in him to walk out of the restaurant and back to his room.

Where he would be alone.

He ran his hand through his hair. God, he felt like he had just been dumped into someone else's bad dream. Which he would more than welcome right now. Because this would mean he'd eventually wake up and everything would be back to how it was before.

But no… this wasn't a dream.

Wearily coming to his feet, he stopped to scribble his name on the check left on the table. He didn't even know why or what he was signing, but his good breeding wouldn't allow him do otherwise.

It was then he noticed the women at the next table were still watching him. No doubt pitying him. But he found he didn't care. In fact, he didn't give a damn what anyone was thinking right now.

Unless of course, the someone was Anna.

One of the women appeared as if she wanted to say something.

Open to any advice on how to get out of this terrible place he'd been thrown into, he sent her a curt nod.

"She'll change her mind." She gave him a tentative smile. "It's obvious she's still very much in love with you no matter what her reason for leaving. So, don't give up hope."

The other woman simply nodded her head in agreement

For Nicholas, with these simple words of wisdom, it all sank in.

Don't give up? But Anna's gone. What else can you do?

He shook his head and turned to walk away.

"Wait! You forgot the gift she made for you." The woman immediately became flustered, her words confirming she and her friend had listened in on his and Anna's conversation.

But this was the least of Nicholas's worries. He stared into space a few seconds before he finally shook his head. "I don't want it. It's Anna I want."

After both women watched him leave, they turned to each other to speak the same words and almost at the same time.

"Oh my..."

There wasn't really anything more to say.

Drawn to the brightly lit window of a jewelry store, Anna walked over to stand in front of it, seeking its illusion of warmth. She was beyond cold, almost to the point she felt completely numb.

After she'd left Nicholas at the restaurant, she kept walking. She had no destination in mind, she only knew she couldn't bring herself to go back to her condo because she didn't want to be alone.

But as she stared at the sparkling snowflake jewelry on display in front of her, the reality of what she'd done hit hard.

She was alone. *So alone* With no one to blame but herself. It didn't matter where she went or what she did. Without Nicholas she was not only alone, but empty, her heart no longer hers.

No, your heart was with him.

Suddenly filled with such a deep and paralyzing grief, she rested her forehead against the window glass and closed her eyes.

An unexpected gust of wind and snow came whipping around the corner of the building, hitting her so hard it almost knocked her down. Bewildered, she gazed around her. When had it started to snow? Accumulating rapidly, the large flakes were covering everything in sight, the ordinarily crowded streets and sidewalks almost deserted.

She needed to go home.

Knowing her chance of finding a taxi would be next to impossible, she wearily started the long walk to her condo.

By the time she arrived at her building, she was chilled to the bone. Her teeth were chattering, she was shaking uncontrollably and both her hair and her coat were soaking wet from the snow.

When Louis met her at the door, he was horrified. After she finally convinced him she would be fine, she slowly made her way up the stairs to her apartment.

After she struggled out of her wet clothing and into her pajamas, she crawled into bed. The chills still rumbling through her, she pulled Mia close for warmth.

She was totally exhausted, her body numb.

But as she drifted off to sleep, her mind refused to let go, plunging her into one haunting dream after another.

CHAPTER 24

The sound of Bing Crosby softly crooning White Christmas was what woke Anna from a deep sleep.

The music lulled her into a feeling of tranquility before the memory of what happened came crashing down on her. She turned to bury her face in the pillow, filled with an overwhelming sense of loss.

Nicholas... oh no, no, no.

When she finally opened her eyes to take in her surroundings, she saw she wasn't alone. Her eyes closed, Marie was seated in the rocking chair she'd pulled up next to the bed.

"Marie?" Her mouth was so dry this came out in a hoarse croaking sound. Startled, Marie opened her eyes. A concerned look on her face, she pushed herself out of the chair.

She put her hand to Anna's forehead. "Chickie! Thank goodness you're finally awake. And it feels like your fever has broken."

Her hand smoothing Anna's hair, she struggled to control her emotions. "Oh Anna, Louis and I have been so worried about you. You've been so sick for the past two days, but maybe now you've finally turned the corner."

She straightened the quilt and fluffed the pillows around Anna. "Now you're awake, you need to eat and I know just the thing, my homemade chicken soup. While I heat some up for you, why don't you try to sit up?"

After Anna had settled back against the pillows, Mia jumped up on the bed to shower her face with wet puppy kisses. As she ran her hand slowly through the little dog's silky fur, the thought of kisses sent a deep longing through her.

Nicholas's kisses… how are you going to live without them?

She slowly shook her head. Her decision had been made. Nicholas was back in London and everything between them was over. She'd have to accept this.

She pulled Mia close, seeking her comforting warmth until she felt Marie's presence, accompanied by the tantalizing aroma of chicken soup.

After Marie placed the soup in front of Anna, she pulled the rocking chair closer to the bed. She watched as Anna began to eat, a satisfied smile on her face. "This will get the roses back in your cheeks. And when you're done, you can tell me what happened."

Unexpectedly, she frowned. "What were you thinking, wandering around the city in a snowstorm?"

An anguished expression coming over her face, Anna started to answer, but Marie quickly shook her head.

"Oh Chickie, I'm sorry. Eat first. I can wait until you're done. Then, you should also check your phone. It rang quite a bit. I'm sure most of the calls were probably from Katy, but you never know. Which reminds me, Katy wants you to call her. She said she had something very important to ask you."

Your phone rang quite a bit? What if even one of those calls was from Nicholas?

Anna snatched her phone from where it was on the bedside table, her shaking fingers struggling to hit the right buttons. She was finally scrolling down through her messages, hoping to find the one message she wanted to see more than anything. From, she realized, the one person she wanted more than anyone.

And finally, there it was… a message from Nicholas, sent Monday evening. She pressed the phone to her ear, the sound of his voice so deep, so familiar and just so Nicholas, she felt almost faint. She listened carefully to each word he said, as if her life depended on it.

Which, she realized… it pretty much did.

> *Anna, love, I hope you get this message tonight.*
> *As you listen, please, please think very seriously*
> *about what I'm about to say.*
> *I'm still here in my hotel room trying to finish*
> *up some work. But I'm finding this is impossible*
> *because my thoughts keep going to you instead.*
> *So, as you can see, you not only have my heart,*
> *you are also always on my mind. Everything I*
> *am belongs to you. I miss everything about you.*
> *Everything.*
> *Our flight was cancelled due to the snowstorm,*
> *but I was able to get new reservations for both*
> *of us tomorrow. All you have to do, is call me,*
> *and I'll make sure you're on that plane with me.*
> *Oh Anna, I'm hoping now that you had time to*
> *think about everything, you see we can make*
> *this work.*
> *And if I don't hear from you? Whatever happens,*
> *know that I'll always be here for you.*

There was a short silence before he spoke again, his voice rough with emotion.

> *Do you remember what we said in the car*
> *yesterday? It was like an exchange of vows,*
> *one I will always honor.*
> *You are in my heart, Anna. And this is where*
> *you will always be. This is my promise to you.*

Then there was only silence.

The phone pressed to her ear, Anna waited desperately for more. But there was nothing. She set the phone on the bed, the ache in her chest so intense, she found it hard to breathe.

She looked over at Marie. "You said I've been sick for two days? So, today is Thursday?"

When Marie nodded, Anna's face crumpled. "Oh Marie, what have I done? And what am I going to do now?"

She closed her eyes, the tears flowing unchecked.

After she reached over to hold Anna's hand, Marie let her cry.

And the chicken soup?

It grew cold.

CHAPTER 25

Nicholas stood at the wall of windows in his office, gazing down at the traffic jammed streets below.

There was no doubt about it, his mood definitely matched the ominous sky and flurry of winter-like precipitation hanging over the city since he returned home.

Usually he felt a sense of pride when he took in this view, thinking about all of the hard work and planning that brought him to this point in his life.

But today, none of this mattered.

In fact, nothing seemed to matter anymore.

He was exhausted.

He was absolutely in no mood to see or talk to anyone.

And more than anything, he was finding it hard to accept he'd failed at getting the one thing he wanted the most.

All said and done, he was a total wreck.

Dear God, will this ever get better? Every hour that goes by you only feel worse. Whoever said time heals all wounds is bonkers. It's only made you realize even more how much you miss her.

He glanced over at the messages stacked in a neat pile on his desk, thinking how he really didn't give a damn about any of them. Because not a single one of those messages was from her.

In fact, what he'd really like to do is take his hand and sweep every one of those pieces of paper into the trash.

Or better yet, to the floor.

Maybe even stomp on them.

He massaged the back of his neck. He was acting like a child, ready to throw a temper tantrum because things weren't going his way.

Come on... you're an adult. So, act like one.

He walked over to his desk and sat down. He put his elbows on the desk, dropped his head in his hands and gave a frustrated groan.

This was insane.

No one should be able to make another person feel like this. And no one should feel this way just because of another person's actions.

But either way, it really didn't matter at this point, did it? Because he was the loser here.

And it hurt like hell.

He leaned back in his chair, closing his eyes.

Kiss me just one more time...

He'd gone over everything in his mind so many times, starting with the whole crazy Marc episode and ending with Anna walking out of the restaurant, he was seriously beginning to think he was going mad.

If he tried to sleep, he tossed and turned, his mind rehashing everything over and over again. If by some miracle he did fall asleep, it was a fitful sleep with dreams that came back to haunt him.

And when he woke up to find the bed empty beside him?

He was filled with such an overwhelming feeling of emptiness he found it almost impossible to even contemplate the day looming ahead.

Right now, his head ached and he felt like he was immersed in a deep fog. He should have stayed home considering the condition he was in. But from the reaction of his house staff, his current behavior wasn't making him very popular there.

Good Lord, he'd swear a cheer went out when he went storming out the door this morning.

There was no doubt about it.

He'd become totally unglued.

A fool in love.

He laughed, almost scaring himself with how harsh it sounded. He'd been dead right when he told Anna this title applied to him. He never understood the phrase before, but he most certainly did now. Those four words described him perfectly. He'd let himself be lulled into the belief he'd found a lasting love, something only dreamers would do. Yep, he thought he was one of the lucky ones.

Yeah, you're lucky all right. If anything, you're more of a fool than you thought you were.

He glanced over at his phone, thinking about what troubled him the most. This being she never called back with an answer to his voice message.

Even if it had only been to tell him her answer was still no.

He sighed. He'd been so sure once she had time to think everything through, she would change her mind.

God, he'd put so much hope in this happening. Even now, here he was, picking up the phone again to see if maybe, just maybe, she'd called since he last checked.

But of course, this hadn't happened. And now there was nothing more to be done. After all, he did promise he would accept her decision. He certainly couldn't go back on his word.

Could he?

No, this was out of the question.

He groaned, running his hands through his hair. Why had he promised such a stupid, stupid thing?

It seems you're a blooming idiot when it comes to relationships. Let this be a reminder to stay away from them in the future.

He leaned back in his chair and closed his eyes.

He was so damn tired...

And so afraid of the man he was becoming.

"Mr. Hanover?"

A timid voice, belonging to one of his office assistants, interrupted the silence. He was pretty sure her name was Victoria.

He refused to move. Or even open his eyes. Instead he let out a very loud and exaggerated sigh. Hopefully this would convince her. to leave?

She cleared her throat. An indication she was still there and determined to wait it out.

Damn...

Well, too bad. He didn't feel like dealing with anyone right now. As far as he was concerned, she could stay there forever if she so desired.

She cleared her throat again, her voice coming out a little louder this time. "I'm sorry to be a bother, Mr. Hanover, but this package came for you."

He sensed she was now standing by his desk. She just wasn't going to give up, was she? He wanted to tell her to take this package she seemed to think was so important, and put it somewhere, anywhere. Or throw it out. He really didn't give a damn what she did with it. In fact, if she wanted to keep it, she was more than welcome to do just that.

He.

Just.

Didn't.

Care.

But he knew this wouldn't go over well. If anything, he was surprised this Victoria had even ventured into his office. He was well aware everyone was buzzing about his foul mood and going out of their way to avoid him.

So, there was no reason for him to add fuel to the fire by throwing a fit over a stupid, stupid package.

Here comes that child in you, acting up again. What could a package have to do with this foul mood of yours?

Giving another melodramatic sigh, he narrowly opened his eyes to look at this Victoria, taking the time to really study her.

She seemed to be an attractive and well-adjusted young woman. Even though she now looked a bit uneasy. Almost as if she wanted to turn around and go sprinting right out of his office.

He leaned even further back in his chair, the next words to pop out of his mouth not at all what he planned to say.

"So, tell me Victoria, do you have a boyfriend?"

Her eyes going wide and her mouth flying open in surprise, it took her a few moments to finally answer.

"Umm... I do."

He nodded. "I see. And how long have the two of you been together?"

This sent a blush to her cheeks. "It will be a year this coming Monday."

A year?

He couldn't even imagine this. He was tempted to ask her how the hell she accomplished such a feat. But again, if this ever got around the office, and he knew damn well it would, he'd never live it down.

He drummed his fingers on the desk, giving her a curious look. "A year, huh? And do you think he is, let's see, how would you put it? The one?"

What in God's name has gotten into you? No doubt you're scaring the girl to death.

Her nervous giggle confirmed this. "Well, we actually just decided to get married." This brought on a brilliant smile. "So yes, I think... no, I know he's the one."

Nicholas continued to study her, nodding his head. "Well, my congratulations go out to you, Victoria. I hope you'll both be very happy."

And yes, he was genuinely happy for her. If only because she and this new fiancé of hers were proof this relationship thing could actually work. The question now, exactly how did one go about making this happen?

He could feel his mouth starting to open again. God help him, what was he going to come out with now?

"Just one more question for you."

A wary look on her face, she gave him a slow nod. So, he dove right in. "What was the one most important thing that made you decide he was the man you want to marry?"

She remained silent for several seconds, considering his question very seriously. This was followed with another brilliant smile. "I know I can always count on him. And I totally trust him. But most of all, I know he feels the same way about me."

Nicholas stared at her. Could this be what was going on with Anna? She still didn't trust him?

He scowled.

Well, he had no idea what else she expected from him. Good Lord, he'd sent Marc sprawling to the floor, possibly breaking his nose in order to defend her honor. He'd asked her to marry him. And the most important thing of all, he told her he loved her. Weren't all of these enough?

He was brought out of this reverie by the sound of Victoria's voice. "Mr. Hanover? Is there anything else?"

He saw she was now backing slowly out of the office. She probably couldn't wait to get back to the safe territory of the main office, where no doubt this conversation would be shared in great detail.

Great... just great. Chalk this up to another reason why getting involved with someone is not for you. Too much personal information gets thrown around.

He cleared his throat, loudly. "Thanks for bringing this, Victoria. I appreciate it." He waved his hand towards the package and gave her a smile. Or what he hoped at least resembled a smile, as he wasn't sure if he even remembered how to pull one off anymore.

Already at the door and no doubt very relieved she was almost free from any more of his questions regarding her personal life, she gave him a big smile. "You're welcome, Mr. Hanover."

She came to an abrupt stop. "And don't forget, Mr. Burns will be here in about twenty minutes."

Stephen?

Twenty minutes?

Damn…

He nodded, vaguely recalling this meeting with Stephen noted on his calendar. To be honest, he'd tried to block it out of his mind, since Stephen was the last person he wanted to see. He was sure to bring up Anna since Katy surely would've called her by now to get the details of the weekend.

He stared off into space, his thoughts again going to Anna. He wondered what she'd told Katy, or if she'd told her anything at all. Obviously, he'd have to play it by ear when Stephen showed up.

He groaned, dragging his hands down over his face. What was happening to his life? He was starting to feel like a character in a soap opera, hurdling his way through one drama filled episode after another.

He sighed. He wasn't used to this. The business world was now looking a hell of a lot less complicated than this relationship thing did

But for Anna?

He'd gladly work it out.

He sighed, and picking up the package Victoria had delivered, he was just about to toss it on the bookshelf behind him when he noticed the return address. It was from the hotel he stayed at in Chicago. Did he leave something there?

Curious, he went about opening it.

Nestled inside on top of tissue paper, was a large white envelope with his name hand-written on the front. He ripped it open to find a note, also hand-written, on a sheet of the hotel's embossed stationary.

According to the date at the top, it was written on Tuesday, the day he flew home.

After a slight hesitation, he began to read.

> *Dear Mr. Hanover,*
> *Let me begin by explaining this note is on behalf of my*
> *friend and I. We were seated at the table next to you in*
> *the restaurant yesterday and witnessed the*

conversation between you and your lovely young lady.

*We hope you won't think we're being too forward in
sending this note, along with the gift you left behind on
the table. Because even though you made it quite clear
you didn't want the gift, we couldn't help imagine you
wondering for the rest of your life what you may
have left behind.*

*We took the gift with us and after much discussion,
turned it over to the hotel clerk who looked up your
signature and room number from the check you signed
at your table. When he found you had already checked
out, he promised to send both the gift and this note to
you.*

*So, it's because of the joint effort of all of us you're now
reading this. And hopefully our interference, in what we
know is a very personal matter, will be forgiven and not
taken as meddling on our part.*

*As strange as this may seem, considering we don't know
anything about either of you, we both feel very strongly
you'll find your way back to each other again. We wish
you both a long life filled with all that you wish for, no
matter how small, or how big, the wish.*
Sincerely, Rebecca Edwards and Sarah Vaughn

Nicholas read the note twice before he slipped it back into the
envelope. He was both surprised and moved these women, who had
not only taken the time to send the gift, but also write such a sincere
note. Almost as if they were bestowing a blessing on him and Anna.

*Ha... if any relationship could use a blessing, it's yours. This is if it's even
considered a relationship anymore.*

Saddened by this thought, he stared at the envelope for a few moments. Then, reluctantly, he pulled the box towards him. After removing the layer of tissue paper, he found as promised, a gift box tied with silver ribbon.

Yes, it was definitely the gift Anna set on the table in front of him. Right before she walked out of his life without a backwards glance.

He stared down at the box, his mind once again reminding him of everything it refused to let him forget. No matter how hard he tried. He didn't get it. What could she have possibly been thinking when she left this with him?

Did she intend it to be a token of their time together? Was it her way of softening the way she ended their relationship? Or possibly the worst reason of all... was it just a simple, it was great knowing you, kind of gesture?

Abruptly coming to his feet, he stuffed the tissue paper and envelope back in the box and shoved it to the corner of his desk. He had a feeling opening it right now would only bring on an emotional response he wouldn't be able to handle.

Closing his eyes, he groaned.

My God, you need to stop torturing yourself like this. You need to move on.

He dragged his hands slowly through his hair. After he took a deep breath, he opened his eyes just in time to see Stephen come sauntering into his office, a big smile on his face.

One look at Nicholas and Stephen came to an abrupt halt, his smile swiftly replaced with an expression of alarm.

"Holy cow! What the hell happened to you? Bad week? Foiled deal? Because it's obvious by looking at you something is very wrong in the Hanover kingdom."

After waving at Stephen to sit, Nicholas sank back down in his chair, a resigned look on his face. "Bad everything, I'm afraid. And this kingdom, as you just referred to it, may also be doomed to hell. Not what you would call a pretty picture, huh?"

The worried expression still on his face, Stephen studied Nicholas.

"That is an understatement, my friend. You look as though you haven't slept for days. Or you're hung over, big time. Which is it? If it's the latter, I hope at least it was top shelf that brought this on."

Nicholas rubbed his hand over his chin to feel the rough growth. Good Lord, hadn't he even shaved this morning? He honestly couldn't remember.

Against his will, his thoughts drifted back to Anna's remarks about how she liked him like this. What were the words she'd used again?

He closed his eyes, a faint smile on his face. Scruffy? Mussed?

Ah yes... and sexy... don't forget sexy.

He scowled.

Ha! I bet she'd think differently now. Because you'd probably scare the hell out of her. Because who's looking like the crazy one now?

Stephen's voice cut into his thoughts. "Hey! What's going on, buddy? I don't want to pry, but..."

Nicholas averted his gaze. He didn't think he wanted to talk about why he was in the condition he was. No, let's be truthful here. He definitely didn't want to talk about it. If even thinking about it brought on such a feeling of despair, he couldn't even imagine what actually talking about it would do to him.

He gave Stephen a weary look. "Then don't."

Stephen, never one to heed the advice of others, got right to the point. "Does this have anything to do with Anna?"

Nicholas didn't answer him. This was because he couldn't, his emotional response to Stephen's query actually leaving him unable to speak.

This was ridiculous.

He was acting like a lovesick kid. Mooning over a woman who didn't want him no matter how many promises he made to her. And he was letting this interfere in every aspect of his life. Not only with him, but in his work and now here with a friend.

He leaned further back in his chair, meeting Stephen's gaze. He could feel the muscles in his jaw twitching in his effort to keep his emotions in check.

After a long whistling breath, Stephen shook his head. "Man, you've got it bad. Really bad. But, you're not alone. Every guy gets hit with this at least once. If you're unlucky, it can happen more than once. Trust me, I know."

Nicholas scowled.

How the hell could Stephen possibly know what he was going through right now? Picking up his pen, he started drumming it on his desk, resisting the urge to fling it across the room instead.

Another childish outburst coming on? How impressive ...

He threw the pen down on the desk, giving a frustrated sigh. "What are you talking about? You seem to be more than blissfully happy with Katy. Hell, you're in love, engaged and probably already planning the wedding. I don't see this at all similar to my situation."

Swiftly holding up his hand, he shook his head. "Our situation I should say. Mine and Anna's."

Stephen gave a short laugh. "Ha... you think it was always like this? Damn, I don't know how many times we almost broke up. It was the most bizarre courtship. You always hear it's the woman who wants to get married, but not my Katy. In fact, the more I brought up the possibility of us having a future together, the more she backed off."

He massaged his chin with his hand, a faint smile appearing at the memory. "Then one day we were arguing about something stupid. I think it was about what she was making for dinner. Tired of discussing something so trivial, I finally said something like, for God's sake, we might as well be married with the way we're acting, arguing about something so stupid. And Bam! She looked at me with this surprised look on her face and said, okay, let's get married. Not very romantic, but I took it and ran with it."

He held his arms wide, a broad grin on his face. "But you tell me, how could any woman refuse all of this? I'm sure my good looks and charming personality had a lot to do with her decision."

Nicholas raised an eyebrow, a slight smile coming to his face. "Your good looks? Charming personality? Awfully full of yourself, aren't you?" Then his expression turned serious. "Well, evidently I must be seriously lacking in those traits, along with so many other things, when it comes to impressing Anna."

He closed his eyes for a brief moment. He wasn't sure he really wanted to share what he was about to say. "I don't even know why I'm telling you this, but I actually asked her to marry me."

At Stephen's look of surprise, he nodded. "But as you can see by my present condition, she wanted no part of that. Which means she wants no part of me, no matter what promises I make. So…"

Briefly closing his eyes, he paused for a few seconds, swallowing hard.

"I've lost her."

The muscle in his jaw twitching furiously, he tried to stop the overwhelming desolation hitting him upon admitting out loud what he never thought he'd even have to think about.

She was lost to him.

My God, get control of yourself. You don't want to start blubbering in front of one of your closest friends, do you?

Stephen was silent, trying to think of an appropriate response. He could also see he needed to give Nicholas a few seconds to regain his composure.

He finally cleared his throat and leaned forward, an inquiring expression on his face. "I take it the events of this past weekend had something to do with this marriage proposal of yours?"

Nicholas narrowed his eyes. What did Stephen know? And where did he get this information?

Damn, this was exactly what you were afraid of.

He raised an eyebrow. "Why? What did you hear?"

Stephen leaned back in his chair, stretching his legs comfortably out in front of him. "Only there was quite a scene at the brunch on Sunday, with Marc winding up on the floor, bleeding profusely. The story going around has you doing quite a bit of damage, possibly even breaking his nose."

He shrugged his shoulders. "I've also received quite a few calls with inquiries about the lovely woman you so ardently fought for. From what I've heard, it seems you made quite an impression."

Seeing the glaring look in Nicholas's eyes, he held his hands up. "Whoa… take it easy. I said nothing, as first of all, I wasn't there to witness what happened. Secondly, knowing you as well as I do, I knew you had a damn good reason for doing what you did. And finally, I know how Marc can provoke a person."

He raised his eyebrows. "I have to admit I'm shocked you, of all people, was involved in something like this. And at a big social event, of all places. It seems so out of character for you." He smiled. "But I'm also quite impressed. And with my usual luck, I missed it. It seems I always miss the exciting events, but never the dull ones."

Nicholas groaned, running his hands though his hair in frustration. "Anna told me she saw Marc the night before, something I should have taken more seriously. Maybe then I wouldn't have left her alone. As it was, there she was, such an easy target."

He reached for his pen and started twisting it in his hands, almost as though he wanted to snap it in half.

"When I came back into the room, he had her backed up against the wall and she looked absolutely terrified. This is when I became so angry and I guess you could say it went all downhill from there. I had no intentions of hitting him like I did. It just happened. And now it looks like I've made a mess of things."

Stephen could see Nicholas thought he was in some way responsible for what happened. This meant he needed to convince him otherwise. But first, a droll smile on his face, he reached across the desk to take the pen out of his hands.

"This is for my own protection, okay? I'm afraid you're going to shoot it in my direction next." When Nicholas only frowned, Stephen took pity on him. "Hey man, don't blame yourself. It's not your fault. You've never had to deal with Marc before. So, how would you know what he's capable of doing? Katy and I witnessed the change in him right after he and Anna became engaged. He began drinking more, his behavior becoming progressively worse. Unfortunately, Anna wound up bearing the brunt of his abusive and sometimes violent behavior. Katy was, and still is, frantic with worry."

His smile was grim. "We thought he would back off after Anna put an end to their engagement. But no such luck. Even now he manages to turn up every once in a while, like he did at that party. Enough to keep Anna in a constant state of fear of when or where he'll turn up again." He frowned. "He's always full of threats. Let's just say he didn't take it very well Anna ended it."

Nicholas leaned back in his chair. His eyes closed, he let all this information sink in before he looked over at Stephen, shaking his head. "This explains a lot. From what little I learned from Anna, I knew he was out of hand. But I guess I didn't grasp how bad the situation is."

A hint of a smile touched his lips. "God, the weekend up until then was incredible. For both of us. I had even managed to convince her to fly here with me. I wanted her to see where I live and meet my family. You know, all the things you do when you're serious about someone."

He stared off into space before he glanced at Stephen, a wistful look on his face. "But after the encounter with Marc, she suddenly became a different person, a shell of the Anna I knew. She wanted to meet at the hotel restaurant. This was when she told me it was over. And of course, I knew this was because of Marc and his threats."

He ran his hand through his hair again. "She's so damn afraid of him. It was so hard for me to see her like this. And though I tried to assure her I could handle him, she wouldn't buy it."

Stephen shrugged. "She knows Marc will want revenge, this being what he likes to do best. She's trying to protect you."

Nicholas response was sharp. "That's ridiculous. I should be protecting her."

In the silence that followed, Nicholas averted his gaze in order to avoid the look of pity on Stephen's face. He finally sent him a faint smile. "Forgive me. I guess I'm having a hell of a time trying to wrap my mind around the fact she walked away from what we had."

He put up his hand again. "What we have, I mean." Then he gave a slow shrug. "I don't know, maybe it's best to let it go."

Stephen shot him a look of disbelief. "I can't believe you're thinking of calling it quits. You never give up when you want something. You fight until it is yours." He waved his hand around at the room. "Hell, this is how you came by all of this!"

Nicholas gave a short laugh. "Well, unfortunately this isn't like a business deal, so I can't use the same tactics. What do you suggest I do, write up a contract and give it to Anna to sign?"

This brought on his genuine smile. "I can only imagine how she would react to this." Then he frowned. "Maybe this is the problem. I only know how to deal with business matters, not those of the heart. I haven't the slightest idea of how to fix this."

When Stephen started to speak, Nicholas held up his hand. "No, I don't want to drag Katy into this, if that's what you're thinking. If there's any chance of working this out, I want it to happen only because Anna wants it as much as I do."

He sighed. "I guess I can only hope. Though being so far apart, now makes it even more of a long shot."

After a few seconds of silence, Stephen spoke. "Well, if you need anything, you know you can count on me. In the meantime, you might start investigating Marc on your own. I know he fell into his father's business a few years ago and rumors suggest he's been slowly running it into the ground. This might explain his behavior. I'll check around, too."

Nicholas smiled. "Thanks, friend."

He caught the pen Stephen tossed over to him. "Now, I don't recall setting up this meeting. Since you did, I assume you have something on your mind?"

Stephen seemed nervous, yet at the same time excited "Well, yes. I have news. A bit of unexpected news, but at the same time, very good news."

Then he just blurted it out. "Katy's pregnant!"

Nicholas jumped up out of his chair and reached across the desk to shake his hand. "My God, this is fantastic news! Congratulations! Did you just find this out?"

Stephen was grinning from ear to ear. "We've known for a little over three months but didn't want to share the news until everything was going well. Katy was having bouts of morning sickness almost around the clock, this the reason we bowed out of the party. She's starting to feel better, but now she worries about what people will say since we're not married."

Nicholas couldn't help but smile back at Stephen's grinning face. "Tell her I'm thrilled for both of you. A baby is always a welcome addition. And hell, you can get married anytime."

Stephen leaned forward, an earnest expression on his face. "And this is why I'm here. We're trying to put together a small wedding, possibly in the next week or so. I feel bad Katy won't get her big wedding, but she insists it doesn't matter. So, if things go as planned, I wonder if you would consider taking over the role as my best man."

He suddenly looked concerned. "I'd really like you to be there, but I know Katy wants Anna as her maid-of-honor. With what you've told me, I won't be upset if you…"

Nicholas held up his hand. "Stop. I'd be honored to be your best man. Anna and I will just have to manage somehow."

Stephen's anxious look dissolved into a big smile. "This is great. And now it's my turn to thank you."

Mulling over this new turn of events, they were silent until Stephen came to his feet, rubbing his hands together.

"So, do you have time for lunch? Since I find it hard to eat when I'm with Katy and she's looking so miserable, I seem to be starving all of the time!"

He chuckled. "Just do me a favor and comb your hair, okay? You're looking a little rough around the edges and I don't want people thinking I'm hanging around with some madman. After all, I need to keep my reputation up to par, now I'm going to be a father."

His head tilted, for a moment he appeared almost shocked by the truth of his words.

Then he grinned. "Again, go figure."

After lunch with Stephen and back in his office, Nicholas tried to concentrate on the work in front of him. But his gaze kept drifting over to the box, still unopened and on the desk where he'd left it.

Oh, what the hell… you might as well open it. Otherwise it's going to drive you crazy.

He tossed the card and tissue paper aside and taking out the gift box, he untied the bow. He opened the box and carefully pulled out a royal blue glass ornament, painted and embellished in great detail.

Anna had painted a man and woman dancing cheek to cheek, the woman's flowing gown embellished with tiny rhinestones. The background was a scattering of crystal snowflakes and stars. A white glittered bow adorned the top of the ornament.

It was a painting of the two of them, as they danced on that amazing night they had together.

He smiled, closing his eyes. He could almost feel her in his arms, the lyrics of the song the orchestra played, an echo of everything he'd wanted to say to her.

> *I found a dream that I could speak to,*
> *A dream that I can call my own.*
> *I found a thrill to rest my cheek to,*
> *A thrill that I have never known.*

For a few moments, he let this memory take over his mind. Then with a slight shake of his head, he carefully examined every detail before he turned the ornament over to find she'd painted a message on the back.

> *Nicholas,*
> *Your kisses drift like snowflakes*
> *into the palm of my hand.*
> *Where I promise to hold on to them*
> *for a million years.*
> *You are in my heart and this is where*
> *you will always be,*
> *Anna*

As he cradled the ornament in his hands, he was filled with a sudden fierce determination.

This wasn't right.

No, this was wrong.

This was so wrong...

He couldn't accept what they had was over. In fact, this wasn't even an option. He was going to find a way to see Anna again. So, he could talk to her and they could make things right.

She was the woman he was meant to be with for the rest of his life. This had already settled deep in his heart and he knew for her, this also held true. In fact, the connection between them was so strong he could feel her love coming through in this ornament he now held in his hands.

She belongs to you.

You belong to her.

And there was nothing more to be said.

After he carefully placed the ornament back in the box, he leaned back in his chair and closed his eyes. He was so damn frustrated. There had to be some way he could convince her to let go of the fear holding her prisoner. Only then would she see they were meant to be together and nothing, absolutely nothing, would ever change this.

Not Marc... not anyone... not anything...

As this all raced through his mind, an idea came to him, one that could be the perfect solution. As a matter of fact, it might be the answer to not only one, but two different dilemmas. He grabbed his phone and after hitting Stephen's number, he waited impatiently for him to answer.

And if this didn't pan out? Well, he would come up with something else.

Because there was no way this was over yet.

Not if he had anything to say about it.

CHAPTER 26

$\mathcal{A}$nna was having a difficult time getting things done.

No matter how much she tried to shake it off, she felt like she was moving in slow motion, unable to accomplish even the simplest of tasks. She would blame it on her recent illness, but she knew this couldn't be the reason for the overwhelming feeling of emptiness inside of her.

No, this was a void only one person could fill.

Nicholas...

Thoughts of him haunted her during every waking moment. Even sleep didn't give her a reprieve, as he was always present in her dreams.

She missed everything about him.

Absolutely everything.

From where she was sitting at her worktable, she could see his tie draped over the end of the shelf. She knew she should've packed it in the box with the ornament she gave him, but she hadn't been able to part with it.

And now it was the only thing she had left of him.

She put her head down in her hands. What had she been thinking, holding on to it like this?

It's just a tie, just a stupid tie. It isn't him.

Suddenly feeling angry, she reached over and grabbed the tie, her intention to fling it across the room. Instead it caught on her arm before it fell on the floor at her feet. She stared down at it, her heart beating a mile a minute, her breath coming hard. She groaned, putting her head down on her arms.

What is happening to you?

She closed her eyes, once again wishing things could be different. And as every other time her thoughts went down this same path, she became filled with such an unbearable sadness knowing, most likely, nothing was going to change.

She needed to move on. She just didn't know how to go about doing this. Or if it was even possible.

She pushed away from the table, picked up the tie and carefully placed it back on the shelf. As she glanced around the room, her eyes fell on the boxes of ornaments by the door, stacked up and ready to be delivered.

In her present state of mind, it had been a struggle to finish them, but now all of her orders were filled and she could finally relax. After all, Christmas was less than two weeks away

Christmas...

This was, by far, her favorite holiday. But this year, she wanted to skip it all together. There was only one thing she wanted for Christmas this year and it just wasn't going to happen.

Nicholas...

She wandered over to the sofa to see Mia was curled up in the corner, fast asleep. She glanced over at the clock, wondering if she should take her for a walk. But this would probably send both Marie and Louis into a panic. The two of them had taken on the job as her personal bodyguards very seriously ever since Marc had shown up unannounced in the lobby of their building. Demanding to see Anna, he'd threatened Louis on two separate occasions. Both times Louis had forced him leave.

Anna shuddered, thinking about what he might be planning to do next. Because he would be back, this she knew for sure.

But she didn't want to think about this either.

She sighed and picked up her phone. Then she quickly set it back on the counter. As much as she wanted, she wasn't going to listen to Nicholas's voice message again. She should have erased it. Instead she'd played it over and over, a sharp ache filling her every time she heard his voice.

When she reached up to tuck her hair behind her ear, she saw her hand was trembling. She sent a desperate glance around the room.

She couldn't go on like this.

She was going to take Mia for a walk. This way she could stop in and see Katy.

If anyone could help her make sense out of everything that happened, it would be Katy.

When the door to Katy's brownstone opened, it wasn't Katy who was standing in front of her, it was Stephen. He cocked his head to one side, giving Anna a long look before he reached out to hug her.

"*Ah... Anna.* Come in. Katy will be glad to see you. She's been so worried about you."

Suddenly tongue tied, Anna could only stare at him. She wanted to ask him, had he talked to Nicholas? And if he had, was he okay? Did he say anything about her? Or about them? There were so many things she wanted to know. But fearful she would only start to cry if she even said his name, she scooped Mia up in her arms and quickly slipped past him to go inside.

Once they were in the great room, an uneasy silence stretched out between them until Stephen took her arm to lead her to the sofa.

"Here, why don't you sit down and relax while l let Katy know you're here. I've been gone for the last three days, so I decided to stop in to see her before going into the office. My flight from London just landed about an hour ago."

Her head jerked up, her eyes anxiously searching his face. The words spilled out before she could stop them. "Nicholas? Did you talk to him? Is he okay?"

He was shaking his head as he sat next her. "Anna, I truly believe he doesn't even know what hit him. You've got…"

"Anna!" With this cry, Katy came running across the room to wrap both Anna and Mia in a big hug. Then she started to cry. "Oh Anna! I've been so worried about you. You weren't answering your phone and when I finally talked to Marie, she told me how sick you were. So, I've been waiting, hoping you'd call. But having you here in person is so much better."

Stephen stood, a resigned smile coming to his face at Katy's tears. "I believe this is my cue to leave. You girls need to catch up and I have work to do."

As he walked out of the room, he turned to wink at Anna. "Hang in there, Anna. I believe fate may be on your side this time."

Katy blew him a kiss. Wiping the tears from her face, she turned back to peer more closely at Anna. "You look okay. Maybe just a little tired. How do you feel?"

Anna was too busy gazing after Stephen, trying to interpret his comment. What did he mean by fate? She wanted to run after him and make him tell her everything he knew. Everything about Nicholas, that is. Instead she forced herself to turn back to Katy, guilt filling her when she saw the worried look on her face.

She smiled. "I'm much better. Now I just need a Katy fix."

Katy responded by giving her another hug. "You must tell me everything. But first I want to apologize for canceling last weekend. It's just… well, I guess I wasn't feeling well."

After Anna put Mia down on the floor and watched her trot across the room to her favorite spot by the fireplace, she turned to study Katy more closely. Why was she refusing to meet her eyes? And why were her cheeks so flushed. Almost as if she was hiding something.

It suddenly dawned on her. "Oh my God, Katy. Are you pregnant?"

Katy dissolved into tears again, flinging her arms around her. "Yes, can you believe this? I'm sorry I'm crying again, but emotionally, I'm a wreck. I'm either crying or laughing. Or doing both at the same time. Poor Stephen, I seriously believe he thinks I've gone insane."

Anna hugged her. "This is wonderful."

An anguished look coming over her face, Katy's next words came out in a wail. "But it's not. Because we're not married. Oh Anna, not once did I ever think this would happen to me."

Anna laughed, hugging her again.

"Well, it did. Oh Katy, just think of the beautiful baby you'll have. I'm so happy for you. And as far as getting married, don't worry, everything will work out."

A radiant smile lit up Katy's face. "Well, it now seems we're actually going to get married next week. I know it sounds crazy, but everything seems to be falling into place. And that's why I wanted to see you. I want you to be there, Anna. You'll be my maid-of-honor, just like you promised, won't you?"

She gave Anna a wistful smile. "Remember the pact we made?"

Anna smiled. "I wouldn't dream of letting you get married without me!"

Katy was looking at her very intently. "No matter where we decide to have the wedding?"

Anna's intuition kicked in. And it was sending her a warning whatever Katy was going to say next, she wasn't going to like it.

Katy took her hand, her words tumbling out. "Stephen was in London on business. While he was there, he went to see Nicholas because he wanted to ask him to be his best man. And now he's just told me Nicholas offered the use of his home for our wedding. It's his gift to us."

A dreamy expression settled on her face. "Stephen has been there a few times and he said it's amazing. It's one of these old English estates. You know, one that's passed down through the family for years. Oh Anna, I'm so excited. It will be so romantic. Like a fairy tale wedding."

Anna closed her eyes, everything in her going into total denial. How could she possibly be expected to go along with this?

She couldn't. It was asking too much. After frantically trying to think up an excuse, any excuse at all, she opened her eyes to stare wildly at Katy. "But you'd have to fly. I thought you were never going to get on another plane again. This is what…"

The pleading expression on Kay's face put a halt to her words.

What are you doing?

This was Katy, her best friend. Katy, who was there for her every single time she needed her. She shouldn't be trying to talk her out of this and she certainly couldn't refuse to be there for her wedding.

She sighed. She didn't have a choice, did she?

"Katy, I'm sorry. Like I promised so many years ago, I will be there. I wouldn't miss this for anything."

Katy threw her arms around her in a big hug. "Oh, Anna, thank you, thank you! It will be wonderful you'll see. And you know I would be crazy to pass up something like this just because of my silly fear of flying."

Anna sighed, a doubtful look on her face. "Yes, I'm sure it will be. At least I know you won't cancel out on me this time."

Katy took her hand again. "Oh Anna, tell me everything."

The look Anna gave her spoke volumes. "Oh Katy, the weekend was so amazing. But then everything was ruined. When I saw Marc on Saturday night, I should've known something awful would happen. He was so drunk, and the things he said…"

She blinked, trying to keep the tears at bay. "Katy, he's taken over my life and I don't know what to do any more. No matter where I go, I worry he'll show up and make a scene. Like he did in front of all those people who were only trying to enjoy the brunch."

She gave Katy a shaky smile. "I can't even imagine what would have happened if Nicholas hadn't been there."

Katy hesitated. "Stephen heard about what happened from some of the people who were there." At Anna's horrified look, she put her hand on her arm. "Oh Anna, they're only talking about it because they're concerned. After all, Marc's behavior over the past few months has caught just about everyone's attention."

She gave Anna a big hug. "I'm so sorry. I wish I would've been there for you. Not that I could've done anything. But like you said, you had Nicholas. And I heard he made quite an impression, coming so gallantly to your defense."

She smiled, a dreamy expression on her face. "It's rather romantic, if you think about it. What girl wouldn't want a handsome man like

Nicholas fighting for her. Like he did for you? Why, it's almost like he galloped in on his horse, defeated the evil villain and scooped you up to whisk you out of danger. Well, maybe there wasn't an actual horse involved, but still … how romantic can you get?"

She saw a hint of a smile on Anna's face before it was replaced with a look of doubt. So, she tried to reassure her even further. "Seriously Anna, think about it. He must care for you so much."

Her eyes blazing. Anna vehemently shook her head."Nothing can ever happen between us, Katy. No, not as long as Marc is around. Because I know he'll go after Nicholas. And I can't let this happen."

Katy sighed. "Anna, you need to have more faith in Nicholas. Like I told you before, trust him. He can handle Marc. My gosh, he's already proved this." She suddenly grinned. "I'm not worried. I know the two of you will work this out. I bet you'll be the next to get married."

She patted her stomach. "Just promise you'll wait until after this baby comes into the world. Because I certainly don't want to be a very pregnant maid-of-honor, waddling down the aisle at your wedding."

Her eyes sparkling, she laughed. "Or should I say matron-of-honor, since in a few days I will be married." She reached over to give Anna another hug. "I'm so excited!"

Caught up in Katy's excitement, Anna almost blurted out about Nicholas's proposal. But she knew Katy would be horrified when she told her how she'd reacted, running off and leaving him in the restaurant.

But how could she expect Katy to understand when she, herself, wasn't sure how all of that came about? It was quite possible, Nicholas now might be feeling the same, wondering what possessed him to ask her to agree to such a ridiculous idea.

But for now? The focus should be on Katy and Stephen's wedding.

She sent Katy a big smile. "Katy, let's talk about your wedding instead, please?"

Katy nodded. "Okay. But remember I'm here if you want to talk. And this would be any time. But for now, we have a wedding to plan."

She picked up a notepad from the table to show Anna the list she'd already started. "I'm really going to need your help because there is so much to do and so little time. Getting my family together, flight reservations, and good grief, a dress! How am I going to find a dress in such a short time?"

Anna grinned. "You already have a dress, if you want it. Mine. After all, you helped pick it out."

Katy eyes opened wide. "I would love to wear your dress! But won't you want to wear it someday?" She grinned. "Possibly sooner than you think?"

Anna gave her a warning look. "Katy! Stop! I want you to wear the dress. After all, we share almost everything, so why not share a wedding dress? Think of it as your 'something borrowed' item."

Katy's sigh was huge. "This is perfect. Another thing taken care of."

She turned to Anna and pointed a finger at her. "And you'll wear what you wore the night you were with Nicholas. I swear that dress was made for you, as it never looked that good on me. I bet he couldn't tear his gaze away from you." She stopped to nod. "He probably didn't want you to take it off."

Thinking of that night and what followed after the dress fluttered to the floor, Anna could feel her face growing hot. She closed her eyes, her sudden longing for Nicholas so overpowering, she almost couldn't breathe.

Oh my God... if you feel like this just thinking about him, what's going to happen when you actually see him again? And this will be in only a few days from now. Lord help you both.

Watching her reaction, Katy grinned. "*Hmm...* or maybe he did?"

"Katy, please..." Her eyes still closed, Anna's plea came out in a soft moan.

Katy reached over to hug her. "Okay, okay. I'll stop. But you've made this decision a very easy one. Your dress has also been decided on."

She tore a page off the notepad and waved it at Anna. "And there we have it, this list is all checked off and we're ready to start a new one. Like I've said, we have a lot of work to do!"

She laughed before she reached over to give Anna another hug. "You're going to be one busy maid-of-honor."

Anna's smile was distracted.

What happened here?

This certainly wasn't what she expected to happen when she made the decision to visit Katy.

Because it now appeared she had a lot of serious thinking to do.

CHAPTER 27

It wasn't until the plane coasted to a stop, for Anna, it finally sank in.

You're here. You're actually in London.

And now, as she slid onto the plush leather seats of the limo that magically appeared as soon as they walked off the plane, she decided it would be best if she ignored this fact altogether.

Instead, she was going to enjoy this unexpected luxury, even if only for a short time. After the hectic pace of the past few days, helping Katy with everything wedding related, she deserved some pampering.

There was no doubt about it. She was definitely earning her title as maid-of-honor. She was also beginning to understand why people chose to elope, forgoing all the hoopla of a big wedding. Who would have thought there would be so many details to work out?

According to the chauffeur, their drive would be about twenty minutes. Enough time to compose her feelings into a semblance of indifference about everything concerning you-know-who.

And yes… this would be Nicholas.

Twenty minutes? Ha, who are you kidding? You know this isn't going to happen.

Certainly not going by the constant state of panic she'd been in since she found out she was going to see him again.

Her heart had begun beating so fast and so hard, it was almost as though it was gearing up. Ready to leap right out of her chest when they finally came face to face.

My God, you're going to drop in a dead faint and right at his feet if you keep up at this pace. Certainly not something you want to have happen again.

She glanced over at Katy and Stephen, relieved to see they were too involved in their own conversation to pay attention to her current state. She rested her head against the back of the seat and closed her eyes. She was going to make a sincere effort to enjoy the rest of the ride.

Yeah, like this is going to be easy.

After what seemed like an incredibly short twenty minutes, the limo began to slow. She opened her eyes to see they were passing by a long stretch of brick wall before turning to coast up a driveway blocked by an ornate rod iron gate.

As if by a secret command, the gate slowly swung open, allowing the limo to pass through. It then closed just as slowly, a subtle clicking sound a clear indication it was locked back in place.

Well... isn't this marvelous. It seems you're not only here, but also locked in for good. Everything keeps getting better and better, doesn't it?

Startled, she jumped when Katy gave a loud gasp and grabbed her arm. "Oh my gosh, Anna... look at this place!"

The building in front of them wasn't what you would even think of referring to as a house, as this would be an insult. If anything, it was more like an English version of an over-the-top Southern plantation. Three stories high, the exterior was a warm, weathered red brick, giving the impression it had been standing forever upon the land it sat on.

Two imposing white pillars flanked the front entryway, anchoring the veranda that wrapped around the front of both sides of the house.

Now the scene of a flurry of activity, there were people everywhere, draping garland and hanging lights. All of this happening at a frenzied pace.

The grounds were immaculate. If there was a stray twig of a blade of grass too high, you sure couldn't see it.

All told, the whole setting was a perfect choice for the cover of any exclusive magazine showcasing the homes of the rich and famous.

A queasy feeling beginning to churn in her stomach, Anna's panic went into overdrive. While next to her, Katy let out a huge sigh. "Oh, my goodness. This is unbelievable. Nicholas's parents must be billionaires, or royalty. Or maybe even a little of both to live in a place like this."

Stephen chuckled. "Actually, this is now Nicholas's home. His parents used to live here, along with Nicholas and his sister, Claire. But once Claire got married and Nicholas came into his inheritance, his parents moved to their home in the country, turning this property over to him."

Katy and Anna turned to each other, their mouths open in disbelief. Then Katy started to laugh. And yes, she also began to cry.

When Stephen rolled his eyes, she swatted him lightly on his arm before she put her hand to her mouth. "I can't believe we're going to have our wedding here!"

Then she launched herself into Stephen's arms to give him a big kiss. "This is like a fairytale. It's going to be amazing!"

She turned to Anna and hugged her, too. "Oh Anna, can you believe all of this?"

A smile pasted on her face, Anna nodded. "Yes, it's going to be wonderful." After all, she really had no choice but to agree. As the maid-of-honor, it was her job to make sure the bride was always happy.

She slowly shook her head, her gaze returning to the house. Her maid-of-honor duties were beginning to feel like a piece of cake compared to what she was up against when it came to Nicholas.

How did she even have a chance of standing her ground when faced with all of this grandeur?

My God, as it was, she was having a hard enough time dealing with him alone.

She nervously twisted her hands together in her lap. It appeared she was a maid of honor who now had a heck of a lot more to worry about than her duties in this upcoming wedding.

With a sigh of relief, Anna closed the door behind the departing housekeeper who'd introduced herself as Mrs. Burrows. Her chatter had been non-stop as she filled Anna in on just about anything she would ever need to know about her stay here in Nicholas's home.

Or, as she kept referring to it, the Hanover's London Estate.

As though she was sharing extremely confidential information, Mrs. Burrow's voice had dropped to a whisper when she told Anna Nicholas had personally chosen this room for her. This way if she needed anything, his rooms were right next door. Anna wondered if she'd imagined Mrs. Burrows put a little bit too much emphasis on the word *anything* when she told her this.

She shook her head

Nope, definitely not your imagination.

She'd also informed Anna Nicholas had left only a short time ago. But he would most definitely be stopping by to welcome her.

Stopping by? And when would this be? Fifteen minutes? A couple of hours? Could she have been more specific?

Now alone in the room, Anna tried to ignore the fact she was more disappointed than she should be about this last bit of information. After all, Nicholas must be very busy and she shouldn't have expected him to be here to greet her when she arrived.

Especially after what happened the last time you saw him.

She gave a frustrated sigh. She just wanted to get their first meeting behind her. Then she'd be able to put him completely out of her mind and focus all of her energy on being the perfect maid-of-honor. Because, once again, this was the one and only reason she was here.

Right?

Hmm... keep telling yourself this.

She wandered over to the window and pushing aside the delicate lace curtains, she peered outside at what she assumed was the back-yard of the house.

As with everything else, this was also a vision of total perfection, the main attraction a large pavilion gazebo centered on a sprawling stone patio. Surrounding this was a maze of perfectly manicured gardens, which even at this time of year, still managed to look lush and green. She could only imagine how beautiful it must be during the summer months when everything was in bloom.

Her eyes closed, she could visualize the guests milling about, the women in their colorful summer dresses and hats, the men in their light summer suits. Their voices and laughter ringing out in the bright afternoon sunshine, they'd be patiently waiting for the bride and groom to make their appearance,

Her eyes flew open.

The Bride and Groom? A summer wedding? Where was all of this coming from?

She shook her head. Another wedding, let alone a wedding here, was not in her future.

Absolutely not.

After she turned away from the window, she wrapped her arms around herself as she gazed around the room. If she weren't feeling so anxious, she'd be so excited to be staying in such beautiful surroundings.

The décor was of a floral theme, giving the illusion of a charming English country cottage. An overstuffed cabbage rose print comforter and pillows covered the bed. The walls were papered in a tiny floral print and a plush hand carved rug was underfoot. A comfy armchair, upholstered in a contrasting plaid chintz fabric, was positioned in front of the fireplace. Right next to the chair was a small lace covered table, all set with an inviting afternoon tea for one.

Anna poured out a cup of the still piping hot tea, breathing in deeply of the fragrant drink, hoping it would calm her. This was when she noticed the simple arrangement of a red rose nestled in baby's breath on the table. Setting the cup down, she opened the envelope addressed to her and propped up against the vase. The wording was simple, yet the message was so clear.

To Anna, with all my love.
As I will be forever and always yours,
Nicholas.

She slowly sank into the chair, the tea completely forgotten.
You shouldn't have come...
Already she could feel her heart gearing up for a fight, determined to betray her. And she didn't know if she had the strength to fight back. No matter the decision she'd already made or what the consequences could be.
No... you should have stayed home.
She gazed into the fire burning in the fireplace. She'd turned down the offer to accompany Katy and Stephen to approve last minute wedding details. With the rehearsal and dinner scheduled to take place later in the evening, this meant she had the rest of the afternoon to herself. After the hectic week, a short nap seemed like a wonderful idea.
Yes, this is what you need. Then you'll feel stronger. And you'll ready to take on anything, Nicholas included.
She pulled down the cashmere throw from where it was draped over the back of the chair and wrapped it around her. Instantly comforted by its warmth and softness, she closed her eyes.
She drifted into a dreamless sleep.

Nicholas glanced in the rearview mirror of his SUV, smiling when he saw his two back seat passengers were now both sound asleep, Clementine's head on Emily's shoulder.
Their silence was a welcome change from their excited chatter and endless questions about the wedding when they first tumbled into the car. The combination of a wedding and Christmas, taking

place in the time span of one week, was like a sugar high to these two.

As he maneuvered the car through traffic, his thoughts drifted to Claire. Picking the girls up from school today, which happened to be their last day before the Christmas holidays, was the least he could do for her. Especially since, at this very moment, she was at his house supervising all of the final details he'd now learned were considered mandatory in pulling off a wedding.

How complicated it all seemed. If you love someone, you should just go off and get married.

Period.

Because, come on… was all of this fuss really necessary?

You know damn well you'd agree to just about anything if you and Anna were to plan a wedding. Admit it.

That there was even a wedding taking place was somewhat of a miracle. Again, this was almost entirely due to Claire. He'd be forever grateful for how she came to his defense when his mother objected so strongly to his plans.

He shook his head, remembering all the ranting and raving that went on. But he should have known his mother was going to react this way.

She couldn't understand why he was going through so much trouble to throw a wedding for a friend. An American friend, mind you. Wasn't it about time he began thinking about planning his own wedding? If this happened, his mother had assured him, she'd be more than happy to help him with whatever his heart desired.

She'd also wanted to know if he had any idea how much work would be involved in setting up this wedding. With all of these strangers descending on him with who knows what kind of demands. Wasn't it enough Nicholas's family already had plenty of their own quirky habits without adding more to the mix?

Then she'd gone on to remind him Christmas was right around the corner, only a few days away. As if he wasn't aware of this. Certainly not the best time to complicate everything with a major event such as a wedding, she'd gone on to inform him.

Finally, she came at him with one last zinger. If this was something he thought up on his own, well, he was clearly out of his mind. It was also proof he needed to find a wife to keep him from making any of the same kind of rash decisions in the future. And this, according to her, was something he needed to do soon. Need she remind him he wasn't getting any younger?

Well, you can't argue with her about your state of mind. But finding a wife? If she only knew

Thank goodness Claire had finally stepped in, reassuring their mother she would help Nicholas and there was no need for her to worry. Which then resulted with his mother feeling insulted, accusing them both of not wanting her help. It had all begun to feel like a no-win situation.

But somehow everything got sorted out and Claire, surprisingly with the help of his mother, took on the job. He just made sure he was there if they needed help. Like picking up the girls from school today.

Now, as he drove up to the front entrance of his house, it was to find a large crew of people stringing more lights and greenery along the veranda.

He grinned. Evidently Claire had decided more is better.

Gently waking both girls, he herded them into the house and through the foyer, now decorated with dozens of poinsettia plants. They were everywhere. There was also a garland of pine and ivy draped along the banisters of the stairs, sparkling with even more lights. This had to be more of his sister's handiwork.

He smiled. His house was certainly beginning to look festive.

As they continued down the hall, a huge container filled with an assortment of red roses and white carnations caught his eye. He reached over to tweak the bows in the girl's hair, smiling down at them.

"How would you like to meet my friend? Remember, I told you she is the bride's best friend? And she is also going be in the wedding? Her name is Anna."

At their nods, he carefully selected two of the carnations and gave one to each girl. "Here... you can each give her one of these."

Clementine grinned at him as she took her flower. "Is she your Sleeping Beauty, Uncle Nicky? If she is, you have to give her a flower, too. But you should give her a red one."

He laughed, shaking his head at her. "Sleeping Beauty? *Ah…* I can only hope. As it stands now, any kind of wake-up kiss is still out of my reach."

After he pulled out one of the red roses, he held a finger to his lips. "Now let's not tell anyone we took these. We don't want to get into trouble."

Clementine began to look a bit worried. "Uncle Nicky, do you think mummy will be mad?"

He pulled her close for a quick hug. "If she does, don't worry. I'll take the blame." He followed this by a look of exaggerated fear.

This set both of them into a fit of giggles just as they arrived outside the door to the room he'd requested for Anna. A room he'd made sure was close to his own suite of rooms.

Suddenly, he was nervous. Very nervous. He had no clue of what kind of reaction he was going to receive from Anna. He only knew he needed to be prepared for just about anything. There was a good chance this first meeting between them might not go as he hoped.

But he didn't care. He just wanted to be wherever she was.

Again? It was this simple.

CHAPTER 28

$\mathscr{A}$ faint knocking interrupted Anna's dreams.

She gave a long stretch and feeling more rested than she had over the past several days, she crossed the room to answer the door.

When she heard what sounded like giggling coming from the other side, she smiled. If it was Katy, she was certainly very happy about something.

She opened the door to find two adorable little girls standing in front of her, each holding a white carnation in their hand. Gazing up at her with enormous blue eyes, they were a mirror image of each other, from the pink polka dot bows in their dark curly hair to the pink sequined UGG boots on their feet.

Enchanted, Anna bent down to their eye level and glanced from one to the other. "Why, hello there... I have a feeling one of you must be Emily and the other must be Clementine. Am I right?"

Their eyes fixed on her face, they both nodded. Then they continued to stare up at her, not a single peep from either of them.

She tried not to laugh, the memory of her first encounter with Nicholas coming to mind.

She wondered, was this a British thing?

Whatever it is, once again, it looks like it's going to be up to you to carry on the conversation.

She gave them a big smile. "My name is Anna. I've come here for the wedding."

This resulted in only more nods. In desperation, she held out her hand. She immediately found herself in possession of the two flowers, along with two very excited smiles.

Thank goodness.

After she gave each girl a hug, she held the flowers to her heart. "These are so beautiful. Thank you so much."

"Uncle Nicky, you have to give her your flower, too."

This excited cry came from Emily. Or was it Clementine? As she glanced from one to the other, Anna had to wonder, how in the word did their parents tell the apart?

Then she stilled.

Wait a minute... Uncle Nicky?

A tremor zipping through her, this was when she realized Nicholas was standing right behind them. Holding on to the door-frame for support, she slowly stood, her gaze traveling from his impeccable grey flannel trousers and up to the ivory cashmere crew neck sweater he was wearing over an ivory, grey and navy pin striped collared shirt. It was a look that was so flawless, so him. This, along with the familiar spicy scent of his cologne, sent a flood of memories rushing right at her.

She took a deep breath and slowly gazed up at his face.

Their eyes locked, his sending her a message of such hope and tenderness. And as if no time had passed since she was last with him, he became her anchor in the sudden whirlwind of feelings that consumed her.

She wanted to go right into his arms. Where she could rest her head against his chest and sink into the safe and comforting sound of his heartbeat. And she wanted him to kiss her.

Oh God... how she so very much wanted to get lost in one of his kisses.

"Uncle Nicky! Uncle Nicky!" With these cries from the girls, Anna quickly came crashing back to earth. She blinked to see Nicholas's eyes were still on her, a wistful smile on his face.

"Uncle Nicky, give her the flower."

With a slight shake of his head, he cleared his throat. "Ah, yes...the flower."

He winked at the two girls and with a slight bow in Anna's direction, his voice was rough as he handed her the rose. "A beautiful flower. For an even more beautiful princess."

Emily and Clementine immediately began jumping up and down, clapping their hands. "Now you have to kiss her, Uncle Nicky. Please?"

At Nicholas's soft chuckle, Anna glanced at him, color flooding her cheeks. Had he put these two little ones up to this? She nervously glanced down the hall, almost expecting to see a horse and carriage come whipping around the corner, ready to whisk the two of them off to the Land of Happily Ever After.

When she glanced back at Nicholas, she saw his eyes were sparkling. He tilted his head and giving her the teasing smile she remembered so well, his next words came at her in a soft drawl. "We certainly can't disappoint Emily and Clementine. Can we, Anna?"

His gaze holding hers, he gently cupped her chin in his hand. This kiss he gave her was gentle, barely a brush of his lips over hers.

"God, I've missed you so, love. Later, when we don't have an audience, I'll kiss you like I mean it." These words, meant for her alone, were a soft whisper against her cheek. He followed this with another smile as he reached for her hand to link their fingers together.

Dropping her gaze to their hands, she made a desperate attempt to unscramble her thoughts.

What the heck just happened here?

Already things were going terribly, terribly awry. This was certainly not the way she'd planned how their first meeting would go. At least not when, as so often in the past few days, she'd gone over and over in her mind how she intended it to take place.

Her plan had her cool and distant, letting him know right from the beginning she was here only for the wedding and nothing more. And even though she knew he didn't want to hear this, she would convince him for one final time, she was right.

A relationship between them was never going to work.

Period.

But what had she just done? She let herself get completely lost in his eyes, his beautiful blue eyes. And this happened all within seconds of seeing him. Which meant nothing had changed. All the time and effort she'd spent over the past few days convincing herself she didn't need him in her life? Well, obviously this had been a total waste of time.

You failed miserably at this, didn't you? So, now what?

Well, it looked like she needed to come up with a new plan. Especially since she'd also become so unraveled from his kiss.

Good grief, it was barely a kiss.

If this simple little kiss made her feel like she was right now, she didn't even want to think of what would happen if he really kissed her. Like he implied he would. But she could only blame herself for this. Evidently this past request of hers was going to keep coming back to haunt her every time he had the chance to remind her about it.

"Nicky?"

Anna glanced up to see a young and attractive woman walking towards them, a tentative smile on her face. At the sound of her voice, both Clementine and Emily whirled around and almost as one, went running over to her. Their excited cries echoed through the hall.

"Mummy! Mummy!"

After she patiently returned their greetings, she glanced over at Nicholas and Anna, her gaze lingering momentarily on their clasped hands.

Anna quickly tried to pull her hand from Nicholas's, but he tightened his hold before he glanced down at her with a smile. Then he winked at her.

Honestly? Now he was beginning to infuriate her.

No surprise here. But remember what happens when you get angry. Not once has it worked in your favor.

She sighed. Again, nothing was going as planned.

Noting the sigh, Nicholas gently squeezed her hand. "Anna, this is my sister, Claire. And Claire, I believe I told you Anna would be here as Katy's maid-of-honor? She and Katy have been friends since they were almost about the age of these two little scamps here." He grinned over at Emily and Clementine after he said this, receiving two identical and enthusiastic grins in return.

Anna managed to pull her hand free from Nicholas's hold to greet Claire, with Nicholas wasting no time in reclaiming his hold. Unable to hide her smile, Claire cleared her throat. "So, what plans do the two of you have for this afternoon? I see you already seem to be well acquainted."

Nicholas sent Claire a warning look. "The girls and I just arrived, Claire. I wanted to introduce them to Anna before the rehearsal." He paused to smile down at Anna. "We've made no plans as of yet."

Claire's look was thoughtful. *"Hmm...* I wonder if you would do me a favor? Katy and Stephen's wedding bands are all engraved and ready to be picked up at Tiffany's. Would the two of you be willing to pick them up this afternoon?" She smiled at Anna. "Consider it a best man and maid-of-honor type of job. You'll still have plenty of time before the rehearsal for whatever else you may have in mind." Once again, she glanced at their joined hands.

Now, Claire didn't intend to keep doing this, but she was finding this outward sign of affection so out of character for Nicholas. She couldn't even remember the last time she saw him holding a woman's hand, if ever.

She decided, as soon as she could, she was going to pull him aside to find out more about this Anna. After all, he was her brother. He should be keeping her up to date about these things.

She shook her head. Leave it to him not to mention something as momentous as this.

Anna shot a quick glance at Claire. She could only imagine what she must be thinking. She certainly hoped Nicholas's behavior wasn't leading her to believe something more serious was going on between them. Because there wasn't. At least this wasn't her plan.

She sighed. This was getting complicated.

Yep, you definitely shouldn't be here. You really shouldn't.

Completely oblivious to what both women were thinking, Nicholas was very pleased with this request of Claire's. Now Anna would have no choice but to spend the afternoon with him. It would be the perfect opportunity for them to make a start at getting back what they'd lost between them.

God, you can only hope...

He nodded over Claire. "Sure, we can do that for you."

Anna quickly chimed in. "Yes, if you need help, please let me know. I'd love to help."

Claire smiled. "I will. But right now, everything is pretty well set. So, you two are free to enjoy yourselves." She smiled. "After you pick up the rings, that is."

She turned to Anna. "It was nice meeting you, Anna. Hopefully, we'll be able to spend some time together so we can talk about this brother of mine." She sent an accusing look in Nicholas's direction. "And everything he's failed to tell me."

She turned to Emily and Clementine. "Come on, you can both be my helpers now that you're here."

Anna and Nicholas watched them leave, with both Emily and Clementine waving and blowing kisses until they all disappeared around the corner.

This was everything Anna had hoped wouldn't happen.

Here she was, not only alone with Nicholas, but still holding his hand. Two things she was having an extremely hard time trying to deal with. It didn't help any bravado she'd possessed only seconds before had abandoned her, leaving her extremely nervous and uncertain.

She didn't know what to say. Or where to look. What she did know was any eye contact with Nicholas was out of the question because it would lead to disaster.

At least for her, it would.

And now they were going to be spending the afternoon together?

This certainly wasn't a good idea. Only because, as much as she wanted to deny this, she couldn't believe how much she was craving his company.

A sign her resolve was slipping fast and she didn't know what to do next.

Or if she should do anything at all.

Nicholas watched the different expressions cross Anna's face. He was so tempted to pull her into his arms, if only to reassure her everything was going to be fine.

How could it not be as long as they were together?

As it was, he was finding it almost impossible to believe she was standing next to him, her hand tucked securely in his. After the past few miserable days, his fear he'd never see her again, it was only when her door opened and she was there in front of him, he'd finally began to feel a glimmer of hope.

And now he wanted more.

He wanted to start by kissing away all of the uncertainty he saw in her eyes. He wanted to bury his face in her hair and breathe in the intoxicating fragrance that was her. He wanted to feel the softness of her pressed against him. And he wanted to tell her everything he'd missed about her while they were apart and how he was so happy she was here.

He wanted all of this.

But most of all, he wanted to tell her how much he loved her. He wanted to be able to tell her this every day for the rest of their life.

A surge of longing swept through him, a feeling so strong it almost blindsided him. If he could, he'd gather her up in his arms and carry her over to the bed behind her. They'd close the door to the rest of the world and make love as they had all during that one amazing night they shared together.

He wanted to bring back the magic. And he wanted to see the fire back in her eyes, a fire that burned with a passion for only him.

God, he craved this more than anything.

"Nicholas?"

Anna's soft query cut into his thoughts. He opened his eyes to find her gazing up at him, a worried look on her face.

Ah... reality check.

He brought her hand to his lips, placing a lingering kiss to her fingers. He smiled. "I told you the girls would love you. My sister, too."

Dumbfounded, Anna could only stare at him until she finally found her voice. "Nicholas, how could they? They were only here for about five minutes. You're imagining things."

He shook his head, his smile growing bigger. "No, trust me. I've never felt so sure of anything in my life." He sent a searching glance behind her.

"Now, where's your coat? You're going to need it."

Nicholas stole another glance over at Anna.

Nope, there was no change.

She still looked like she wanted to bolt. Right out of his SUV and as far away from him as possible. He could actually feel the tension swirling between them, most of which seemed to be coming from her side of the car.

He was definitely beginning to feel a sense of *déjà vu* here.

Anna knew she was acting like a child, something she'd become quite good at over the past few weeks. But determined to keep a safe distance between them, she knew it would be best if she didn't talk to, or even look at Nicholas.

But this was so not what she wanted.

Because, seriously? It was just about killing her.

She looked down and saw because of the anxious state she'd worked herself into, she'd twisted her gloves into a wrinkled wad of leather. She shot a quick glance over at Nicholas, hoping he hadn't noticed.

Ah ... but of course he had.

She watched as he reached over to take the gloves from her. After he placed them on the console between them, he reached for her hand. "I'm so happy you're here with me. But at the same time, I'm afraid you're going to jump right out of this vehicle. And as much as it pains me to say this, I know this would be to get away from me."

His smile was teasing. "This isn't at all how I envisioned it would be when we got back together again."

Back together again?

And just like that, she was furious. Because he had to be kidding, right?

Did he actually think you would fall right back into his arms? Did he even remember anything that was said in the restaurant on that awful day?

She snatched her hand back, so caught up in her anger she didn't even notice his startled reaction. She opened her mouth, her intent to remind him of what he should already know. Instead, all of her pent-up emotions decided this was the perfect time to make a much more dramatic appearance.

And she burst into tears.

Nicholas swiftly pulled the SUV into a parking space on the side of the street.

He turned to her, completely bewildered. "Anna, whatever is the matter?"

She could only shake her head. When she began using her hands to wipe away the tears, he dug into his pocket for a handkerchief.

He cleared his throat. "Tell me what's going on, love."

This tenderness in his voice only brought on more tears and it was only after a few minutes she was able to answer him. "Oh Nicholas, I don't think I can do this. I just can't."

His eyes searching her face, his expression was genuinely puzzled. "Do what? Pick up the rings?"

She stared at him in disbelief. *Seriously?* Then she slowly shook her head. "No, it's not that. Oh Nicholas, no. It's everything. Everything to do with us. And no matter what I think, or you think, I…"

She looked down at the handkerchief in her hand and took a deep, shuddering breath. Her words were barely audible. "I never should've agreed to come. Most of all, I shouldn't be here with you."

He closed his eyes, these words from her the worst possible thing she could say to him. As he desperately tried to think of how to answer her, she continued. "Don't get me wrong, I think it's wonderful what you're doing for Katy and Stephen. And I know they're both so excited. I'm happy for them, I truly am. But I can't do this. I can't be here with you. Not with these scared and mixed up feelings inside of me."

She gave an almost hysterical-sob-like laugh. Her hand going to her mouth in an attempt to keep her emotions under control, she met his gaze. "But I can't even leave. My God, Nicholas, I feel like I'm being held prisoner with those huge iron gates and brick walls surrounding your house."

Unable to bear the look of pain and confusion in his eyes, she turned to stare blindly out the window. This left them sitting in silence, their frustration a daunting barrier between them.

Nicholas dragged his hand through his hair. At a loss, only one thing registered in his mind

She wanted to leave?

He couldn't believe she felt this way. But then again, he could. He had been so intent on getting her here, he'd completely blocked out the possibility her fears might tag along instead of staying behind. The same fears which tore them apart to begin with.

You certainly haven't handled this very well, have you?

He closed his eyes, shaking his head.

Anna was beginning to feel uneasy. She was also regretting her remark about being a prisoner. I mean, come on, could she have been any more dramatic? This was a perfect example of why she was better off keeping her mouth shut when she was with him.

She stole a quick glance over at him. He looked completely miserable, his eyes closed and the muscle in his jaw clenched. And, as usual, she was the one who brought him to this state.

She sighed.

She just couldn't do it. Stay silent, that is. She needed to say something.

"Nicholas? Can't you at least see my side of this?"

Deep in thought, Nicholas almost didn't hear her. He was trying to think, desperate to fix this rift between them. He didn't want these unresolved feelings to be a part of them anymore. Not when she was finally here, close enough for him to take her into his arms and kiss her until everything righted itself again.

God, was this really too much to ask?

Her hands clenched in her lap, Anna waited, becoming more anxious by the second.

Finally, and much to her relief, he spoke. "Anna, you're absolutely right to feel this way. I shouldn't have put you in this position. I'm so sorry, love." He studied her for a few seconds. "It's just that, well... I had no idea I could miss someone as much as I missed you. Every single minute of every single day we were apart. And though I'm pretty new at all of this and it seems like I don't know what the hell I'm doing, there's one thing I do know. And this is you've completely taken over my heart."

He smiled wistfully at her.

"I guess I was only thinking about how much I wanted you here, like we'd planned. So, when Stephen told me he and Katy were getting married, but not with the big wedding Katy always dreamed of having, offering my home for the wedding seemed like the perfect way to make this happen. I know this might seem a little drastic, but to tell you the truth, I was desperate."

He shook his head. "But this is also very much about Stephen and Katy. Over the past few years my friendship with Stephen has become such a big part of my life. So, giving them the wedding they'll always remember is my way of showing both of them how much they mean to me."

He shrugged. "And so here we are..." A glint of humor suddenly appeared in his eyes. "Good Lord, I'm beginning to feel like the wicked villain here. One who's spirited you off to his castle and as you've just implied, is holding you captive. Thank God, my house doesn't have a tower or you would've run off long before this."

At the small flicker of a smile on her face, he hesitantly reached over to run his fingertip down her cheek. "Here all along I hoped I was your prince. Your knight in shining armor and maybe even your hero."

His expression uncertain, his words came out almost in a sigh. "I don't understand… what happened?"

She shook her head. "Oh Nicholas, I don't know. I…" She quickly closed her mouth, her bottom lip starting to tremble.

He viewed this with alarm. Dear God, he certainly didn't want her to start crying again. He reached for her hand and slowly began drawing small circles in her palm with his thumb.

He smiled when he saw her look down at their hands, almost in a trance. "Look at me, love."

She turned to him, her eyes deep pools of turquoise, shimmering with her tears. And, if possible, he found he was more in love with her than he'd been before, everything he wanted shining back at him in her eyes.

And this was when he knew he'd been right in bringing her here. And he was going to do everything he could to keep her here.

Everything…

His voice was soft, pleading. "Oh, Anna, I'm finding it so hard to accept we can't be together. I sincerely believe it's already been decided for us. Written out in the night sky, shining brightly in the stars. Please, trust me on this."

She blinked. Why did these words sound so familiar? The brightly shining stars? The night skies? She couldn't quite place them.

He brought her hand to his lips. "I want to make a deal with you. Any free time we have while you're here, I want to spend it with you, only you. And I promise to be on my best behavior. The entire time."

The expression on her face made him smile.

It was more than obvious she wasn't buying what he said.

He chuckled. "Okay, maybe I should rephrase that. How about I promise to give it my best shot? And it will be your call, you'll be the one in charge. Whatever you want. Do you think you can agree to this?"

Though what he was proposing sounded so simple, she knew it wasn't. The last thing she should do is spend time with him. But since they needed to get along, if only to get through this wedding maybe this deal of his might work?

She regarded him very seriously. "Just promise me you…" And this was as far as she got before his mouth captured hers in a kiss.

After a slow brush of his lips over hers, he waited for her to open her eyes before he gave her a guilty smile. "I, ah… I do believe I needed to get that out of my system. Consider it like a handshake on our deal. Which starts right now."

Anna was trying to recover from the kiss. It was obvious she had been wrong. This wasn't a good idea after all. Because the only thing she could think about was how much she wanted him to kiss her again.

Absolutely not. Put this completely out of your mind.

She frowned, turning to him. "Please don't…"

But he was already out of the car. And by the time he opened her door, he'd already decided he was going to ignore her request because it was a promise he wouldn't be able to keep. The kiss he gave her was proof of this

He took her hand. "Come on, let's go pick up those rings. Then I think this might be the perfect time to finish the Christmas shopping I've been putting off. I still have quite a few gifts to buy and seeing how you did such a good job with Clementine and Emily's, I thought maybe you could help me out again? We might even be able to fit in tea, a glass of wine or whatever else your heart desires. Sounds innocent enough, doesn't it?"

He was pleased to see this brought a genuine smile to her face. He was also very happy she was still holding his hand.

She gave him a sideways glance. "I'm beginning to think when you're involved, nothing is innocent."

He chuckled. *"Hmm…* I guess you'll have to hang around to see if there's any truth in that."

A mischievous twinkle appearing in his eyes, he pulled her against him in a quick hug.

"Or at least until I decide to unlock the gates and set you free."

CHAPTER 29

After Nicholas checked in with the kitchen staff to confirm the dinner plans were in order, he'd wandered over to the atrium, where both the wedding ceremony and reception were going to take place.

He shook his head in amazement as he gazed around the room, taking it all in. He had to hand it to Claire, she'd had outdone herself, transforming the space into a winter wedding wonderland.

Lights were twinkling everywhere. They were in the flocked pine trees scattered along the perimeter of the room and in the iridescent netting floating across the ceiling. White poinsettia plants were scattered among the trees, along with large gold and silver candles of varying heights. The rows of white satin covered chairs were lined up in front of an altar made from a trellis covered with ivy, pine boughs, frosted ornaments, white satin ribbon and of course, more lights.

Surrounded by the beauty and tranquility of the room, Nicholas was filled with a sudden longing, instead of Katy and Stephen, Anna and he would be the bride and groom standing under this trellis tomorrow, pledging their love to each other.

"So, what do you think?"

He turned to see this was coming from Claire. When she reached his side, to link her arm with his, he smiled at her. "Claire, this is absolutely brilliant. I owe you."

She studied him for a few moments before she gave him a teasing smile. "I'm glad you approve. And as you can see, I don't need much notice. So, keep this in mind in case you need to plan a wedding in the future. *Hmm... like maybe your own?*"

"Ah, Claire, who knows what lies ahead for me?" He drew her into a hug. "But I promise, if things change, you'll be the first to know."

She peered up at him. "Anna seems to be very nice, Nicky. The two of you are so perfect together. And I can see by the way you look at her, your heart in your eyes, you care for her very much. It's also quite obvious she feels the same about you."

"Claire, you've seen us together, for what? Five minutes?" His look incredulous, he laughed. "Believe me, Anna has me running in circles when it comes to knowing what she's thinking about me."

A baffled expression appeared on his face. "I never thought I'd fall so deeply in love with a woman who would be such a challenge."

Immediately realizing what he admitted out loud, he wanted to snatch it right back. But when he glanced over at Claire, her mouth dropped open in surprise, he knew the damage was done.

He'd just blurted out his feelings for Anna.

Again.

How was it, after he'd already declared his love for Anna to Stephen, here he was, revealing the same to his own sister?

What the hell was happening here? He'd never been one to share his feelings, or anything concerning his personal life. Never. Not with anyone. At least not until these last few weeks, he hadn't.

What next?

Good Lord, he wasn't becoming one of these love-sick blokes who rambles on about every detail of their love life to anyone who'd listen, was he? Or, an even more frightening thought, what if he professed this love for Anna to one of his parents? All hell would break loose if he did. God knows his mother would never be able to keep something like this to herself.

He observed the excited expression on Claire's face, the knowledge even if he tried to make light of what he said, she wouldn't believe him. She knew him too well.

He shook his head.

Admit it. It's actually a relief to say it out loud. You love her. Now, if you could only get her to realize she feels the same.

Her face one big smile, Claire threw her arms around him. "Nicky! Oh my gosh, I'm so happy for you!"

He held her away from him, slowly shaking his head. "Whoa… hold on. There are still quite a few things to be worked out. So, promise me this will remain between the two of us, okay? I don't want the rest of the family descending on her for information. This would send her running right out the door."

And, he thought with a smile, scrambling right up and over those iron gates she's so worried about.

Claire was smiling. It was a huge smile, in fact. "I'll make sure they behave." She reached up to pat his cheek. "But Nicholas, this is just so exciting! Might she stay for Christmas? If so, I'll need to get her a gift. And the girls! They'll be so excited! I was listening to their chatter this afternoon and heard them referring to Anna as Sleeping Beauty. How they came up with this, I have no idea."

Nicholas shot her a startled glance. Then he smiled. "You know their obsession with fairy tales. And please don't get ahead of yourself with plans for Christmas. Knowing Anna, the way I do, anything could happen between now and then. I don't want your hopes dashed."

Or yours … Christmas with Anna? Your mind can't even fathom that.

He suddenly wanted to be with her. If only to know she was still here. "Speaking of Anna, I need to go. Love you, Claire. And again, thank you."

After a quick kiss to her cheek, he left.

A smile on her face, Claire raised her fist in celebration.

She also made a mental note to buy a Christmas gift for Anna.

She had a good feeling about this.

CHAPTER 30

$\mathcal{A}$nna studied her reflection in the bathroom mirror.

The dress she'd chosen, a full-skirted and emerald green chiffon cocktail dress, shimmered in the light as she moved. Her hazel eyes, echoing the same shade of green, were sparkling. While her cheeks were still flushed from the cold winter air and the wine she'd shared with Nicholas.

Now she only needed to wait for Katy and Stephen to stop by so they could walk together over to where the rehearsal was being held. As she absent-mindedly ran a brush through her hair, her thoughts drifted to Nicholas and the afternoon they spent together.

He had been the perfect gentleman, just as he promised.

After they picked up the rings, they had embarked on what could only be described as a whirlwind of a shopping excursion. This involved selecting gifts for what seemed to be a very long list of Nicholas's family and friends. After the last purchase was made, with the promise everything would be wrapped and delivered by the end of the day, they decided to celebrate their hard work with a glass of wine.

They stopped at a cozy little wine bar where Nicholas did most of the talking, filling her in on details of the wedding and what she could expect from the members of his family who would be attending. Reluctant to leave, they finally made it back with just enough time to get ready for the rehearsal.

It had been the perfect afternoon. With the perfect man.

She sighed. How easily she could get used to having him in her life. It would be like the best of beginnings to the end of a fairy tale. And, as crazy as this sounded, this was exactly what she felt she was living right now.

Nothing felt real.

She, of all people, knew life wasn't made up of fairy tales.

No, life was about everything real, both the good and the bad. Nothing like this enchanted bubble she and Nicholas had become caught up in. Both of them living, what seemed like, their perfect dream.

There was a knock on her door. Assuming it was Katy and Stephen, she called out for them to enter. After one final check in the mirror, she walked into the room and twirled around. This sent her dress floating up into a cloud of shimmering green chiffon.

"So, what do you think? Is this the proper attire for a maid of honor?"

She stopped in mid twirl, her mouth dropping open in surprise. Because it wasn't Katy and Stephen who were now in her room.

It was Nicholas.

Nicholas was almost hypnotized by this vision of loveliness that was Anna.

His Anna.

Yes, his.

Because in this very moment he knew she was, and always would be, his.

His eyes never leaving her face, he swiftly covered the distance between them. Reaching for her hands, he brought them up to his lips to place a soft kiss in each palm. "*Ah ... o*nce again you've outdone yourself. You look stunning, love."

He smiled, unable to resist teasing her. "And you're definitely the most appropriately dressed maid of honor I've ever seen. Certainly, the only one I want to be with tonight."

And always.

As she began to straighten his tie, a ritual that had become so important to her, she suddenly stepped back and smiled up at him. "Wait… there's something I need to give you."

She left to search through her suitcase. When she returned, she was holding the tie he'd left in her condo.

He chuckled. "*Ah…* I wondered what happened to that. I thought I might have left it in my hotel room."

Her cheeks growing flushed, she stumbled over her words. "No, you left it in my condo that night. I… I guess I've been holding on to it. I wanted…" Her words trailing off, she looked down at the tie.

She was about to tell him the tie was the inspiration for the ornament she gave him. But what if he didn't even have ornament? Instead, he'd left it behind in the restaurant.

She pressed the tie in his hands. "I know I should have given it to you, but I couldn't, I mean… well, here it is."

When he saw the wistful expression on her face, he pulled off the tie he was wearing to replace it with the one she gave him. As he began to adjust it, she put her hands over his to stop him. "Please, let me do it for you."

Mesmerized by nearness, the heady scent of her perfume and the light touch of her fingers, it was a struggle not to pull her into his arms.

He closed his eyes.

Ah… why did you promise to be on your best behavior? Because it's not looking like a great idea right now, is it?

"Nicholas?"

At the sound of her voice, he opened his eyes.

She smiled up at him. "You're perfect."

So, so perfect.

The unmistakable look of longing he gave her was almost her undoing. And it was at this moment she realized she was up against something far more powerful than anything she'd ever experienced before in her life.

If this was a dream, she never wanted to wake up. If she was living a fairy tale, she wanted to keep turning the pages, holding on to the promise of a happily ever after.

She wanted this with Nicholas.

You want it all.

The thought of this making her almost dizzy, she stepped back, to almost stumble. He reached out to steady her, but she put her hands out to stop him. "Nicholas, you promised."

If he touched her now, she knew she would be lost.

Reaching out to run his fingers lightly down the side of her face, the groan he gave spoke volumes. "Oh sweetheart, I know I did. But you're making it so damn hard."

He reached for her hand. "I guess we should go. As much as I'd rather stay right here with you, we have a wedding to rehearse."

When Anna and Nicholas entered the atrium, a hush fell over the crowded room.

Amused, but not the least bit surprised, he tightened his hold on her hand. After all, he'd warned her this was exactly the kind of behavior she could expect from his family. But this close scrutiny still had to be pretty overwhelming.

It was obvious everyone was surprised, or maybe even more in shock, to see Nicholas in the company of a woman. That he was holding her hand was also raising eyebrows all around.

Even more mind boggling, she was a woman they knew absolutely nothing about. Who was she? She certainly didn't look familiar. How long had Nicholas known her? And why hadn't he mentioned she was obviously more than just the maid-of-honor in this wedding? At least to him, she was.

When the silence continued to grow, Nicholas glanced over at Claire, sending her a silent plea for help.

She bent down to whisper something to Emily and Clementine.

This sent them running over to envelope Anna in a big hug, almost knocking her over in the process. This broke the silence, the buzz of conversation and laughter again filling the room.

At the same time the girls began pulling Anna over to where most of Nicholas's family were gathered, a member of the catering staff came to him with a question. So, he waved the girls and Anna on, watching as she became swallowed up in their midst.

He frowned. Dear Lord, it was almost as if she'd been lured into their den, ready for the kill. He needed to get to her as soon as possible. If there was ever a knight-in-shining moment for him, this could very well be it.

He quickly dealt with the catering dilemma, but was once again pulled aside, this time by members of Katy and Stephen's families. So, by the time he was finally able to make his excuses and go to Anna, he was more than relieved to find his family was on their best behavior and Anna was holding her own.

In fact, she was deep in conversation with his mother, of all people.

He slipped behind Anna and rested his fingertips lightly on her waist. A tremor going through her at his touch, he impulsively pulled her closer. The urge to press his mouth to the sensitive place he remembered all so well, right below her ear, raced through him like fire.

But with his reputation on the line and everyone watching his every move, he settled for a quick kiss to the top of her head. And even though he tried to act very casual about this, the reaction this received, proved he'd fooled no one.

And how was his mother dealing with all of this?

She was eagerly taking it all in, a big smile on her face. Completely surprising him, she planted a big kiss to his cheek. This public show of affection was so far from her usually reserved behavior, he had every reason to be worried.

So, when she opened her mouth, he could only hold his breath and hope for the best.

"Nicholas, why haven't you told us about your delightful friend?

She was just telling us the story of how you met." After smiling warmly at Anna, her gaze slid back to him... and she winked.

Nicholas was flabbergasted.

Good Lord, did your mother really just wink at you? What next?

He glanced down at Anna, his mind scrambling for a response before his lips curved into a teasing smile. "Yes, I guess you could say she fell for me pretty hard. But I fell just as hard, if not more. So here we are... isn't this right, love?"

And now it was Anna who didn't know what to say.

Oh no...

She glanced around the group, Nicholas's mother's expectant expression the first to jump out at her. Even Emily and Clementine got caught up in the moment, their eye going wide as they watched the grown-ups

Oh no, no, no...

Desperately searching for something to say, she glanced down at Nicholas's hands on her waist. But knowing she wouldn't be able to give his family the answer they were looking for, she gently slipped from his hold. Her eyes pleading with him to understand, she turned to face the eager faces.

She shrugged. "Somehow Nicholas always manages to pick me up when I need help. Far too many times, I'm afraid."

She reached over to pat his cheek, smiling to soften her next words. "He's such a good friend to have. And always so charming. He's going to make some woman very happy one day."

After a slight hesitation, Nicholas reached for her hand, his tight grip the only sign of his disappointment. His voice was dry. "Ah, yes... one can never have enough charming friends, can one?"

She found she couldn't answer. The hurt in his eyes wouldn't let her. In fact, no one had anything to say. There was only a long silence as everyone tried to interpret this confusing exchange of words.

His mind in a turmoil, Nicholas gazed around at the group.

What just happened here? Good Lord, please don't let anyone come out and say some-thing really stupid.

He turned to Claire, sending her another plea for help. She

scanned the room before loudly clapping her hands for attention. "It looks like everyone has finally arrived. So, let's have everyone take a seat and we'll get this rehearsal underway."

As everyone reluctantly began take their seats as Claire had instructed, Anna seriously wondered if this might be a good time to make her exit. She'd just turn around and walk right out of the room. Even run, if need be. Whatever was needed to get as far away as possible from this uncomfortable situation she managed to create.

Iron gates and brick walls be damned.

Once again, she'd let her emotions take over. But this time she'd basically shot Nicholas down in front of his whole family.

What must they be thinking?

And Nicholas ... aren't you wondering what he's thinking?

She stole an anxious glance over at him. At the bewildered expression still on his face, she moved closer, her voice cracking with emotion. "Nicholas? I'm so sorry. I don't know why I said what I did. I think I panicked. I didn't want people to think... well, you know. And then the words came out before I could I stop them. I told you this wasn't ..."

His fingers were at her lips. "Ah, no, no ... Anna. Please, not another word."

Then he smiled, slowly shaking his head.

And even though he told her everything was fine, it wasn't.

Because the smile he gave her was not the smile she loved.

It wasn't real.

The warmth was gone.

CHAPTER 31

$\mathcal{N}$icholas leaned back in his chair, his gaze roaming over the guests seated around the long dining table. He was pleased to see everyone seemed to be having a good time.

Everyone except him, that is.

But then he really wasn't in a party frame of mind right now. Nor did he foresee this mood of his would be changing anytime soon.

He shook his head. Nope, this wasn't going to happen.

Not until he figured out what to do about this latest setback with Anna.

Ah... Anna.

His intriguing and so unpredictable Anna.

With Stephen and Katy seated between them during dinner, he hadn't been able to talk to Anna at all. Or, for God's sake, at least have the option of holding her hand. And this was something he really wanted to do after he'd so foolishly kept his distance from her during the rehearsal.

But give him a break. At the time, he had still been reeling from what she said, this taking place in front of almost everyone here, no less.

So, can you blame him?

But now, after more than enough time to think things over, he was regretting his behavior.

Damn.

He was seriously beginning to think he was losing his mind.

Yes, nothing seems to be making much sense, does it?

Fueling his frustration even further, it appeared Anna was having a wonderful time without him. From what little he'd been able to observe, she seemed to be enthralled with everything Katie's brother had to say. Seated next to each other during dinner, they had chatted almost the entire time.

He searched his memory, trying to remember the guy's name.

What was it? Kevin? *Ah, yes … Kevin.* An all-American athletic type of guy. From what Stephen told him, he was a baseball player and very close to making his debut in the big leagues.

His eyes narrowed, Nicholas studied him. Exactly how close was Anna to this Kevin? Should he be worried? Because it did seem as thought she enjoyed his company.

He frowned and reaching for his glass, he downed what was left of the wine. Immediately, a server was at his side to refill it.

Great, just great. Go ahead and get wasted. Maybe it will dull the pain of your bruised ego.

He leaned back in his chair, absently fingering the stem of his wine glass. Now what was he to do? Because, honestly? He was at a loss here. After Anna stunned him with her comment implying they were only friends, he was more confused than before.

He was beginning to wonder what the hell he was doing. Maybe he wasn't cut out for this relationship thing? There were those who went through life alone and seemed to be perfectly happy with their choice. Maybe he was destined to be one of these people?

He shook his head.

Nope. Definitely not for you. Not after Anna.

But he wasn't used to this feeling of uncertainty. This up and down roller coaster sensation that had him hopeful and on top of the world one moment. To then go plummeting into despair and confusion the next.

He groaned, the sudden urge to throw his head down and bang it on the table a couple of times. If only to knock some sense into it.

Good Lord, could he be more melodramatic? Was this what falling in love does to a person? And here all along, he thought women were the more emotional.

Well, let's hope years from now, you'll be able to look back and still see the humor in this.

But for now?

He was done.

Things needed to change.

Anna had reached her breaking point. She also appeared to have lost her appetite. Pushing the food around on her plate with her fork, she glanced around the table. The servers were now busily clearing the table, a sign the dinner was coming to an end.

Thank God.

Since her unfortunate outburst, the evening had passed in an agonizing blur. This was because, from that point on, Nicholas had acted like they were complete strangers.

During the rehearsal, he'd treated her with an almost polite indifference, only speaking to her when it was required of him.

She'd begun to worry.

During dinner, her one and only attempt to make eye contact with him had been met with a blank stare.

This had sent her worried state into a heightened sense of panic.

So now, as far as she was concerned, this dinner couldn't end soon enough. So, she could escape to her room. Where she could be alone.

And is this what you want? Really?

"Anna?" Kevin's voice broke into her thoughts. Startled, she smiled over at him. "I'm sorry, did you say something? I'd also like to apologize. I haven't been that great of a dinner partner tonight, have I?"

Though for her, he'd been perfect. Never at a loss for words, Kevin had been perfectly happy to carry the conversation.

He patted her on the shoulder before he rested his arm along the back of her chair. "It's okay. It's obvious you have something on your mind. But then you've always been the dreamer of our little group, haven't you?" He grinned, shaking his head. "I only asked how well you know Nicholas, our host and the best man?"

His question came at the exact moment a brief silence had fallen over the room, his words reaching out to everyone. And suddenly, it was as if they all wanted to know the answer to this. Almost as one, the members of Nicholas's family actually leaned forward in their seats, all conversations coming to a halt.

And once again, all eyes were on Anna. As she glanced around the table, her gaze fell on Nicholas, who appeared to be extremely irritated about something.

Uh oh, this can't be good.

Yes, Nicholas was very annoyed. From what he could see, this Kevin had had now moved closer to Anna, slipping his arm around her.

This was unacceptable.

Okay, so maybe his arm was only on the back of her chair, but he was still too close.

And now what the hell was he doing? Caressing her shoulder?

Evidently, he needed to know Anna was off limits. And if anyone was to inform him of this, Nicholas decided it might as well be him.

He loudly cleared his throat to get everyone's attention. Forcing a smile on his face, he gazed slowly around the table.

He nodded over at Kevin. "Well, Kevin… it is Kevin, right? I think I can answer your question." His deep drawl reached out to everyone in the room. "How well do I and Anna know each other? If you must know, it's only been for a short time. But we've become very close. After all, you don't spend a weekend with someone without getting to know that person quite intimately. So, in answer to your question, I'd have to say we know each other well… very well."

Abruptly, he shut his mouth.

My God, what are you doing? This isn't like you at all.

Where was this I'm-a-macho-kind-of-guy act coming from?

More importantly, what was he trying to prove?

What happened between Anna and him was too private and too special to be flaunted in front of everyone.

Good Lord... almost the whole Hanover clan, no less...

He slowly leaned back in his chair, running his hand through his hair. Unable to even imagine what Anna was thinking, he sent her a tentative glance.

Met with the stunned expression on her face, he slowly shook his head, his eyes pleading for forgiveness.

You need to fix this. And you need to fix it now.

His gaze held hers. "For me, it was the best weekend of my life. One I know I'll never, ever forget. I can only pray she feels the same."

Anna's first impluse was to run right out of the room. But locked in place by the message in Nicholas's eyes, she couldn't move.

To make things worse, the room had become deadly silent. But this was probably because no one really had any idea of what to say.

Yep, if ever the saying—you could hear a pin drop—would be applicable, this would be that moment.

Anna sent a desperate glance over at Katy. Zeroing in on Anna's unfinished dinner, she began babbling. "Anna! You hardly ate any of your dinner. You need to eat. Especially after you were so sick last week. And running around with all this wedding stuff ..."

Her nervous chatter trailed off in mid-sentence. Looking over at Anna, she shrugged.

Anna looked down at her plate.

Well, that certainly didn't help, did it? One minute it's implied you've seduced the host, the next you're being scolded like a child for not finishing your dinner. My God, Nicholas's family will be talking about this for years.

Nope, no one was ever going to forget this night. Certainly, not for a very, very long time.

Nicholas didn't even have to look to Claire for help. She was already on it. With a big smile pasted on her face, she shot up out of her chair.

"Coffee, after dinner drinks and desserts will now be served in the drawing room, everyone."

Nicholas tore his gaze from Anna long enough to respond to Claire. "You go on ahead. I'll stay here with Anna while she finishes eating."

He had a feeling Anna wasn't going to react very favorably to this suggestion. But he was determined to keep an eye on her. Having already watched her walk away from him twice, he wasn't going to let this happen again.

After he finished the wine in his glass in one swallow and pushed the empty glass away, his gaze returned to Anna.

She was still watching him, the expression on her face unreadable.

So, the only thing he could do was wait.

Anna's nerves were just about shot.

For the second time this evening, she'd become the center of an uncomfortable situation, all eyes on her. And she didn't like this one bit. She also wasn't sure how she felt about Nicholas making decisions for her. So, she should be very angry. Instead, she couldn't stop thinking about what he'd said for everyone to hear, the words dancing around in her head.

Claire came to rest her hand on Anna's shoulder. She gave her a nervous smile. "Anna, I'm sure Nicholas will take good care of you." She gave a furtive glance in his direction. "But if you need anything, please don't hesitate to let me know."

Her expression turned earnest. "Oh, Anna, Nicholas has always been protective and overly opinionated with the people he loves the most. And now you've come along, bringing out all these emotions he didn't even know he was capable of feeling. So, please, try to be patient with him."

After she gave Anna a hug, she began herding the few remaining guests out of the room. Anna had to smile when she saw her send a glaring look at Nicholas on her way out.

But then her smile faded.

She took a deep and calming breath.

She had a feeling she needed this for what was to come.

The room now empty of guests, Nicholas slowly moved around the table to sit next to Anna. A quick glance at her face confirmed she wasn't in a very welcoming mood.

At least not when it came to him.

There was no smile for him like the smile he saw her give Claire. Nope, if anything, she looked like she wanted to murder someone.

He sighed, wondering why it always came down to him being that someone.

After what you just did, you're surprised at this?

His uneasiness growing, he dragged his hand through his hair. Then he removed his jacket and tossed it over the back of the chair next to him.

He glanced over again at Anna.

She was still ignoring him.

Damn.

He ran his finger under his collar. It seemed to have become much tighter over the course of the evening. Wondering if it would help to loosen his tie and unbutton the top two buttons of his shirt, he decided to give it a try.

Ah ... much better.

But it didn't take away from the fact Anna was still refusing to look at him.

He opened his mouth to say something, but then closed it. Then he gazed up at the ceiling, shaking his head.

Dear God, you've definitely got your work cut out when it comes to fixing this.

The silence continued. Unable to take it anymore, he cleared his throat. "Anna?"

She looked up at him, a quick flash of anger in her eyes, something he was almost relieved to see. After all, this was an expression he'd seen more times than he wanted to count. Almost to the point he was used to it.

But he'd swear he also saw a glimpse of something else. Tenderness? Compassion?

Hopefully he wasn't imagining this.

Anna gave a long, exaggerated sigh. "Nicholas… how could you have shared something so personal? With everyone. Your family, our friends… good grief, just everyone. I can't even imagine what they must be thinking."

He leaned back in his chair, giving her a long look, a thoughtful look on his face.

Wait a minute here…

What about him? Had she already forgotten how she practically threw him under the bus with the comments she made to his family only a short while ago?

Good Lord, how had that made you look?

He shook his head. Not good. Not good at all. So, what he said in return had merely been his attempt to save face.

Surely, she could understand this?

He crossed his arms over his chest. "*Hmm* ... I guess you could say the words popped out before I could put a stop to them." He raised an eyebrow. "Sound at all familiar, sweetheart?"

She said nothing. But he'd swear he saw her mouth turn up in something resembling a smile. Which made him think there might be hope for him after all.

God, you hope so.

There was another long silence, with him now leaning forward in his chair in an attempt to get closer.

He gave a frustrated sigh. Why was it, he never felt he was close enough? So, he could pull her into his arms, the memory of how good it felt to have her curled up next to him so vivid in his mind.

Unfortunately, the still slightly angry expression on her face had him slightly hesitant of trying this.There was also that daft promise he'd made. The one about being on his best behavior.

Again, what had made him think this was a good idea? Because it wasn't. This was sure as hell proof of this.

He cleared his throat again. "I guess I was also a bit bothered with how Kevin was getting so familiar with you."

She sighed. "Oh, Nicholas, I've known Kevin since I was little. He's a good friend, that's all."

Nicholas gently cupped her chin in his hand, bringing her face close to his. "*Ah...* and we know how important it is to have a good friend around, don't we?"

There it was again, and this time he was sure.... it was another smile. Encouraged, he leaned in to just barely brush his mouth over hers, smiling when she swayed towards him, her lashes fluttering shut.

His next words came at her almost as soft as his kiss. "And is he also... what was it you told my family I was? Charming? Yes, I do believe this was the word you used. Charming. Is he also charming, Anna?"

Anna was having a hard time breathing, overwhelmed by his nearness. And his voice, she forgot how seductive it could be.

When she felt a nervous laugh coming on, she reached up to remove his hand from her chin.

Avoiding his gaze, her response was a breathy muddle of words. "Oh Nicholas, don't let that comment go to your head, because it isn't necessarily a compliment. And yes, Kevin is very charming. But again, he's only a friend. Certainly not my type at all."

He captured her hand and bringing it up to his lips, he placed a slow, openmouthed kiss to her wrist.

"*Hmm...* I see. So, tell me, Anna, where would this put you and me? Could I possibly be your type?"

As had become the norm, for Anna, everything began to spin out of control. She should still be at least a little upset with him, shouldn't she? But this simple kiss he gave her, on her wrist of all places, was making this very hard to do. If anything, she considered it a miracle she was still able to concentrate on what he was saying.

She wanted to melt right into him.

Instead, with a great deal of effort, she dragged her hand from his. Nervously licking her lips, her next words came out in a breathless rush. "No. You are not my type. My God, Nicholas, if you really want to know, I think the only thing we have in common is that we are good at driving each other crazy. You have me so I can't think straight. I say stupid things. I do stupid things. And sometimes I can't even catch my breath because you make me so angry."

She paused long enough to take a long, shaky breath. "So, in answer to your question, I'm pretty sure you are not the man for me. Definitely not when you make me feel like this."

For an split second they stared at each other before she quickly looked away.

Did any of what she just said even make sense?

At the amused expression on his face, she had a sinking feeling it didn't.

He leaned in to brush his lips over hers again. He knew he was pushing his luck, but he couldn't resist. When he was this close to her, all sense of reason eluded him. And from the impassioned speech she just gave him, he was pretty confident she was feeling the same.

"I see." He nodded, smiling. "Would you like to know what I think? I think you're in denial." An expression of surprise coming over his face, he leaned back in his chair and crossed his arms over his chest. "My goodness, could it be I'm actually right about something? What do you think, Anna?"

The mischievous glint in his eyes made it clear he was teasing. But all kidding aside, she needed to put an end to this conversation. Exactly how had it gone from her being rightfully angry to a discussion about how she felt about him? She didn't need a reminder of how she was feeling right now. And she certainly didn't need this to be coming from him.

She sent him a pleading look. "Nicholas, stop. Please..."

His gaze roamed over her flushed cheeks, ending at the pulse beating rapidly in her neck. And suddenly, it took everything he had to keep from pulling her into his arms.

He wanted this so *damn* much.

He closed his eyes, taking a deep breath. When he opened them, it was to find she was watching him. And she looked very worried.

Good Lord, you're beginning to scare her. Say something. You want to love her, not scare her to death.

He cleared his throat. "Ah sweetheart, I'm only trying to figure out why you're so intent on denying we would be so good together. Then maybe I would be able to understand your reasoning. That's all."

Unable to come up with an answer to this, she picked up her fork. Maybe if she started to eat, he would stop talking. Something she so desperately needed.

As she stared down at the now cold and unappealing food still on her plate, she was almost relieved when he reached over to take the fork out of her hand and set it on the table. Tucking her hair behind her ear, there was a concerned look on his face. "And what's this about you getting sick?"

Her gaze was on her plate as she answered. "I got chilled and it almost turned into pneumonia. But I'm okay now."

When he remained silent, she glanced over at him. He still looked worried. She sighed. "Oh, Nicholas … really, I'm fine. But this should prove to you what a disaster I am. Running into things, fainting spells, crazy ex-fiancé… and now you can add illness prone to the list."

She shrugged her shoulders. "And who knows what might happen next? I could drag you right down with me. So, it may be in your best interest to get as far away from me as possible. While you still can."

He tilted his head, his expression doubtful. *"Hmm…* let me think about this. You? A disaster? I don't see this." He adamantly shook his head. "Maybe it was a little rocky when we first met, as it wasn't the best of meetings. But it was a very memorable and unusual encounter, wouldn't you agree? Definitely a good story to pass on to future generations."

He reached for her hand, merely nodding at her startled reaction to what he said. Then his gaze slowly traveled over her before finally ending at her face, sending a shiver through her.

Anna was hopelessly trying to keep it together. She glanced down at their hands to see she was gripping his as though she was holding on for dear life.

Which, she realized, was exactly what she was doing.

His voice was so soft. She closed her eyes, letting his words flowing through her. "*Hmm...* and these many faults you're claiming? Nope, I don't see this." Here he gave a big sigh. "If anything, I would say you're absolutely perfect."

Then he laughed. Concerned, she opened her eyes to his grin. "Maybe there is one fault. And this is you can't seem to accept I'm your type. But I'm sure we can work on this."

He smiled at her. "And finally? You think I should go away?"

He shook his head in the negative before he brought her hand to his mouth, lightly brushing his lips over her knuckles.

"This isn't going to happen, sweetheart. So, don't get your hopes up. If I'm going to be 'dragged' anywhere, I've already decided I want this to be with you."

His fingers caressing hers, his expression became serious again. "When were you sick?"

She gave him a blank look. When was she sick? For the life of her, she couldn't remember. And this was probably because she'd finally reached her limit.

She was done. The only thing she wanted was to throw herself into his arms. In fact, she was trying so hard not to make any move at all, afraid if she did, she would do exactly that.

"Anna?" He reached over to run his fingertip down her cheek.

She blinked, the words tumbling out. "It was Monday. The day you were supposed to leave. After I left the restaurant I got caught in that snowstorm. When I finally made it home, I collapsed into bed. And this is all I remember. Marie and Louis took care of me over the next few days. They told me I was pretty ill."

His eyes searching her face, he seemed to have nothing to say. She shrugged her shoulders, giving him a hesitant smile.

He gave her one of his slow smiles in return.

Finally...

His smile.

It was back.

She closed her eyes, breathing a sigh of relief.

His voice was pulling her in. "Could this be why you didn't return my call?"

"No… Yes…" Anna shook her head. "Oh Nicholas, I don't know. Maybe?"

At his silence, she slowly opened her eyes. She could see by the look on his face, he already knew the answer. An answer she couldn't deny even if she tried.

Let's face it… you're lost… so, so lost.

Her reply came out in a whispery sigh. "Yes…"

He was now holding both of her hands as he leaned in closer, his response also a whisper. "I almost didn't get on that plane, Anna. I kept waiting. And hoping. I was so sure you would call. To let me know you had changed your mind and were on your way to me. *God, sweetheart…* I was a mess when I finally realized this wasn't going to happen. I felt like the bottom had dropped out of my world."

He bowed his head for a moment. Then he looked up at her before he exhaled a long drawn out breath. "It was by far the worst flight I ever took in my life."

Their eyes locked, they didn't move. Or even take a breath. Then everything suddenly became crystal clear, the tension and uncertainty swirling around them swept up in a sweet surrender. Leaving behind only their deepest feelings revealed in their eyes.

An unfamiliar threat of tears welling up in his eyes, Nicholas could see the same mirrored in hers. Emotion clogging his throat he waited.

Almost in a daze, Anna slowly let out the breath she was holding. Haltingly running her fingers in a feather-light touch down the side of his face, her words spilled out in an unsteady whisper.

"Nicholas… I'm so sorry. So, so, *so* sorry. I never wanted to hurt you. I didn't. I was so scared. I'm…"

Her words were swallowed up in his kiss. A kiss they held on to for as long as they could. His mouth brushing over hers, he gave a deep sigh. "Oh, love… it's okay. That's all in the past and you're here now."

The hint of unsteadiness in his voice was replaced with a sudden sureness. "We're meant to be together, love. And this is something that will never change. You just need to stop fighting it. Then you'll see how wonderful it is. And it's only going to get better."

Then he was kissing her again, a smile touching his lips when she leaned into the kiss with a whispering sigh, her hands moving up his arms to hold on.

Like she never planned to let go.

Finally...

"Anna? Nicholas? Are you two all right?"

The sound of Claire's voice, coming from behind them, shattered this spell they had fallen into. They glanced over at her, with not the foggiest idea of who she was or where s had even come from.

A smile lit up her face. "Well, I see you're both doing just fine."

She put her hand on Anna's shoulder. "I wanted to make sure you weren't being bullied by this man, Anna. Trust me, as his little sister I know how bossy and domineering he can be. Even so, there's not a thing I would change about him."

Then she turned to Nicholas, her hands going to her hips. "Unless it would be to curb your tendency to shake things up with your shocking remarks."

She shook her head. "Nicky… seriously? I can't believe what you said. At what, up until then, had been a flawlessly turned out and uneventful dinner party.",

She laughed, swatting him lightly on his arm. "You are so bad! Mum is all in a dither. You know how prim and proper she can be. Of course, it didn't help that Aunt Mary accused her of being a prude. Let's just say the conversation turned out to be quite interesting, if not a little overheated after that."

At the concerned look on Anna's face, she laughed. "Oh Anna, not to worry. You'll find out soon enough this family loves drama, the more scandalous, the better. If anything, you've given them something to talk about instead of their usual squabbling."

She gave each of them a kiss on the cheek. As she turned to leave, she was still smiling. "I'll see you both in the morning! I can't wait. It's going to be a beautiful wedding!"

After they watched Claire leave, Nicholas grabbed his jacket from the chair before he turned to Anna, holding out his hand. "Come, love… come with me."

Hand in hand, they walked out of the dining room. When she stole a quick glance up at him, she was met with another one of those heart-stopping smiles of his.

She wanted to stop right where they were. So she could go into his arms and ask him to kiss her. She didn't care that they were in the middle of the hallway. Or if all of his family suddenly gathered around to watch.

In fact, if they were out on the roof, with the whole city looking on, she just wouldn't care.

She just wanted him to kiss her.

Nicholas paused to glance into one of the rooms lining the hall-way. Finding it unoccupied, he put his hand to the small of her back and guided her inside.

They were in a library. Books covered every available space, over-filling the shelves that lined the walls, and reaching all the way up to the high ceiling. A well-worn burgundy leather sofa and two matching chairs were arranged in front of an ornate wood paneled fireplace, the mantle draped with evergreen branches tied with green and red plaid fabric bows.

With the scent of freshly cut pine perfuming the air and the mesmerizing glow of the crackling fire, the room was like an oasis of calm in the now hectic household.

After Nicholas closed the door behind them and tossed his jacket on the sofa, he took her hand to pull her over to one of the chairs. And just like the night of the Christmas party in Chicago, he sank into the chair, taking her with him. But this time, before she even had time to react, he cradled her face in his hands and covered her mouth in a deep hungry kiss. Just when she thought the kiss was about to end, he pulled her even closer, devouring her mouth in another breath-stealing kiss.

It was obvious he was making up for all the time they had been apart.

He finally rested his forehead against hers with a long, contented sigh. "*Ah* Anna… I've been waiting to kiss you like this from the very first moment I saw you today. I don't even want to think of how many times in the past few days I've sat in this very chair imagining this."

He gazed around the room before he pressed a kiss in her hair. "This room was where my grandfather spent so much of his time. I would sneak in here to be with him and we would talk, I'd do my homework or read books or whatever. I miss those days and still come here when I need to think things through. Or even just to bring a little peace and quiet into my life." He gazed down at her, a thoughtful look on his face. "I know he would have liked you. He once told me, whatever I did, I should find a woman who was spirited and would challenge me. Then my life would never be boring."

His eyes suddenly sparkling with humor, he smiled at her. "I have the feeling boredom will never be an issue when I'm with you. You've definitely proved this to be true so far, love."

Her answer was to give him a quick kiss to the corner of his mouth.

He pulled her closer, burying his face in her hair. "*God,* Anna… how I've missed you. I don't want to be away from you again."

"Nicholas …" The ever-lingering fear kicking in, a hint of panic sounded in her voice.

He quickly put his finger to her lips. "Shush. It's okay. For now, just let me hold you. We've already exchanged too many unintended words tonight and look what's happened. It seems our emotions have gotten the best of us."

She sighed and resting her head against the reassuring beat of his heart, her next words slipped out on their own accord. "I've missed you, too. So much. I wish … oh, how I wish we could stay like this forever."

Nicholas's heart skipped a beat. Did he hear right? Or was this only his imagination, what he so badly wanted to hear?

He smiled as he trailed his hand through her hair. "Well, I'm sure you've noticed there's plenty of room in this house, more than enough for just one person. And you don't seem to take up much space. Look how nicely you fit in this chair with me."

Anna's answer was only a slight shake of her head, his euphoria fading, frustration pushing its way in.

Damn. You should've known it was too good to be true. But remember, it's going to take time.

He continued to run his fingers through her hair, keeping his voice casual. "I bet one of these many rooms could easily be turned into a studio for you. A place for you to create ornaments or whatever else your heart desires. I would like this."

Her smile was wistful. "That would be wonderful. It's always been a dream of mine to have my own studio, but never would I have imagined it could be in such beautiful surroundings. How lucky you are to live here, Nicholas. With so much history. And even more memories."

He shrugged. "I suppose you're right, love. But now, it's only a house. I'd want it to be a home, one filled with family. With children laughing and running through the halls. Just like Claire and I did when we were small."

He smiled down at her, pressing a kiss in her hair. "Yes, so many family memories were made here. And now It's time to start making new ones."

As he said this, it came as a surprise to him how much he really wanted this. And this sudden yearning was all because of her.

She stirred in his arms, lifting her face to his. Caught up in his gaze, the smoldering look in his eyes had her breathless. "I… oh my, what are you thinking?"

Nicholas cleared his throat. She'd started to finger one of the buttons on his shirt, this simple act bringing every nerve in his body to attention. The last time she did this was the beginning of a night that changed his life forever. The night he had fallen so deeply in love with her.

And now she was here. In his arms and where she belonged. Her eyes pulling him in and her lips parted, waiting for his kiss. It was almost too much to take in.

Still running his fingers lightly through her hair, his voice was low and soft. "Sweetheart, my thoughts are only about you. How incredibly beautiful you are. And how you fit so perfectly here in my arms, leaving me almost dizzy from the intoxicating scent that is yours. And your eyes, love… how they draw me in with the hope I might see straight to your heart."

His fingers stilled, the deep timbre of his voice sending a tremor through her. "How I want to remove every bit of clothing hiding your beautiful body. So I can kiss every inch of you, from the top of your gorgeous head to your exquisite toes. Then we would make mad, passionate love, each time more amazing than the last. Here in my home and in my bed, love. It would be like it was the first time. But oh, so much sweeter this time around."

He eased her fingers from the button she was now gripping so tightly to raise her hand to his lips. After he placed a slow, hot kiss in her palm and folded her fingers over the kiss, he placed their hands together over his heart.

"And this, love, is what I'm thinking about. You. Loving you. Always and only you."

Anna had gone completely still. His words reaching deep, they had sent her heart beating so furiously she wondered if he could feel it pounding between them.

She closed her eyes. She didn't want to fight this anymore. It was too powerful, this connection between them. And now the next move was up to her. What he promised would only happen if she gave him a sign she wanted this as much as he did. Gently removing her hand from his, she slowly reached up to link her fingers behind his neck.

Nicholas tilted his head, holding her gaze. The frantic beat of her heart, almost an echo of his, was like music to his ears. And though it was taking every ounce of control he had, he waited.

He wanted the Anna who had given her love to him so freely that night in Chicago. He wanted all of her, heart, body and soul. He wanted this so badly, the aching need that filled him was overwhelming, almost to the point of pain.

With a whisper of a sigh, her lips traveled slowly up his neck before going on to brush over his mouth. She brought her hands to his shoulders, her plea as soft as her sigh.

"Oh, Nicholas ... just kiss me."

Gladly...

His hands tangling in her hair, he tilted her face to his. The kiss he gave her was deep, yet gentle. Sweet, but passionate. It was a kiss that was a promise of everything he'd just said. She melted against him, the kiss carrying her away to a place she never wanted to leave.

He cupped her chin in his hand. "Anna..."

Her lashes fluttered open to his smile. "Love, we can't stay here. I don't know if all of the spirits still lingering here after all these years can handle what I want with you. And more than anything, I want you in my bed."

A shudder ran through her. "*Oh, my God...* Nicholas..."

She was struggling here, trying to come back to earth. She wanted to tell him what he was doing to her. How when she was in his arms, nothing else mattered but him. He was her safe haven, his strength surrounding her to keep everything else at bay. His every kiss, each touch and every whisper reached deep into her heart, drawing her into him again and again.

But in the state she was in, words were elusive. So she framed his face in her hands, pressing soft, urgent kisses everywhere. Across his cheeks, his jaw, his forehead.

Just everywhere...

He buried his face in her hair, his response coming in a groan. "I know, sweetheart, I know. Let's..."

A sudden commotion out in the hallway was the only warning they had before the door flew open, Emily and Clementine bursting into the room.

In their pajamas and running at full speed, it was obvious neither of them had any intention of going to bed quite yet.

"Uncle Nicky! Uncle Nicky! Mummy is looking for you!"

His fingers reaching up to massage his forehead, Nicholas groaned. While Anna laughed, caught up in the girl's excitement.

From what she'd observed of the girls so far, Emily was the spokesperson and most outgoing of the two. While Clementine tended to be more serious and observant. She also seemed perfectly happy to let Emily take the lead.

Her hands on her hips, Clementine was closely studying Anna and Nicholas. Her eyes growing wide, a huge grin lit up her face. "Anna! Is Uncle Nicky telling you a story?"

Nicholas burst out laughing. Shaking her head, Anna placed her hand over his mouth just as Claire came into the room.

The girls immediately started dancing around her, clamoring for her attention. "Mummy, Uncle Nicky is telling Anna a story! Just like he does for us!"

After a quick glance over at Nicholas and Anna, Claire tried to hide her smile as she addressed the girls. "Yes, it does look that way, doesn't it? And I'm sure it's one of your Uncle Nicky's better stories."

She sent Nicholas and Anna an apologetic smile. "I'm so sorry we came barging in on you like this, but I've been trying to find you, Nicky. A Jack Duffy is here and waiting to see you in your office. He knows he doesn't have an appointment and it's late, but insists he has something important to tell you. Do you want to see him or should I tell him to come back another time?"

Nicholas stood, pulling Anna up with him. He gave Claire a brief nod, his expression unreadable. "No, I'll see him."

After he slipped into his jacket, he turned back to Anna. "When I get back, I'll finish the story I was telling you, love. I know you're looking forward to the ending." He gave her a boyish grin, following with a quick kiss.

He turned to Clementine and Emily. "Girls, I want you to take Anna back to your room. I bet you can convince her to read you a story. As soon as I can, I'll come to tuck you in." He winked. "Just promise me you won't let her run away."

After they gave him their solemn nods, he left the room. After smiling over at Claire, Anna held her hands out to the two girls.

"Since I don't know where your room is, you'll have to lead the way."

They left the room, Claire's comment meant for Anna alone. "Anna, I do believe you've completely bewitched my big brother. It's about time someone has. God bless you."

CHAPTER 32

*N*icholas was leaning against the door frame. His arms crossed, he was captivated by the scene in front of him.

Anna, sitting on the bed with Emily and Clementine cuddled up on either side of her, was reading aloud. No doubt it was a story all about a princess, her prince, castles and of course, a magic potion or two.

All three of them were so engrossed in the story they hadn't yet noticed his presence.

This was fine with him. He would be happy to stay right where he was, for as long as he could. He smiled.

This is what is missing in your life.

As he had told Anna earlier, he wanted this house to become a home. He wanted it to be like this vision in front of him, a safe haven from the hectic pace of the outside world. A home filled with laughter and bedtime stories. A place where love held everything together.

The sudden constricted feeling in his throat was such an unexpected surprise he had to close his eyes. And this is how he remained, lulled by the sound of Anna's voice as she read the last page of the book.

"The handsome prince pulled the beautiful princess up on his horse and

wrapped her in the shelter of his arms. With the moon and the stars guiding their way, they galloped down the winding road to his castle. Where they lived happily ever after. The end."

Anna closed the book with a flourish. She glanced down at both of the girls. She was pretty sure it was Clementine who was having a hard time keeping her eyes open. While Emily, still wide awake, was now bouncing on the bed.

Emily suddenly stilled, a serious expression on her face. As serious as a six-year old child could pull off, that is. She tilted her head and gazed over at Anna. "Anna, are you Uncle Nicky's Sleeping Beauty?"

Startled, Anna could only stare at her, while Clementine sat straight up, her eyes now wide open. Nicholas, still manning his post by the door, chuckled.

This should be interesting ... but quite the norm when it comes to these two.

After a huge yawn, Clementine rolled her eyes. "Of course. she is, Em." She looked over at Anna. "We asked Uncle Nicky why he didn't find someone to marry like daddy found mummy. He said when he found a Sleeping Beauty to wake up with a kiss, he would marry her."

Emily began bouncing up and down on the bed again, her voice high with excitement. "So be careful if you fall asleep, cuz if he wakes you up with a kiss, you'll have to marry him!"

Clementine gave Emily what could only be taken as an incredulous look. And once again she rolled her eyes. "But she would want to marry him, silly. Like mummy wanted to marry daddy."

Then she turned to Anna, her eyes wide. "You would, wouldn't you, Anna?" The tone of her voice was quite anxious.

Nicholas was almost holding his breath as he waited to see how Anna was going to answer this.

How was it this little duo of six-year-olds, whom he now thought of as extremely clever with their brilliant observations, had made everything seem so simple? According to them, a simple wake up kiss was all that was required to live happily ever after.

Ah... If only it was this easy.

With the girls waiting for her answer and overwhelmed with the direction the conversation was going, Anna began to gaze around the room as if the answer she was seeking might possibly be found there.

She found Nicholas instead.

Caught up in each other's gaze, they didn't move.

Nicholas, because he was still trying to rein in his emotions. Anna, because she was seriously beginning to wonder if she'd been caught up in a modern-day fairy tale. With Nicholas playing the part of the handsome and gallant prince.

Even Emily and Clementine remained silent, sensing something momentous was taking place.

It was Nicholas who finally broke the silence. Clearing his throat, he pushed away from the doorframe to make his way over to the bed. "It looks like I've arrived just in time, huh? Otherwise who knows what other secrets you two little scamps might've shared with Anna."

He studied them before he slowly shook his head. "Em, I know you may not be tired, but I can see Clemi is ready to drop. You both really need to go to sleep. We don't want two tired and crabby little girls moping around in these beautiful dresses tomorrow, do we?"

He gestured to the two sparkling tulle dresses hanging on the closet door, one red and one green. This brought a concerned look from Clementine and a somewhat apprehensive one from Emily.

He softened his next words with a smile. "Come on, let's get you both tucked in."

Anna watched as he settled both girls in their beds before planting an enthusiastic kiss to their foreheads and making them giggle.

Nicholas turned to her and held out his hand. After blowing a kiss to the girls, she slipped her hand in his and they left the room, Nicholas softly closing the door behind them.

The girl's explanation of what it meant to be Nicholas's Sleeping Beauty had completely thrown Anna off balance. The first time he referred to her as this was the morning she woke to find him in her condo. Had he been so sure of his feelings for her even back then?

Oh, no … this couldn't be possible. Why, they hardly knew each other then. And he certainly couldn't have been enamored by the way she treated him during that time. Good grief, only when she'd been passed out at his feet had he been free from her crazy behavior and wild accusations.

No, she certainly hadn't acted like a princess searching for her prince, let alone waiting for a kiss from one. If anything, she fell more into the category of a princess gone bad.

Horribly, terribly bad.

Just thinking about this, she suddenly longed to let him know how sorry she was. About everything.

She turned to him. And as their eyes met, she realized her apology would have to wait. Because right now, there was something she wanted even more.

She wanted him.

Nicholas was unsure of what his next move should be.

Was he surprised at this? Of course, he wasn't. Not with the way he'd handled everything up until now. But, as he had vowed at dinner, it was time for things to change.

My God, you just want time alone with her.

But the faint shadows under her eyes were a reminder she still hadn't completely recovered from her illness. So, his first concern should be she got a good night's sleep. But he wanted her with him and if this came to pass, something still looking highly unlikely right now, sleep was not at all what he had in mind.

Giving a frustrated sigh, he ran his hand through his hair. He needed to do the right thing.

At that moment Anna turned and their eyes met, the longing in hers so apparent, the decision was made for him. Scooping her up in his arms, he carried her the short distance down the hall to his suite of rooms.

Surprisingly, it appeared he'd made the right decision. Completely relaxed and her fingers linked behind his neck, she rested her head on his shoulder. She followed this with a long, sensuous sigh.

The sigh rocked him to the core, awakening the memory of the last time he'd carried her in his arms on that magical night they shared in Chicago. It was a memory too vivid for him to ignore.

Almost overcome by the strong wave of desire that engulfed him, he went striding into his suite, kicking the door closed behind him. Leaning back against the door, a deep groan escaped him right before his mouth came down on hers with a hunger almost out of his control. When he felt a deep tremor run through her, he pulled her roughly up against him, his kiss becoming more demanding, more urgent, this sudden deep need of his taking them both by surprise.

Almost completely thrown off balance by the intensity of this sudden show of passion, Anna could only hold on as she gave back all she had. Her body pressed to his, she struggled to keep up with the kiss, one that was more demanding than any they had shared up until now.

With this kiss, he was staking a claim on her, giving her the utmost reminder, she belonged to him.

It was a kiss proclaiming, together, they were one.

It was in somewhat of a daze Nicholas finally removed his mouth from hers. Reluctant to lose his hold on her, his hands guided her as she slowly slid down against him to the floor. Even with her feet on solid ground, she leaned into him. Her hands gripping his arms for support, she was almost lightheaded from the overwhelming force of what they just shared.

He held her against him and resting his head back against the door, he closed his eyes. With the frantic pounding of his heartbeat echoing in his ears, he gave a long, shaky breath in an attempt to slow his breathing.

Good Lord, where the hell had that come from? Never before in your life have you kissed anyone with such passion.

He slowly shook his head, once again amazed at how she was able to make him become so completely undone.

When he felt her start to push away from him, he swiftly reached out to pull her back. But her hands came up to stop him.

"Katy. I need to call Katy."

And, yes. These were the exact words to come tumbling out of her mouth.

What? Where did that come from? Oh God, he's going to think he's been right all along. You're crazy! Why else would you bring up Katy after he kissed you like he just did?

She gazed up at him, an expression of complete horror on her face. While Nicholas, his head tilted in confusion, struggled to understand.

Katy? What the hell? Why does she need to talk to Katy? And why now?

Her hands going to her forehead, Anna vigorously shook her head. "No, no... I'm sorry. I don't know where that came from. I didn't mean to say... Oh God, Nicholas, after that kiss I can't even..."

She closed her eyes, taking a deep breath. "It's just that it's Katy's last night. I mean since tomorrow... Oh, Nicholas, I'm sorry..." Her voice trailed off as her eyes met his, begging him to understand.

Nicholas continued to stare at her, the confused expression still on his face.

Then with a slight shake of his head, he reached out to pull her into his arms.

"Hush. It's okay, sweetheart. I understand. That kiss was... well, let's just say it was quite a surprise to me, too."

He rested his forehead against hers, running his hands gently up and down her arms until he felt her trembling begin to fade. He could still feel the frantic beat of her heart, but he smiled when he realized his was beating just as wildly, if not even more so.

His voice came out almost in a sigh. "But this is what you do to me, love. You have definitely put some kind of spell over me."

He traced her lips with his finger, a distracted smile on his lips. "But now tell me, what's this about Katy?"

Her hands drifting down his arms, she linked his fingers with hers. She suddenly found it impossible to let go.

"Oh Nicholas, it's just that I don't know if she wants me to spend the night with her tonight. The bride and groom are not supposed to see each other the night before the wedding. And Katy really believes in all of the traditions and superstitions about weddings. Since I haven't talked to her since dinner, I should check with her. As the maid…""

He cut her off in mid-sentence. "I know, I know. You take your role of maid-of-honor very seriously." His smile resigned, he pulled his phone out of his pocket. "Here, take my phone. I know you won't rest until you've talked to her."

While Anna was on the phone, Nicholas walked over to the fireplace, where he tried to stay busy, adding a few logs to the fire. He stared down at the flames, exhaling a long drawn out breath.

Dear God. Another interruption.

He thought once they were in the privacy of his rooms, they would be safely away from everyone.

He didn't think he was asking too much.

But evidently, he was.

Nope, they hadn't had a single moment to themselves.

Well, you did have that time in the car and look what you did there. Not one of your best moves, coming up with that ridiculous promise you made.

Again, he really didn't need to be reminded of this. He knew it was not one of his better decisions. But lately, when it came to bad moves, he was on a roll. Not something he wanted to think about.

He removed his jacket and tie and tossed them over the arm of the chair. His hands shoved in his trouser pockets, he stared into the fire. At least they made it this far. He should be thankful for this, right?

Now, he only needed to be patient

But he wasn't feeling very thankful.

And it was obvious he'd reached the end of his patience. Proof of this was the kiss he just gave her.

Good Lord, you're still reeling from that. And with the way things are going, you'll all but devour her when you finally get the chance to love her.

He sighed.

This certainly wasn't painting a very pretty picture, was it?

As usual, things weren't going as planned.

CHAPTER 33

Anna came up behind Nicholas, the scent of her perfume floating over him in an intoxicating cloud. Her arms encircling his waist and one hand holding his phone, she leaned against him.

"I thought you might like to read Katy's message."

Was that a smile he heard coming through in her words?

God, he hoped so.

He took the phone from her to read Anna's text first.

Katy, do you need me for anything? Do you want me to stay with you?

This was followed by Katy's reply.

No. Come to my room tomorrow morning around eight. I'm pretty sure there's someone else that needs you more right now. Oh Anna, be happy!

Nicholas closed his eyes in a silent prayer of thanks. He owed Katy big time for this.

He tossed the phone on the chair and turned to Anna, the vulnerability in her eyes so transparent he was filled with the sudden need to reassure her.

He pulled her into his arms. Resting his cheek in her hair, he held her close until he felt her begin to relax against him.

He leaned back to smile into her eyes. "So here we are... and we have the whole night ahead of us, just the two of us. No more interruptions. At least, I sincerely hope not." He paused to press a soft kiss to her forehead. "You know with us it's not just about tonight, don't you? And it's still your call, sweetheart. Whatever you'd like, whatever you say, I'm yours."

Her mouth curved into a small smile. "If I recall, you did make a promise to me."

A smile tweaked the corner of his mouth. "I did? *Hmm...* and what was this promise again? Refresh my mind.

The solid strength of his embrace, the caressing tone of his voice and the fact they were in his private suite had completely stole her ability to think, let alone speak. She could only gaze into his eyes.

His beautiful blue eyes...

He patiently waited, his eyes never leaving hers.

She finally found her voice. "A fairy tale... I mean a story. The rest of the story."

With a sigh, she placed her hands against his chest. "This is what I feel we're living right now. A fairy tale. Everything seems to be too good, too perfect. What if it all falls apart?"

At the anxious look in her eyes, he gathered her hands in his and placed them over his heart. "Feel my heartbeat. Feel how it's beating for only you, love. And you don't even need to ask, as it is already yours. And has been since the very first time I saw you."

She rested her cheek against their hands, his name coming out in a sigh. *"Nicholas..."*

His next words settled even deeper inside of her, touching her heart. "Yes, our love may seem like a fairy tale, but it's so much more. Because it's real. And it will never fall apart. Not as long as we're together."

Emboldened by this promise. she slowly began undoing the buttons of his shirt. "Oh, Nicholas, I've missed you. How I've missed us. So, so much."

He pressed the softest of kisses to her forehead, his voice a husky whisper. "Tell me, love. Tell me what you want."

She wanted the promise he was giving her with his eyes.

She wanted him…

Her hands going up to frame his face, her answer was shining in her eyes. "Oh, Nicholas… the magic. I want the magic back."

She pulled his head down for a kiss.

It was a kiss confirming everything he'd longed for was now his.

And this was all he needed.

His mouth never leaving hers, he unzipped her dress, sending it to the floor in a pool of fabric. He began moving them towards the bedroom, and with her help, they left a trail of clothing on the floor behind them.

All barriers removed he eased her onto the bed. His hands roamed over her, everywhere. His lips hovering over hers, his whisper came in a soft brush of breath against her mouth. "I'm finding it almost impossible to believe you're really here with me, love. My God, I feel like I've dreamt of this so many times, this could be just another dream."

Anna clasped her hands behind his neck. "Oh Nicholas, this can't be a dream. A dream couldn't possibly make us feel this way."

He buried his face in her shoulder, once again swept up in the intoxicating sensation of how it felt to be with her. He claimed her mouth with one hungry kiss after another, while his hands caressed every inch of her.

Just as he'd promised he would.

To be with Nicholas again was everything as Anna remembered.

Matching him kiss for kiss, as desperate for him as he was for her, she let him take her even beyond where they had gone before. He captured her heart, while at the same time he filled her soul.

And in that final moment, right before she fell apart, she knew she would always be his.

In a daze she opened her eyes to find he was gazing down at her. His expression almost one of awe, he claimed her mouth in another deep kiss.

This sent her soaring again, her hands reaching out to him.

She would always want more.

As long as it was with him.

Nicholas had been right. This time was so much sweeter. To be with her… here… now… never before had he felt so alive. And never before had he wanted anything as much as this moment with her.

The knowledge he was able to kindle such passion in her was overwhelming to him. And now, he only wanted to give her more.

He wanted to give her everything.

Holding her in his arms, he watched her lashes slowly flutter open. Their eyes locked and it was too much.

But this time, he took her with him.

After their long journey, they had finally made it home.

CHAPTER 34

The whisper of her name drifted into Anna's consciousness. Curled up against Nicholas, her mouth curved into a smile at the sound of his voice.

"Anna?"

There it was again. But she didn't want to move. Not yet.

No, she wanted to freeze this moment in time. So, they could stay as they were, wrapped up together in this cozy haven they had created, hidden from the rest of the world.

"Mmm…" Her hand drifting over his chest, she rubbed her face against his shoulder. She reveled in being able to touch every inch of him, his solid strength so achingly familiar.

It was like awakening from an incredible dream to find it wasn't a dream after all.

"Anna?"

She gazed up into his face, met with his expression of such tenderness. Unsure of how to deal with this sudden rush of emotions, she closed her eyes.

His response was to brush his mouth over her eyelids. "Open your eyes, love."

This time, when she opened her eyes, it was to his smile.

His voice was hushed, his words a soft vow. "Anna, I love you. I know I've already told you this, but I want to say it now that you're here with me. In my home, in my bed and in my arms. Every minute, every second I'm with you, I fall even more and more in love with you. I will always be here for you, love.

Knowing those three little words would not come easy to her, he wasn't expecting an answer. But when this finally happened, he knew she would be his. So, until then, he was more than willing to wait.

He smiled. He wasn't going anywhere.

If need be, he had the rest of his life to wait.

When he sensed she was struggling with a response, he pressed a slow kiss in her palm. "You don't need to say anything, love. I'm not looking for your promise right now. All I ask is you're here with me. Nothing more."

He rested their hands over his heart, a smile in his voice. "Except maybe a kiss now and then?"

She reached over to give him a quick kiss before she settled back against him with a long, contented sigh. He could see she was fighting a losing battle to keep her eyes open. The combination of jet lag, and what had turned out to be such a long and emotionally draining day, was taking its toll.

He sighed deep in response before he whispered in her hair. "Sleep, love. You'll be safe here with me."

With a smile on his face, he drifted into a dreamless sleep.

Anna opened her eyes, taking in her surroundings.

The past few hours she'd spent with Nicholas playing in her mind, she smiled. As her eyes adjusted to the dimness of the room, illuminated only by the flickering fire in the fireplace, she saw Nicholas was sprawled out in the chair, sound asleep.

She tossed aside the quilt and, picking up his shirt from the floor, she slipped into it as she crossed the room to kneel next to his chair.

She smiled.

He looked so relaxed and at peace, his hair all tousled and a small smile hovering on his lips. Hesitant to wake him, she remained silent, her gaze slowly traveling over him. And even though she tried not to stare, she decided her assessment of him had been right all along.

He was perfect.

Every single, amazing inch of him.

A shiver running through her, she lifted her head to see he was awake. His smile deepened before he reached for her hand to pull her into his lap.

"Anna." This came out in a long sigh as he nuzzled his face in her neck. Then he chuckled. "So, tell me, sweetheart. Did you find everything to your satisfaction?"

Oh, dear God.

Thank goodness, because of the dimness of the room, he couldn't possibly see the color flooding her face. Flustered, she stammered out a response. "Why yes, yes, I believe I'm quite happy with everything I've seen so far, thank you." She followed this with a dramatic sigh. "I missed you."

"*Ah...*" Thoughts of any further teasing forgotten, he pressed a kiss in her hair. "I'm sorry I wasn't there when you woke. It wasn't what I had planned."

She slipped her hand in his. "That's okay. Did I kick you out of bed?"

He laughed softly "*Ah...* I assure you, it would take more than a kick to get me out of a bed you're in, love. I added more wood to the fire and while I was waiting to make sure it was burning properly, I guess I dozed off."

He didn't tell her how he'd stayed where he was, for the longest time, his eyes wide open and staring into the fire. His fear was he would drift off to sleep and later awaken to find it was all a dream. She wasn't with him after all.

But he did fall asleep.

And she was still here.

His gaze settled on the shirt she was wearing. "And now look at you, looking so sexy in my shirt. I do believe you wear it so much better than I ever could." He slowly pushed the shirt down over her one shoulder, his lips brushing across her skin before they trailed up to whisper softly in her ear. "I will never be able to get enough of you. Never…"

This sent a tremor through her, almost as if her body was humming at his touch. Overcome by a sudden shyness, she hid her face in his shoulder.

"*Ah,* Anna…" He was smiling as he rested his cheek to the top of her head.

She abruptly pulled away to stand in front of him. Clutching the fabric of his shirt together for cover with one hand, she held out her other hand. "Come… come back to bed with me and make love to me again. Before the morning comes and everything gets crazy. Please?"

He stood, throwing out another one of those smiles that had her almost diving into his arms. She sighed, reaching up to wind her arms around his neck. "Oh God, Nicholas. When you smile at me like that, I'd do anything for you."

He leaned back, a thoughtful look on his face. "*Hmm…* I'll definitely have to hold on to this bit of information for future reference." He grinned. "I do seem to remember you telling me this exact same thing on a night not so long ago. Of course, at the time, the wine may have influenced what you said."

She sighed against him. "That was not one of my best nights. I can't believe you even wanted to see me again."

He chuckled at her embarrassment. "Ah, I knew a good thing when I saw it. But, be warned, as long as you're with me, these smiles will keep coming, sweetheart."

Relinquishing his hold on her, he began gathering up the quilt and pillows from the bed. After he spread them out on the floor in front of the fireplace, darn if he didn't throw another one of those smiles at her.

This had her wondering if she'd made a mistake, reminding him of what they did to her. Because it appeared he was already using this information to his advantage.

But this was completely forgotten when he pulled her down with him into the soft nest of bedding. Lost in the sensation of being completely surrounded by him, she eagerly welcomed the kisses he showered on her - across her cheeks, her eyelids and traveling along her jaw - before he finally ended with a gentle kiss to her mouth.

His expression almost shy, he gazed down at her. "I've always wanted to make love to a beautiful woman in front of the roaring fire of a fireplace." After sending a quick glance over at the barely flickering flames, he gave her a droll smile. "So, this one isn't exactly roaring, but it will do."

His voice dipped to a husky whisper. "Because I'm with a very, very beautiful woman. A woman I'm so deeply in love with, nothing, not even a dying fire, could ruin this moment for me." His eyes held hers. "I want for nothing but you, love."

And if what he said wasn't enough, he followed this with a deep, passionate kiss.

And once again, Anna was lost.

Completely and forever lost.

She could only gaze up at him, so swept away by the love shining in his eyes she was afraid she was going to cry.

Her hands drifting up his arms, she searched his face. "Nicholas, I…" Unable to go on, she closed her eyes.

His whisper was against her cheek. "It's okay, love. I understand."

Then he was gently pushing her down into the soft bedding, his hands and lips moving over her with a familiar touch.

He become the center of her world.

And the words gone unsaid?

It appears they really hadn't needed to be said after all.

CHAPTER 35

"*H*ey Sleeping Beauty, wake up."

These soft words were accompanied by a kiss. Followed by a second kiss before Anna's eyelashes slowly fluttered open to find those blue eyes gazing directly into hers.

Nicholas traced her lips with his finger. "Good morning."

She pressed a sleepy kiss to his finger before, closing her eyes, she sighed, burrowing her face in his shoulder.. "Please don't tell me it's already morning and time to get up."

He chuckled, pressing a kiss to the top of her head. "It depends on how much time you need before you have to meet up with Katy. I've already asked for breakfast to be set up in Katy's room for all of you. And I had all of your belongings from your room brought over here."

A startled look on her face, her lashes flew open. "Oh Nicholas, what are they going to think?"

"Who? The staff?" He laughed, his eyes smiling into hers. "They aren't going to think anything except that I want you here with me. Which is the absolute truth."

Seeing the skeptical expression on her face, he smiled. "Anna, I know what you're thinking. And believe me when I say you're the only woman I've had in this room and most definitely the only one to ever share my bed. In fact, I'd be willing to bet, far as my staff is concerned? A lot of high fives are being shared right now. With everyone in agreement it's about time. If I love you, they'll love you, too. It's that simple."

She shook her head. "But what if..." Pressing her face back against his shoulder, she grew silent.

Nicholas's jaw clenched. Here it was again, that roller coaster feeling. With this ride having made more than enough twists and turns.

Well, as far as he was concerned, it was time to get off. So he and Anna could start their life together, both their feet and hearts together on solid ground.

He exhaled a long, drawn out breath. "Let's just plan on getting through one day at a time, love. Starting with today, Stephen and Katy's wedding day."

As his fingers trailed lightly through her hair, he started thinking about all of the wedding festivities looming ahead. With everyone arriving in just a few hours, he and Anna really wouldn't have much time together.

Certainly not alone.

Why the hell didn't you take this into consideration when you set these plans in motion?

How nice it would be if they could forget about the wedding and stay right here in this room. He'd hang a 'Do Not Disturb' sign on the door, take Anna into his arms and, well... love her.

Until she was completely convinced she couldn't live without him.

A man could dream, couldn't he?

But seriously, was it really necessary he and Anna needed to be present for this wedding? They picked up the rings, wasn't this enough?

He groaned. He might as well accept it. The world wasn't going to cater to them alone. He glanced over at the clock on the bedside table. "Anna, you have a little over an hour."

She gave a sleepy stretch before she settled back against him. "I only need twenty minutes. Can I stay here with you until then?"

He closed his eyes.

Can she stay here with you?

There were so many things he could say in answer to this. Instead, he brought her hand to his mouth for a kiss before he placed their hands together over his heart.

He watched as a small smile settled on her face, her lashes slowly fluttering shut.

But now he was wide awake. This was because he couldn't stop thinking about what she said.

Let's just say he had responded. What would his answer have been?

He was damn sure he would have told her yes. Because he was counting on her spending the rest of her life doing exactly that.

Yes, he knew this was a little thing

But it was a start.

CHAPTER 36

Totally-crazy-and-out-of-control.

This was the only way to describe the scene greeting Anna when she walked into Katy's room. It reminded her of when she and Nicholas had first walked The American Girl Store, this a grown-up version of the same kind of chaos.

She was suddenly in the company of entirely too many women who were all trying to be heard. And unfortunately, this was happening all at the same time.

She made her way over to where Katy was having her hair styled. Once she was able to get her attention, Katy jumped up out of her chair and greeted her with a big hug. "Anna! Thank goodness you're here. Come on. Let's get out of here."

Taking Anna by the arm, she pulled her over to the door of the adjoining room. Waving off all the comments and questions yelled in her direction, she grabbed two Mimosas off the buffet table. After handing one to Anna, she shouted over to the hairdresser. "Do my mom's hair. Or take a break. Whatever. I need to talk to Anna."

Once they were in the other room, she locked the door. Leaning back against it, she let out a long sigh of relief. "Oh my God, Anna. It's been crazy like this for over an hour. Absolutely insane. I love my

298

family, I really do. But they have an opinion about everything. And this wedding has put them over the top. Right before you came, I told them everyone has to be out of the room by ten o'clock. No exceptions, no excuses. Then it will be just you and me. I can't wait."

She grinned, holding her glass out to Anna. "But enough of that. Let's toast to us. And to my wedding day!"

She threw herself on the bed, patting the space next to her. "Now tell me, what's going on with you and Nicholas. I want every single detail."

Anna joined Katy on the bed. "Oh Katy... I feel like I'm living a dream. Or I've stepped right into a modern-day fairy tale. With Nicholas as my prince, and here to wake me from the awful nightmare I've been living for the past year."

She began twisting her hands together. "But what if it isn't real? I think back to when I believed in Marc, to then have everything fall apart. So, I'm scared. More like terrified. So much so, that I can't give Nicholas what he wants to hear."

Katy was shaking her head. "Oh, Anna, it's so obvious Nicholas is madly in love with you. Even Stephen commented on this and he never notices these things. And, come on... after what he shared about the two of you last night at dinner? In front of everyone? How can you even doubt his love?"

When she saw the start of a smile on Anna's face, Katy pressed on. " Why, I'm a thousand percent positive the love you and Nicholas have for each other is more than enough to overcome any problems with Marc. You do love him, don't you?"

Anna's answer came out in almost a whisper. "I think I do. I only know I've never felt like this before. He makes me feel so, oh God, Katy, I don't know. I can't get enough of him. His kisses... Oh God, Katy, when he kisses me... Or he looks at me with those blue eyes of his... I'm lost. And when he gives me one of his smiles? I would do anything for him."

She shrugged, a wistful smile plying over her face. "But most of all, he makes me feel safe. With him, I know I can be me. I never thought I would find this with someone."

Wiping away a tear, she sent Katy a shaky smile. *"Oh, geeez...* here it's your wedding day and I'm ruining it. I never thought a person could cry so much, but I feel like this is all I've done over the past few weeks. I'm surprised Nicholas hasn't already taken off running. If only to get away from my dramatics."

Katy pulled a tissue from the box on the nightstand, nodding as she handed it to her. "I'm beginning to think we should buy stock in these. But Anna, be serious... you really think Nicholas is going to leave? Trust me, there's no way this is going to happen. In fact, I think it's time I finally show you something."

She hopped off the bed and began rummaging through her suitcase. She returned, holding in her hand the same photo she showed to Nicholas.

The photo that, if you stop to think about it, is responsible for this whole love story.

She handed it to Anna. "Remember this?"

Anna smiled as she gazed at the photo. "Yes, I remember that night. How happy we look."

Her hands clasped together, worry creased Katy's brow. "I've been waiting for the right moment to show you this. And I think this is it, even though you might want to kill me after I finish telling you what happened."

Ignoring Anna's anxious expression, her words came spilling out. "Do you remember when Stephen and I came here a few months ago for vacation? Well, one night when we were out with Nicholas, we started talking about our childhood and I showed this photo to Nicholas."

She looked at Anna, her expression almost one of awe. "Anna, I will never forget his reaction. It was as if he felt this immediate connection with you. And this was only from seeing the image of your face. A stunned look on his face, he said he wanted to meet you. No, it was more like he insisted he had to meet you. Period. Anna, he wouldn't let it go."

She nodded at Anna's look of disbelief. "So, we set a date for a cocktail party the next time he came to Chicago. This was so the two of you could meet. This was the same party you decided to pass out at his feet. For the second time in less than, what was it? Maybe twenty-four hours?"

She smiled. "So, something is going on here, Anna. I don't know what it is, but I think it's far greater than the both of you. Is it fate? Who knows? But whatever it is, I think you should take it seriously. It's obvious Nicholas already has."

Anna stared down at the photo.

She didn't know what to say.

Nervously waiting for Anna to say something, Katy sent her a timid smile. "Anna, are you okay? You're not mad at me, are you?"

Anna's smile was brilliant. "Oh, no… but I'm at a loss, finding this so unbelievable. But at the same time…" She brushed her fingertip over the photo, shaking her head. "Can I keep this?"

Relieved her part in all of this was finally out in the open, Katy's sigh was huge. "Of course, you can! But please, think carefully about what you decide. You and Nicholas can work this out, I know you can. To have someone love you as much as he does?" She sighed. "My goodness, Anna, it's like you've been given this amazing gift."

She jumped up off the bed. After taking a big gulp of her Mimosa. she grinned. "Yum. I know I shouldn't be drinking this with the baby and all. And I know I may sound sappy, but it is my wedding day. So, I'm pretty sure I'm allowed to act this way."

Clasping her hands over her heart, her expression turned serious. "Anna, Nicholas is offering you his heart. Take it and give him yours in return. Once you do, everything else will fall into place. I know it will. You just need to take the first step."

Anna slipped the photo in her pocket before she reached over to give her a hug. "Oh Katy, thank you. What would I do without you?"

Suddenly feeling almost deliriously happy, she laughed. "But enough about me! Come on, you're about to get married and we're going to make you the most beautiful bride ever!"

Finally, there was silence.

All of the relatives and friends had left, giving Katy and Anna sole possession of the room.

The glance Katy sent Anna was shy. "Well, what do you think? Do I look like a bride?"

Anna shook her head, her eyes going wide in an attempt to keep the tears from spilling over. When this didn't work, she grabbed a tissue. "Good grief, here I go again. This has got to stop."

She took a deep breath to steady her voice. "You look absolutely beautiful. Stephen is going to have a hard time keeping it together when he sees you. Oh Katy, I'm so happy for the both of you. And so grateful I get to share this day with you."

Brushing away the tear sliding down her cheek, Katy reached for the tissue Anna held out to her. "Please, stop. Or my makeup will be ruined before I even walk down the aisle."

She finally managed a smile. "There's no way I would be doing this without you. And I should be the one thanking you, for letting me wear this beautiful dress. I hope when you wear it, you'll be as happy as I am."

She grinned. "What am I saying? I know you will."

Anna only response was her smile as she began gathering up the items they would need to take with them for the ceremony.

At the soft knock on the door, thinking it was one of Katy's family members, Anna went over to open the door.

But, it wasn't.

It was Nicholas.

The look of tenderness on his face had her breath catching in her throat. Her grip tightening on the door handle, she gazed up at him, her heart in her eyes.

The first to move, Nicholas reached out brush her cheek with the back of his hand. "Hi, beautiful. Is it safe for me to come in for a minute?"

At her nod, he slipped into the room.

Her gaze sweeping over him, a smile lit up her face. He was

wearing the snowflake tie she brought to him. She moved closer, her fingers lightly skimming down over the tie before she reached for his hands.

She gazed up into his eyes. "Oh Nicholas... you're more than perfect."

So much more...

His gaze was more thorough, slowly sweeping from the flowers pinned in her hair to her rhinestone-embellished high heeled sandals.

He smiled as he put his finger under her chin, lifting her face to his. "And you, my love, look even more beautiful than the last time I saw you in this dress. It will indeed be an honor to be your partner for this wedding today."

And for the rest of your life...

Yearning for his touch, she moved closer, her hands drifting up his arms. He pulled her against him, resting his forehead to hers.

At the sound of Katy clearing her throat, Nicholas made his way over to her, taking Anna with him. Slowly shaking his head, he smiled. "My God, Katy, you look stunning. Stephen is going to be blown away when he sees you. He's a lucky man."

He pressed a kiss in Anna's hair, to then give Katy a sheepish grin. "Do you mind if I steal your maid-of-honor for a few minutes? Let's just say there's a sort of best man and maid-of-honor thing we need to talk about."

Katy smiled, while shaking her head at the same time. "Nicholas, you're such a charmer. I was just telling Anna how lucky she is to have you. Of course, you can whisk her off for a bit. I'm pretty sure everyone is gone from the room next door."

Once the door to the room was closed behind them, Nicholas swept Anna into his arms, claiming her mouth in a deep kiss.

He rested his forehead against hers. "My God, Anna. What have you done to me? We've only been apart for a short time and already how much I've missed you."

She gave a soft little sigh. "I know. I've missed you, too."

And just like every other time she gave one of those little sighs of hers, he could only stare at her, his mind having gone completely blank. His mouth then curving into a smile, he put his hands on her shoulders to turn her around.

She was curious. "Nicholas?"

She could hear a smile in his answer. "Just hold on for a second, love."

His fingers grazed the back of her neck as he fastened the clasp of a necklace. She turned to smile at him before she hurried over to the mirror to see it was a delicate sterling silver chain with a snowflake pendant.

But it wasn't an ordinary snowflake. No, this snowflake was covered in diamonds. As brilliant as the stars in a clear night sky, they sent flashes of light in every direction, with her every move.

When Nicholas came from behind to wrap his arms around her, she leaned back against him and smiled up into his face. "Thank you. It's so beautiful."

His lips brushed her cheek. "I got it for you when I was in Chicago. I wanted to give you something that would bring only good memories of the weekend we shared."

He swallowed, his voice rough. "I hope you wear it forever, love. I was beginning to wonder if I would even get the chance to give it to you."

She turned in his arms and leaning against him, her eyes searched his. "I will treasure it forever. But Nicholas, I don't need anything to bring back memories of that weekend. I'll always remember how wonderful it was."

She pressed the lightest of kisses to his mouth. "Because I was with you. And because of you, it was magic."

He closed his eyes as he held her against him.

Magic?

Ah… it was so much more than magic. And he wanted to be the one to show her this.

Forever, if he could…

Anna reached up to stroke his cheek lightly with her fingertips.

Her voice was hushed. "I better get back to Katy. And you should be with Stephen, no?"

After one more kiss, he turned to leave. But as he started to open the door, he was surprised to find she'd come to stand beside him. She took his hand and after placing a kiss to his palm, she folded his fingers over the kiss. Exactly like the kisses he gave her all those times before.

She gazed up at him, her bottom lip slightly quivering. "I believe it's your turn to hold on to a kiss from me." Then she gave him an impish grin. "I believe you've more than earned it!"

He chuckled as he reached out to run his fingertips down her cheek in a caress. "*Ah*, maybe I've finally got it right?"

When she nodded, the look he gave her was one of such love, it filled her completely, body, heart and soul. And she went right back into his arms.

He framed her face in his hands and gazed deeply into her eyes. "I will hold on to it forever."

After one more kiss, he was gone.

CHAPTER 37

*G*ood grief, what was wrong with her?

Anna squeezed her eyes shut and took a deep breath. You would think she was the one who was getting married. Halfway through the ceremony, her hands were still shaking, the bouquet she was holding quivering as if it had a life of its own.

This was all because of Nicholas. It just wasn't fair he was looking so amazingly handsome, his light grey suit making his eyes an even more incredible shade of blue.

Every time she glanced over at him, which was happening more times than she wanted to count, his eyes were right there to meet hers. This was invariably followed by one of those killer smiles of his.

Which meant she became completely undone.

Again… and again… and then again.

How could she even have a chance of keeping it together with those two things coming at her? And almost at the same time?

She couldn't.

It just wasn't possible.

For heaven's sake, get a hold of yourself. Or you'll give everyone even more to talk about. His family already doesn't know what to think of you. Let's not make it any worse.

She knew most of Nicholas's family, the number in attendance now suspiciously having grown in number since last night, were watching her with a great deal of interest. After the rehearsal and the dinner last night, this was understandable. After all, she certainly hadn't made a very good impression during that time.

But, suddenly this all seemed so unimportant.

Because honestly? There was only one person whose opinion mattered.

This would be the same person who'd managed to turn her world upside down by completely capturing her heart.

Nicholas...

She glanced over at him… and their eyes met.

She gave him a brilliant smile.

Nicholas was now a firm believer in the magical power of fairy tales. How else would you explain what was happening to him? He was bewitched, this had to be what it was.

Yes, whatever spell Anna has cast over you, it's worked. Big time.

When he told her earlier her how beautiful she looked, he meant every word. In fact, this was all he was able to think about.

He wanted to be able to touch her. He wanted to kiss her. He wanted to whisper sweet nothings to her. He wanted all of this, if only to let her know how much he loved her.

So, even though they were only inches apart, these inches were more like miles, as none of what he wanted was a possibility right now. Certainly not while they were in full view of everyone in the room.

Which, by the way, was something he found quite puzzling. Had they really invited all of these people? He was beginning to suspect his mother had something to do with this sudden increase of guests.

In an effort to get his mind back on the ceremony, he took a deep breath and bowed his head. His gaze went right to his fingers. They were pressed into his palm as though they were still holding on to the kiss Anna had placed there.

He smiled, a big, goofy smile.

It was official… he'd definitely gone off the deep end.

Just don't do anything stupid. Like kissing the maid of honor right here in the middle of the ceremony.

Hmm… this was a thought. He was tempted. But there was something he'd like even more.

He wanted what he had with Anna to be permanent.

And he was starting to feel hopeful she was feeling the same. There had been a change in her this morning. A new softness in her gaze. A deeper longing in her voice.

But he wasn't going to push it. More than anything, he wanted her to commit to him on her own.

He glanced over at her to be met with a brilliant smile.

Good Lord, he was a complete goner.

Katy and Stephen were about to exchange their vows. As they'd rehearsed, Nicholas moved to stand next to Anna. He reached for her hand, an option definitely not up for discussion during the rehearsal, but now feeling very right to him. When he felt her fingers trembling, he slowly began tracing small circles in her palm with his thumb.

And she slowly began to relax.

They both listened as Katy and Stephen recited their vows, the love they had for each other shining radiantly in their faces for everyone to see. It was when Nicholas stepped forward to hand over the rings, a tear slowly began to trickle down Anna's cheek.

She began blinking furiously.

But these tears are to be expected, right? After all it's your best friend who's getting married. And you are the maid-of-honor.

Noting the tears, Nicholas reached into his jacket pocket for his handkerchief. As he went to hand it to her, he stopped.

Oh, what the Hell…

He gently wiped away the tears with the handkerchief before he tucked it into her hand. When she smiled up at him, leaning into him, he put his arm around her and rested his cheek in her hair.

Once again, not the usual protocol for the best man and maid-of-honor during the ceremony. But, if you stop to think about this, with them, when had anything been at all normal?

This was also the exact moment Nicholas came to the decision he'd had enough.

He was done with waiting...

Done with guessing...

Done with thinking...

It was time.

As if on cue, music began to fill the room as an announcement was made. "With the authority invested in me, I present to you, the new Mr. and Mrs. Stephen Burns. Stephen? Let's have a kiss for your beautiful bride."

Stephen pulled Katy in for a crowd-pleasing kiss before he scooped her up in his arms. Flashing a huge grin, he sauntered down the aisle with her hanging on for dear life. She was waving her bouquet in celebration, a radiant smile on her face.

Anna and Nicholas followed right behind. But their smiles were only for each other.

And he was still holding her hand.

With the waiters now making their rounds with trays of tempting appetizers and the bar all set up and ready to take orders, the receiving line had dwindled down to only a few stragglers.

Anna decided this was her chance to find a place where she could be alone, if only for just a few minutes. Where there were no crowds and no noise. No new people to meet, names to remember and no more speculating looks. A quiet place where she could take some time to think clearly about everything.

She laughed aloud.

She had to be kidding, right? She'd completely lost her ability to think, let alone clearly, since the very first time she let herself get caught up in Nicholas's eyes. He'd completely swept her off her feet. And she hadn't come back down to earth since.

She was tired of fighting with herself. She was also beginning to wonder why she was trying so hard to resist what she wanted so badly. It was obvious her heart had already made its feelings very clear. So why couldn't she do the same?

Since Nicholas still hadn't returned, having excused himself to take a phone call, Anna began wandering down the hall. She came upon a towering Christmas tree on display. Every branch completely covered with ornaments and lights, it was absolutely breathtaking.

As she gazed up at the tree, her breath suddenly caught in her throat.

It couldn't be...

She blinked.

But it was.

The ornament she'd given Nicholas in the restaurant on that terrible day in Chicago was hanging almost in front of her, centered right in the middle of the tree. She moved closer, hesitantly reaching up to see if she could touch it. If only as proof it was really there.

Please, oh please... don't let this be a figment of your imagination.

"Be careful there, young lady. Most of those ornaments are very fragile. Why, some are much older than I am, if you can imagine this being possible."

This sharp voice coming from behind her was so unexpected, she immediately jerked her hand back to her side. She whirled around to find an elderly woman behind her, leaning on the support of her cane.

The woman haltingly moved closer to peer into Anna's face, her eyes magnified through the thick glasses she wore. After a thorough inspection, her face lit up in recognition. "*Ah...* you're the bridesmaid my nephew was so besotted with during the ceremony. Do you remember me from last night? I'm Aunt Mary. As crotchety and meddling as they come. I'm sure anyone in the family would jump at the chance to confirm this."

Not wanting to be rude, and not sure how to respond, Anna gave her a tentative smile.

"You'll do." She grinned. "Though, I must say, after I saw the way Nicholas looks at you, I don't think anything I'd have to say would matter. I was ready to bet my latest winnings at the track he was going to kiss you right there in front of everyone during the ceremony."

Her laugh was deep and boisterous. "So, I guess I would've lost that bet. But it won't stop me from betting on him in the future, as everyone knows when a Hanover goes after something, it's a sure bet it's theirs for the taking. The competition simply doesn't stand a chance."

She winked, gently nudging Anna with her cane. "And from what I've seen so far, it looks like you're the one our Nicholas wants. Which means you must be pretty special."

She shook her head. "Up until now, he hasn't shown any interest in settling down, no matter how many women have tried to snare him."

Her expression abruptly changed, another nudge of her cane coming at Anna. "I certainly hope you feel the same way about him, my dear."

Anna smiled, deciding it might be best to change the subject. "Nicholas is very special to me, too. And yes, I do remember you from last night. My name is Anna, by the way."

She gestured to the tree. "I was admiring this tree. It's so beautifully decorated, the ornaments all so unique."

Her attention going to the tree, Aunt Mary waved her cane about in a large arc. When it swiped one of the branches, Anna tried to hide her smile as she quickly reached out to steady as many of the wildly swinging ornaments as she could.

Completely oblivious to this, Aunt Mary continued to wave her cane about as she spoke. "Ah yes, each ornament on this tree is special, some over a hundred years old or more. And each has a story to tell. I guess you could say it's the family tree of our Christmas past."

She pointed her cane right at the ornament Anna had made. "I see there's a new one. So pretty. I wonder what the story is on this one."

A story...

Anna smiled as she gazed up at the tree. Wouldn't it be wonderfulif her ornament continued to hang on this tree and in this very room for years to come? Becoming part of a story shared by family and friends every Christmas?

It would be a story about you and Nicholas. A story about love. A fairy tale kind of love.

As she continued to gaze up at the tree, she knew this is what she wanted.

And she wanted to be here with Nicholas to see this happen.

Admit it. You are in love with him, so very much in love with him.

This sudden revelation was so unexpected, it almost took her breath away.

How could she have been so blind? This love she'd been trying so hard to deny had been a part of her since the first time she gazed into his eyes. Or heard his voice. Or when he gave her one of his smiles. She could go on and on and on …

And it was always going to be with her, with each and every single beat of her heart.

He was her everything. Her home, her haven and her place in this world.

Hadn't Nicholas been the one to tell her their fate had already been decided? They were destined to be together, he'd told her. This message spelled out in the stars shining in the night skies?

Who are you to argue with this?

A calmness settling over her, she smiled. And as the smile began to grow, she could feel it settle with a long sigh of relief deep inside her heart.

Nicholas... you need to find him so you can tell him this.

As she turned to tell his Aunt Mary this, someone called out her name.

It was Katy's brother, Kevin. Sprinting towards them, he waved.

"Hey, Anna… wait up!"

CHAPTER 38

Kevin came to stand next to them, out of breath and a serious expression on his face.

Anna eyed him curiously. "Kevin, is everything all right?" When he seemed reluctant to answer her, she turned to Nicholas's aunt. "Aunt Mary, this is Kevin. He's the bride's brother."

Giving her a quick smile, Kevin shook Aunt Mary's hand. "It's so nice to meet you. I can't tell you how grateful we are for your family's hospitality. Everything has been amazing. But now I wonder if I could steal Anna away? I really need to talk to her."

Before he even received a response, he took Anna's arm to lead her down the hall. Leaving behind a very confused Aunt Mary.

Anna glared at him. "Kevin, what are you doing? That was so rude!"

Without responding, he led her to a more deserted area of the hallway. He turned, and tightly grasping both of her hands, now even more seriou

Anna peered more closely at him. This wasn't the Kevin she knew. "Kevin, you're scaring me. Tell me what's going on."

"Anna, I'm sorry. It wasn't my intention to be rude. This is about Marc. I just heard from a very reliable source he was in an accident yesterday. From what I was told, he was drinking and got involved in another one of his stupid fights before he took off in that sports car of his. He was driving at a high rate of speed and lost control, crashing head on into an embankment."

He tightened his grip. "Anna, his injuries were so severe, he didn't have a chance. He died a few hours ago."

The color slowly began to drain from her face. Afraid she was going to pass out, he tightened his grip on her. "Oh Anna, I know this is terrible news. But I think we all expected something like this might happen. I guess we should be thankful no one else was with him." He searched her face. "You won't have to live your life in fear anymore. Marc will never be able to threaten you again."

When she didn't respond, he led her over to one of the chairs lining the hallway. But even when she was seated, she continued to stare at him, a dazed expression on her face.

This was when he became very worried. "*Damn*... maybe I shouldn't have told you this now. But Anna, it's going to be all right, really it is."

She closed her eyes, slowly shaking her head,

Kevin tried to think. Water. He would get her a glass of water. This was what people usually did in these kinds of situations, wasn't it? Yes, this is what he should do.

He nervously ran his hand through his hair. "I'm going to get you a glass of water. I promise I'll be back as quickly as I can."

He gave her one more worried look. "Stay right here."

Still in shock, Anna watched him leave.

Marc was gone?

Where was Anna?

Nicholas wandered down the hall, a troubled expression on his face, He was couldn't understand where Anna could have gone. He'd checked every room he passed and found no sign of her. So, he was now on his way back to the atrium.

This was when he saw Kevin come flying around the corner.

He called out to him. "Kevin! Have you seen Anna? I can't seem to find her. My Aunt Mary just told me she was having a conversation with her when a handsome young man came along and spirited her away."

He chuckled. "Let me guess. This young man is you?" His amusement made way for concern when he noticed the worried expression on Kevin's face. He grabbed his arm. "What's wrong?"

Kevin groaned, running his hand over his face. "Oh man, I think I've gone about things all wrong."

Nicholas remained completely silent while Kevin told him what happened. He'd already been notified about the accident when Jack Duffy, the private detective he'd hired to keep an eye on Marc, came to the house last night. Since Marc's condition at the time was still listed as critical, Nicholas decided to wait for a further update.

Shortly after the ceremony this morning, he received the call Marc had succumbed to his injuries. Since then he had been trying to determine when and how he should give Anna this news.

Well, it looks like you no longer need to worry about this. But what will this do to her?

Kevin was still visibly upset. "Hell, Nicholas, I'm sorry. I guess I thought it would be good news for her. Evidently, I was wrong, as she appeared to go into a state of shock. I found her a place to sit right outside of the library. I was on my way to get her a glass of water."

Now his concern only for Anna, Nicholas gave Kevin a quick pat on the shoulder. "It's okay, you meant well. But let me take care of her now, okay?"

With Kevin staring after him, he went striding down the hall to find the area where Kevin had left Anna was now deserted. Becoming concerned, he broke into a run, heading back towards the atrium. Maybe she'd gone there looking for him?

His mother was chatting with a group of Katy's relatives right outside of the atrium. As he passed by, she called out, stopping him in his tracks.

"Nicholas, stop running! My goodness, what will people think? If you're looking for your Anna, we saw her go out the French doors to the patio. Maybe she needed fresh air, but she's going to freeze without a coat. Why, we just noticed it's beginning to snow."

He turned to head in that direction, but then swiveled back to remove the cashmere shawl his mother had draped over her shoulders. "I am going to borrow this, okay? Thanks." After pressing a quick kiss to her cheek, he was off and running before she even had a chance to respond.

She stared after him for a few moments before she slowly began to smile. He might beg to differ with this, but as his mother, she knew him better than anyone.

And from what she could see, he was acting like a man in love.

Deeply and madly in love …

CHAPTER 39

$\mathcal{A}$nna was having a hard time believing what Kevin told her was true.

Marc was gone?

Images of him began to fill her mind. But they weren't of the Marc the last time she saw him. No, these were how she remembered him when they had first met and before they became engaged.

He had been so different then... so happy, so handsome and so full of life. Attentive to her every need, he'd treated her like she was the most important person in his life. He promised to love her forever and together they had made so many plans for the future.

But then everything began to spiral so horribly out of control. He became moody and secretive, responding with only sarcasm or in anger when she tried to talk to him. His drinking increased, his behavior becoming so volatile, she was terrified to be around him.

When she ended their engagement, he refused to let it go. She didn't think it was because he still loved her. No, what he felt then couldn't have been love. Certainly not like the love she so desperately tried to give him.

And now he had finally taken one too many chances, this last one costing him his life.

She slowly rose to her feet. She needed find a place away from the curious glances of the guests as they passed by.

She came to a set of French doors that opened to the patio with the gazebo. She opened them and slipped outside.

The cold hit her instantly, shocking her senses. Almost in a daze, she watched as big, fluffy snowflakes began to drift lazily down from the sky, landing on her bare arms and shoulders.

She started to shiver. Wrapping her arms around herself for warmth, she made her way over to stand in the shelter of the gazebo.

Her head bowed and her eyes closed, she said a prayer for the Marc she used to know, her only hope he was now more at peace than he had been in the last months of his life.

This was when she heard her name coming in almost a whisper. By the one person, who right now, she wanted and needed the most.

Nicholas...

Not wanting to frighten her, Nicholas softly called out her name as he walked up behind her.

His plan had been to take her into his arms. But when she whirled around to face him and he saw the haunted look on her face, he gently draped his mother's shawl over her shoulders instead. He reached for her hands, cradling them in his.

His voice was soft as he gazed directly into her eyes. "Anna, Kevin told me he gave you the news about Marc."

She gave him a slow nod, her eyes searching his face.

His heart aching for her, he gripped her hands even tighter, hoping she would be able to draw strength from this. Again, his voice was soft. "Sweetheart, what happened to him has nothing to do with you."

Her face suddenly crumpled and she began to cry, big gulping sobs. "Oh Nicholas, I didn't want him to die. I really didn't. I just wanted him to leave me alone. He wasn't always such a bad person. He wasn't, you know."

With these words, a horrified expression began to spread across her face. "It's me, isn't it? Something terrible always happens to the people I love."

She closed her eyes, swaying towards him. When she opened them again, they were sending a plea for help. "I can't take any more, Nicholas. I can't. What if something happens to you? I couldn't handle this. I can't lose you, too. Not now. Not when…"

She pulled her hands from his and frantically clutched the lapels of his jacket. A terrified look in her eyes, she searched his face before her words came at him in an anguished cry.

"Oh my God, what would I do if something happened to you?"

This is when he decided now was probably as good a time as any to finally take her into his arms, as she was crying so had she couldn't even stand. As she began to sag against him, he gathered her up in his arms and made his way back to the house.

He was surprised to find Claire holding the door open, a worried look on her face. She held the door open for him. "Mum told me she thought something was wrong. Oh Nicky, what happened?"

She had to run to keep up with him as he strode down the hall, all the while giving her a brief explanation. It was only when they arrived at his suite, he finally gave her a reassuring smile.

"It's going to be okay. But once again, I need of your help. I want you to keep the party going. Start up the music. Bring out more drinks. More food. Do whatever is necessary to keep everyone happy. I can't promise you anything, but hopefully Anna and I will join you in a bit. And please tell Stephen and Katy not to worry."

He placed a soft kiss in Anna's hair before he smiled wistfully over at Claire. "Together, Anna and I will get through this."

Nicholas sat in the chair by the fireplace, holding Anna in his arms while she continued to cry as if her heart was breaking. Feeling completely helpless, he pressed soft kisses to the top of her head, all the while running his fingers lightly through her hair.

He whispered everything was going to be fine. He was here for her. He would always keep her safe. He'd never leave her. Never. He loved her. Oh, how he loved her and always would. Over and over, he whispered these promises to her.

His hope was this outpouring of grief would wash away the pain and fear still claiming a hold on her. He leaned his head against the back of the chair and closing his eyes, he sent up a silent prayer this would finally bring that part of her life to closure.

Her crying had dwindled down to a few occasional sniffles. The tremors running through her had faded and now there was only her slow, even breathing.

He handed her the box of tissues now miraculously setting on the table next to them. He smiled, willing to bet Claire was the person responsible for this.

After he placed another soft kiss in her hair, he cleared his throat. "Anna, I wish this hadn't happened, and on today of all days. But what happened has nothing to do with you, love. Absolutely nothing. We'll never know what was going on in Marc's mind. But the outcome was something he brought on himself."

Blotting her face with tissues, Anna nodded against his chest.

After his unsuccessful attempt to straighten the flowers in her hair, now hanging down at an unfortunate angle, Nicholas smiled tenderly at her. "I believe you've been holding everything inside for so long, the life you've been living hasn't been a life at all. Now you can put all of the fear and anxiety behind you. There is no one to hurt you and if any harm does come your way, I will be right here by your side to keep you safe. You know this, don't you?"

She blew her nose before she gave another nod. When she rested her head on his shoulder, he placed a soft kiss to her forehead. "And you're certainly never, ever going to lose me, not if I can help it. Good Lord, I've spent entirely too much time falling in love with you to let this happen. We're just getting started, love."

Anna reached for his hand, bringing it to her lips. "Oh Nicholas, what would I do without you?"

He placed another kiss in her hair. "It works both ways, you know. I can't imagine what I'd do without you either."

She leaned back against him, reaching over to finger one of the buttons on his shirt. He smiled, thinking how such a simple thing as this had now come to mean so much to him.

Her fingers stilled against his shirt. She gazed up at him, her eyes luminous from her tears. "I'm so sorry. I'm so, so sorry about everything. Oh Nicholas, what have I done? I've treated you so badly and yet you're still here."

Her voice became choked with new tears. "And then I almost let Marc ruin what we have. Even after I realized I was so much in love with you."

He felt as though every ounce of breath had been snatched from his lungs at her words. His throat thick with emotion, he cupped her chin in his hand. He searched her face, relief pouring through him when he saw in her eyes, the fire that burned for only him. A fire he'd been so afraid he would never see again.

But he still needed to hear her say it. He had waited so long. And so patiently. He wanted to hear the words from her telling him she was completely his, just as he already belonged to her. Without her even asking this of him.

His eyes held hers. "Anna, say it."

Anna had to close her eyes, almost blinded by the love she saw blazing in his.

He gave her a gentle kiss, just barely brushing her mouth with his. Her name on his lips was a soft plea. "Anna?"

Her hands going up to his shoulders, she gazed right into his eyes. "Oh, Nicholas. I love you, I do. So, so much. I think I fell in love with you right from the very beginning, the first time I looked into your beautiful eyes. But I kept fighting it because I was so afraid of being hurt again. I know now, what I truly believe I've known all along, you will never hurt me."

She placed a soft kiss to the corner of his mouth, her next words a whisper against his lips. "I should have listened to my heart, as it was yours from the very beginning. I love you. And I will never stop loving you. This will always be my promise to you."

His mouth captured hers and together, they became lost in the kiss.

It was a kiss that erased all of the fear and uncertainty that almost tore them apart.

It was a kiss that was the promise of a new beginning.

And finally, it was a kiss that was a solemn pledge of their love for each other.

For always...

Everything in Nicholas's world had now settled in place. A smile on his face, he brushed his fingers over Anna's lips. "I'll never tire hearing you say those words, love. And I'll never stop saying them to you. I will always love you."

She took his hand in hers and placed a kiss to his fingers before she rested her head on his shoulder. "I love you, too."

She gazed up at him, a wistful expression on her face. "Oh God, Nicholas, all those people out there. I don't want spend the time with them. I want to stay here with you."

He laughed, a happy, carefree laugh. She reached up to trace his mouth with her fingertip, her eyes searching his face. She drank in every detail, finding it hard to believe what they had was real.

But as far as fairy tales went, theirs' was as real as you could get

He smiled down at her. "*Ah...* as tempting as this sounds, you know we have to get back to the reception. Claire's probably at her wits end right about now, trying to keep things moving along. And after today we'll have the rest of our lives to be together, love." He sighed. "Even though, today, I'm going to be counting the minutes until we can be back here."

She suddenly grinned and putting a finger to her lips, she nodded towards the door to the room. Nicholas turned to see it was partially open, two small faces peering in at them.

He smiled. "Hey girls, what's up?"

The door flew open with Clementine and Emily almost tripping over each other in their haste to get across the room.

As usual, Emily was more than excited to be sharing their message. "Mummy sent us. She wants to know if you are going to come to the party. She said to tell you she really, *really* hopes it's soon.

She scrunched up her face in thought. "She said she's running out of something, but I forgot what it is … onions, maybe?"

Nicholas laughed. "My guess is she said options, not onions." He reached out to tweak her nose. "But you were close, very close."

As usual, Clementine was silent. She was studying Anna, a very concerned expression on her face. "Anna, were you crying? Did Uncle Nicky yell at you?"

Nicholas groaned. "Why, please tell me, am I always the bad guy? Yes, Anna was crying, but she's feeling much better now. And no, she wasn't crying because I yelled at her."

A soft giggle escaped Anna as she reached over to stroke his cheek with her fingertip. "*Ah …* but if you remember, you did yell at me. Crazy, huh?" He gave her a slow smile before he leaned in to give her a kiss. His whisper was for her only. "Crazy for you, yes. Always."

Emily rolled her eyes at this. "Oh brother, you're getting all silly like mummy and daddy do when they think we aren't watching."

Clementine was still not quite finished with her observations. She gave Anna another troubled look. "Anna, are you going to fix your eyes before you come back to the party?"

With a startled laugh, Anna scrambled out of Nicholas's lap to hurry into the bathroom. There she found her eye make-up was in dire need of a touch up, her mascara all smudged under her eyes. As she began repairing the damage, the two girls joined her, giggling as they made faces at each other in the mirror. She smiled at them.

"I can't believe your uncle didn't tell me I looked like this."

Nicholas had come over to lean casually against the door, his hands in his trouser pockets. His head tilted, his gaze went to Anna. When their eyes met in the mirror, his smile came right at her.

She stilled. His expression was so full of love, it was pulling at her like a magnet. She tightened her grip on the edge of the counter to keep from running right to him.

His eyes held hers. "You always look beautiful. Right, girls?"

They nodded, curiously watching Anna, who was staring dreamily into the mirror, the mascara wand still in her hand. It was only when Nicholas tactfully cleared his throat, she blinked, giving them a bright smile. She then went back to applying her mascara. concentrating on this as though her life depended on it.

She fixed the flowers in her hair and after adding a touch of lip gloss, she applied a dab to both Emily and Clementine's lips. They were thrilled, admiring their new look in the mirror.

Slowly shaking his head, but with a smile on his face, Nicholas motioned to them. "Why don't the two of you trot on back to the reception. You can tell mummy Anna and I will be there in just a bit. And if she says anything about you wearing lipstick, make sure you tell her this was Anna's doing, not mine!"

He smiled at Anna over their heads before he watched them run out of the room. When he turned back to Anna, again their eyes met in the mirror. And this time, when he smiled, she walked right into his arms.

Pressing a kiss to the top of her head, Nicholas gave a long, drawn out sigh. "We need to go. I guess we should remind ourselves of all we have to look forward to from this moment on." He pressed a kiss to the top of her head. "A life with no more fears. No more ghosts. No more regrets. Just you and me, love."

She nodded against his chest. "Just you and me. Oh, how I love the sound of this." She rose up on her toes to catch the corner of his mouth with a kiss. "Oh, Nicholas. I do love you. So, so much. It feels so good to finally say it. I love you with all of my heart."

Her smile was shy. "Remember what we promised each other in the car?"

He nodded, his eyes searching hers.

"You are in my heart, Anna. And this is where you will always be."

Her eyes shining with her promise, she smiled.

"As you are in my heart, Nicholas. And will always be."

CHAPTER 40

*H*er hand in his, Anna and Nicholas walked into the atrium.

She gazed around the room before she smiled up at him. "Oh Nicholas, this is so beautiful. Claire did such a wonderful job."

The transformation was amazing.

Gone were the rows of chairs and the makeshift altar from the ceremony. The room was now an elegant reception area.

The tables were covered in crisp white linen, the hand-cut crystal glassware and fine white china plates, rimmed with silver, sparkled in the light of the multi-candle centerpieces. At each place setting, there was a single red rose, adding the perfect touch of color.

Miniature lights, twinkling like stars in the sheer netting draped across ceiling, gave an almost magical glow to the room. Trees of all different sizes, strung with even more lights, along with clusters of both white and red poinsettia plants, were scattered throughout the room.

In one corner, a quartet was playing, the soft classical music providing the perfect background for the pre-dinner conversation among the guests.

Embarrassed by the enthusiastic reception they received, Anna let

Nicholas guide her through the maze of tables to where Katy and Stephen were seated. As soon as she sat down, Anna tried to apologize, but Katy put her hand on her arm, shaking her head.

"Oh Anna, no. It's okay. I know I shouldn't even be saying this, but I am just so relieved that part of your life is over and you can move on. Starting with this handsome guy of yours, who looks even more in love with you than he was before. If this could even be possible. I'm so happy for you."

She laughed, giving Anna a big hug. "This has all been so wonderful, the perfect dream wedding."

At the same time, Nicholas was deep in conversation with Stephen. Whatever they were discussing, it brought a huge smile from Stephen before he gave Nicholas a quick hug. When Nicholas saw Anna was watching him, he came over to sit beside her. He brought her hand to his mouth for a kiss before linking his fingers with hers.

Anna gazed down at their hands. She couldn't stop smiling.

She wanted to stand up and twirl around in circles like Emily and Clementine. Laughing out loud, the two girls were making themselves almost dizzy as they watched their dresses float around them in clouds of sparkling red and green tulle.

The dark clouds hovering over her for the past several months had lifted, leaving her now floating on cloud nine. Where she'd found a love she never thought possible, along with the promise of so much hope for the future.

She turned to Nicholas. She wanted to tell him this. But when their eyes met, she realized this wasn't necessary.

The message in his eyes told her he already knew.

Anna smiled over at Katy and Stephen as she stood in front of the wedding guests, about to make her maid-of-honor speech. She didn't dare look at Nicholas. If she did, the words she planned to say would probably fly right out of her head. And since this speech could be the start towards redeeming herself in front of his family, she didn't want to goof it up.

She took a deep breath. "Hi, I'm Anna. I've known Katy since second grade when we made a pact to be best friends for life. Over the years we've become more like sisters, always knowing we'll always be there for each other, in both good times and bad."

She grinned over at Katy. "But there have been so many good times. Let's talk about the one when Katy and Stephen went on their first date. Katy came home from that date in a horrible mood, ranting and raving about everything to do with Stephen. I definitely got the impression this Stephen could do nothing right."

She laughed as she glanced over at Stephen. "I bet you had no idea, did you? But since we're here today, you can relax. Because it's obvious she now feels much differently."

She turned back to the guests. "I let Katy ramble on, as we all know when she has something to say, there's no stopping her until she gets it all out." She sent Katy an apologetic smile. "I finally said to her, I take it there will be no second date? She looked at me with this big smile on her face and said, "Of course there will... I've already decided he's the man I'm going to marry!"

Once the laughter died down, Anna turned to Katy and Stephen to raise her glass in a toast. "I can't thank you enough for allowing me to be a part of your special day. I hope you'll always be as happy and in love as you are today. I wish you the best of everything. All my love to both of you."

After she made her way back to Nicholas, he took her hand and placed a kiss in her palm before he closed her fingers over it.

I love you.

She leaned in to give him a kiss.

I love you back.

It was now Nicholas's turn to make his best man speech.

After a quick kiss to Anna's cheek, he hesitated slightly before he whispered in her ear. "I hope you're ready for this, love."

Before he turned to walk away, he winked.

Anna was mystified.

Ready for what? Does he know something you don't?

Casually pacing back and forth, Nicholas gazed around the room.

His eyes finally came to rest on Anna.

When he smiled at her, she knew she was probably grinning from ear to ear, leading everyone to wonder what she was up to, but she didn't care.

He grinned right back at her before he turned to Stephen and Katy. "Ah, Katy and Stephen. What a wonderful day this is! I'm sure I speak for everyone here when I tell you how happy we all are for you."

Then he shook his head, giving a soft chuckle. "After hearing Anna's version of Katy and Stephen's first date, I think you'll find it very amusing to hear mine." He winked over at Katy. "Shortly after this same date and during a phone conversation with Stephen, I asked him if there was anything new in his life. He told me he had met this girl, her name was Katy, and he was pretty sure she fell for him hook, line and sinker."

At the laughter that broke out, he held up his hand. "Yes, these were his exact words. When I laughed, he said, "Seriously, Nicholas, I'm pretty sure she's the only woman I know who loves everything about me. I may just have to marry her!"

Katy leaned over and gave Stephen a big kiss, bringing a loud round of cheers and applause.

Once this died down, Nicholas turned to smile at the both of them. "It's obvious this marriage was destined to happen from the very beginning. The love you have for each other shines not only in your faces, but in everything you do. You're an inspiration to all of us."

He raised his glass. "So, I'd like to propose a toast to a long and happy marriage ... and what the hell, let's raise our glasses a second time to a house full of children to keep you forever young!"

His speech at an end, instead of making his way back to Anna, he remained where he was. Anna watched, mystified, as he sent an apprehensive glance over at Stephen, receiving a thumbs-up in return,

He then took a deep breath, a look of determination on his face.

After holding his hand up for silence, he sent a smile around the room.

"With Stephen and Katy's permission, I'm going to do something a little out of the ordinary. But in order to make this work, I'll need the help of my two very young and charming assistants."

He glanced over to where Emily and Clementine were seated and held out his hand to them. "Girls, are you ready?"

They both jumped out of their chairs and came running over to stand by him, identical grins lighting up their faces. Curiosity building, the room became even more silent.

Anna felt a nervous flutter start up in her stomach, her heartbeat quickening. Her hands tightly clasped in her lap, her gaze never wavered from Nicholas.

What is going on? And why do you have this sudden feeling you are a big part of what is about to take place?

Nicholas's eyes slowly scanned the room. Once again, they came to rest on Anna where they lingered for a few seconds.

A bemused look on his face, he gave a slight shake of his head before he turned to address the room. "I don't know if any of you are aware both Emily and Clementine are very much the experts when it comes to fairy tales. They always cheer when the princess finds her prince. Isn't this right, girls?"

They both nodded. Emily was hopping up and down with excitement, while Clementine stood silently next to Nicholas, taking her role very seriously.

Nicholas grinned at them. "Now, the three of us have had many discussions about this, their biggest concern being I haven't yet found a princess of my own. And now they've become even more worried about the fact I'm not getting younger."

Emily grabbed his hand for attention. "But Uncle Nicky, like mummy said, you're already *waaaaay* over thirty!"

Amid the laughter this brought, Nicholas glanced over at Claire, an eyebrow raised. She merely shrugged before she blew him a kiss.

He turned back to the guests and massaging the back of his neck with his hand, he gave a very dramatic sigh.

"*Ah...* so there you have it. Not only am I at the advanced age of 'way over thirty' there is also no princess or a happily ever after in sight. Unlike Stephen here, with his now forever princess, Katy."

He reached up to massage his chin. He appeared deep in thought.

He gazed slowly around the room, his eyes again resting on Anna. "*Hmm...* but maybe this isn't necessarily true? Maybe things have changed?"

He squatted down until he was eye level with Emily and Clementine. He looked puzzled. "So, girls, what do you think? Is there a chance there might be a princess waiting for me? And maybe, just maybe, she could possibly be here in this room?"

They both began to jump up and down, crying out in unison. "Yes! Yes! Yes, Uncle Nicky! Sleeping Beauty!"

Nicholas stood, a smile coming through in his words. "*Ah...* yes. Sleeping Beauty, the beautiful princess waiting to be awakened with a kiss from her forever prince."

He slowly began to weave his way around the tables, the two excited girls hopping and skipping beside him. He finally came to stand in front of Anna.

"*Nicholas...*" Her voice coming out in a breathy whisper, she reached for his hand.

He smiled and taking her hand, he turned to address the two girls. "And what did we say should happen when I found my Sleeping Beauty, girls?"

Emily grabbed on to his arm. "You said you would marry her, Uncle Nicky!" Clementine grabbed his other arm. "Ask Anna to marry you, Uncle Nicky!"

His gaze fixed on Anna, Nicholas was vaguely aware of a very loud and excited shriek from somewhere in the room. In the laughter that followed, he knew he could safely bet his house and everything in it his mother was the one guilty of this.

Aw, give her a break! You know she's been waiting for this.

When he saw the color flooding Anna's face, he gently squeezed her hand before he turned to the two girls. "Well, girls. I have to say, this sounds like the best advice I've received in a long time."

He then glanced over to where his mother was seated. She was clearly embarrassed, her face hidden behind her hands. He shook his head, a huge grin on his face. "If we go by what we just heard, it appears this also meets the approval of another very important person here with us today."

After he gently pried his hand from Anna's shaky grip, he gave both Emily and Clementine a hug before he turned back to the guests. "So, it looks like I now I have a plan. But first, how about a round of applause for my lovely assistants?"

After an enthusiastic response, a big part of it in response to the girls very elaborate curtseys and the kisses they blew to the guests, silence once again descended on the room, all eyes on Nicholas and Anna.

Anna was mesmerized by the look in Nicholas's eyes. His beautiful blue eyes. Sending a message of so much tenderness and love, they were all she could see. It was as though the rest of the world had simply disappeared, leaving only the two of them sheltered within their love.

With a smile so real it made her heart ache, he got down on one knee. He reached into his pocket and reaching for her left hand, he slipped a diamond solitaire engagement ring onto her finger.

His eyes blazing with the promise of his unconditional love, his voice was rough with emotion.

"My Sleeping Beauty, my Anna, my love. Will you marry me?"

She was in his arms before he could even get out the last word. "Oh Nicholas, *yes... yes... yes.*"

She rested her cheek against his.

"A million times, yes!"

SO, WHAT ARE YOU DOING NEW YEAR'S EVE?

*N*icholas added another log to the fireplace.

He stepped back to watch as it caught fire, sending flames shooting into a shower of sparks up the chimney. Once he was satisfied the fire was burning steadily, he turned to Anna.

He smiled.

Curled up in the chair, she was wearing only his shirt, her engagement ring and the snowflake necklace, both the ring and necklace sparkling in the light of the fire. A faraway expression on her face, her eyes were closed.

He leaned down, his lips leaving a trail of kisses across her cheek before they brushed over her mouth. She opened her eyes, reaching up to stroke his cheek with her fingers.

She gave him a lazy smile. "Oh God… I'm so in love with you."

Nicholas gently pulled her up out of the chair and into his arms, burying his face in her hair. As he breathed in the intoxicating floral scent he'd come to love, he was at once filled with such a deep feeling of contentment. And so much love. Both of these, still so new to him, were almost overwhelming at times.

Like now...

"As I'm so in love with you." This was a whisper in her hair as he settled into the chair, pulling her onto his lap. He smoothed the hair back from her face. "This is my favorite place to be. I'm so glad we left the party early."

Anna was frowning. "Oh Nicholas, what must everyone think? We were there such a short time and I only met a few of your friends. Then we left without saying goodbye to a single person, not even the host and hostess."

He glanced over at the trail of clothing scattered across the floor from the door to the bed before he smiled down at her. "I'm sure they'll figure it out. We'll have plenty of opportunities to meet up with friends in the future. But this year, I want to welcome in the New Year with you, not at a crowded party. In fact, every moment I have, I want to share it with you."

Curling into the warmth of him, Anna's answer came out in a sigh. "I know. Me, too."

Caught up in their thoughts, they were both silent. Anna was the first to stir. "Katy sent a text earlier. They love Paris and are having a wonderful time. She sends her love. I can't believe their honeymoon is almost over."

Nicholas chuckled. "I don't think the honeymoon will ever be over for those two. They are perfect for each other."

Smiling the slow smile that evoked many different feelings in her, always all so extremely pleasurable, he ran his fingertips lightly down the side of her face. "Speaking of honeymoons, Claire has asked me, for what seems like at least a dozen times, if we've set a date for our wedding. I told her this was your call. Wherever, however and whatever you decide, I'm in. The only request I have it will be soon. I just want to be married to you, love."

Anna caught his fingers in her hand to bring them to her lips. "*Hmm...* so many things we need to think about and so much to plan. Do you think we could invite the women who sent the ornament? I will never forget how I felt when I saw it hanging here on your tree. And the note they sent was so nice. I know they might not come, but I'd like them to know everything worked out and we're engaged. After all, they had such a big part in making this happen."

A worried expression flooded her face. "Oh Nicholas, what if things hadn't happened like they did? If they didn't take the time to the ornament? Or I decided not to come for the wedding? Oh God, there are so many things that could've gone wrong."

Nicholas had pulled her even closer, the last of her words muffled against his chest. "Love, everything is fine, more than fine. Look at us, together and so much in love. And I promise this will never change. I've kept every promise I've made to you so far, haven't I?"

Anna nodded, again letting herself be lulled by his promise, his strength and most of all, his love.

Nicholas brought her left hand up to his mouth, kissing the finger that wore his ring. "And, beautiful fiancée of mine, I would have found a way to get us back together, wedding or not. I knew from the very beginning you were the one for me and there was no way I was going to let you get away." He chuckled. "Even if I had to pull on my rusty armor, get up on my aging horse and set out in a brave, yet feeble attempt to kidnap you."

Anna sat up, her hands going to clasp behind his neck as they both started to laugh. "Oh Nicholas, I do love you! You are definitely my knight in shining armor, my prince and my hero all rolled into one!"

His mouth swooping in to cover hers, her laughter was swallowed in his kiss. When the kiss ended, he shook his head. "*Ah*, Anna. I think we should just be thankful it hadn't come to that."

When she settled back against him, her head on his shoulder, he gazed down at her. "But now, where were we? In the middle of planning a wedding, I believe? And, yes to your previous comment. Of course, we'll invite them. What else, love?"

She tilted her head to smile at him. "Pink or blue. Which do you prefer?"

He laughed. "Oh no, you don't. That's your department. When it comes to wedding details like colors, flowers and so on, I'm completely at a loss. That's why I cajoled Claire into doing most of the planning for Stephen and Katy's wedding. Which, by the way, she is more than eager to help with ours if you're interested."

She continued to smile as she gazed into his eyes. *"Umm... that's good to know. But I'm asking you again. Pink or blue?"*

He was confused. He had no idea what she was asking of him.

Pink or blue? Aren't these the colors people usually associate with babies?

And with this one simple thought, it hit him.

Tears came to Anna's eyes she watched his expression go from shock to one of complete joy. He framed her face in his hands and gazing into her eyes, his struggle to find his voice finally resulted in an outpouring of words. "Anna! My God, Anna! A baby? How? When? Are you really sure, love?

She reached up to stroke his cheek. His excitement such a change from his usually reserved behavior, laughed, happiness filling her. "How? Nicholas, really? Do I really need to tell you how?"

Her laughter was silenced almost at once as his mouth claimed hers in another kiss. Then he searched her face, a bemused expression on his. He was waiting for more.

She reached up to stroke his cheek. "Well, let me see. Of course, you know when it happened. And as far as being sure, unless the pregnancy tests I took were defective, they all showed I'm definitely going to have a baby. The three times I actually did the test, that is."

She grinned. "I had a hard time believing it then, and almost still can't believe it now. It's early, still so very early, Nicholas. But I had to tell you. I couldn't keep something like this from you."

Her arms slowly crept up around his neck. "Since this is so unexpected, are you really happy about this?"

Nicholas pulled her closer, his lips in her hair. "Anna... I can't even begin to tell you how happy this makes me. As it is, I'm still trying to take it all in." He grinned. *"My God,* love. The luckiest day of my life was when you came into my life, running like a wild woman through the streets of Chicago." He leaned back, his smile teasing. "In fact, now that I think about it, I believe that had to be one of my best knight-in-shining-armor moments. Wouldn't you agree?"

Anna tried to look as insulted as she could.

But she couldn't seem to stop smiling. "I'm not only crazy, but wild, too? *Hmm...* I'm beginning to wonder how much of a part you had in determining how all that went about. If only to flaunt your super hero powers. Admit it."

Her expression changed, a tenderness sneaking into her smile. "But as long as we're reminiscing about how we met, there's something I'd like to ask you."

She left him to return with the photograph Katy gave to her. Once she was settled back in his arms, she handed it to him. "Katy gave this to me. She told me what happened. Nicholas, how did you know?"

He enfolded her in a hug, a long sigh coming from him. "Oh love, I'm not all that sure. I only know when I saw your face in this photograph, I knew I had to meet you. Something bigger than the both of us was telling me you were meant to be a part of my life. And I had no choice but to listen."

He brushed his fingers down her cheek. "And once we did meet, even with all the ups and downs we struggled through, I knew I would never be able to let you go." He shrugged. "And so here we are."

A huge smile lit up his face. "And now there's a baby on the way, sweetheart. *A baby…*"

The clock on the mantle began to chime. After it rang out twelve times, they looked at each other and smiled. But before he claimed her mouth with a kiss, his voice held the promise of everything good.

"Happy New Year, my love."

THE WINDY CITY

At the time most Londoners were ringing in the start of a new year, in Chicago, Illinois, the festivities hadn't even yet begun.

There, it was only six o'clock in the evening.

Kevin Kardell stepped out of the shower. After toweling himself dry, he turned on the hair dryer to dry his hair.

He had plenty of time. He wasn't due to meet his friends at their usual downtown hangout for at least another hour.

Once he finished getting dressed, he picked up his phone from where it was charging on the nightstand.

He saw he had two text messages. The first one was from Katy.

> *Hey, it's only me,... your newly*
> *married sister, Mrs. Katy Burns.*
> *I just love how that sounds, don't*
> *you? I wanted to wish you a Happy*
> *New Year from Paris. Have fun,*
> *but not too much fun. I know how*
> *crazy your friends can get. I'll call*
> *you when we get back.*

Love you, xoxo

After he texted back his message, he checked the second text to see it was from his agent, Kyle.

He shook his head. He couldn't get used to this agent thing. That he even had an agent was mind-boggling to him. He played baseball. This didn't qualify him as a celebrity. Certainly not one who needed an agent.

But he was open to whatever it took. He just wanted to play ball.

He read the text.

> *Hey Kev, great news! You've*
> *been picked up by Cleveland!*
> *They're eager to sign the papers*
> *to get things in order and ready*
> *for Arizona in February. I'll call*
> *you on the second with the details.*
> *It looks like this could be your year!*
> *So, get out there and celebrate!*
> *Happy New Year!*

Kevin read the message again. Then, just to be sure, he read it one more time.

He was grinning like crazy.

He sent a text to Kyle, along with another to Katy, sharing his good news. After he grabbed his jacket from the closet, he was out the door.

He was ready to celebrate.

The new year couldn't come fast enough.

Would you like to know what happens next?
It's all in Book 2 - For the Love of July

ABOUT THE AUTHOR

L. B. Joyce lives in Chagrin Falls, Ohio. A freelance artist by day, with designing Christmas ornaments her specialty, she's also a writer by night. She loves getting lost in a good book, has redecorated almost every room in her house more times than she'd like to admit, loves baking up a storm in her kitchen, hates housework with a passion and will drive just about anywhere because of her fear of flying.

To keep up with news of the first seven books of the Twelve Months, Twelve Love Stories series — *A Million Decembers*, *For the Love of July*, *February's Angel*, *Promise Me November*, *An Unexpected June*, *A January to Remember*, *September's Moonlight Serenade*, and *Goodbye Heartbreak, Hello May* - along with the first book of the new *Holidays in White Oaks Valley* series, *A Grand Slam Kind of Christmas* — check out the website/blog at: lbjoyceauthor.com
Facebook: https://www.facebook.com/LBJoyceAuthor/
Email: lbjoyce12@gmail.com

And finally?
Let's give credit where credit is due:
At Last, Lyrics/Music by Harry Warren and Mack Gordon
Cover by Soxsational Cover Art